THE MIDWIFE'S LONGED-FOR BABY

BY
CAROLINE ANDERSON

ONE NIGHT THAT CHANGED HER LIFE

BY
EMILY FORBES

MILLS &
BOON

Caroline Anderson is a matriarch, writer, armchair gardener, unofficial tearoom researcher and eater of lovely cakes. Not necessarily in that order! *What Caroline loves:* Her family. Her friends. Reading. Writing contemporary love stories. Hearing from readers. Walks by the sea with coffee/ice cream/cake thrown in! Torrential rain. Sunshine in spring/autumn. *What Caroline hates:* Losing her pets. Fighting with her family. Cold weather. Hot weather. Computers. Clothes shopping. *Caroline's plans:* Keep smiling and writing!

Emily Forbes is an award-winning author of Medical Romance for Mills & Boon. She has written over 25 books and has twice been a finalist in the Australian Romantic Book of the Year Award, which she won in 2013 for her novel *Sydney Harbour Hospital: Bella's Wishlist*. You can get in touch with Emily at emilyforbes@internode.on.net, or visit her website at emily-forbesauthor.com.

THE MIDWIFE'S LONGED-FOR BABY

BY
CAROLINE ANDERSON

MILLS &
BOON

HarperCollins
PUBLISHERS
— Since 1817 —

Published in Great Britain 2017
By Mills & Boon, an imprint of HarperCollins*Publishers*
1 London Bridge Street, London, SE1 9GF

© 2017 Caroline Anderson

ISBN: 978-0-263-92665-1

Dear Reader,

I felt moved to write this book to try and understand the rollercoaster of emotions that is infertility. My daughters are of an age when they and their friends are having families, and it seems that for quite a few of them the road is far from straightforward.

What do they go through? How do they feel? How on earth do they cope with the endless setbacks, the inevitable despair that every failed attempt at pregnancy must give rise to? And when it takes its toll—as it often must—what then?

For Nick and Liv, with a brilliant marriage and so much love to share, working in the business of babies means they are constantly surrounded by the 'success' of others whilst they are 'failing'. And they do what many couples seem to do: they stop communicating, withdraw into themselves, and in doing so destroy their marriage.

Do they miss each other? Yes. Do they miss the endless rounds of hope and despair? Not at all. And that's the stumbling block. They aren't happy apart, but they weren't happy together.

So what now? I had to get them back together and throw them headlong into a situation where they have no choice but to talk. Enter fate—me playing God again and then sitting back and waiting for them to work it out. But it wasn't easy for any of us.

Did I succeed? I hope so. I'll let you be the judge…

Caroline x

For all those whose infertility stories have touched my heart, and for the very many more whose stories I have never heard but who are themselves travelling this emotionally challenging road with courage. My heart aches for you.

Books by Caroline Anderson

Mills & Boon Medical Romance

Yoxburgh Park Hospital

Their Meant-to-Be Baby

From Christmas to Eternity
The Secret in His Heart
Risk of a Lifetime

Mills & Boon Cherish

The Valtieri Baby
Snowed in with the Billionaire
Best Friend to Wife and Mother?

Visit the Author Profile page
at millsandboon.co.uk for more titles.

CHAPTER ONE

'LIV, HAVE YOU got a minute?'

She hesitated, about to say no, but Ben wasn't one to waste time and if he wanted to talk to her…

'If it really is only that? I need to check on a mum soon.'

'That's fine, it won't take long. I just want to run something by you. Can we go in my office?'

His office?

'Is this about Jen?' she asked as Ben closed the door.

The fleeting smile didn't quite reach his eyes. 'In a way. Did you know she's got cancer?'

'Yes, Simon told me yesterday. I was gutted. She's such a lovely person and it seems so unfair. He said they're moving home so their families can help with the children while she's having treatment. So what is it you want me to do?' she asked, thinking flowers, a gift voucher, something for the kids—

'Nothing, but what I do could affect you, because yesterday was Simon's last day and his compassionate leave's pretty open-ended so we need a locum, and I'd like to talk to Nick about it.'

'Nick?'

Of all the things he'd been going to say, her ex husband's name was so far down the list it wasn't even on it, and just the sound of his name made her heart beat faster. And he wasn't officially ex, because she'd never quite been able to follow through on that—

'Are you still in touch?'

Ben nodded. 'Yes, we're in touch. I speak to him quite often. He always asks about you,' he added gently.

Her heart lurched. 'Does he? How is he?' she asked, trying not to sound too needy and failing hopelessly.

'He's OK. He's well, keeps himself busy.' He frowned, hesitating, then went on, 'I know it's none of my business, Liv, and I'm not asking any questions, but I was really sorry when you two split up.'

She felt her eyes fill and blinked as she looked away. 'Me, too, but it wasn't working.' Any more than this was, this awful aching emptiness where her love for Nick had been…

'I know. I could see there was something wrong, so I wasn't surprised, just saddened for you both. Look, don't worry about it. I'll try and get someone else. I only thought of him because he'd be perfect for the job, but I don't want to make things difficult for you—for either of you, really.'

The shock had worn off now, swamped by a tidal wave of mixed emotions that she couldn't quite work out. Longing? Dread? She didn't have a clue. Both, maybe, but confusion was fighting its way to the top of the pile.

'I don't understand how he could do it anyway. Doesn't he have a job?'

He must have. He was paying the mortgage on their house—

'Not any more, as far as I know. His existing locum

post's about to come to an end and I haven't heard that he's got anything else lined up so I wanted to get in soon if we were to stand a chance, but it's probably too late anyway.'

He was *locuming*? He'd been made a consultant at Yoxburgh Park Hospital a few months before they'd split up. How had he ended up working as a locum? Although it was only a year ago since he'd left. Maybe nothing had come up, nothing as good anyway. Nothing that would do him justice...

'Can I think about it? Before you ask him, or get anyone else. It's just—it's the last thing I expected you to say and I can't quite get my head round it.'

'I know, I can see that. And I realise you might need to talk to him first.'

No way. She hadn't spoken to him since that horrible day that she'd regretted ever since, but this wasn't the time or the way to do it. She shook her head. 'No, I don't need to do that. How long can I have?'

Ben shrugged. 'The rest of the morning? I'm sorry, I know it isn't long, but if you think you can deal with it I really don't want to hang about in case we lose him. It's right up his street—mostly obstetrics, but there's some of the fertility clinic work as well, which is why I thought of him.'

That stopped her mind in its tracks, and she felt her jaw drop. She just couldn't picture him in a fertility clinic, of all the ironic places, but of course Simon's job partly involved it.

'I didn't realise he knew anything at all about infertility.'

Apart from their own, but she wasn't saying that to Ben.

'Yes, that's one of the reasons why we want him, because of Simon's role here. Plus he's a damn good obstetrician, of course, but he's a perfect fit. He's been running the fertility clinic in his hospital since last May, and it shuts any day now.'

Her heart was beating so fast she could feel it thudding against her ribs. Of all the things for him to do, running a fertility clinic was so out of left field she'd never have seen it coming. Why would he choose to punish himself in that way? *Unless he'd had no choice.* Had he been driven to it just to earn a living? Her guilt over the mortgage ramped up a notch.

'I had no idea,' she said numbly. She took another moment, letting it all sink in a little, and then took a deep breath and made a decision she just hoped she didn't regret.

'Talk to him, Ben. Ask him if he's interested. If he is—well, I'm sure we can be civilised about it.'

'Are you sure? I realise it's a big decision for you.'

'But it isn't really mine to make. It's yours, and his, and if he's the right man for the job, who am I to stand in the way? And anyway, it's not permanent. Ask him, Ben. Just keep me in the loop, OK? I don't want any surprises.'

'Of course I will.' He opened the door and stared down thoughtfully into her eyes. 'Thank you, Liv. I do appreciate it and I know it can't be easy for you.'

Did he? She wondered how much he knew about their break-up, about the why and the how. Had Nick spoken to him about it? Surely not. If there was one thing her marriage had taught her, it was that Nick didn't talk about his feelings. Not to her, and certainly not to his boss.

She found a smile from somewhere. 'You're welcome. Just let me know his reaction.'

'I will.'

'Nick? It's Ben Walker. Are you OK to talk? I want to ask you something.'

'Yeah, sure. What d'you want to know?' he asked.

'Nothing. I'm headhunting you. I know your clinic's shutting any time now, and we need a full-time locum consultant to cover Obs and Gynae and some of the fertility clinic workload and I thought it sounded right up your street, unless you've got your next job lined up already?'

Ben was asking him to go back? With Liv still there? At least, he assumed she was. He hadn't heard otherwise and Ben would have told him, he was sure. Would he be working with her?

His heart rate rocketed, and he hauled in a deep breath and let it go, consciously engaging his brain instead of his adrenal glands.

'Whose job is it? It sounds like Simon's.'

'It is. His wife's got cancer and he's gone off on compassionate leave with immediate effect. They're moving back to their home town so their parents can help with childcare.'

'Oh, no, that's horrendous. Poor Jen. Poor all of them. And poor you, because it's obviously left you in the lurch, but I'm not sure I'm the man for the job. Does Liv know you're asking me?'

'Yes. I asked her first. She said she thought you could be civilised about it.'

Civilised?

He'd be right under her nose, working with couples to solve the very thing that had left their marriage in tatters. *Civilised* wasn't the word he would have applied to that situation.

A minefield, more likely.

Or an opportunity to build bridges? He knew so much more now than he had then, but the pain was still raw and no amount of knowledge was going to make that go away.

Could he do it? It wasn't as if they'd be working together, and it was only temporary in any case. They could keep out of each other's way if necessary, but it might give them a chance—

'So, are you still free?'

'Yes, technically. I haven't got anything lined up yet, at least, and I'm seeing the last patients today, but I had thought I'd take a break. When would you want me to start?'

Ben made a sound that could have been laughter. 'Tomorrow? And by the way, that was a joke, but—ASAP, really. We can cover it for a few days but after that it'll get really tricky. Every woman in Suffolk seems to be pregnant or trying to be at the moment.'

His chest tightened. Not quite every woman. Not his Liv...

'Why don't you come and talk to me about it?' Ben went on. 'See how you feel?'

He had no idea how he'd feel. Confused? Desperate to see Liv? Afraid to see her, to find that she was happily settled without him when he was still miserable and lonely and struggling to make sense of it all? But maybe she *was* happy, which would mean he'd done the right thing by leaving without a fight. Maybe he needed to know that so he could move on?

There was no real reason why he couldn't go. When

the clinic closed its doors at five that evening, he'd be jobless. He'd planned a holiday, something reckless and adrenaline-soaked, but he hadn't booked anything and now Ben was dangling this opportunity to go back to Yoxburgh right in front of his nose.

Yoxburgh, and Liv.

They'd been so happy there at first in the pretty Victorian seaside town, but it had all gone horribly wrong for them and now the only memories he had of it were sad ones. Did he really want to go back?

He'd made changes in his life, tried to get it back on track, but although his diet and lifestyle had undergone a radical overhaul, his heart hadn't moved on. He'd just shut it away, buried it under a massive pile of work and endless runs around an inner-city park, and going back was bound to open a whole new can of worms. Did he really want to do that? The sensible answer was no— or was that just the coward's answer?

And Ben needed him. He had no commitments or ties, no reason why he couldn't go, except that Liv would be there, and maybe that wasn't a good enough reason to stay away.

Even though it was a minefield, even though they hadn't spoken in over a year, even though he knew it was rash and stupid and ill-considered, he realised there was a massive part of him that wanted to see her again.

Needed to see her again.

It was high time they had the conversation he'd been putting off since they'd split up. The conversation he owed her—and the one she owed him, like why after more than a year she still hadn't started divorce proceedings…

'Let's just go for it,' he said, suddenly decisive. 'I

can't do tomorrow, but why don't I come up on Friday? That gives me a day to tidy up here and pack, and if I can sort everything out with your HR first thing on Friday morning I can start work right away. My paperwork's all in order, so once HR have seen it I'll be good to go. Then you'll only have to deal with tomorrow, and I can spend the weekend finding somewhere to live.'

'Are you sure?'

'Yes, absolutely,' he said without giving himself time to back out of it. 'Let's do it. I'll drive down early so I'm with you for eight and I can be in HR as soon as they open.'

'Nick, thank you. I can't tell you how grateful I am,' Ben said, and the relief in his voice made Nick realise just how much pressure his old clinical lead was under. 'And don't worry about finding anywhere to live,' Ben added, 'you can stay with us as long as you need to, Daisy'd love to have you. Come here, to the hospital. You know where to find me. They'll page me when you get here.'

'Sure. Thanks. I'll see you then.'

He hung up, slid the phone into his pocket and stared blankly across the room.

He was going back.

He wasn't sure he was ready to see Liv again, because he'd never managed to get any emotional distance and his heart was still as raw as it had been the day she threw him out, so it was going to be tough. Very tough. But maybe he could use the opportunity to find out if she was happy without him, because he sure as hell wasn't happy without her...

There was a knock on the door and a nurse popped

her head into the room. 'Mr Jarvis? Mr and Mrs Lyons are waiting to see you.'

He nodded, gave himself a mental shake and got to his feet. 'Show them in, please.'

He was coming back today.

Taking Simon's job, at least in the short term. She still couldn't work out how she felt about that. Confused, more than anything. Confused and nervous and tingling with apprehension. Lots of that.

She found a slot in the staff car park, got out and headed for the maternity unit on autopilot, her mind whirling.

Would she see him today? Did she want to? Did *he* want to see *her*? Their last exchange had hardly been amicable. Well, her side of it anyway. He'd hardly said a word but then he hadn't needed to, the evidence had spoken for itself.

She reached the kerb and glanced up, checking that the road was clear, and saw a car approaching.

Nick's car.

She recognised it instantly, and her heart started to thud as he drew closer, their eyes meeting as he slowed down.

To speak to her?

For a moment she thought he was going to stop, and then he raised his hand in acknowledgement and drove on, and she hauled in a breath and crossed the road on legs like jelly.

Her heart was tumbling in her chest, her lips dry, and she was breathing so fast she could have been running. Ridiculous. He was just a doctor, here to do his job, and she was just a midwife doing hers. The fact that they were still married was neither here nor there. They could do this.

She just had to work out how.

Nick parked the car and sat there for a moment, waiting for his heart to slow down.

He'd known it would be odd to see her again, but he hadn't expected the thunderbolt that had struck him when he'd met her eyes. It was like being punched in the gut, and it had taken his breath away.

Jaws clenched, he took the key out of the ignition, picked up the briefcase containing his stethoscope and the file with all the documentation for HR and got out of the car, following her towards the maternity unit.

Why the hell had he said yes? He could have turned Ben down, walked away, gone and had the holiday he'd been promising himself. Then he wouldn't have been here, he wouldn't have seen her and ripped open the wound left by the abrupt end to their marriage.

Not that it had taken much ripping. It had barely skinned over in the last year and a bit, but he was here now, the damage was done and he might as well just get on with it. And anyway, she needed the truth. They both did, and maybe then they could both move on.

The door slid open and he strode through it, went up to the maternity reception desk and asked them to page Ben.

'Morning, all.'

'Oh, Liv, I'm so glad I've caught you. Can you do us a huge favour? Would you mind covering an antenatal clinic this morning? Jan's called in sick and you're the only person who's not already involved in a delivery.'

She felt a little shaft of relief and smiled at her line manager. 'No, that's fine, I'll head straight down.' And she'd be nicely tucked out of the way so she wouldn't run the risk of bumping into Nick.

Which was stupid, really, because it was going to happen sometime, but she'd had less than forty-eight hours to get used to the idea of him coming back and judging by her reaction to him in the car park, it had been nothing like long enough.

She'd spend the morning giving herself a thorough talking-to, and then by the time he actually started work she'd have herself firmly under control.

Good plan.

Except it wasn't.

The clinic receptionist welcomed her with a smile of relief and then comprehensively trashed her peace of mind.

'Thank heavens it's you, Liv, we need someone who knows the ropes. There's a bit of a delay because the locum who's covering for Mr Bailey is still in HR, but he'll be down soon, apparently, so if you could make a start that would be amazing.'

Simon's clinic? That meant she'd be working with Nick all morning, before she had a chance to shore up the walls and get all her defences in place. Great. Fabulous.

Her heart had started to pound, and she hauled in a breath, picked up the first set of notes with shaking hands and pasted on a smile.

'No problem. I can do that,' she said, as much to herself as the receptionist. She walked out to the waiting area, glanced at the file and scanned the room.

'Judy Richards?'

* * *

'Nick! Welcome back!'

He recognised Jane, the motherly but ruthlessly efficient woman who acted as Ben's secretary as well as Simon's, and greeted her warmly.

'Hello, Jane, it's good to see you again. How are you?'

'I'm fine. I've been expecting you. HR said you'd be up here shortly. They said you were very well organised, ironically.'

He laughed. 'It just so happens I had a file ready with the relevant paperwork in it because I knew I'd need it soon, but don't let that lull you into a false sense of security. I hate admin.'

She smiled knowingly. 'I haven't forgotten that. Don't worry, I'll make sure you do everything you have to do.'

'Can you read my mind?' he asked, and she just laughed.

'If necessary. That's what I'm here for.'

'Good. I don't suppose you've got Simon's schedule handy, have you? I really need to hit the ground running. Ben said something about a clinic and I've got a list this afternoon.'

'Yes, I've printed it all out for you here. First on your list is the antenatal clinic, as you know. It's still in the same place and they're expecting you. And your elective list starts at two, so you should just about have time after the clinic to meet your patients before you start in Theatre. The notes are on the ward.'

'Jane, you're a legend.' He hung his stethoscope round his neck, left his briefcase in her care and went.

At least in the clinic he was less likely to run into Liv,

because she'd be safely tucked away on the midwife-led unit. And even though in a way he'd wanted to see her, their brief encounter this morning had shaken him more than he'd expected and he could do without any more surprises.

Yes, a nice, busy clinic was exactly what he needed. Just until he got his head round the idea of working in the same building as her...

'Liv...'

She was standing in the empty corridor with an armful of notes when she heard him say her name, and she turned slowly and met his eyes.

Anguish, love, regret—and then nothing, as he got control of himself again and slammed the shutters down. He'd had plenty of practice at that, he'd got it down to a fine art in the last year of their marriage, but he'd been too slow this time and his reaction exactly mirrored her own.

'Hello, Nick,' she said, her voice sounding scratchy and unused. The words *how are you* hovered on her tongue, but she couldn't speak because it had glued itself to the roof of her mouth so she just stared at him.

His face was leaner, she realised, the crows' feet more pronounced, the frown lines shallower. Because he was happier? He hadn't looked happy, but he looked more like the old Nick, the man she'd fallen in love with, fit and well and healthy but with a touch of grey at his temples now. Stress, or just age? He was thirty-nine now, nearly forty, and he wore it well apart from that.

Not that the silver threaded through his dark hair did anything to dim his subtle but potent sex appeal—

Her heart was beating so fast it was deafening her,

her breath was lodged in her throat, and she had to clamp her lips together to stifle a sudden little sob.

She blinked fiercely and adjusted the folders in her arms before looking back at him, and as she met those beautiful, smoky grey eyes again her heart thudded, but his gaze held her eyes and she was powerless to look away.

'I wasn't expecting to see you down here,' he said after a second of silence that seemed to scream on for eternity, and his gruff voice set her free and she breathed again.

'Ditto, but it's just as well you're here now, we've got a lot of work to do.' She pretended to look at the notes in her arms. Anything to get away from those searching eyes when her own were bound to be too revealing. 'I take it you managed to tick all HR's boxes?'

'Yes. I have a file I keep up to date. It comes in handy when you're a locum.'

That again. *Why hasn't he got a full-time job?*

He hesitated, as if there was something else he wanted to say, but after a moment he looked down at the armful of folders she was holding. 'So, what's that lot?'

'The ladies who've had their BP and fundal height measured and their urine tested, so they're all ready for you.' Her voice was almost normal again, and she nearly laughed. If he had any idea what was going on in her chest—

She led him into the consulting room and handed him the folders, and as he took them his hand brushed lightly against hers and the heat from his skin sent a wave of longing through her. She almost dropped the files but he had them, and he turned swiftly away and dumped them on the desk.

'Anyone I should be particularly aware of?' he asked, his voice a little taut and very businesslike, so she followed his lead. Anything to help get herself back under control before her heart gave out.

'Yes, Judy Richards,' she said briskly. 'She has a history of early miscarriage. This is her fourth pregnancy, she's thirty-two weeks which is the longest she's ever gone, but her fundal height hasn't changed since her last appointment a week ago and that wasn't as much as it should have been, so it might be that the baby's found a new position, or it could be that it's stopped growing for some reason. She's on the top of the pile.'

He frowned thoughtfully, all business now. 'Right. Good. Has she been tested for APS?'

'Yes, after her last miscarriage. The test came back negative.'

'Hmm. OK, well, she'd better have another scan before I see her, if we can do it without worrying her too much.'

'It's done. I knew you'd ask for it so I told her it was because it was a new consultant, and she didn't question it. The results are on here,' she said, handing him the department tablet.

'Great. Thanks.' He scrolled through and studied the results, then handed it back, frowning thoughtfully.

'OK. I think I'm going to admit her. Can you call her in, please, and I'll check her over and break the news?'

'Sure.'

And oddly it was fine, because Judy Richards and her baby needed them, they had a job to do and so they just got on with it, slipping seamlessly back into the familiar routine as if it had been yesterday. Not that she was relaxed in any way, but it was a joy watching him with Judy, and a stark reminder of how good he was at his job.

She'd forgotten how intuitive a doctor he was, and how caring. Kind, gentle, thorough—and from his first greeting onwards, Liv could see Judy had utter faith in him.

'Mrs Richards—I'm Nick Jarvis, I've taken over from Simon Bailey. I've had a look at your notes, and also the scan you had done today. It doesn't really shed any light—which is good news in a way, I suppose, but it still leaves some unanswered questions and I don't like that, so I think I'd like to admit you and do a few more tests, get a closer look at your baby and the placenta and retest you for APS—antiphospholipid syndrome. Has anybody discussed that with you yet?'

'Yes, Mr Bailey did, but he didn't think I'd got it.'

'He may well be right, but I'm erring on the side of caution, so if that's all right with you, I'll ring the ward and make the arrangements for you to be admitted now, and then maybe someone could bring some things in for you later.'

'I can't go home and get them myself?'

'You can, of course, but I'd like to get the tests under way as soon as possible and I'm in Theatre this afternoon, so I'd very much rather you didn't because I'd like to look after you myself rather than hand you over to someone else in my team.'

By the time he'd convinced Judy to come in immediately for closer monitoring, she was still calm and relatively relaxed, which considering her obstetric history was nothing short of a miracle.

If only *they* were as calm and relaxed things would

be fine, but they weren't. Liv felt like a cat on hot bricks, and she wasn't sure he was faring any better.

They got through the morning by keeping out of each other's way as much as possible, avoiding eye contact, restricting conversation to a minimum and all work-related, but fun it wasn't and her nerves were in bits, so the second the clinic was finished she made her escape.

He closed the door as Liv went out with the last patient, leant back against the wall and closed his eyes, letting his breath out in a long, slow huff.

Well, they'd survived, if you could call it that.

Not that it had been easy, but they'd got through it by sticking to business and getting on with the job, and they'd done that well, working together as a smooth, well-oiled team just as they had in the old days. Except in the old days they'd enjoyed it, and he was pretty certain neither of them had enjoyed it today, and the tension between them could have been cut with a knife.

It couldn't go on like this, though, and he knew he had to do something to break through the icy politeness and careful distance between them or it wasn't going to work. At all.

He shrugged away from the wall, picked up the last set of notes and left the room, scanning the clinic for Liv, but there was no sign of her.

'Seen Liv?' he asked at Reception as he handed over the file, and was told she'd gone for lunch.

Which meant, unless she'd changed her habits, she'd be in the café that opened onto the park.

Good. He could do with a nice, strong coffee, with caffeine in it for a change. It might help him get through what was sure to be a deeply awkward conversation.

CHAPTER TWO

'MIND IF I join you?'

She might have known he'd find her here. She should have gone to the other café, or the restaurant—or even better, gone off-site.

Too late now. She looked pointedly at the two free tables, then up into those beautiful, unreadable eyes that were studying her knowingly. Too knowingly. She looked away.

'Is this about work?'

'In a way.'

He didn't wait for her to invite him, just put his cup on the table and sat down, his gaze meeting hers again, but this time she didn't look away because his eyes looked guarded and a little wary still, and she realised he was—nervous? No, not nervous, that didn't sound like Nick. Uncomfortable, maybe. That didn't sound like him, either, not the Nick she knew and loved anyway, but maybe he'd changed. Maybe she'd changed him by cutting him so brutally out of her life, but she'd been so hurt...

'Liv, I realise this is awkward, but I do think we need to clear the air if we're going to work together,' he said quietly, 'unless you being in the clinic this morning was just a one-off?'

She shook her head. 'No, it wasn't a one-off, but I wasn't meant to be doing the clinic today and I didn't realise you'd be starting work so early. I thought it would take longer with HR.'

'Ah, well, that's the file for you,' he said with a slight smile that didn't reach his eyes. 'Answers all the questions in an instant. So, getting back to us, I'd assumed when Ben asked me that you'd still be in the midwife-led unit?'

She shook her head again. 'No, I only moved there while you were working your notice, and after you'd gone there was no point in me staying there, so I switched back to the consultant unit when there was a vacancy. I've been back six months.'

He frowned. 'I didn't know that. I'm sorry, I would have talked to you first if I had. Obviously I knew we'd see each other anyway from time to time, but that's not quite the same as having to work together. Are you going to be OK with that?'

Was she? OK with spending day after day bumping into him, working alongside him on deliveries, their hands, their bodies touching as they brushed against each other in the confines of the delivery room? OK with hearing his voice, catching endless glimpses of him around the maternity unit, hearing him laugh? He had a wonderful laugh, warm and rich and never, never unkind.

Would she really be OK with all of that?

She let out a soft, slightly shaky sigh. 'Nick, it's fine. We managed this morning and as I said to Ben, I'm sure we can be civilised.'

'I'm sure we can, but that still doesn't make it easy.'

The despairing little laugh escaped without her permission. 'What, you thought you could come back into my life after a year and it would be *easy*? Get real, Nick. We're not married any more, in case you hadn't noticed. Of course it won't be easy.'

He winced slightly—so slightly that anyone who didn't know him as well as she did wouldn't have spotted it, but when he spoke it was without emotion.

'We *are* still married,' he corrected, his voice carefully controlled, 'but I haven't forgotten for a single moment that we're not together. That's not what this is about. But we are going to have to work together, and we never had a problem in the past and I don't want us to have a problem now.'

'Did we have a problem today?'

'With the work? No. With the atmosphere, definitely, and I'm not sure I can do it unless we can find some middle ground. We used to be such a brilliant team, and I want to find a way to get that back.'

'Seriously?' she asked, slightly incredulous, but he nodded.

'Seriously. I realise it's not going to be the same, but it needs to be better than it was this morning, and I just wanted to clear the air, break the ice a bit and get rid of the awkwardness, so that we're more at ease next time.'

In his dreams. There was no way she was going to be at ease with him. She only had to hear his voice or catch a glimpse of him and her heart started racing, but he was here and she was stuck with it, for now at least, and he had a point. They did have to be able to work together, although she still had questions about that, so she went for the first one on the pile.

'How come you were available to locum anyway?' she asked without preamble. 'I'd imagined you tucked up in a nice little consultant's post somewhere picturesque.'

Probably with another woman. She didn't add that, because he was trying to pour oil on troubled waters and it wouldn't help at all if she threw petrol on the fire instead. And besides, it was none of her business any more who he chose to sleep with.

He glanced down, stirring his coffee on autopilot even though she knew it wouldn't have sugar in it.

'I didn't want to tie myself down,' he said, finally putting the spoon back in the saucer and meeting her eyes again. 'After I left here, I just wanted to get away, let the dust settle, work out where I wanted to go. I thought maybe New Zealand, but my parents are still alive and they're getting older, so I took a two-month locum post covering maternity leave fairly close to them while I worked out what I wanted to do, and then when that was coming to an end they asked me to cover the fertility clinic until it shut because the services were being centralised and the consultant had left, so I did. I saw my last patients two days ago, on the day Ben rang, and I had nothing else lined up, so I'm here.'

'Why on earth did you say yes?'

'To Ben? Because I need a job, so I can eat and keep a roof over both our heads.'

She felt another pang of guilt. 'I didn't mean that, Nick, but if the mortgage is an issue—'

'It's not an issue, Liv, it's a fact, and I'm not going to make you homeless under any circumstances so let's just ignore that. So what *did* you mean?'

'I was talking about the fertility clinic job. I couldn't

believe it when Ben told me that's what you'd been doing. It seems such an odd choice to make, under the circumstances, and I couldn't understand why on earth you'd do it.'

His eyes flicked away, then back to hers, curiously intent. 'Because I needed a job, as I said, and I was already in the hospital, I'd made a few friends, it meant I wouldn't have to relocate—and maybe, also, because I thought it might help me understand what had happened to us.'

Her heart thumped. 'And did it?'

He smiled sadly. 'Well, let's just say it made it blindingly obvious that we weren't the only couple struggling.'

His expression wasn't guarded now, just full of regret, and she lowered her head, unable to hold those clear grey eyes that seemed to see to the bottom of her insecurities.

'How about you?' he asked softly. 'What have you been up to since I went?'

She picked up her spoon and chased the froth on her cappuccino, stalling just as he had. 'What I'm doing now, pretty much. What did you expect?'

'I didn't. I had no idea what you'd want to do.'

Cry? She'd done so much of that after he'd gone, but she wasn't telling him that, although he could probably work it out. Fix it? Impossible, because the thing that had been wrong was the thing they hadn't been able to fix, so she'd just got on with her life, putting one foot in front of the other, not even trying to make sense of it because there wasn't any sense to be made.

'I didn't want to do anything,' she said sadly, watching the froth slide off the spoon. 'I just wanted peace, that was all. Peace, contentment, and the satisfaction of a job well done instead of the endless spectre of failure—'

'You didn't fail, Liv!'

She dropped the spoon with a clatter. 'Really? So what would you call it? Month after month, all our hopes and dreams flushed away—and then, just to rub my nose in it, you go off and sleep with your ex. That doesn't exactly make it a success in my book—'

She pushed back her chair, grabbed her bag and walked swiftly away from him, out of the café into the park, hauling in the cold air as if she'd just come up from the bottom of the ocean.

Don't cry! Whatever you do, don't cry—

'Liv! Liv, wait!'

She turned and looked up at him, right behind her, his grey eyes troubled, and she had the crazy urge to throw herself into his arms and sob her heart out.

Don't cry!

'Leave it, Nick,' she said, hoping her voice didn't show her desperation. 'Just leave it. I don't mind working with you, I said that to Ben, and I'm sure we can keep it professional, but I don't need any cosy chats or in-depth analysis of where it all went wrong for us. We both know exactly where it all went wrong, and if I'd gone to the conference with you that weekend then you would never have slept with Suzanne—'

'I didn't sleep with her.'

She stared at him, stunned. *'What?'*

'I said, I didn't sleep with her.'

Shock robbed her of breath.

'I don't believe you. You're lying!'

'No, I'm not, Liv. I didn't touch her. Honestly.'

She took a step back, struggling for air, for sense, for understanding, but they all eluded her.

'That's not true. It can't be true. Why would you suddenly come out with this now?'

'Because it *is* true, and I should have told you at the time.'

How did he do that with his eyes? Make them appear utterly unguarded and shining with sincerity?

'But—you admitted it!'

'No. No, I didn't Liv, I just confirmed that she'd spent the night with me in my room,' he told her. 'That was what you asked me, and I said yes because it was the truth. She did spend the night in there with me. You didn't ask why, though, or what for, because by the time I came home you'd spoken to Beth, you'd found the note Suze had left in my luggage and you had me hung, drawn and quartered and hung out to dry before I even stepped over the threshold, so you wouldn't have believed me anyway.

'You just assumed I'd slept with her,' he went on, his voice heavy and tinged with sadness, 'and I let you, because in that split second I felt that you'd thrown me a lifeline, a way out of a marriage that was tearing us both apart, so I just grabbed it and ran. And I'm sorry. I should never have done that to you. I should have told you the truth there and then, and made you listen.'

His words stunned her, the shockwaves rolling through her, bringing a sob to her throat.

'How could you do that?' she asked, her voice a strangled whisper. 'How could you let me believe that for all this time? I've spent a whole, agonising year believing that you slept with her, that I wasn't enough for you, that you didn't truly love me any more—you're right, you should have told me the truth then, Nick, instead of letting me think that you'd spent the night making love to—'

She broke off, unable to say her name. 'You let me end our *marriage*, on the grounds that you'd slept with that *whore*—'

His eyes hardened. 'She's not a whore, she's a friend, a damn good friend, who told me to pull myself together and go home and sort out my marriage.'

A sob rose in her throat, threatening to choke her, but she crushed it down and pulled herself together. 'Well, you did a great job of that—'

Her voice cracked and she pushed past him, shaking his hand off as he tried to stop her. She went back inside, cutting through the café to the main hospital corridor, then out on the other side bordering the car park, deliberately going the wrong way to throw him off the scent and lose him because if she had to spend another moment in his company she was going to cry, and she wasn't prepared to give him the satisfaction.

So she kept on going, and she didn't stop until she was back on the ward.

She'd gone.

The corridor was empty and he stood there, kicking himself for letting the conversation stray into such dangerous territory—especially in a public place and right in the middle of the working day.

Idiot!

He had to talk to her, to explain why he'd let her believe what she had, how he'd felt, why he hadn't stood his ground and told her the truth at the time. The *real* reason.

But not now. This afternoon he had a—mercifully

short—elective list, so his first port of call was the wards, to make sure Judy Richards was settled in, and to meet the patients he was going to operate on and read through their notes before he was due in Theatre. And if he was lucky, Liv's shift would be well and truly over by the time he'd finished.

He'd go and see her at home later, to apologise, to explain, to try and help her understand.

If he could get her to listen, and judging by the way she'd just reacted, that was by no means a foregone conclusion.

Liv was tied up in a delivery for the afternoon, the nice straightforward labour of a woman having her sixth baby. She'd haemorrhaged after the last so she'd been admitted directly to the consultant-led unit with this one just in case, but so far everything was going fine.

Just as well, because Liv's concentration was totally shot.

How could he have done that to her? Let her believe he'd betrayed her like that if he hadn't? And why then, when she'd just found out that *yet again* she wasn't pregnant, so she'd been at her most vulnerable? She'd spent over a year living with the bone-deep certainty that he'd been unfaithful to her, and now she didn't know what to believe—

'I need to push.'

'OK, Karen. Nice and steady. That's good.'

But Karen's baby wasn't going for nice and steady, and three minutes later, half an hour before the end of Liv's shift, a lusty, squalling baby was delivered into her father's waiting hands.

'It's a girl,' he said, laughing and crying as he lay

their daughter in his wife Karen's outstretched arms. 'Finally, it's a girl!'

Liv's eyes filled, and she had to blink away the tears as she gave Karen the oxytocin injection to help her uterus to contract down.

If this had been them, if she'd been able to give him a child, then maybe that would have been enough to keep him...

Liv checked the baby quickly as she lay in her mother's arms, making sure that all was well, but the baby was lovely and pink, her pulse steady and strong, her skinny little arms and legs moving beautifully. She'd stopped crying now and was staring up at her mother, riveted by the first face she'd ever seen.

It was a beautiful moment, one Liv never tired of seeing, and she watched the two of them staring into each other's eyes and falling in love and felt a familiar lump in her throat.

'Apgar score ten at one minute,' she said, her voice miraculously steady. 'Congratulations. She's lovely.'

She checked her again four minutes later, by which time the cord had stopped pulsating, so Liv clamped and cut it and handed the baby back to her mother.

'I take it this is your first girl?'

Her father's grin was wry. 'Yes, so hopefully we can stop now. Six is getting a little crazy, but we did want a girl so we thought we'd have one last try.'

'We may live to regret it when she hits puberty,' Karen said with a laugh, her hands cradling the naked baby tenderly at her breast.

Liv laid a warm towel back over them both and tucked it round the baby. 'She'll be fine, and she'll have all those big brothers to look after her. She's latched on well,' Liv added, struck yet again by the miracle of birth and the naturalness of this wonderful bond between mother and child. The bond she would never know…

'Yes, and thank goodness I've never had any problems with feeding any of them,' Karen said with a laugh. 'There's way too much to do in our house without sterilising bottles and making up feeds. Ooh, I can feel a contraction.'

'OK, Karen, that's good, you're nearly done. Gentle push for me when you're ready?' she said calmly, but Liv felt her heart rate pick up, because this was the moment, as the placenta separated from the uterine wall, that the haemorrhage would happen, and she really, really didn't feel ready for that.

Didn't feel ready for any more stress today, and the last thing she needed was Nick striding in there to take over like the cavalry after he'd just destabilised her fragile status quo with that bombshell about Suzanne.

Concentrate!

The haemorrhage didn't happen. To everyone's huge relief, the placenta came away cleanly with hardly any blood loss, so after they'd sorted Karen out and Liv was happy that her uterus was contracting down well and that all was as it should be, she left the other midwife to fill out the notes and headed for the changing room, only an hour late.

Tomorrow was Saturday, and with any luck she wouldn't run into Nick again today which meant she was unlikely to see him again until Monday. That would give her two clear days to get her emotions in order.

Except it didn't, because she walked out of the lift at the bottom of the building and ran slap into him.

'Sorry—'

She stepped hastily back, and they stood transfixed in awkward silence as the lift doors hissed shut behind her, cutting off her retreat.

'I gather your delivery was all right?' he asked, breaking the silence. 'I've been on standby in case she haemorrhaged again.'

'Oh—yes, it was fine, thanks. No problems. How's Judy Richards?'

'Settling in. I think I've reassured her.' He paused, his eyes searching hers. 'Look, Liv, are you done for the day?'

'Yes,' she said firmly, holding his eyes with a determined effort and clutching her coat in her arms like a shield. 'And I'm going home.'

'Can we talk?'

Her heart sank. 'Again? Nick, there's nothing you have to say that I need to hear. If there's a shred of truth in what you said, you should have told me then, not saved it for now, and I really don't want to discuss it. For heaven's sake, just leave it. It's not relevant any more anyway.'

She pushed past him and walked out of the door, but of course he couldn't leave it, could he? She could barely hear his footsteps behind her but she knew he was there, his voice calling her name as she made her way across the car park, but it was almost drowned out by the pounding of her heart.

She dodged between the rows of cars, reached the kerb by the access road to the main car park and was about to cross it when she felt his hand on her arm.

'Liv, please, let me talk to you. Give me a chance to explain.'

But she'd had enough to deal with already today, so

she turned back to face him and shook her head. 'No. I can't do this now just to ease your guilty conscience, Nick, and I'm not going to. Please, just leave me alone!'

He caught her shoulders and held her. 'Liv, I won't take much of your time, but there's something I need to tell you and you need to hear it—'

'No! No, I don't!'

She tried to spin away from him, but his grip suddenly tightened and he tried to pull her back.

'Liv, no!' he yelled, his voice urgent, but the urgency was lost on her as she wrenched her arm away and stumbled backwards off the kerb out of reach.

She saw the look of horror on his face, heard the blast of a horn, saw the car as it clipped her and sent her spinning, and then her head hit the ground and everything went black...

He watched helplessly as the car struck her, saw her fall, saw her head bouncing off the kerb as she came to rest just inches from the front wheel. The big SUV had ground to a halt and the driver stumbled out, other people ran towards them shouting, but his eyes were only for Liv.

She was lying motionless on the edge of the road like a broken doll, her head level with the front wheel, her feet partly under the car just inches from the rear wheel, and for a terrifying second he thought she was dead.

Her hair had tumbled over her face and he dropped to his knees beside her, sweeping the hair aside to check for a pulse in her neck, but his own heart was beating so hard he could scarcely feel hers and his breath jammed in his throat.

'Liv? Liv, talk to me, for God's sake!'

He found a pulse and dragged in a breath, digging out the doctor instead of the lover, running his hands over her quickly, checking that she was breathing, scanning her for injuries, but her limbs were all straight, her pupils were equal and reactive, her breathing was normal. For now. But she was unconscious, and that could mean anything.

He needed help, and fast. He tugged his phone out of his pocket with shaking fingers and rang the ED direct. 'One of our midwives has been knocked down near the staff car park and she's unconscious. Send a team out here now, please, fast. Tell them they'll need a collar and board and a pelvic band. And hurry.'

She started to stir, and he dropped the phone and reached out, bracketing her head carefully in his hands and holding it steady, feeling the stickiness of blood on his fingers as they burrowed through her hair. No...

'Easy, Liv. Try not to move. I've called for help. Just stay as still as you can.'

'Nick?'

She knew him. Thank God...

'It's OK, Liv, I've got you, my love. I've got you. They'll be here soon. You'll be OK. Just keep still for me, sweetheart.'

'My head hurts...'

'I know, darling, I know, but they'll be here soon. Just hang on another minute. It won't be long.'

'Over here,' someone yelled, and then the crowd that had gathered around them parted as the trauma team arrived.

He looked up without moving his hands. 'She was KOed briefly, she's got a head wound, and you'll need a collar and a board. GCS three at first, now fourteen.

She's concussed, almost certainly whiplashed and she could have pelvic and spinal injuries—and mind her legs. I don't know if they were hit,' he said unsteadily, and then someone took over the control of her head and neck and he found himself gently shifted out of the way. Someone backed the car away very carefully to give them better access, and as soon as her spine was immobilised they moved her onto a stretcher, then up onto the trolley for the short trundle to the ED doors.

He scooped up her bag and coat and went with them, still issuing instructions on autopilot. 'Try and keep it smooth,' he said, putting his free hand on the trolley to steady it. 'She'll need a head and neck CT and a full trauma series—'

'It's OK, you can leave her with us now,' someone said, but he shook his head.

'No way, she's my wife,' he said, for the sake of economy, and he followed them into Resus without waiting to be invited. The team closed around her, nobody he recognised, no one he could connect with, and then a door swished open and someone said, 'OK, what have we got?' and the voice from his youth was so familiar he could have cried with relief.

'Sam,' he said, his voice choked, and Sam stopped in his tracks and did a mild double-take.

'Nick? What are you doing here?'

'My wife was knocked down in the car park, right in front of me. Her name's Olivia—Liv. She's a midwife here.'

'Liv's your wife?' Sam's face creased into a frown and he bent over her so she could see his face without moving. 'Hi, Liv, it's Sam Ryder. Remember me? You delivered our baby last year.'

'Of course I do. How is she?' she mumbled, and Nick let out a sigh of relief because if she remembered that, it was a good sign—wasn't it?

'She's fine. They're both well.' Sam turned to him. 'What can you tell me about the accident? Speed, angle of collision, how far she travelled?'

He made himself focus. 'Um—low speed collision, probably less than ten miles an hour at the most? She stepped out backwards in front of a big SUV. She was hit from her left side and spun as she fell, but not far. Her head hit the kerb pretty hard. There's a cut on the left side just behind the temple. GCS three initially, then fourteen after a brief loss of consciousness—'

'How brief?'

He shrugged. 'I don't know. Not long, but long enough to be significant. A minute, maybe, at the most? I'd done a cursory check and called for help before she stirred.'

'Did her head hit the bonnet before she fell?'

'No. No, it really wasn't that fast and the front wing just clipped her. She just—spun and fell, but really hard so she'll need a CT and her head's bleeding so she could have a fracture there where she hit the kerb, and she might be whiplashed and her spine needs checking thoroughly—'

Sam lifted a hand. 'OK, we're on it. Can you give us her details so we can be getting her notes up? And then maybe you need to go and get a coffee while we check her over.'

'I can't leave her—'

'Yes, you can. Don't worry, we'll keep you updated. Make sure we've got your number.'

Sam turned back to Liv, taking her hand in his, focusing intently on his patient as Nick stood numbly and watched them, hardly daring to breathe.

'OK, Liv, can you tell me where it hurts?' Sam asked softly.

'Everywhere.'

'Well, that's not very useful,' he said with a grin. 'Can you try and be a little more specific?'

'My head?'

'Anywhere else?' He carried on chattily assessing her while Nick watched tensely from the sidelines, then he straightened.

'OK. That's all good. Can we get some IV paracetamol on board, please, and get a full trauma screen to rule out any fractures and then we'll send you down for a head and neck CT, Liv, OK? And can we run a FAST scan, please, while we're waiting?'

Nick felt himself relax a fraction. Despite his light-hearted banter, Sam was looking after her properly, and all the time the nurses had been working, linking her to a monitor, getting IV access ready, cutting her clothes away so Sam could see her injuries.

He could see them, too, and the bruises on her smooth, pale skin made him wince. She could so easily have been killed—

'Mr Jarvis?'

He turned his head, finally becoming aware of the nurse who'd laid a hand on his arm and was shaking it gently to get his attention.

'If you could give me her details that would be very helpful.'

'Of course. I'm sorry.' He forced himself to focus, rattled off her name, date of birth, address, GP—

'OK, I've got her. You're her next of kin?'

'Yes,' he said firmly, although he didn't know if that was still true, strictly speaking, because the ex-ness made that all a little unclear...

'Same mobile phone number?'

'Yes.'

'Is that her stuff? Would you like me to look after it?'

He looked down and saw the coat and bag, clutched in his hand like a lifeline. He'd forgotten all about them. 'Yeah, thanks.' He handed them over just as the door behind him opened again and swished shut, and he turned his head and met Ben Walker's worried eyes.

'What's going on? I heard Liv had been run over.'

'Not run over,' he said, his voice suddenly hollow. 'She was knocked down. She's got a head injury.'

Ben frowned, crossed over to the bed and exchanged a few words with Sam, then leant over her. 'Hi, Liv. Anything I can do?'

She mumbled something, and Ben nodded and straightened up, squeezing her hand as he left her side.

'Don't worry, I'll look after him.'

He turned to the nurse who was printing up Liv's labels for the notes. 'Page me if you need us,' he said, and hooking his arm around Nick's shoulders, the bluff Yorkshireman gently but firmly led him away.

CHAPTER THREE

BEN STEERED HIM through the department and out of the doors on the park side of the building.

The cold March air hit him, and he hauled in a breath and gagged.

'I feel sick,' he said, and doubled over, retching emptily.

He felt Ben's hand on his back. 'Come on. We'll find a bench where you can sit down and I'll go and get us a drink.'

He nodded and straightened up, following Ben obediently across the grass on legs that weren't quite steady. 'I thought she was dead, Ben. She was about to step out in front of this massive SUV, right in front of my eyes, and I tried to hold her but she pulled away and fell backwards and it smacked into her and then she was lying there, so still, her feet just inches from the wheels—'

'Nick, she's alive and conscious and talking, and Sam will be doing everything he can to make sure she stays that way. Now sit down before you fall down.'

They'd reached a bench, and he didn't need telling twice. He dropped onto it and propped his elbows on his knees, trying to slow his breathing and regain control of his emotions. After a few seconds he straightened up and glanced across at Ben, who was sitting beside him watching him thoughtfully.

'Better?'

He nodded. 'Yeah. Sorry.'

The hand on his shoulder was warm and firm and comforting. 'Don't be. You're in shock, and I'd be just the same if it was Daisy or one of the kids. How do you take your tea?'

'Coffee, for a start, black, no sugar—and if you put a ton of sugar in it, I'll pour it on the grass, so don't even try.'

Ben grunted and got to his feet without bothering to comment. 'Have you eaten today?'

'Not since seven. I didn't manage to get lunch.'

Too busy trashing what was left of his relationship with Liv...

'Right. I'll get you something to eat, as well. Stay here.'

He didn't think he had a choice. He was seriously unsure his legs would hold him if he tried to get up, and he swallowed on another wave of nausea.

Shock, he realised numbly. He was in shock, as Ben had said, but Liv was alive, Sam was looking after her and if he was as good a doctor as he was a sailor, she was in safe hands.

All he could do was wait.

So this is what it's like in a scanner, she thought, but she felt curiously detached, as if it wasn't really happening to her.

It didn't take long, and then she was wheeled back to the ED, lying on her back staring at the ceiling as it whizzed past and feeling disorientated. She knew the route well, but she'd never seen it from this angle. Weird.

They went through several sets of doors, and came to rest at last in Resus. She was glad they'd stopped. Her head was spinning and even the slight jiggle of the trolley along the smooth corridors had made it hurt more.

'OK?' Sam asked, smiling down at her, and she tried to smile back but it felt like a pretty poor effort and she just wanted Nick.

'I think so. My head aches a bit.'

'It will. You've had quite a bump, Liv, but nothing's broken and there's no evidence of a brain injury. You might be pretty sore for a while, though, but your spine's OK and so's your pelvis, so we can get rid of all this stuff and someone'll come and clean you up a bit and then I'll get you moved out of Resus.'

'What happened to my clothes? I don't remember anyone taking them off.'

'We cut them off you,' he said, frowning slightly. 'When you were brought in.'

'Oh.' She thought hard, but came up with nothing. 'I didn't register that. I suppose you had to. Where's Nick?'

'I don't know, but when I find him he's going to ask me questions and I gather from Ben that you're not together any more, so do I have your permission to talk to him about your results, or would you rather I didn't?'

Her results? 'Yes—yes, of course. If you don't tell him he'll only ask me anyway so you might as well.'

Sam chuckled. 'That sounds like him. OK, I'll go and find him while we get you sorted. He won't be far away.'

* * *

He was in the relatives' room where Ben had left him when Sam came in. He tried to get up, but Sam put a hand on his shoulder and pushed him gently back down. It wasn't hard. His legs felt like jelly and he thought he was going to be sick again.

He opened his mouth to ask how she was, but he didn't need to, Sam got there before him.

'She's OK, Nick. She's doing all right.'

He let his breath out in a rush and crushed the sudden urge to cry. 'No brain injury?'

Sam sat down beside him and shook his head.

'No. Not as far as we can see but we'll watch that. Her CT was clear, her X-rays didn't reveal any fractures, but she's got a small cut on her scalp which I'm going to glue, and she's going to have some colourful bruises. There's the odd superficial graze from contact with the ground, of course, and she's going to be sore, but all in all she's got away with it pretty lightly. Assuming there's no silent head injury waiting to show itself, she should be fine in a day or so but she might be a bit concussed. She's got a headache, so I want to keep an eye on that, but it's probably a bit of whiplash.'

He nodded, swallowing. 'Can I see her now?'

'In a minute. I'll get someone to take you to her as soon as she's ready. I'm going to keep her on fifteen-minute obs for a while, and I'm probably going to admit her overnight, just in case. She didn't seem to remember we'd cut her clothes off, but that might just be shock. She was still in the neck brace so she might not even have realised what we were doing, but I don't want to make assumptions and miss anything.'

Nick tried to smile. 'Don't worry, I won't let you.

I'll be right there by her side and I'll be watching her like a hawk.'

'Good. I'll let you know when she's ready. Oh, and the police want to talk to you about the accident. I'll get them to come and see you now. Don't move.'

It seemed to take an age before the police were finished with him, but finally he was able to go and see Liv. She was in a bed in the small observation ward, her lashes dark against her pale cheeks, and she looked so frail and vulnerable that his heart wrenched. It could so easily have been so much worse. It might yet be...

The chair creaked as he sat down, and her lids fluttered open and her head turned towards him.

'Nick?'

He stood up and moved to her side, gripping the cot sides on the edge of the bed as he stared down at her ashen face. A bruise was coming out on her cheekbone, blue against the pale skin, and he swallowed hard. 'Yes, it's me, Liv. Is that OK, or do you want me to leave?'

'No, stay with me, please?' Her hand fluttered, and he reached down and slipped his fingers through hers and they curled around his and clung.

'How are you feeling?' he asked, aware of how gruff his voice sounded but unable to do anything about it.

She shrugged slightly, and winced. 'Sore?' she said, sounding weak and tired and nothing like his Liv. 'I've got a banging headache and everything's feeling a bit tender. Sam said I was lucky not to break anything, but it doesn't feel lucky from where I'm lying.'

'It's lucky,' he said fervently. 'Trust me, it's lucky. I watched that car hit you, and for a minute there—well, whatever. If I hadn't followed you—'

'Nick, it wasn't your fault I stepped out in front of it.'

'Don't, Liv. I don't want to think about it. It's all I can see as it is, and it *was* my fault, I should have listened to you and let you go.' He lifted her hand to his mouth and pressed a long, lingering kiss to the back of her fingers. 'Is there anything I can do for you, anything I can get you?'

'A taxi?' she joked weakly. 'Not that I can go anywhere. They cut my clothes off.'

He frowned. 'They had to, Liv. They had no idea what injuries you had, and anyway, hitting the tarmac won't have done them any good. And as for the taxi, you're going nowhere,' he said firmly. 'Sam's talking about admitting you overnight for observation and I think it's a good idea.'

'No-o. I don't want to stay in,' she moaned softly. 'It's so noisy here. I just want my own bed.'

'OK. Maybe later. I'll talk to Sam,' he murmured to stall her, although he knew darned well what Sam would say, and so, apparently, did she.

'My parents used to do that,' she said, her voice tailing off. 'I'll ask your father. I'll see what your mother says. All stalling tactics. The answer never did change…'

Her lids drifted down, her lashes coming to rest against her bleached skin, and as her hand relaxed he laid it down gently, let his breath out on a slow, silent huff and lowered himself onto the chair again, never taking his eyes off her.

She'd get better a lot quicker, Liv thought, if they'd only leave her alone to sleep, but she knew why they were doing it, and it was reassuring in a mildly irritating way.

The nurses came intermittently to do her obs, and

after a while Nick told them not to bother, he'd do them. It meant he had to touch her, to feel the pulse beating in her wrist, to check her pupils with a pen light, and although he was doing exactly what the nurses had, somehow his touch was different.

Not quite so clinical as theirs, lingering a little longer than was strictly necessary, and his voice was quiet and soothing but also filled with an emotion that he either didn't or couldn't disguise. And when she had to stare into his eyes so he could test her pupil reflexes, there was a tenderness there that made her want to cry.

A nurse brought him a cup of tea at one point, and a couple of times Sam popped his head round the curtain, glanced at her chart and exchanged a few words with them, asked her questions, made her squeeze his hands, push against him, wiggle her toes, shone a light in her eyes to check her pupil reflexes and accommodation, but all of it with an appropriate clinical detachment which just made Nick's touch all the more obviously different.

It was weird having him there with her. He was so gentle, so quiet and unobtrusive, and yet even when he was sitting silently beside her, she was aware of him with every battered cell in her body. She'd been so desperate to get away from him that she'd nearly died, and now that seemed ridiculous because she actually wanted him there, crazy though it was.

Because she still loved him, despite the lie? Maybe even *because* of it—because of the fact that he hadn't, after all, slept with Suzanne.

Why not? She wouldn't have blamed him—or Suze, come to that. She was a beautiful woman, and he was a beautiful man. Why wouldn't they want each other?

It wasn't as if it would have been the first time—and it wasn't as if things had been exactly peachy in the months leading up to it, and that was her own fault as much as his.

She'd spent the last year blaming herself for shutting him out and driving him to it, but he'd shut her out, too, and their relationship had been crumbling for months before it had reached crisis point.

He was right, they did need to talk, but not now, and not here, in probably the busiest department of the hospital. Now, with her head hurting and every part of her starting to ache, all she wanted was to go home.

Sam, though, had other ideas. Before he'd discuss it he wanted a urine sample to check for blood, presumably to see if she'd sustained kidney damage.

'I'll get a bedpan,' Nick said, but she was ready for that and dismissed it instantly.

'No way. Or a commode. The loo—as in proper plumbing, running water, and a door that shuts.'

'I don't think—'

'Good. Don't bother,' she said, trying to sound firm and failing miserably. 'Seriously, Nick, if you won't let me walk, then get me a wheelchair, and if you won't do that then I'll crawl on my hands and knees. Please don't make me, because I will do it.' Her voice cracked, and she bit her lips and waited.

She watched his internal battle, and then to her relief he sighed quietly and got to his feet. 'Still as stubborn as ever, then,' he said mildly, and went, presumably to find a wheelchair.

'Going somewhere?' Sam asked as Nick wheeled it in.

'Yeah. It has to be the loo, apparently.'

'Well, stay with her.'

'I will.'

'Over my dead body,' she said, and Sam just laughed, but Nick frowned, his face a mask.

'Can we not talk about your dead body, please?' he said tightly, and she felt a chill run over her. If that car had been going a little quicker, she might not be here now. There'd been a fraction of a second when everything had gone into slow motion, and she'd been sure she was going to die. What must it have been like for him to watch it all happen and be unable to prevent it? To feel that he'd caused it, even?

Horrendous, and it was only by the grace of God that she wasn't dead or far more critically injured. No wonder he was fussing over her. After all, he'd loved her once, and maybe, in a way, still did. And despite their problems, he was a good man. Way too good to have deserved the way she'd treated him.

'Sorry,' she said soberly, cutting him some slack. 'If you could just wheel me there, please, I can do the rest.'

He had an opinion, of course, but in the end she won and he hovered outside the door until she'd finished and then took the urine sample off her and wheeled her back to bed.

'OK?' he asked as she sank back against the pillows with relief.

'Mmm. Thanks. Could you give that to Sam and ask him when I can go home?'

'You can ask me yourself,' Sam said, appearing at the foot of the bed and giving her a wry smile. 'You won't like the answer.'

'Oh, no, Sam, really? I'm fine—'

'No, you're not, Liv,' Sam told her gently. 'You're

doing OK, but you're not fine, and if you've got a silent head injury—'

'Then I'll call someone.'

'Not if you can't,' Nick growled from beside her. 'You need monitoring all night.'

'No, I don't! I'm fine, Nick, and if you won't discharge me, Sam, I'm going to discharge myself.'

'Liv, I really—'

'No, Nick! This is none of your business. I appreciate your concern, both of you, but I don't want to stay in. I've got a few bruises—'

'You were out cold!'

'For seconds—'

'It still counts, Liv,' Sam interjected, but she just glared at him.

'I. Want. To. Go. Home,' she said, stressing every word as if she was talking to a pair of idiots, which frankly she felt she was. Her head was killing her, everything hurt and she just wanted out. Now. Before she broke down and let out all the emotions that were building inside her.

Sam looked at her, looked at Nick and looked back at her again—and gave in.

'OK,' he said, to her astonishment. 'On one condition.'

'Anything,' she said rashly.

'Nick stays with you.'

'No!'

They spoke together, but Sam just arched a brow and shrugged. 'Your choice. It's that or nothing.'

'I'll discharge myself.'

Nick felt sick again. She would, he knew that. The

woman was stubborn enough for anything, even if it worked against her. He'd learned that years ago, and he'd given up fighting it.

But this was different. This was her life they were talking about, and her safety was more important to him than anything else and he'd done enough to compromise it today already.

'I'll do it,' he said. 'If you insist on going home, I'll do it.'

'No. It's not necessary.'

'Take it or leave it, Liv,' he said flatly. 'Either I'm there with you, or you're here, which is definitely my preferred option.'

'It's not your option to have, and you can't make me—'

'Watch me. I've already seen you nearly get killed once today because of me. I won't stand back and watch you have another go. As I said, take it or leave it, but that's the way it is.'

She frowned, lifting her hand to her head and pressing it against her forehead as if she was trying to push away the pain. Finally her arm dropped in a gesture of defeat.

'OK. You win. Come home with me if you think you have to, but it's totally unnecessary and I'm not happy about it.'

'Tough. At least I'll be able to live with myself,' he told her.

Sam rolled his eyes and grinned. 'Right. Now that's sorted, I'll go check this urine for blood, and if it's OK I'll authorise your discharge so that we can all go home tonight,' he said, and Nick watched her close her eyes with a sigh.

'I'm still not happy,' she grumbled, but he wasn't going to argue. He'd won this round. For now, that was enough.

It was almost ten that night before he pulled up on the drive of the home they'd shared for three years.

When they'd bought it just over four years ago, a bright future lay ahead of them. Little had they known how it was all going to pan out, but those happy days—and nights—now seemed a lifetime ago and he'd almost forgotten what home meant.

'Keys?' he said to her, and she rummaged in her bag and held them out to him.

'The burglar alarm's set. My code's 0901—and there's a mortice lock on the door now, too.'

The security lights triggered as he got out of the car, which was just as well, as he had to find the new keyhole.

Why the new lock? To stop him getting back in? And changing the code? She hadn't needed to do that. She should have known he wouldn't have invaded her privacy. Maybe he should have done, should have stuck it out and had the rest of the conversation she'd cut off at the ankles when she'd thrown him out, and maybe then he'd still have been with her, instead of drifting around in limbo and living alone in a box no bigger than their double garage.

He let out a tired sigh and swung the door open, stepping into the hall with a curious sense of déjà vu. He didn't know what he'd expected—that she would have changed the decor, or moved the furniture—anything, really, apart from nothing, which was what confronted him.

The same colour walls—not quite white, a soft touch

of earthy grey taking the edge off it—the same striped
stair carpet in muted greys and neutrals, the chair that
sat randomly in the corner for no apparent reason—
even the basket of carefully pressed and folded washing on the third step waiting for her to make a journey
upstairs and take it with her.

It could have sat there untouched since the day she'd
thrown him out—on the ninth of January. Hence the
code for the burglar alarm, he realised belatedly.

Swallowing the lump in his throat, he turned it off
ran upstairs with the washing basket and put it on the
floor in their—correction, *her*—bedroom, and ran back
down to help her out of the car.

Too slow.

'Liv, what are you doing?'

She lifted her head and frowned at him. 'What do
you think I'm doing?' she asked, levering herself to her
feet. 'It's obvious.'

Stubborn woman. 'Here, let me help you—'

Her level stare stopped him in his tracks, her pride
obviously overriding common sense. 'Nick, relax, I can
manage. You're only here because Sam insisted. I don't
need you to help me.'

Which would have been fine, had she not then
swayed against the car and let out a stifled groan.

He didn't wait to be asked. She'd be on the floor before she admitted she needed him for anything at all,
so he just stepped in, laid her right arm carefully over
his shoulders and put his other arm around her waist
to steady her.

'Headrush?' he asked quietly, and she nodded.

'Mmm. It's OK now.' But she didn't try and shake
him off, which she would have done if she'd truly been

OK, so he walked her carefully to the front door, helped her over the doorstep, and then lowered her gently to the chair. He'd never seen the point of it until now, he thought wryly, watching as she sat silently on it with her eyes shut and a tiny frown creasing her brow.

The bruise on her cheekbone was spreading, coming out nicely in a black and blue stain that extended up into her hair and round the edge of her eye, steadily creeping across her eyebrow and down onto the lid. The only reason her face wasn't scraped was that her thick, dark hair had tumbled across her cheek and protected it as she'd hit the tarmac, and it had been further back on the side of her head that she'd taken the brunt of the fall. Hence the dried blood matted in her hair—

Her eyes opened again and she lifted her head and looked at him, the frown deepening. 'What?'

'What do you mean, what?'

'You were looking at me funny. You still are.'

He clenched his teeth, swallowing the horror he'd been reliving, the sight of her crashing to the ground, the way her head had bounced off the kerb—

'You're imagining it,' he said dismissively. 'Where to? Up or down?'

She looked at the stairs, her eyes running up the flight as if to assess the enormity of the task, then back to him as the fight went out of her. 'It all looks like too much effort but I suppose I really ought to go to bed before I can't get there.'

'Is there anything I can do to help you?'

She shook her head. 'No. I'll manage, Nick.'

She shrugged off her coat, took a deep breath and tackled the stairs. They seemed endless but she made it, only because she didn't really have a choice if she was going to be comfortable, but her head was pounding and she felt dizzy halfway up and had to lean on him.

'Just a few more steps to go,' Nick murmured, his warm, solid body reassuringly close behind her, and she gritted her teeth and made it up the last ones, pausing to lean on him for another moment before tackling the short distance across the landing to the bed.

He flicked back the covers, and she sat down gingerly on the edge with a sigh of relief, cold sweat beading on her forehead.

'OK?'

'Yes, I'm OK. I'm up here anyway. Maybe I should have some painkillers. My head's banging like a drum now.'

'Maybe you should. Let's get you comfy and I'll sort you out a drink to take them with.'

He shifted the pillows, stacking them up so she could lean back on them while she kicked off her shoes and then swung her legs up.

'Oh, that's better.' She sighed, settling against the pillows. 'I just feel a bit battered all over, and my head aches. I keep telling it I feel better, but it hasn't got the memo yet.'

He gave a wry huff of laughter, and he ran downstairs and brought her back a glass of water to take the paracetamol.

'Have you had any other drugs today? Any other pain relief?'

'No, I haven't. You know I don't take drugs. Only the IV paracetamol they gave me this afternoon, and that was hours ago. Just give it to me, for heaven's sake, and don't fuss.'

'I wouldn't dream of it,' he said drily, handing her the water and holding out his hand with the pills in.

She took them, washed them down with water and handed the glass back with an apologetic sigh. 'Thank you. I'm sorry I've been so bitchy. I just...'

'Forget it,' he said softly. 'Tea? Coffee? Something to eat?'

'Tea would be lovely. And some toast, maybe? I'm starving. I don't know what happened to lunch.'

He did. He'd messed it up, like he'd messed so many things up. He put the glass on the bedside table and went back down to the kitchen. It hadn't changed any more than the rest, and he glanced across to the family room, his eyes settling on the sofa where it had all unravelled.

It could have been yesterday, he thought, if it wasn't for the wrenching heartache that had filled every day since she'd told him she wanted a divorce—a divorce that had never happened, for some reason.

He rested his hands on the edge of the worktop, hung his head and let out a shaky sigh. He so hadn't wanted to do this, to be here with her in this way, forced together by circumstances and Sam's well-meant interference, but he was the best candidate for the job.

He knew every inch of the house, could find his way round the kitchen in the dark, and, more importantly, knew Liv well enough to override her when necessary. That didn't mean he was going to enjoy it, and he knew it wouldn't be easy, not if she had anything to say about it—and he was sure she would, in spades.

Oh, well. One thing at a time.

He straightened up, hauled in a bracing lungful of air and put the kettle on.

CHAPTER FOUR

'DOES BEN KNOW you're not staying there tonight?'

He glanced up at her, taking his eyes off the midwifery journal he'd been pretending to read. As if she hadn't realised that. He hadn't turned a page in the last few minutes and his face had been like a frozen mask.

'Yes. I rang him just before we left the hospital. He's been fretting about you. He took me for coffee and force-fed me a disgustingly sweet chocolate muffin when Sam kicked me out of Resus, but then he had to go back to work. He's been bombarding me with texts ever since, asking how you are.'

She laughed softly and then winced, and he frowned.

'You OK?'

She nodded. 'My stomach muscles hurt a bit. I guess being flung around like that'd cause all sorts of odd aches and pains.'

He frowned again at that, no doubt reliving the accident, and she regretted mentioning it.

'You probably tensed up to protect yourself. Are the painkillers working yet?'

She would have laughed under normal circumstances, but she'd tried that once. 'Not so you'd notice,' she told him. 'I need to get out of this lot,' she said, plucking at the horrible hospital gown and the borrowed scrub bottoms they'd lent her in the ED.

'Really? I thought it was rather fetching. The little NHS logo all over the gown goes really well with your eyes, but it's your choice.'

'Good of you to remember that,' she said drily. 'There's a long pink T-shirt with short sleeves in the second drawer, on the left.'

'Do you really need it?'

He sounded puzzled, and she forced herself to look up and meet his eyes. 'Yes, I do, because you're going to be here and we're not together any more,' she told him bluntly.

He rolled his eyes. 'Jeez, Liv, give me credit. I just thought you'll be more comfortable with nothing on. I'm hardly going to take advantage of it.'

'It's nothing to do with that,' she said, remembering when he'd taken every opportunity to do exactly that, but that was a long time ago, well before she'd thrown him out. Their problems had started long before then. She sighed. So much water under so many bridges…

'Nick, I can't be bothered to argue,' she told him. 'Just find it, please, could you, and then leave me alone? The bathroom's just here, not ten feet from the bed. I'll be fine.'

That sounded churlish, and she didn't mean it to. She let out a shaky sigh and shook her head. 'Sorry. That came out all wrong but I'm too tired to play games and I just want to go to sleep.'

She looked up at him, and saw sorrow etched on his face.

'It's OK, Liv. I understand,' he said softly. 'I know

you don't want me here, but it's not for long. You'll be
fine in a day or two.'

He was wrong. She did want him there, but not like
this. Not shackled by duty and guilt, but there because
he loved her.

He found the T-shirt, put it on the bed beside her and
went out of the room. Not far, she knew that from the
creaks on the landing, but far enough. He was probably
sitting on the top step. She swung her legs over the side
of the bed as she sat up, then unfastened the hideous
hospital gown and tried to peel it off her shoulders, but
they protested and she stifled a whimper.

Come on, girl, toughen up.

She got there in the end and pulled the long top on,
then stood up, but as she bent over to push the trousers
down she felt her head start to swim again.

She let out a little wail of frustration as she sagged
back onto the bed, and the door swung open and Nick
walked in.

'Feel free to knock,' she grumbled, but he ignored
it and crouched down in front of her, his hands resting
lightly on her knees as he looked up at her.

'What happened?' he asked gently. 'Another headrush?'

'Mmm. My head started swimming again when I
bent over to take the scrubs off.'

'I'm not surprised, you've got concussion,' he said,
easing them off over her feet as his eyes scanned the
bruises that were coming out on her legs. His voice was
calm, but she was sure he didn't feel calm. She could
see the pulse beating in his throat as he looked at the
bruises, and she knew he was holding his feelings in.
Maybe it was just as well. She was on the brink of los-

ing it as it was, and if he'd been nice to her, shown the slightest sign of caring, she would have crumpled like a wet tissue. Might anyway...

He stood up. 'Let me check your obs again,' he said, all business now suddenly, as if that was the easiest way to cope. He probably wasn't wrong.

He took the pen light he'd raided off Sam out of his pocket and turned it on, crouching down in front of her again. 'OK, look at me,' he said, and flashed it in her eyes in turn while she stared straight back into his. He had such beautiful eyes, and there'd been a time not so very long ago when they'd looked at her lovingly. Now, it was all business.

'OK, follow the pen.'

She followed it dutifully, overwhelmingly conscious of his left hand on the edge of the bed close to her right hip, steadying himself as he balanced on the balls of his feet. He was so close to her that she could feel the warmth coming off his body, smell the faint and yet unmistakable scent that was uniquely him.

She'd missed that, missed snuggling up to him, missed his arms around her, his heart beating under her ear—

'OK, your eyes are fine. Squeeze my hands?'

His grip was sure but gentle, and after she'd squeezed and relaxed he let her fingers lie in his. Only for a moment, but longer than was strictly necessary, then he let them go and stood up briskly, and she felt cool air sweep in where his warmth had been.

'You'll do,' he said, his voice suddenly gruff.

'I could have told you that. I need the loo now.'

'Can you manage on your own or do you need my help?'

'No, I can manage,' she said, mustering her feeble

reserves. *Gosh, she was so tired.* She stood up, tugging the long tee down, and headed through the door, closing it behind her and waiting for his voice.

'Don't lock it.'

Right on cue. 'I won't,' she promised wearily. Not so long ago they'd never bothered to shut the bathroom door, but those days were long gone, and for what? Just a lonely, aching wilderness of wasted emotion.

Her eyes prickled and she screwed her eyes up and swallowed hard. She was *not* going to cry. Not, not, not.

And then her head swam again, and the sob she'd tried to suppress wasn't having any of it, and it broke free in an anguished wail.

He opened the door and found her still sitting there, her hand clamped over her mouth. Holding down the sobs? Pointless, because they were escaping anyway and tearing him apart.

The darkening blue tinge of her bruises was starting to show more clearly against the pale skin of her leg. When they really came out it would be black from top to bottom. He dragged his eyes away and swallowed hard. How she hadn't broken anything...

'What's up, sweetheart?' he asked gently, the endearment slipping out past his guard as he went over to her.

'I feel dizzy and I daren't get up and I feel so stupid—'

Her voice cracked, and his hands cradled her head tenderly against him while he told her she wasn't stupid, just hurt, letting her lean on him in a rare moment of weakness while he struggled to keep his own emotions in check. She didn't give him long, though. A few precious seconds at most, and then she pulled herself together, straightening up and using his hands to lever herself to her feet, her independence fighting fit again.

'Thank you,' she said, aiming for the basin, but he headed her off.

'No. Bed,' he told her firmly, wheeling her out of the room towards it. Independence be damned. 'I'll wash your hands, and then I'm going to find us something proper to eat because I think you're probably feeling lightheaded because of low blood sugar as much as anything else. What do you fancy?'

She sat down on the bed and shrugged. 'I don't think there is much. I'd be fine with more toast.'

'That isn't enough, not for either of us, and I haven't eaten all day apart from that muffin which really doesn't count. Don't worry, I'll find something in the freezer. You just settle back and get comfortable and leave it all to me.'

He went back into the bathroom and noticed a tiny crumpled heap of something on the floor beside the pan. The hideous disposable paper pants the hospital had given her, he realised, and stooped slowly and picked them up. She used to wear gorgeous undies—delicate lace that offered tantalising glimpses of her body.

He dropped them in the bin, turned on the tap, ran it until the water was hot and squeezed out her facecloth in the water, adding a touch of soap.

'Here,' he said, picking up her hands one at a time and washing them meticulously. The right one was fine, the left a little grazed and bruised on the outside edge where she must have landed on it, and he worked carefully round the sore place, then rinsed the cloth and wiped them again before patting them dry. Such a simple thing to do, and yet strangely symbolic. If only he could wash away their sadness and make them whole again...

'Thank you,' she whispered, and he looked up and saw the sparkle of tears in her eyes and felt his own fill. 'Thank you for looking after me. I know I've been horribly ungracious, but I really couldn't have managed without you, and I'm sorry.'

'Oh, Liv—' His voice cracked, and he squeezed her hands in his. 'You don't have to apologise to me for anything.'

'Yes, I do, for so many things—'

'No. Not now. Now, you need to rest, and you need some food, and then you need to sleep,' he said gently, his voice sounding like sandpaper.

He took the towel back into the bathroom and caught sight of his face in the mirror. He looked haggard, his eyes a little wild, his mouth a grim line. No wonder. She could have died under those wheels, so easily. Another foot—

He hung up the towel, rinsed the facecloth and wrung it out so hard he nearly tore it in two.

Nick went downstairs to make some food, and she rested her head back and closed her eyes. She was exhausted, but even on the normally very comfortable bed she couldn't get truly comfortable. She must have dozed off, though, because she woke with a little groan to find he was there again, straddling the small bedroom chair he'd turned around, arms folded across the back, watching her with those intent, searching eyes.

'Hi,' he said, his voice sounding a little rough and unused for some reason.

'Hi. I didn't hear you come back up. Have I been asleep for long?'

'Ten minutes, perhaps?'

'Oh. Right. Not long, then. Did you find any food?'

His mouth kicked up in a wry smile and he shook his head. 'Not really. I had a look in the freezer, but it's not exactly over-stocked. How about a takeaway?'

Her stomach rumbled, and she realised she was ravenous. No wonder she was dizzy. 'That would be lovely.'

'Is the Chinese restaurant on the front still open?'

'Yes. And they deliver free.'

'Special chow mein?' he asked.

Gosh. Had she really been so predictable? It felt odd, especially considering she hadn't had one for at least a year, or maybe two. Not since long before he'd left. She dredged up a smile. 'Please.'

'Banana fritters?'

'That's disgusting,' she said, trying not to be tempted.

'But you love them.'

'Loved,' she corrected. 'I'm eating much more healthily now.'

'Still having chow mein.'

'Says the man whose entire diet today has been a slice of toast, a chocolate muffin and black coffee—and this whole takeaway thing was your idea, remember, not mine.'

His mouth twitched, but he let it go and pulled out his phone, looking for the number.

'Seven six four, three two nine,' she said, and he laughed as he keyed it in, the sound wrapping round her and cloaking her in grief for all they'd lost.

'You always did have the memory of an elephant for irrelevant detail,' he teased, and she felt her smile falter.

'It's not just the irrelevant things I can remember,' she told him sadly, and he swallowed hard and looked away.

'Frankly, today, I'm happy that you can remember anything—yeah, hi, can I order a special chow mein and chicken chop suey with boiled rice, please?'

That made her blink. Normally he'd have had king prawn balls in batter with special fried rice, and drenched the lot in lurid orange sweet and sour sauce, but maybe she wasn't the only one to address her diet. She ran her eyes over him, reassessing the changes she'd noticed earlier. He'd lost a little weight, but it was more than that—the difference between healthy and letting yourself go. He looked fit and toned again, as if he'd taken up running or rejoined a gym. Gone was the man she'd been married to when it had all fallen apart.

Taking care of himself at last? He must be, and about time. He hung up and turned back to her.

'It'll be here in ten minutes.'

'Great. Thanks. Can you help me sort out the pillows? I can't sit up straight enough to eat and my neck's just not comfortable like this.'

'Sure.'

He sat her up, rearranged the pillows and settled her back against them as if she was made of fragile china.

'Better?' he asked, and she nodded.

'Yes, much. Thank you.' She rested her head back and frowned. 'I feel so guilty. Ben and Daisy were expecting you and she will have cooked, you know what she's like.'

'I know, but it can't be helped and Ben knows I'm staying here and why, and it's just until you're all right.'

'I am all right, Nick. I'm fine—'

His quiet snort of disbelief cut her off. 'Really? So fine you can't get off the loo without help? So fine you can't even move in your sleep without waking up because of the pain?'

He came over to her, perched carefully on the edge of the bed and wrapped her hand in both of his, a frown furrowing his brow.

'Liv, look at yourself,' he said softly, his voice oddly raw. 'You're going to be black and blue, your head's banging like a drum—how bad do you have to be before you'll let go of this ridiculous pretence that you're fine and just accept my help? For God's sake, you could have died—'

His voice cracked, his fingers tightening on hers, and in the moments before he looked away, she saw the fear that he must have felt for her, the guilt that because he'd followed her when she was trying to get away, she'd stepped out in front of the car. And he'd only wanted to talk to her. How much would it have hurt her to stop and listen, give him a chance? Not this much.

'Nick, I didn't look where I was going. It's my fault, not yours.'

He let go of her hand and stood up, pacing to the window.

'Of course it's my fault. It's all my fault. It's my fault our marriage went wrong, it's my fault you threw me out, my fault you got hit—'

'That's rubbish. And it's not your fault our marriage went wrong; I shut you out, I wouldn't let you help me, and if I'd gone to the conference with you instead of sending you on your own, none of this would have happened and I wouldn't have kicked you out.

You can't take the blame for everything, Nick. I was horrible to you.'

He sat back down on the bed, taking her hand again, his warmth curiously comforting.

'No, you weren't. You were just unhappy, and so was I, and we took it out on each other instead of getting help, and it just got into a downward spiral and I don't think we knew how to stop it. And it happens so often with couples who have difficulty conceiving, but one thing my job's taught me is that struggling on alone isn't the answer and we were barely even communicating by the end. We got so lost that we couldn't find a way out and we just stopped talking to each other.'

'Why us?' she asked forlornly, but he just shrugged.

'Why anyone? It's the luck of the draw, Liv, and we got unlucky, but it was our own fault we let it destroy us and we both should have known better and tried harder instead of building walls around ourselves.'

The doorbell rang, and he let go of her hand and went downstairs, and she dropped her head back against the pillows.

Was that what they'd done? Built walls? Probably. They'd had an amazing marriage, filled with love and laughter and tenderness, and then bit by bit it had all slowly disappeared, eaten away by the bitter disappointment of their repeated failure to make a baby. And with every bit that went, they'd added another brick to their walls.

Nick was right. It was nobody's fault, and they'd been helpless to help themselves, and by the end they weren't even trying to, they'd just let it all wither away to dust.

A tear trickled out of the corner of her eye, and she

swiped it hastily away as he came back into the room with two bowls and a couple of forks.

He plonked himself down on the bed next to her, propped himself up against the headboard and handed her the chow mein. 'There you go, wrap yourself around that.'

It smelt amazing, and there'd be plenty of time to talk later. 'Gosh, I'm ready for this,' she said, finding a smile from somewhere, and dug her fork in.

'Where are you going to sleep?'

He glanced at her, looked around the room and shrugged. 'On the floor, I guess.'

'Nick, there are two other bedrooms—'

'Three.'

She looked away. 'Two. I turned the little room into a study.'

The room that had been destined to be a nursery. The room that had haunted her until she'd had the guts to address it and claim it as her own, instead of waiting for something that would never happen.

He frowned slightly. 'There's a study downstairs.'

'But that's yours,' she said simply, 'and I wanted my own space.' One where she wasn't constantly bombarded by reminders of him. 'I'm doing a course on natural childbirth and pain relief in labour. I'm studying hypnosis at the moment. And it wasn't as if it was needed for anything else.'

He closed his eyes briefly, and when he opened them she could see the anguish in them.

'I'm sorry, Liv,' he said heavily. 'I'm so sorry it didn't work for us, that we never needed that room. I'm sorry I couldn't give you a baby. And I'm so sorry I wasn't there for you, sorry I shut you out, sorry I let you shut me out. It wasn't meant to be like that. Not at all. It was all going to be perfect—'

'Oh, Nick, don't—' She felt her eyes fill and looked away, blinking hard. They'd been so happy, had so many hopes and dreams, and it had all come to nothing and in such a horrible way.

'So anyway,' she went on, putting that firmly out of her mind, 'you have two other rooms to choose from tonight, both of them better than sleeping on the floor.'

'Not for keeping an eye on you, which is after all why I'm here.'

'It's not as if you'll be far away, and anyway, I'm—'

'If you tell me once more that you're fine, I might just strangle you. And I'm not leaving you alone, Liv. Not for anything. I told Sam I'd look after you because otherwise he wouldn't have let you come home, so humour me, for God's sake.'

She gave a choked little laugh. Anyone less physically violent than Nick she'd never met, and he was obviously worried sick about her and she knew he'd only lie awake all night.

'Oh, for goodness' sake, if you're going to insist on being in here, why don't you just sleep in the bed?' she said softly.

After a pause so long she thought he hadn't heard, he turned his head and met her eyes.

'You'd let me do that?'

She frowned. 'Why not? It's not like I can't trust you. You wouldn't be here if I didn't trust you. I would have stayed in hospital.'

'That's not what I meant. I just thought you wouldn't want me that close. It's not much more than an hour since you insisted you needed nightclothes on, and that's when you thought I'd be in another room.'

'That's nothing to do with this.'

'Isn't it?'

'No. It's because I didn't want to—' She didn't know how to describe it. Flaunt herself? In front of Nick? Ridiculous. He knew every inch of her. Expose herself to humiliation, then, perhaps, because he'd certainly lost interest in her body by the end…

He let out a weary sigh. 'Liv, it's OK. I'm sorry, I don't want to argue. Of course you want to wear a night-dress, you're entitled to your privacy. And it doesn't matter where I sleep. I'll sleep anywhere.'

'So sleep here,' she said, patting the mattress beside her. 'Near to me. Just in case—you know…'

He frowned. 'Is your headache worse?'

She tried to shake it, and thought better of it. 'No. No more than it was, and maybe less, but I know you'll be getting up and down all night because you'll be worried about me. If you're here you can just prod me and ask if I'm all right and go straight back to sleep.'

Fat chance.

He hovered over her while she washed, then did a quick neuro check before he settled her in bed and lay down beside her, but he was reluctant to move in case he hurt her or disturbed her, and his head was too full of the endless re-run of the accident to let him sleep.

Beside him Liv was restless and he wasn't sure she was asleep, either, despite the fact that she must be exhausted. Too sore? Or too cold?

The heating must have gone off and the room was growing steadily colder. It hadn't been over-warm in the first place—to save money? He propped himself up on one elbow and peered at her in the dim light spilling in from the landing, and realised she'd kicked the covers off, and she was going to be stiff and sore enough when she woke in the morning.

He checked his phone for the time. Nearly one o'clock. Time for another check. He turned towards her, pulling the covers back over her as he woke her.

'Liv?'

'Mmm?'

'Talk to me, sweetheart. It's time for another check. Are you OK?'

'I'm fine,' she said. She sounded tired rather than sleepy, and he wondered if she'd been awake, too.

'Do you hurt?'

'No, not so much now. I'm a bit cold.'

'You'd kicked the covers off, but I've put them back now, you'll soon warm up.'

He'd propped himself up on one elbow to flash the pen light in her eyes, and it gave him a chance to study her face. The bruise around her eye had invaded the lower lid now, and he could see further bruising along her cheekbone.

Without thinking, he leant over and touched his lips lightly to the bruise. 'You've got a real shiner now,' he said softly. 'The neighbours are going to think I've come back for revenge and beaten you up.'

'You'd never hurt me,' she said quietly. 'Not physically, at least.'

No. She was right, he wouldn't. Couldn't. But it hadn't stopped him walking out on their broken marriage and he knew how badly that had hurt her. Hurt both of them. He sighed softly, lifting his hand and trailing it lightly over her cheekbone and down her jaw. 'Do you need painkillers again?'

'No, not really.' She hesitated, her gaze holding his, then said quietly, as if she was afraid of his reaction, 'Do you know what I really want more than anything? A hug. I've really missed your hugs.'

A tear slid out of the corner of her eye and ran down into her hair, and his eyes blurred.

'Oh, Liv—'

His voice hitched, and he put the pen light back and lay down, reaching out his arms and folding them gently round her, and as she wriggled closer he pressed his lips to her forehead and squeezed his eyes tight shut to try and hold back the tears.

She wasn't the only one who'd missed this, and the feel of her body against his made something deep within him, something that had been out of kilter for one or maybe even two years, fall back into place.

He felt her hand slide up his chest and settle against his jaw, her fingertips resting against his neck, right over the pulse.

'What happened to us, Nick?' she asked sadly, her fingertips stroking soothingly over the beating artery. 'How did we end up in this mess?'

He swallowed hard. 'I have no idea. I just know I miss you every single day.'

'I miss you, too. You were my best friend.'

'Don't—'

His arms tightened round her, cradling her against his heart, and he blinked away the stinging tears and pressed another kiss to her hair.

It was stiff and smelt of blood and antiseptic, and he thought of how close she'd come to death, lying there almost under the wheels of that big, heavy car, and the tears squeezed past his lids and trickled across his temple and onto the pillow by her head.

'I nearly lost you today, Liv,' he whispered into the darkness. 'That car was so close—'

Her arms tightened round him, her lips finding his cheek and feathering soft kisses over the damp skin. 'Oh, Nick. I'm sorry I scared you. I was scared, too. I thought I was going to die—'

Her voice cracked, and he cradled her head tenderly against his shoulder. 'Don't be scared any more. You're not going to die, sweetheart, you're going to be fine,' he murmured gently, 'but you need to rest, my love. Just go to sleep. You're safe now. I've got you.'

She made a sleepy, contented noise and settled against him, and he felt the tension going out of her limbs, her breathing growing slow and deep and regular as she drifted off to sleep, but he didn't sleep for a long, long time.

He just held her, feeling the slow rise and fall of her chest with every breath, the warmth of her body against his, and wondered where on earth they went from here.

CHAPTER FIVE

HE WOKE TO the soft, yielding warmth of Liv's body draped over his.

He'd checked her a couple more times in the night and the last time she'd rolled away, but at some point she must have rolled back. He hadn't woken, but his arm was round her and her head was on his shoulder and it felt so familiar, so *right*...

Her arm lay loosely over his chest, her knee wedged down between his thighs, and her body was so close to his he could feel her heart beat.

Which would have been fine, except his body was apparently very happy to have her pressed up tight against it and he wasn't sure they were quite ready for that yet. At least he'd kept his underwear on. It gave him a little privacy, but not nearly enough, and it wasn't going to get any better unless he could somehow ease his leg out from under hers and move away.

He could always wait, he thought. She'd wake up at some point and then he could get his arm out from under her head and unravel the potentially embarrassing tangle of limbs.

But she didn't wake, and she was overdue for another check. He touched her cheek.

'Liv, wake up.'

She made a funny little noise and snuggled closer, her right arm curving down over his ribs, her fingers tucking under his side.

He closed his eyes, swore softly and took her wrist in his hand and eased it back again. 'Liv! Liv, wake up. I have to check you again.'

But she didn't move, just moaned slightly, and his heart went into overdrive. Why couldn't he wake her? Did she have a brain injury after all, and he'd slept through it and missed the signs?

'Liv! Come on. Wake up. Now!'

He shook her arm roughly and her eyes flickered open, blinking in the daylight that seeped in around the curtained windows. She made a soft noise and shifted her head back so she could get him into focus. 'Don't shout at me. What's the matter?'

Relief flooded him and he closed his eyes and sucked in a breath. 'Sorry. I'm sorry. I couldn't wake you, and I thought…' He couldn't say it, couldn't voice his fears out loud, but he didn't need to.

She blinked again, as if she'd just worked out where she was and what had happened, and she let out her breath on a little sigh and settled back against him. 'Oh, Nick, I'm fine,' she said softly, her hand coming to rest over his heart. 'A bit sore, but my head's much better now. I was just really heavily asleep.'

He felt himself relax, but not much, because their legs were still wrapped together and he really, really needed to get away before she realised quite how much his body was lapping it up.

'Good. I'm glad you're feeling better, but I need to

get up. My arm's gone dead and I need to phone the hospital about Judy Richards.'

'Oh. Sorry, you should have said.'

He gave a soft, frustrated laugh. 'I just did. That's why I was trying to wake you.'

'Oh. Right. OK.'

She put her hand on his chest and shifted her leg, and as she moved it she brushed against him and her eyes widened and she froze.

'Nick?' His name was a soft out-breath, teasing against his skin, and her hand curved against his cheek, the delicate touch unbearably erotic.

Damn. He closed his eyes. 'Sorry. Ignore it, it's just a normal, physiological response,' he muttered, his voice gruff. 'It doesn't mean anything—'

Her lips brushed his. 'Oh. And there I thought you were pleased to see me,' she murmured, a hint of mischief in her voice, but it was a touch husky and he knew if he didn't get out of there soon he was going to lose the plot.

'Very funny,' he said, but she just laughed softly and curled her hand around the back of his head, easing him closer. Her lips met his again, the touch so sweet, so familiar, so agonisingly dear that he let out a soft groan and kissed her back.

Not for long. Just long enough that he knew if he didn't get out of there fast this was going to get well out of control and it was every kind of a bad idea.

He dragged his mouth away from temptation. 'Liv, no,' he said, his voice as firm as he could make it. 'I have to get up.'

'I thought you were,' she said mischievously, but before he could react she laughed again and rolled away.

'Better?'

'Yes, thank you.'

Liar. It was much worse, because he wanted her right back where she'd been, and it wasn't going to happen. He retrieved his arm and groaned.

'What?'

'Just my arm dropping off.'

'So long as that's all…'

He gave a despairing chuckle, swung his legs over the side of the bed and stood up with his back firmly towards her. He hadn't seen Liv in this teasing, mischievous mood for years, and the urge to get back into bed and haul her into his arms was killing him.

'I'll go and phone the hospital and I'll get you some tea while I'm at it.' He grabbed his shirt and headed for the door, shaking his right arm to get the circulation going. 'Ah, dammit,' he muttered again as the blood started to flow back into it.

'Wimp,' she called after him, and he paused on the top step, shoving his arms into the shirt.

'Me, a wimp? You should listen to yourself. The fuss you've been making, anybody would think you'd been hit by a car.'

The sound of her laughter followed him down the stairs to the kitchen, and he couldn't help but smile. She sounded so much better and the relief he felt was profound. For a moment there, when he hadn't been able to wake her—

He cut that thought off before it dragged him back in, phoned the hospital about Judy while the kettle boiled and took her tea up to her, his body now back under control.

She was in the bathroom when he got there and he

put the mug down on the bedside table as she opened the door and came out.

'Are you OK?'

'I'm fine, considering I was *hit by a car*. Much less sore than I deserve to be,' she said with a wry grin.

'Good. And you don't deser—'

She reached out and pressed a finger to his lips, stopping the words. The grin softened to a smile, and he felt his heart thud against his ribs as she dropped her arm and took another step towards him. She was close enough now that he could smell the toothpaste on her breath and feel the warmth radiating off her skin, and she put her arms around him and rested her head on his chest and hugged him.

'Thank you for looking after me last night,' she murmured, and he wrapped his arms around her and dropped a gentle kiss on her matted, bloodstained hair, every cell in his body aware of the soft press of her breasts against his chest, the warmth of her body luring him, reeling him in. Such a bad idea, but his body thought it was great. He dropped his arms.

'You're welcome,' he said gruffly. 'I've put the tea on your bedside table. I'm going to get my stuff out of the car. I could do with a shower and shave.'

She lifted her hand and rubbed the palm over his jaw against the lie of the hair; he heard the stubble rasp against her skin, saw her pupils darken, felt his body react. 'Shame. I rather like you with the morning-after look,' she said with that slightly wicked smile he'd missed so much for so long now.

Her hand was just there, her thumb against his lips. He could turn his head and press his lips to her palm, ease her back into his arms—or he could just step back out of reach and keep what was left of his sanity.

'Liv, don't do this, please. It's hard enough as it is.'

'Mmm. I noticed.'

He groaned and took a step back out of reach, his control at breaking point. 'It's not funny, Liv,' he said gruffly. 'It's so not a good idea. You're hurt, and it's not what I'm here for.'

Her eyes widened and she blinked, her hand falling slowly to her side.

'No. No, I'm sorry. I wasn't—I didn't mean—'

She couldn't finish the sentence, maybe because like him she didn't know quite what to say, what the protocol was in this really rather awkward situation.

'It's OK. It's just—I don't really think…'

Now it was him who couldn't finish, so he gave up on the conversation, pulled on his trousers, ran down-stairs and let himself out of the front door, kicking him-self every step of the way.

She watched him go, beating what could only be called a hasty retreat, and bit her lip.

He'd seemed so uncomfortable with her touch, as if she'd crossed an invisible line that had somehow ap-peared between them since they'd got out of bed. Or maybe it had been there all night, and she'd crossed it then too without realising.

She'd certainly been close enough to him when he'd woken her, close enough to feel his reaction. It wasn't un-usual, just a spontaneous physiological response, as he'd said, and in the good old days, before the bad ones, they would have taken advantage of it. But today he couldn't get away fast enough, and he'd seemed embarrassed.

And all she'd done was tease him, when actually she'd wanted him to wrap her in his arms again and make love to her like he used to.

She hadn't even thought about it when she'd suggested he share the bed, and although he'd protested, he hadn't refused, and he'd willingly held her most of the night. He'd obviously only done it out of concern because of her head injury, though, and then she'd gone and wrapped herself all round him, and then hugged him and touched him in a way she no longer had any right to touch him.

And maybe he'd moved on. Maybe there was another woman in his life now, a woman who had those rights?

She felt a wave of humiliation, then a hollow ache inside, and without permission her eyes filled with tears. She hadn't even thought about it, but maybe he'd found someone to love, someone who could give him babies, or just someone to have fun with, as they'd had fun in the early days, before it all became about ovulation tests and body temperature fluctuation and counting days on the calendar?

Not that it was any of her business now, since she'd kicked him out without giving him a second chance.

'Oh, Nick…'

She shifted the pillows into a pile and crawled back onto the bed, leaning back against the pillows and kicking herself for reading too much into his kindness last night. Because that was all it had been, of course. Just kindness.

But he said he'd missed her every single day. Was that kindness talking? It hadn't felt like it, and she was sure there had been tears on his cheeks at one point. That didn't seem like simple kindness, and the way he'd held her, as if she was the most precious thing in the world…

She could hear his voice outside through the bathroom window, and wondered who he was talking to at this time of the morning. Bert, probably. Oh, lord. That would open a whole new can of worms.

It was her own fault. She should have stayed in hospital like Sam had wanted her to instead of making such a fuss—or better still, asked Ben not to contact Nick, and then none of this would have happened.

But then she wouldn't have seen him again, and somehow that felt immeasurably worse…

'Morning, Nick.'

Damn. He looked up and saw their old neighbour clipping their rose hedge. Liv's rose hedge, he corrected himself. He supposed he should be grateful Bert was looking after her, but instead he felt resentful and distinctly underdressed.

'Morning,' he grunted, unlocking the car and opening the door, wincing as he stepped back onto a sharp stone in his bare feet.

Bert's voice followed his head into the car. 'I see you're back, then. Hope you don't mind, I'm just tidying up a few bits and pieces I missed. First clip of the season, so she gets the best flowers.'

He ducked his head back out as Bert took a step towards him, shears in hand. 'Back for good, are you?'

He gave a mental sigh and put the old man straight.

'No. Liv had an accident yesterday. I'm just looking after her for a day or two.'

Bert lowered the shears, settling in no doubt for a

nice long chat and a few juicy details. 'Oh, I'm sorry to hear that. I hope she'll be all right. Car, was it?'

'No.' Well, it wasn't. Not hers. 'She fell,' he said, which was being massively frugal with the truth, but it was none of Bert's business. 'She's just got a few bruises and scrapes.'

'Oh, dear. Poor Liv. I'll tell Gwen, she'll pop round—'

'No, Bert, really, it's fine. She just needs to rest.'

'Oh, well. Give her our best, then. And you'd better get back inside before you catch your death with those bare feet.'

'Yes, indeed.'

He lifted his overnight bag out of the car, locked it and headed back inside, hearing the irritating click-click-click of the shears as Bert went back to work on the immaculate hedge. He ran upstairs, pausing at the bedroom door.

'I'm going to have a shower, if that's OK?'

'Of course. Was that Bert?'

'Yes. He'd obviously spotted the car and he wanted to know if I was back. I told him you'd fallen and got a few bruises. He was threatening to send Gwen round, probably to interrogate you. God knows what she'd make of your black eye, but I'm sure I'd be implicated. I told him you needed to rest.'

Liv rolled her eyes. 'Good. Thank you. They mean well, but—Gwen kept asking questions when you went, saying things like, "It's such a shame he's gone, we were so looking forward to the patter of tiny feet," and I just didn't know what to say to her.'

'Tell her to mind her own business,' he said roughly, the mention of those elusive babies catching him on the raw. 'He's cutting the hedge again, by the way, though why he needs to do it before eight o'clock on a Saturday morning defeats me. It doesn't look as if it needs it anyway.'

'It doesn't. He only did it last week but he was saying he'd missed a bit. I couldn't see it. I've told him not to bother, I can do it myself and anyway, I quite like it when it gets a bit wild, but he insists I won't get the best flowers unless it's done early, and I just can't be that churlish.'

Nick snorted, hefting the bag in his hand. 'I'm damn sure I could. I'm going to shower and get dressed, and then I'd better give Sam an update and phone Ben.'

He scooped up his shoes and socks and took everything to the other bathroom, grabbing a towel on the way and locking the door firmly behind him. Not that she was likely to follow him in, but he just needed some guaranteed privacy while he got his thoughts into order because frankly, between watching her almost get killed and then having her plastered over him all night, his head was a mess and his body wasn't much better.

And her touching him like that, hugging him, kissing him, running her hand over his stubble and looking at him with those melting eyes that threatened to lure him in again—

He stared at the shower controls, contemplated cold and decided against it. He'd never been a masochist, and the last twenty-four hours had been tough enough. He turned on the hot, tested the temperature and stepped into the cubicle under the wall of steaming water.

It pounded down on him, and he dropped his head forwards and felt the tension drain away, but it was replaced by relief that she was still alive, and anguish that she'd been hurt at all, by the deep sorrow left in the wake of their break-up and the grief he still felt that he'd never been able to give her the child she so desperately wanted. Might never be able to.

She'd asked what had happened to them, and the answer was nothing. No pregnancy, no baby, no family.

That, rather than Suzanne, was why their marriage had fallen apart. The business with Suze had just been the trigger, the last straw, and if he was honest, he hadn't cared at that point, because he'd been at the end of his tether with their broken relationship.

By asking for a divorce she'd handed him a perfect way out, or so he'd thought, but then she'd never done it, never started divorce proceedings, just left him in limbo waiting for the other shoe to drop. He'd thought she'd be better off without him, but he hadn't been better off without her, and walking out of her life had left a wound that time didn't seem about to heal.

And getting too close to her again too soon could be a disaster, so no more snuggling up in the night, no more hugs, no more tender touches breaking through his defences and laying him wide open to hurt again.

And what about the job? How were they going to cope with working together every day when they were obviously still so attracted to each other? Could he manage to keep his distance?

Did he really want to? Or was he just being a coward, afraid to try again? Frankly, he had no idea.

He reached for the soap, scrubbed away the memory of her body against his, towelled himself roughly dry—and discovered he'd forgotten to pack his razor.

Damn.

He ran his hand over his beard, hearing the rasp of it against his skin, feeling the touch of her hand against it earlier, and swore softly and comprehensively at himself.

He could always borrow hers, he supposed, but she'd be unlikely to have a new one and the one in the shower would be worse than useless, he knew that of old. And the intimacy of it...

He'd go and buy some later. Just so she didn't get any more ideas about his morning-after look.

He dressed quickly, packed up his things and took his bag down to the hall. There wasn't really any need to stay here again tonight, he could quite easily go to Ben and Daisy's as planned. Much safer.

He ran back up and stuck his head round the bedroom door. 'OK?'

'Yes, except I'd love more tea. Oh, and Sam rang, by the way. He's on his way over to check up on me. Says he doesn't trust you.'

'Damn cheek. Do you have any decent coffee?'

'I think so, in the freezer. If not there's an unopened packet of ground coffee in the larder cupboard. I might not have a lot of milk. I was going shopping on the way home.'

'I'll check. What do you want for breakfast?'

She shrugged. 'Anything. Toast is easy. And marmalade. It's in the fridge door. And forget the tea, I'll have coffee if you're making it for Sam.'

'OK.'

He ran downstairs and put the kettle on just as the doorbell rang, and he opened the door to his old friend.

'Sam—come in. Thank you so much for yesterday.'

'You're welcome,' Sam said, stepping into the hall and wrapping Nick in a fierce and affectionate hug. Yesterday he'd been a professional but today he was a concerned friend, and he dropped his arms and stepped back with a wry smile, studying his face.

'It's really good to see you again. I'm just sorry it was under those circumstances. How is she? And come to that, how are you? It must have been pretty tough to witness it.'

He shrugged and closed the front door. 'I'm fine. She's a bit sore, but her head seems OK and that was the real worry. I've just put the kettle on. Can I get you anything?'

'Coffee would be good. I've been up since before six with Isadora.'

'Your baby?'

'Yes. She was born last October.' Sam smiled ruefully. 'She's gorgeous, but she's an early riser, and Kate's not a morning person.'

'Are you?'

Sam laughed. 'After years in the army, believe me, getting up for a smiley baby is a walk in the park.'

Nick gave a dutiful laugh, then turned away. 'Yes, I can imagine,' he said. 'Why don't you go on up and see Liv? She's on the right at the top of the stairs. I'm just getting her breakfast and I'll bring our coffee up.'

He headed back to the kitchen, trying hard not to think of the joy of being woken by a baby with a beaming smile at any time of the day or night.

Liv hadn't wanted to go to the conference because everyone would be talking about their children, and she'd been right. They were at the age where their friends nearly all had families, and the fact that they'd kept their problems a secret just meant there'd been nobody to share it with, no one to offload on when it all became too much.

Except Suze, and look where that had got him.

He put bread in the toaster, checked the milk situation and found the new packet of coffee and the cafetière.

Core business, he told himself. *Stick to what you're here for, and forget the rest.*

'Well, good morning. How's the patient?'

'Much better but cross with myself, thank you,' she told him, and then asked the question that had been niggling at her since yesterday. 'How come you know Nick?'

'We grew up together. He was my best friend, but we drifted apart once life got in the way.'

'Ah. You're that Sam—the one who taught him to sail,' she said, all the little pieces falling neatly into place.

'That's me. Can we talk about you, now?' he said, smiling a little wryly. 'That's a cracking black eye you've got there.'

'Isn't it just? At least it's only the colour. I can still open my eye more or less fully, and I feel fine now.'

'Really? The eye doesn't say so, and I'm pretty sure your body's at least as colourful.'

'I'm fine, Sam. Really. Yes, I hurt a bit here and there, but I'm alive, no fractures, I haven't got a serious head injury—what more could I ask for? Apart from the common sense not to have stepped backwards off the pavement. That would have helped.'

Sam chuckled, then his smile faded as he studied her. 'How is Nick? I haven't seen him for years. The last I knew he was working in Surrey.'

'He was, but that's six or seven years ago. It's where

we met.' She swallowed and looked away. 'And I don't really know how he is. I haven't seen him since last March, and I hadn't spoken to him then since we split up in the middle of January because we weren't working together and we were avoiding each other. He came back yesterday because he's going to locum for a bit, but that was the first time we'd spoken, so yesterday was a bit of a trial, one way or another.'

Sam looked shocked. 'Gosh, Liv, I'm sorry. If I'd realised that, I wouldn't have suggested he stayed here with you, but you seemed to want him around and he certainly wasn't going anywhere, but no wonder you both objected. Ben mentioned that you weren't together now, but I just assumed you had a working relationship—kids, probably, and shared custody, not total radio silence.'

She tried to smile, but it was probably a sad little event and she gave up. 'No kids,' she said, trying to keep the wobble out of her voice. 'We just—it wasn't working, so we split up.'

She didn't elaborate, just left him to conclude whatever he liked from that, because by the end nothing had been working for them, not the relentless striving for a child, or their crumbling relationship.

'I'm sorry,' Sam said again. 'I shouldn't have interfered without knowing more about your situation.'

'Sam, it's fine,' she said, swiftly changing the subject to one she was more comfortable with than the slow and painful disintegration of her marriage. 'Tell me about your baby.'

'Isadora?'

'Is that what you called her? What a lovely name. Have you got any photos?'

Of course he did, and he pulled out his phone and scrolled around for a moment and then handed it to her. 'Swipe from right to left. That's her yesterday morning, helping me eat my breakfast. She kept stealing the spoon, so I think we're going to have to start weaning her soon.'

'She's just like you.'

'I generally have better table manners.'

Liv felt a lump in her throat, and with a choked little laugh she scrolled through the photos, only handing the phone back when Nick came in with a tray laden with toast and coffee.

'Room service,' he said lightly, putting the tray down on the top of her chest of drawers and turning to Sam. 'Black, white, sugar?'

But her head was aching, and she knew the men would have lots to talk about, so she caught Nick's eye. 'Actually, I could do with a nap. If you could leave me some toast and coffee, maybe you two would like to catch up downstairs for a while?'

Sam stayed for an hour, telling him about the baby, his wife, their house, the fact that he'd just bought, done up and sold a wooden ketch and was now looking for a much more sensibly sized sailing dinghy.

'I thought I might get a Laser or a Firefly. You'll have to come out with me when I get it. I'd trust you not to tip us both over the side,' he said with a wry grin, and Nick laughed, remembering the time Sam had taken a girl out sailing and she'd done exactly that.

'I can still hear that girl scream as she hit the water,' he said with a chuckle, and Sam grinned.

'Lizzie. Yeah. She never really forgave me for that.'

His smile died, and he searched Nick's face with eyes that knew him far too well.

'I'm sorry about you and Liv. She's a lovely woman.'

'She is,' he said, that lump back in his throat, 'but it just wasn't working any more.'

'Yes, she said. Shame.'

'It is, but it's over, we've moved on, and—well, that's it, really,' he lied, glossing over a whole world of messy emotions.

'So I gather you're going to be locuming here for a bit.'

'Yes.' He looked away, pretending to study his hands. 'I don't know how I feel about it. Coming back here, I mean.'

'How does Liv feel?'

'I don't know. I tried to talk to her about it yesterday but it didn't go well. I didn't realise we'd be working together, I thought she'd be in the midwife-led unit still, so yesterday was a bit fraught, and since I almost killed her by letting her fall under a car, we've had other things to think about.'

Sam put his cup down and got to his feet.

'I'll leave you in peace. It'll be good to have you near for a while, though, and let's not lose touch this time. It's been way, way too long and I didn't realise how much I'd missed you.'

He hugged Nick again, the gesture saying more than words ever could, and Nick waved him off and closed the door. The lump in his throat was so big now he could hardly swallow. What on earth was wrong with him today? He was an emotional wreck—

'Has Sam gone?'

He turned slowly and looked up the stairs at Liv. She

must have showered, because her hair was wet and she was wearing a loose, comfortable dress that fell to her ankles. He was glad about that. It covered her bruises, which meant he wouldn't be constantly reminded of them. If he didn't look at her face…

'Yeah, he's gone. I thought you were napping? Did he say it was OK to wash your hair?'

She nodded. 'He said it would be fine so long as I didn't soak in the bath, so I just showered to get the blood off, really. I feel much better now. Much less sore and a lot less grubby.'

'Good. Will you be OK if I go out? I need to see Judy Richards, and Ben wants to talk to me about the job and what it entails which he was going to do yesterday evening, so I thought I'd walk to the hospital, then I can pick up your car after I'm done.'

'Good thinking. I'll get a parking fine if I don't move it but I'm not sure I should drive yet. You know what insurance companies are like,' she said, making her way carefully down the stairs. 'And you also need to apologise to Ben for me for messing up your weekend—and don't tell me again it was your fault.'

He ignored that. 'I'll pick up some more milk while I'm out. Is there anything else you want?'

She nodded. 'Maybe some salad for lunch and something to have with it? Oh, and probably bread. I don't have any decent bread.'

'OK. Text me a shopping list—and I need the car key.'

'I'll just give you my set. There's a house key on there as well, so you'll be able to let yourself back in, just in case I have a nap on the sofa.'

She found them in her bag and then hesitated before

she dropped them into his outstretched hand, as though she was afraid to touch him. Very wise. He closed his fist around them, nodded, and let himself out.

CHAPTER SIX

SHE SPENT THE morning dozing on the sofa in the sitting room.

It was the sofa she'd always thought of as his, the only one she used now. It had the best view of the garden, if you didn't count the one from what they'd optimistically described as the family room, and she hadn't been able to bring herself to sit in there since their final showdown.

Too many painful memories.

But it had been glorious in the sitting room today, the sun streaming in and bringing the promise of spring with it, and between that and her sleepless night she'd struggled to stay awake, but lying awkwardly hadn't done her neck any good so she'd retreated back to the bedroom for a nap.

She was contemplating getting up and taking a walk around the garden when she heard the scrape of the key in the lock and his soft, 'Hello? I'm back,' as he closed the door.

'I'm up here,' she called, and she heard him run lightly up the stairs, tapping on the door as he walked in.

The Nick she'd fallen in love with wouldn't have knocked, and he would have bent down and kissed her, but this Nick didn't, and it was shocking how much she'd missed that. How much she'd missed him.

'I'm sorry I've been so long. Have you been OK?'

'I've been fine. Sleeping, mostly. How's Judy?'

'Good. Everything's stable, the baby's got a lovely strong heartbeat, her blood pressure's fine and the placenta scan was OK. It's just watch and wait until the blood test results come back. I got milk. Do you want a coffee?'

'That would be great. Thanks.'

He disappeared for a little while, and she could hear the kettle boiling and the sound of the fridge door being opened and shut as he put the shopping away, then after a moment he came back up the stairs with the coffee and a packet of almond thins.

'My favourite biscuits!'

He opened the packet and handed them to her, his smile a little crooked. 'We aim to please.'

'How did you get on with Ben?'

'All right,' he said thoughtfully. He put the biscuits down on the bed and propped himself up against the headboard beside her, his face troubled. 'There's a possibility Simon won't come back.'

'I did wonder. Was Ben trying to talk you into staying?'

He chuckled quietly. 'How did you guess? I said I'd do the locum partly to help Ben out of a bind and partly because I knew I needed to see you again, but we haven't exactly got off to a flying start and I wouldn't contemplate coming back permanently if you didn't want me to, Liv. That wouldn't be fair on either of us.'

'No. No, it wouldn't.' She bit her lip, wondering what it would be like if he came back, and she realised she was hoping—desperately hoping—that it would happen. But only if he came back to her as well, and there was a question that was burning a hole in her, even though she wasn't sure she'd want the answer despite agonising over it the whole time he'd been out—well, when she hadn't been asleep, at least—but it was sort of relevant so she said it anyway.

'That would depend on if there's anybody else in your life now, because that would change things a lot. You know—someone you're seeing? Suzanne, perhaps, or someone new?'

His laugh sounded like disbelief, and he shook his head firmly. 'No, Liv. Absolutely not, and certainly not Suze. I haven't even seen her since the conference. I've been working in a different field so our paths don't cross any more, and even if they did, our relationship was over seven years ago. Why would I want to go back to it? And, no, there isn't anyone else, either. There hasn't been anyone else. I'm not interested.'

She stared at him, shocked by that admission. Her relationship with Nick was—or had been—physical. Very physical. Until it all went so horribly wrong.

'No one at all?' she asked incredulously. 'Not even a minor fling, in more than a year?'

He shook his head. 'No. Why would I?'

'For sex?' she offered, stating the obvious, and got the same sad, slightly disbelieving laugh.

'With someone I don't really want? No. Sex is just an itch, Liv. I can scratch it myself, and the only woman I really want threw me out, so that's not a goer.'

He held her eyes with his, the sincerity in them so believable she couldn't doubt it, and after an age she sucked in a breath and looked away, letting it all sink in, but still it didn't quite stack up, because always in the background was this thing with Suzanne that she couldn't quite believe.

'If that's really true, can we scroll back to the conference, because it doesn't seem plausible that you'd be in your room with Suze and not sleep with her, and I'm obviously not the only person who thought that. I knew something had been going on because Beth rang me on Sunday morning and asked if everything was all right, and there was just something in her voice that told me it wasn't, and when she said Suzanne was there and she'd seen you together at breakfast, it all sort of fell into place. But breakfast alone wouldn't make her think that, surely, so she must have seen you going into your room together, and I'm really struggling with that because I know you, Nick, and I know sex is a hugely significant thing in your life, so if it wasn't to sleep with Suze, then what the hell *was* it for?'

He was staring down at his coffee, his face a mask, shutting her out again.

'I just needed to talk to her,' he said eventually.

'So why couldn't you do that downstairs in the bar or something? Why your room? And what on earth were you doing that made Beth suspicious enough to ring me?'

He let out a weary sigh and scrubbed his hand through his hair, then he lifted his head and met her eyes, and his were raw with pain and grief.

'She saw us waiting for the lift. I was in the bar on my own wallowing in self-pity, and Suze came over and asked me if I was all right, and I got so choked I couldn't answer her, so she suggested we took it upstairs. She grabbed the bottle of wine off the table and hauled me out of the bar, and I didn't stop to analyse what anyone might think of it. I just wanted to leave before I made a total idiot of myself, and then we ran into Beth by the lift—me, Suze and the bottle. God knows what she thought we were up to but it must have looked pretty incriminating. Anyway, she asked how we were and I mumbled something and then the lift came and we got in it. Then the following morning she came into the restaurant after we'd already met up there, saw us having breakfast together and I guess put two and two together and came up with five.'

'Well, of course she would—who wouldn't?'

'Exactly. And under any normal circumstances and with anybody else, she would have been right, but it wasn't normal, I wasn't normal, and Suze realised that. That's why she got me out of there, and I can promise you sex was absolutely the last thing on my mind at the time.'

'So why didn't you just tell me that?'

'Because you wouldn't have believed me, and because for that fleeting moment it seemed like an escape route and I was desperate for one. It was a split-second decision, Liv, and I've regretted it ever since, and I know it's too late now to undo all the hurt, but I really need you to believe that nothing happened between me and Suze.'

'So—what did you do? You just drank the bottle of wine and talked? And if so, how did she come to write you that note? "Always here if you need me"? I don't buy it. That's a lover's note, Nick.'

'Or a friend's. If she hadn't been there that night I don't know what would have happened to me, because I was on the brink of a total meltdown and if it hadn't been for her I don't know what I would have done. And I know she's not a saint, but she's not a whore, and that was a cheap shot yesterday, Liv.'

She felt a wash of shame. 'I know. I'm sorry, I should never have said that but I'd spent a year hating her—'

'No. You've spent seven years hating her, being jealous of her, and I've never understood it.'

'What? She's gorgeous, Nick. She's got that amazing lush figure and come-to-bed eyes and you were together for years. And I know she's still in your phone contacts, and she sends you a Christmas card every year—it really wasn't such a stretch to think you would have slept with her again. A lot of people wouldn't even count it, sleeping with an ex.'

'But I would. Which is why I couldn't have done it, because she's a *friend* now—and anyway, what makes you think she's any more desirable than you are?' he asked, shifting so that he was facing her.

'Because I'm not blind?'

He laughed softly and shook his head. 'Liv—seriously, you have nothing to worry about in that department. Yes, we were lovers, of course we were, but she didn't want what I wanted, she didn't see life and family and the future in the same way as me, but you did, and right from the beginning I knew I needed to be with you. You're the one I married, you're the only woman I'll ever want.'

'But you didn't want me then! We hardly ever made love any more, only when the time was right, and it wasn't as if you hadn't slept with her before, so why not?'

'I've just told you that—and I did still want you. I just couldn't touch you without breaking down, and I was trying to be strong for you but I just couldn't do it any longer. I was breaking my heart over us, Liv, and Suze realised it, and the moment the door was shut and she said, "What's wrong?", I fell apart. She sat me on the bed and held me, and I unravelled all over her.

'When I finally ground to a halt she made us coffee and let me talk. Which I did, for hours. I lay on the bed next to her and poured my heart out, told her everything, and then I fell asleep and when I woke up, she was gone. She must have written the note and put it in my bag before she left, but I didn't see it until you showed it to me.

'She told me over breakfast to come home to you and sort things out, to do what I could to mend our marriage, but I'd hardly got through the door before I had to go into the hospital to deliver Amy Zacharelli's baby, and by the time I got back you'd already spoken to Beth, you'd found the note, and you'd made up your mind. From that point on, I didn't stand a chance.'

Tears welled in her eyes, and she looked down at her hands, the fingers clenched together, trying not to cry for everything they'd lost. Or thrown away.

'I'm so sorry. Sorry I've been mean about her...sorry I didn't trust you. I should have trusted you, but the evidence was so clear, Nick, and I felt like such an idiot. That was why I was so shocked about Suzanne, so angry, because even though I was jealous of her I thought I knew you wouldn't do something like that, not once we were married, and then suddenly it looked as if you'd just run back into her open arms and I wondered if I really knew you at all.'

His hand reached out and cradled her cheek gently. 'Of course you know me. There's not much to know.

I'm pretty straightforward. You should have trusted your judgement—and I should have told you the truth there and then.'

'But I didn't make it easy for you, did I? As you said, I'd made up my mind, and I'm so sorry, because it's all my own stupid fault. I should have come with you. It should have been me you broke down with, me you poured your heart out to. If I'd only come with you, maybe you would have done that and then all this business with Suze would never have happened,' she whispered, her voice cracking, but he shifted closer, disentangling her knotted fingers and wrapping them in his warm, strong hands.

'No,' he said gruffly. 'It's not your fault, it's mine. I can't let you take the blame for that. I shouldn't have gone, but I was just at the end of my tether with it all and I couldn't cope with it any more. I'd had the day from hell, and then I came home and found you distraught because you weren't pregnant again and I couldn't take it any more, couldn't bear your pain any more. It was the last straw.

'I never should have left you alone like that. I should have stayed with you, talked about it properly, faced the truth instead of just running away to the conference be-cause it was the easiest thing to do—'

'What could you have done? We'd talked about it endlessly. Every month, for nearly two years. What more was there to say? We'd said it all.'

'No, we hadn't. We'd said the same things over and over. It'll be all right. It'll happen soon, we just need to give it time. We're still young. There's no hurry. Lots of people have this trouble. We've been too busy. We missed the date—every month, the same excuses, the same justification for our failure to conceive, but we never once admitted that we might have a problem, that we needed help, that it wasn't working and wasn't going to work, because we didn't want to admit it. It was as if saying it out loud would make it real, and we couldn't bear to do that.'

She didn't answer, because she didn't need to. He was right, all their talking had got them nowhere because neither of them would admit that they needed help, and maybe there would have been a simple answer if they'd only ever asked the right question.

She'd started running for an hour every day to escape from the truth, from the mess her marriage was in, from the endless recurring sorrow of her infertility, and yet the running itself might have made the situation worse. Why hadn't she realised that? She'd got so thin, scrawny almost. That wasn't healthy, but it hadn't stopped her, and there had been the odd month when the ovulation test hadn't reacted positively. Was that why?

His thumb traced idly over the back of her hand, sweeping backwards and forwards, over and over as the silence hung in the air between them until finally he broke it with a shuddering sigh.

'I wish I'd felt able to talk to you, Liv. I never really told you how I felt, did I? Not really. Not honestly. I never told you how I grieved for us every time we failed, how I ached for you, how I blamed myself for not being able to help you when I was working in the same field. Why couldn't I? I'm a doctor, an obstetrician. My job is babies, and yet I couldn't even give you a baby.'

'You weren't alone, Nick. My job's babies, too, and I couldn't give you one, either. And I couldn't talk about it—not to you, not to anyone. I don't think that helped us.'

'No, I don't think it did. I meant to, when I got back from the conference, but then the whole thing just escalated and overwhelmed me, and I wasn't thinking clearly anyway. I'd had virtually no sleep, I knew I had a mountain to climb to get our marriage back on track, and then you told me to go and I realised there wasn't any point in talking about it, because you'd made up your mind, so I did the easy thing. Again. It was about the only thing I was any good at.'

'So why not talk to me after that?' she asked. 'You were still here for nearly three months, working your notice. You could have given me time to cool off, and then told me the truth. I waited and waited, and you never said a word in your own defence. It felt like you'd slunk away with your tail between your legs, and it just made you look even guiltier, if that was possible.'

'I know, and it was deliberate, even though it was killing me. I thought it would be easier that way, easier for both of us—give us a fresh start. I thought we might be able to move on, but I haven't. I haven't moved on at all. Have you?' he asked, his voice low, the question hardly voiced as if he wasn't sure he wanted the answer. 'Have you met anyone?'

She shook her head. 'No. No, of course not.'

'There's no "of course" about it. You're a beautiful woman, Liv. Why not?'

Because no one else was Nick. She'd had other relationships before she'd met him, but once he'd come into her life she'd realised he was the only man she'd ever really loved, the only man she'd ever really wanted. Nothing would change that.

She shook her head. 'I'm not interested. I've never been one for casual sex, and even if I'd met someone I really liked, I wouldn't have done anything about it, because the last thing I needed was another relationship. I just can't see it happening.'

'Because I hurt you so badly,' he said heavily.

'No, not you. Our marriage. The way it slowly crumbled away beneath us. That was so hard to take, and it wasn't even as if we'd fallen out of love. We'd just stopped communicating.'

'We had, you're right. And we shouldn't have done, but I was afraid if I was honest and told you how desperate I was, you'd just feel even guiltier, and I knew how that felt.'

She looked up at him, searching his eyes while she asked another question, one which had been plaguing her since Ben had told her what he'd been doing.

'I know I've already asked you this, but why *are* you working in infertility? I would have thought you'd run screaming from it, taken any other job in the world, almost, to avoid it.'

He shrugged and shifted on the bed, and she wriggled closer and rested her head on his shoulder.

'I don't know, to be honest,' he murmured. 'It was partly by accident, really. As soon as he knew it was destined for closure the consultant left to set up his own private clinic, and they were left in the lurch without a proper job to offer, so recruiting someone permanent wasn't possible, and I'd just come to the end of one job, it was in the same department, I knew some of the people—I suppose I felt I owed them, in a way, and they talked me into it. I didn't really want to do it, but it wasn't long term, there was a definite end-date, and

I thought it would give me time to look for something I really wanted. And it meant I wouldn't have to move again for a while. So I said yes, and then after a bit I realised I'm actually ideally placed to do it.

'I know what it's like, I know what they go through, how hard it can be to cope with the endless see-saw of emotions, the hope, the fear, the despair, and in a way it helped me to understand what had happened to us. As I told you yesterday, I realised we're definitely not alone. There are marriages and relationships falling apart all the time because of the pressure couples put on themselves, and for the ones who stick together, if I can help them get pregnant, then maybe I can save them going through what we did, and if I can't, I can empathise. I can give them advice, point them in the direction of support groups, talking therapies, relationship advice—'

'We never had any of that,' she pointed out sadly.

'No. No, we didn't. Nor did we go through the endless investigations, or try any one of the many options which might have helped us in one way or another, and I'm still not really sure why, because it was getting blindingly obvious that we needed help. Maybe it was because we felt there wasn't enough there to start with, that our marriage just wasn't strong enough to survive what might lie ahead.'

She sucked her breath in, shocked by that. 'Nick, we had a good marriage,' she said, her voice little more than a whisper. 'You know we did.'

'I thought so. I'd always thought so, so why couldn't I support you when you needed me?' he asked despairingly. 'Why wasn't I there for you every time it didn't happen? Why did I go to the conference without you that weekend—and why did you believe the worst of me and not even question me about Suze?'

'I did!'

'No. You asked me if she was in my room. You never asked me why, or what we did. You just assumed I'd slept with her, and yes, I could have explained, but it was as if you'd already made up your mind, and in the next breath you told me you wanted a divorce as if you'd been waiting for a reason to get rid of me. Why would you do that if our marriage was so good?'

'Because it wasn't by then,' she admitted, her eyes filling. 'It was awful. You know what it was like. We hardly spoke to each other, we never hugged or kissed or laughed together. We just had sex at the right time— never at the wrong time, never just because we wanted to. I can't remember when we last made love, but I can remember just about every time we had sex to make a baby that never happened.'

He was silent for an age, and then he drew in a ragged breath and rested his head against hers.

'I'm sorry. I never meant it to be like that, but this room became such an emotional minefield that I almost dreaded going into it. I felt as if that was all you wanted from me, that I was just a sperm donor, that my only reason for being there was to get you pregnant, and I couldn't do that, and when you said you wanted a divorce, it gave me a way out of a situation that was tearing me apart.'

'Which was why you didn't tell me the truth about that night, because you wanted out.'

'Partly. I knew I still loved you, and I was coming home to try and make it work, but in my heart of hearts I knew I couldn't live with you any more, not the way

it was. And I don't want to go there again, Liv, I really
don't. I won't get back on that merry-go-round of hope
and despair until I'm sure we're strong enough to take
the next step. It's too destructive, and I can't do it. It
just hurts too damn much.'

'Have I asked you to?'

He shook his head. 'No. No, you haven't, but I didn't
want you building any dreams of that happening on
the vague possibility of me coming back here to work
permanently. That's not what I'm here for, and I don't
know if we could ever be strong enough to try again
for a baby.'

Her heart jolted, a shock of disappointment coursing
through her, and she realised she'd foolishly allowed
herself to hope…

'So why did you say yes to Ben? Why did you come
back?'

'Because I have to earn a living?'

She waited, but he said nothing more for a long time,
then eventually he shrugged his shoulders as if he was
asking himself the same question.

'I don't know,' he said at last. 'Yes, I needed to work,
but I could have taken any one of a number of locum
jobs. I wasn't even going to start looking until I'd had a
holiday, but then Ben rang, and—I don't know why I'm
here really, Liv. I just know I'm not happy, that my life
outside work doesn't really exist, that I'm lonely and I
miss our old friends.'

He turned towards her, and she shifted her head so
she could look into those sad, stormy eyes.

'And I miss you,' he went on softly. 'All the time.
I know I hurt you, and I know you hurt me, but I still
miss you, and I never stopped loving you, which doesn't

mean I see us getting back together, but maybe we can find something else, forge a friendship—I don't know. I don't have the answers, Liv, I wish I did. I just know that what I have now isn't working for me, either in terms of job satisfaction or personally, and I want more. I want something better. And one way or another, I want you in my life.'

She held his eyes, her own filling. 'I want you, too. I've missed you every single day. And even though it was horrible by the end, I still loved you. I'll always love you. And I want something better, too, because there has to be something better than this.'

He gave a quiet, heartfelt sigh. 'That's why I came back, but just because we love each other doesn't mean it works, Liv, and we've hurt each other enough already. The last thing I want is to make it any worse.'

She gave a soft huff of empty laughter. 'I don't think that's possible,' she said honestly, and he sucked in a breath, his fingers tightening on hers.

'Don't say that. I didn't want to hurt you. I never wanted to hurt you.'

Their eyes were locked, his sorrow and regret plain to see until in the end he sucked in a shuddering breath and looked away.

'Oh, Nick. Come here,' she said softly, and he shifted, putting his arms around her with such fierce tenderness it made her want to cry. She turned her face into his chest, breathing in the scent that was so unmistakably Nick, holding him close.

'I miss you so much,' she admitted. 'My life's so empty without you. All I have is my work, and I love it, but I'm still empty because you aren't here.'

His arms tightened a fraction, his chest shifting as

he sucked in a deep breath, then let it out on a ragged sigh. 'I'm empty, too, but I don't want to go back to what we had.'

'Then let's not. Maybe we should try again, Nick. Not for a baby, but for us, to see if we can make each other happy like we used to. Because we did. We were very happy, once. Maybe we could be happy again, if we wanted it enough. Maybe we just didn't try hard enough at *that*.'

He lifted his head and searched her eyes, then his closed and he swallowed hard.

'I don't know. I don't know if we can even remember *how* to be happy any more.'

'But we should try. We owe ourselves that much.'

She drew his head down, touching her lips to his, and with a quiet sigh he kissed her back, a gentle, lingering kiss, not platonic but not passionate, either.

An apology, from both of them, for all that had gone before?

Then he pulled back a little, staring down into her eyes. 'I'm sorry I blew it,' he said quietly. 'I honestly never meant to hurt you. I thought leaving would make it easier for you, but it didn't, did it? And I don't want to risk hurting you again.'

She sighed quietly, wishing she could see an easy way forward, dreading how she would feel if they couldn't. 'Life hurt us both, Nick, but only because we let it. We're older now, wiser. Why don't we just see where this takes us? You're here for a while now. Maybe we just need to turn back the clock far enough, rediscover what it was about each other that we fell in love with. Maybe that's all we've ever needed. And if we can't have children, we have our jobs and they're filled with babies, all the babies we could ever want. Maybe that should be enough for us. We need to find what it was we had, and then perhaps we'll be able to make sense of it all.'

'Maybe. But I'm not making any promises. Not yet. And I don't want to rush into anything, either. As you said, I'm here for a while. Let's just take our time.'

He dropped another kiss on her lips before rolling away from her and standing up—to distance himself from a conversation that was becoming uncomfortably deep? Probably, because he changed the subject then, his voice firmer, deceptively casual.

'By the way, did you know Daisy's pregnant again?'

'Yes. I'm really pleased for her. She had a miscarriage a few months back, and they were gutted. It's really good news.'

'Ben didn't tell me that,' he said quietly, his attempt at casual banished in an instant. 'That's really sad. Miscarriage is horrible.'

'It's obstetrics, Nick. It happens. Pregnancy is never a certainty until you've got a healthy baby in your arms, and that's just the start of all the trouble. They have to grow up safely, and that can be a challenge. Their little boy Thomas fell out of a tree last year and broke his arm.'

'I didn't know that, either. I can't believe he's old enough to climb trees.'

'No. You disappeared off the radar, Nick, not just for me but for everybody. It would be so good to have you back, even if it was just as a friend. I've really missed your friendship.'

She reached out a hand and he took it, folding it in

both of his, bowing his head to press a firm, lingering kiss on her knuckles.

'Let me think about it, Liv. Don't let's rush this. The last thing I want to do is make any more mistakes.'

She nodded, not wanting to give him time but knowing she had no choice if she was going to stand a chance to win him back. And she really, really wanted him back. She knew that now, with bone-deep certainty.

But first, it was time for a change of scenery, a breath of air, a bit of emotional space for both of them.

'I need to walk around for a bit or I'll just seize up. And I'm starving. How about some lunch?'

CHAPTER SEVEN

SHE WANTED HIM BACK—and he wanted her. That had never changed.

But to try again? He wasn't sure if what he felt was trepidation or anticipation.

Or both. But there were still things she didn't know, things he wasn't sure he wanted to tell her until he knew it was relevant, and the knowledge was eating a hole in him.

He made them lunch, just a simple salad with the things he'd picked up in the local shops on the way back, while she sat in the garden munching almond thins and drinking her tepid coffee on the swing seat under the tree where they'd often sat together in the good old days.

Not so much in the bad old days. She'd tended to retreat to it then, and he'd let her.

A mistake? Probably, but he'd been struggling to stay afloat himself then, and it had all been about self-preservation. He picked up the plates and went out to her.

'Can you manage this on your lap? It's pretty much fork food.'

'That's fine—it looks lovely. Thank you.'

'You're welcome. How are you feeling now?'

'OK. I feel a bit woozy if I bend over, but not bad. I can move around which has to be a good thing. I might go for a stroll later. I don't want to seize up.'

'Don't overdo it.'

She rolled her eyes and went back to her salad, and when she'd finished eating she went into the sitting room to watch the television while he cleared up the kitchen and dealt with his emails.

Mostly spam and trivia, but there was one from Ben with the detailed job description attached, dangling the carrot under his nose again. He read it through carefully, more and more sure that he wanted it if Simon didn't come back—so long as this thing with Liv didn't blow up in both their faces.

He'd do his best to avoid it, but his track record wasn't great. Could they pull it off? He really, really wasn't sure, but the best way to make it work was to take it slowly and give themselves time to adjust, to get used to each other again rather than jumping in the deep end. That way at least they could still be friends, and anything more would just be a bonus.

He stayed there that night, justifying it to himself on the grounds of her head injury—which, considering how well she looked, could have seemed a bogus excuse, but he wasn't prepared to risk it. At the very least she had concussion, and it wasn't too late for a slow, encapsulated bleed to flare into a full-blown crisis, so he talked himself into it and slept in the spare room with the door ajar—just in case.

He woke in the night and went to check on her, and found her fast asleep with her arms wrapped round a pillow.

Better that than him, he thought morosely. A lot, lot safer. Safer still if he found himself a flat. He'd check online tomorrow, see what there was. He went back to bed, ridiculously jealous of the pillow, and finally fell asleep again, to be woken by the brush of her hair over his face and the touch of her lips on his cheek.

'Rise and shine, sleepy-head. I've brought you a cup of tea. I thought you might want it before you go back to the hospital to see Judy Richards again.'

Judy! He struggled up out of the bedclothes, stifling a yawn and the urge to pull her down into the bed with him and take advantage of his early-morning erection. 'What's the time?'

'Eight thirty.'

'Damn. No time for tea. Shoo.' He grabbed the bed-clothes, gave her a pointed look and waited until she was out of the room before throwing them off and getting out of bed.

He definitely needed a place of his own.

He showered in record time, went to the hospital and satisfied himself that Judy was all right and her baby was stable, then on the way out his phone rang.

'Nick? It's Sam. What are you up to?'

'I've just seen a patient and I'm leaving the hospital now—why?'

'Because I've been thinking, Ben said you were supposed to be staying with them until you could find a flat, but you didn't sound overjoyed, and after talking to you and Liv yesterday it's pretty obvious you feel awkward staying with her, so why don't you come and live here while you do your locum? We've got a cabin in the garden that's doing nothing and you'll love it— it's right by the sea wall. You probably know it, it used to be James and Connie's house and I lived in the cabin when I first came up here, before I bought the house off them. It's got everything you'd need—a shower room and a small kitchen, a decent bed, free wi-fi, and it would be great for you.'

A place of his own? He felt a wash of relief, but held it down. For now. 'I didn't know you'd bought it— but then I don't know anything about your life now, so that's hardly a surprise, is it? And hadn't you better ask Kate before you start offering me the cabin? She might hate me.'

'Nah, of course she won't. She's itching to meet you, and anyway, it was her idea. Why don't you come down now? I'll make you a fancy coffee and Kate'll feed you cake while I talk you into it. Five minutes?'

'Sam, I haven't even had breakfast yet!'

'Perfect. Nor have I. You can have a bacon roll *and* cake.'

He laughed and gave in, trying not to let himself get too excited by the idea of a place of his own. 'OK, but I need to tell Liv I'm not going back yet. I'll see you shortly.'

Sam was right.

The cabin was exactly what he needed, bigger than the studio flat he'd lived in for the past two years and right by the sea, as he'd been told. It didn't overlook the water, set down as it was behind the sea wall, but with the windows open he could hear it, and it was instantly soothing.

After he'd been introduced to Kate and the delightfully smiley Isadora, they'd settled down in their big sitting room with the sea stretched out in front of them as far as the eye could see, and eaten fat, juicy bacon rolls followed by cake washed down with copious coffee, and then Sam took him up onto the sea wall.

They strolled along to some railings and leant on them, listening to the soft suck of the sea on the shingle and watching the gulls wheeling over the water. 'Look at that—how can you resist it?' Sam asked with a grin, and Nick laughed.

'I don't even want to try. What sort of rent are we talking about?' he asked, and Sam looked incredulous.

'What? You're the best friend I've ever had. Why the hell would I charge you money to stay here?'

'Because I'll be using electricity for heating and hot water, I'm invading your privacy—it's not fair.'

'It is fair. You can come sailing with me when I find a boat. Then I won't have Kate on my case about going out alone.'

He laughed and gave in. 'Well—if you're sure, and if Kate doesn't mind—'

'She doesn't. She really likes you. She says it'll be fun.'

He smiled at Sam. 'I really like her, too. You're well suited. How long have you known her?'

'Oh, not long. We met last January, but I didn't see her again until I started work here in April. Liv said you left in March, so I must have just missed you.'

'Yes, you must. So how does the maths work?' he asked, his mind ticking. 'Because Isadora's—what, five months old?'

Sam grinned. 'Yeah. Well, let's just say it was love at first sight and leave it at that. Whatever, we couldn't be happier. So, when are you going to move in?' he asked, changing the subject, and Nick shrugged.

'I don't know, but to be honest I need to get out of there, for all sorts of reasons and the sooner the better. I'm working all week and I'm probably on call next weekend, but I'm not doing anything today, and Liv seems fine now. I could go and empty my flat and come straight back here tonight. Is that OK, or is it too soon?'

'No. Whenever. Makes no difference and if Liv's worried she can always call me. I'll give it a clean this morning, and you can have it as soon as you like. Do you need a hand with moving your stuff?'

'No, I'll be fine. I don't have a lot, it'll easily go in the car. And don't worry about sheets and towels, I've got all that.'

'Great. I'll give you the key now and then it's all yours.'

'How did you get on with Sam?'

He smiled fleetingly. 'Good. It was a bit weird going down to the harbour. I didn't realise how much I'd missed the sound of the sea—it sort of felt like I'd come home.'

There was something sad about the way he'd said that which tugged at her heartstrings. 'It could be home again,' she said, a little tentatively because she didn't want to push it, but he just nodded.

'Maybe. I hope so. The cabin's lovely, by the way, and Sam said I can have it as soon as I like, so I thought I'd go and empty my flat and move in there today, if you're feeling OK?'

He was moving out today? She'd thought—or maybe not thought, just hoped—that he'd stay a little longer.

'Yes—yes, of course, if it's what you want, but is

there really that much of a rush?' she asked, curiously reluctant to let him go so soon. Or maybe at all? 'Why not leave it till next weekend? And what about Judy Richards?'

He was silent for a moment, then his eyes met hers fleetingly and flicked away again. 'Ben's going to keep an eye on her—he's on call this weekend anyway, and Sam says you can call him if you're worried or need anything. I'm working all week and I might be on call next weekend but I've got the opportunity today and I don't know when I'll get another one. And there's no rush, but now you're feeling better it might be wise for us not to be spending too much time alone together.'

'Wise?' Why *wise*?

'Yes. *Wise*.'

His eyes met hers again, and this time she saw the slow burn deep in the back of them, and heat flooded her body. She looked away hastily.

'I want you, Liv,' he said softly, 'but we're not ready for that yet. We need to take our time, be sure before we commit. And it's not as if we don't know how good it used to be.'

He was right, of course, but she felt a stupid surge of disappointment. 'So how about lunch, then, before you go?'

'Actually, I might just go now,' he said. 'We had bacon rolls and then Kate fed me a ton of cake so I really don't need to eat. Which reminds me, will you have enough food or do you want me to shop for you before I go?'

'No, it's fine, there's still some food in the fridge and I suspect the second your car's off the drive Gwen'll be round with a casserole or an apple pie to get the low-down anyway.'

He gave a wry chuckle. 'I don't know how you tolerate it.'

'Oh, they mean well, and I know it seems nosey but it's quite harmless. They're sweet, really, and they've been very kind to me.'

'Which is more than can be said for the hedge. He's tortured it into submission.'

She laughed, and once again his eyes caught hers and she saw the heat flaring in them. This time it was him who looked away.

'Are you sure you'll be all right if I go?'

'Nick, I'm fine. I'm better. I'm going back to work tomorrow.'

He frowned. 'Really? So soon? Are you sure?'

'Yes, I'm sure. I haven't even got a headache today. And I'll be fine. Go, get your stuff, get settled in. It's a good idea.'

He held her eyes for a second, then nodded. 'OK. Right, I'll get my bag,' he said. He ran upstairs, and she heard the slight creak of the boards as he went into the spare bedroom overhead, then moments later the stairs again as he came back down.

'That was quick.'

'I travel light. Don't get up. I'll let myself out.'

'No. I want to give you a set of keys before you go.'

She found them in the study—his study, in the top drawer of his desk—and handed them to him. It felt weirdly symbolic.

'So you can come and go whenever you want,' she said. 'No strings.'

He hefted them in his hand, met her eyes, his own unreadable again, and slipped them into his pocket.

'Thank you.'

'Don't thank me,' she said, shaking her head. 'I should be thanking you for looking after me—'

'It was my f—'

She cut him off, her fingers pressed over his lips. 'No. No more blame,' she said softly, and then she curved her hand around the back of his neck, drew his head down and kissed him.

For a second he froze, then his mouth softened, coaxing, tempting her until her lips parted to welcome him, his hand cradling her cheek as he deepened the kiss, tasting, searching, his tongue duelling with hers in a gentle, sensuous dance filled with promise.

Then he eased away, long before she was ready to let him go, opened the front door and turned on the step. 'Don't do anything rash, Liv,' he said gruffly. 'Don't forget you've got concussion. The signals in the brain can be disrupted for a month.'

'Nick, I'll be fine. Go. And ring me when you get back.'

He opened his mouth as if he was going to argue, then gave a rueful smile and nodded. 'Will do. Take care.'

And with a fleeting smile, he got into his car, fired up the engine and drove away.

She was on tenterhooks for the next twelve hours. Ridiculous, considering the number of times he must have been on the road in the last two years and she'd never given it a second thought.

It was different now. Now, she was letting herself

care about him again, starting to forgive him—not for being unfaithful, because she'd done that long ago when she'd realised that she'd shut him out, but for letting her believe it all this time.

And she had to forgive herself, too—for making their lives a misery, for shutting him out, for putting him in a position where he'd been happy for her to think that he'd betrayed her trust because it gave him a way out of a situation that had become intolerable.

Why hadn't they talked? Because they were talking now. They'd done little else in the past forty-eight hours, and already the wounds hurt a little less.

Like the physical ones, from Friday. Every hour saw another patch of skin go black as the bruising came out, but it looked much worse than it felt and it really didn't hurt any more and nor did her head.

She pottered in the garden, tried a little weeding and gave up because bending over induced a headache and she didn't want to push it, even though her concussion had only been mild. Maybe Nick was right and she should take it easy.

Her phone pinged at midnight, with a text to say he was back at Sam's and see her tomorrow, and for the first time in hours she let herself relax.

Then on Monday morning just before eight, he rang her.

'Are you really coming in to work?'

'Yes, I am, but only light duties from nine to three. Are you still fretting about me?' she asked mildly.

'No, not at all, but I've put Judy on steroids. I've got a funny feeling about her—until we get the antiphospholipid result we won't know why she's had problems, but at least if the steroids have matured the baby's lungs it'll have more chance if we do need to deliver her in a hurry. I just thought you'd like to know.'

'Mmm. Thanks. Poor Judy. How is she?'

'Scared? She might appreciate a visit, if you've got a minute.'

She smiled. 'I'll drop in on her. And before you ask, no, I'm not driving, I'm going to walk in.'

'Good,' he said, sounding relieved. 'I'll see you later. Text me when you get here.'

So much for keeping their distance, she thought with a smile, but at least if they were at work there'd be no cosy moments to derail them.

To his surprise she walked onto the antenatal ward half an hour later, just as he went to check on Judy again.

'Gosh, two of you! It's like buses.'

'Mine's only a social call, Judy,' Liv said, turning towards her. 'I just popped up to say hi.'

'Oh! Your eye! What have you done?'

'Ah, yes. Minor accident on Friday.'

Nick snorted softly, and Judy glanced from him to Liv and back again, studying their nametags. 'You're both Jarvis,' she said slowly. 'Are you married, or is that just coincidence?'

He opened his mouth, looked at Liv and left it up to her.

'We were married—and no, he didn't hit me, it genu-inely was an accident,' she said, and gave Judy a twisted little smile.

'Oh, gosh. Why did you let him go?'

Nick snorted again and picked up the board at the end of the bed, scanning her charts with half an eye while he waited for Liv to reply to that one.

'Yes. Bit silly, wasn't it?' she said eventually, and the silence grew a little awkward.

'Right, now we've established that I'm not a wife-beater, can we get back to business, please? Judy, how are you feeling?'

All trace of humour vanished from her face. 'Worried, if I'm honest, because there's something I didn't tell you that maybe I should have. I've been taking aspirin since just before I got pregnant.'

'Aspirin?' he asked, frowning, and glanced at Liv, who just shrugged and looked as stunned as he felt.

'Yes. I've been really worried about this APS thing but the test I had after my last miscarriage was negative so I thought I'd be all right, but then I read up about OAPS and it just seemed to fit, you know, and it said take aspirin, so I started taking it after my last period, and I don't know if it's coincidence but everything seemed to be going fine until I stopped—'

'You stopped? When?'

She nodded. 'About three weeks ago, because I was bruising so easily and I thought I might be doing more harm than good and I was a bit worried about having a haemorrhage, and it's all gone wrong since then.'

She pressed a hand over her mouth. 'It's my fault, isn't it? I shouldn't have stopped. I should have said something.'

'Yes, you should, because stopping it could certainly explain the baby's slow growth in the last few weeks,' he told her thoughtfully, 'but taking it could also have stopped you miscarrying in the first place, so, no, I don't think it was the wrong thing to do, but yes, you probably should have told us because had we known I would have put you back on aspirin on Friday as a precaution.'

'I'm so sorry—'

'No, don't apologise, Judy, it's OK, because I think it's just made everything a lot clearer, so here's what we'll do. I'm going to chase those results, because it's quite possible you *have* got obstetric antiphospholipid syndrome, which unlike normal APS only affects you when you're pregnant, hence the negative result before. Basically what happens is the blood clots in the capillaries in the uterine wall and can prevent implantation of an embryo, prevent the placenta developing, or cause it to fail later on, which may be what's happening with your baby now, but if that's what it is, it's utterly treatable and we can stop it in its tracks, so I'm going to put you back on aspirin just to be on the safe side, and we'll see what the results come up with and go from there. OK?'

She nodded, looking on the verge of tears. 'I'm sorry. I should have told you I'd been taking it, but I didn't want to look hysterical. I know doctors frown on people self-medicating.'

'There's nothing hysterical about it, Judy, and you may have done exactly the right thing. You've lost three babies already, but this one's still alive, and I'm going to make very, very sure that we do everything we can to keep it safe. OK?'

Her eyes filled, and she nodded. 'OK. Thank you.'

'My pleasure. Let's just hope we get some answers soon.'

Liv got to her feet. 'I'll leave you to it. I think there's a stack of filing with my name on it. I'll pop back and see you later if I get a minute, Judy.'

'That would be lovely.' Judy watched her walk away, then said, 'You ought to take care of her, she shouldn't be here, not with that eye,' and he met her reproachful eyes over the top of the charts and felt a twinge of guilt mixed with frustration.

'Tell me about it.' He sighed, and hung the charts back on the end of the bed. 'OK. I'll chase up the results, get you some aspirin and I'll be back later. Yell if you feel any different. They'll page me. And don't worry about Liv, I'm keeping an eye on her.'

'You do that. She's a lovely woman.'

As if he hadn't noticed.

He appeared in the ward office some time after she started sifting through the clearly non-essential paperwork, most of which needed shredding, from what she could see.

'Sorted Judy?' she asked, and he nodded.

'I wish she'd told us about the aspirin, I would have put her back on it prophylactically on Friday, but she's on it now and hopefully it won't be too late. Got time for coffee? I haven't had breakfast yet and I've been here since seven.'

'Yes, I've got tons of time,' she said with a wry smile, getting to her feet. 'Nobody will give me anything to do. I think they're all terrified by the black eye, so it's a good job they can't see my leg.'

'Probably, it was bad enough on Saturday and it can only be worse by now. Judy told me to take care of you, by the way, and said you shouldn't be here with that eye. I agreed with her.'

'Is that why nobody'll give me anything to do except filing, because you've been sticking your oar in?'

'I hardly needed to do that. One look at you is enough.'

She made a disgusted sound. 'Whatever, I'd like to kill whoever invented filing. I'm beginning to think it's possible to die of boredom and I've only been doing it for half an hour.'

He chuckled. 'I think you're trying to get out of a dull job.'

'Rumbled,' she said with a laugh, and they walked down to the café in a companionable silence.

He ordered their coffees and picked up a cereal bar and a banana. 'Want one?' he asked, waggling the banana at her, and she nodded.

'Yes, please. There wasn't much left in the house so I only had toast for breakfast. Gwen didn't rock up with a casserole, by the way, but I did see her through the window and waved. I think the black eye might have scared her off.'

He winced. 'Perhaps you'd better explain about the accident before Bert comes looking for me with his garden shears.'

They found a table by the window, and he sat down and stretched his legs out. 'Before I forget, I put a food order in this morning so you'll have something for breakfast tomorrow. It should arrive at yours this evening between six and seven. I take it you'll be there?'

'You ordered food for me?' she said, puzzled.

'Yes. Well, some staples for you to save you having to shop, but I got some stuff for us to share, as well. I thought, if we're going to take this seriously and try and get to know each other again, maybe we should spend the evenings together when we can, and the kitchen in the cabin's a bit basic so I thought maybe we could do it at the house? I'll do all the cooking, so it should be easier for you, too. Unless you have any objections?'

'No, that sounds great. Why would I object to being waited on? Did you order wine, by the way? I'm sorry I didn't have any over the weekend.'

'I don't drink any more,' he said. 'I still have the odd glass if I'm with friends, but I never buy alcohol routinely, and I absolutely never drink on my own. And I go to the gym, and I'm running again, and I've cleaned up my diet—too little, too late, but...'

He tailed off, leaving her to absorb all that for a second, and she shook her head.

'I thought you looked better,' she said quietly. 'Fitter. Healthier. More like the man I married—except you don't look like the man I married, because the man I married was happy, and you're not happy any more and that's my fault.'

'Liv, it's not your fault.'

'Yes, it is. I've destroyed your life, messed up your career, trashed everything, and I'm so sorry. I shouldn't have believed that you'd been unfaithful to me, because it was so unlike you, but when I thought about it, it didn't seem such a stretch to imagine that you'd turn to someone else, because you weren't showing any interest in me by then and I couldn't see what I had to offer you any longer. It was all so horrible—'

He gave a soft sigh, his voice quiet, his smile gentle, but he looked troubled, as if there was something he wanted to say. He didn't, though, just took her hand and squeezed it. 'Hey, no more, come on. This isn't the time or the place. Let's concentrate on the here and now—and right now, I'm operating in an hour and I haven't gone through the notes properly yet, so I'll take my coffee and go. You take it easy, I'll catch you later.'

She watched him go and sat there a moment longer,

soaking up the sun, but then her phone rang, making her jump. It was Sam, checking up on her and asking if she felt she needed physio.

'No, Sam, I'm fine, but thank you. I'm back at work already.'

'Seriously? You've got concussion, not to mention the bruises.'

'Sam, I'm fine, really. And thank you for putting Nick up. It's very kind of you. He seems really happy with the cabin.'

'Good. You're welcome. Sorry, I've got to go, I'm needed in Resus but you know where I am. Shout if you need anything and don't overdo it.'

The phone went dead, and she slipped it into her pocket, finished her coffee and went back to the tedious filing.

Overdo it? Chance would be a fine thing.

CHAPTER EIGHT

SHE WAS SENT down to cover for Jan again in the antenatal clinic after lunch, and Nick took one look at her and told her to go home. 'You're white as a sheet and you look shattered. Go on, out of here.'

'I'm fine. I'm only working till three. Don't fuss. How's Judy?'

'OK, but she has got antiphospholipid antibodies.'

'So she's definitely got OAPS?'

He gave a frustrated sigh. 'It looks like it, and I'm kicking myself for not putting her on aspirin on Friday when I admitted her. The more I think about it, the crosser I get.'

'Why? She'd already had a test that was negative, and Simon hadn't picked it up.'

'No, but his wife had just been diagnosed with cancer, so I doubt his mind was in the right place, and I wasn't firing on all cylinders either after finding we were working together, but two wrongs don't make a right.'

'No, they don't, but she'd withheld vital information, and anyway, it was a judgement call, Nick.'

'And I made the wrong judgement. Hence the expression "human error", but it's unforgivable when a baby's life's at stake. Still, I'd admitted her and she'd been monitored so we know nothing happened over the weekend. I suppose that's something to be thankful for. Right, Amy Zacharelli.'

She felt her eyes widen. It was Amy's baby he'd gone to deliver by emergency C-section on the day she'd thrown him out. Of all the coincidences…

'Amy's pregnant again already?'

'So it would seem.'

'Is she going for another section?'

'I don't know. I'm going to talk to her now I've seen her latest scan images. I'm hoping not. Simon's written "Query VBAC" in her notes, so it's obviously been discussed. Would you like to call her in?'

'Sure.'

She went out to the waiting room and called Amy, and a good-looking couple got to their feet. She'd never seen Amy, but she would have recognised Leo blindfolded. He was a celebrity chef, and she was a massive fan of his cookery show.

'May I come, too?' he asked with a coaxing smile, and she smiled back and hoped she didn't look too fangirly.

'Of course, if Amy's happy. Mr Jarvis won't mind,' she said as she ushered them into the consulting room.

'Mr Jarvis?' Amy said, and her face lit up as she saw him in there. 'I thought you'd gone for ever.'

'So did I.' He got to his feet and smiled, shaking their hands. 'It's good to see you again, and not before time. I owe you both a massive apology. I promised to come back and make sure you were OK when I delivered your last baby, but I got caught up in something and then I was off on leave and I didn't even get a message to you. I'm really sorry.'

Caught up in something? On leave? One way of putting it when your wife calls time on your marriage, Liv thought, and wondered if she was the only person who could see what was going on under the surface of his calm, professional demeanour. She hoped so, for his sake, but both she and Nick were well aware that she'd found Suze's note while he'd been delivering Amy's baby.

'There's no need to apologise,' Leo was saying. 'I'm just sorry that we never had a chance to thank you, but I've never forgotten how kind you were to Amy, and how much we owe you.'

'You don't owe me anything,' Nick said, brushing it aside. 'It was a pleasure. So, how is your little girl? Is she doing well?'

'She's wonderful. Naughty, but wonderful,' Amy said with a laugh, 'and she's been fine, thanks to you and Mr Walker.'

'Do you know what this one is?'

'A boy,' Leo told him, his smile saying it all, and Liv felt the familiar shaft of pain like an old friend, but Nick's smile was convincing. If you didn't know better...

'Perfect,' he said. 'So, what are your birth plans? I see from your notes there's a suggestion you want to try for a normal vaginal delivery.'

'I want to, if I can. Mr Bailey said he was prepared to let me try, but he's apparently gone off on indefinite leave so I'm in the lurch again. I seem to have that effect on people.'

His smile was a little strained. 'I'm sure you can't

take the blame for either of us abandoning you, but you're not in the lurch, unless I don't count? I'm replacing him for now, so I'll be looking after you for the rest of this pregnancy and I'm happy to let you try if everything looks OK.'

'You are?' Her face lit up, and she pressed her hands to her mouth. 'Oh, that's amazing! I was so worried, I thought his replacement might say no.'

'No. They're going to be close together, of course, only about fifteen months apart, but it's over a year so technically speaking that's not a problem. Why don't you hop up on the couch and let's have a look at your scar?'

All was well, he was relieved to see. The scar was a fine, tidy line, her uterus under the skin felt smooth, with only the slightest hint of a ridge over the incision site, and he could feel nothing to worry him.

'OK, Amy, I'm all done.' He snapped off his gloves and propped himself up on his desk. 'It's looking good,' he said. 'The head's engaged, everything looks fine, and I think I'll be quite happy to let you try. I'll make sure I'm here when you're admitted, but I don't see any reason why you shouldn't succeed. Liv?'

'No, I'd be happy to deliver you, Amy. I might be a bit less happy if it was a home birth, but provided you're here and we're keeping a close eye on things, I don't see a problem at all.'

'Oh, that's brilliant,' Amy said, tugging her clothes straight and picking up her bag. 'I feel so much happier now.'

He grinned at her enthusiasm. 'Good. I like my mums to be happy. I'll definitely make sure I'm around when you go into labour, and I'll do my best to give you the delivery you want, but the safety net is there. We'll make sure of that.'

'Thank you,' she said fervently, and then to his astonishment she went up on tiptoe and kissed his cheek. 'Thank you so much.'

'My pleasure. I'll see you in two weeks, if not before. I wouldn't want you to go over, but we'll see how it's going, and you might need a membrane sweep to chivvy things along, but so far, so good. You take care. It's good to see you both again.'

'You, too,' Leo said. 'Welcome back to Yoxburgh.'

Nick smiled and watched them go, wondering again what it would be like to come back here permanently, to see his patients extending their families, getting to know them over the years.

Maybe he'd get to find out?

He turned to Liv. 'Right, you, time to go home. I can manage the rest. They'll find me a nurse. Shoo. Go.'

She went, much more tired than she'd expected, and the short walk took her twice as long as usual. She let herself in and curled up on the sofa, her body tired and achy, her legs like lead. She'd just got settled when the doorbell rang, and she dragged herself off the sofa and opened the door.

Flowers.

Beautiful flowers, hand-tied and in a lovely vase, so she didn't even have to arrange them. There was a card, and she pulled it out of the envelope.

N xxx

Nothing more, but he didn't need to say more. His phone went straight to voicemail, so she left him a message thanking him, and spent the rest of the afternoon either dozing or staring at them with a silly smile on her face.

He cared. Still, after everything that had happened, he cared. And tonight couldn't come soon enough...

He looked tired but happier when he turned up, and although he'd shaved this morning she could see the dark shadow of stubble on his jaw again, and it sent a shiver through her.

He hugged her briefly, kissed her cheek and let her go, shoving his hands in his back pockets. To keep them out of trouble? Probably wise, she thought regretfully.

'So, did the shopping come?' he asked.

'Yes. And the flowers. They're beautiful. Thank you.'

'You're welcome. How are you?'

'Tired,' she admitted. 'I wasn't expecting to feel like this. It's not even as if my head aches.'

'Concussion's a weird thing. You need to take it easy. What about the rest of you?'

'All right. My bruises hurt if I touch them, but otherwise I'm fine.'

'Well, there's an easy answer to that,' he said with a grin.

He wandered through to the kitchen and started poking about in the fridge.

'So, what did you do this morning while I was filing?' she asked, following him.

'Oh, gynae surgery. All the usual stuff. Pretty dull. I like the babies.'

She laughed sadly. 'Me, too. We really chose the

right careers, didn't we? So what do you reckon Amy Zacharelli's chances of delivering successfully are?'

'I don't know. She's due in sixteen days, but I don't want her to go over, really. It would be lovely if she went into labour spontaneously so we don't have to induce her but that could complicate things so I'm not holding my breath.' He pulled his head out of the fridge. 'How do you fancy a Thai chicken curry with cauliflower rice?'

She felt her eyes widen. 'That's a bit healthy. And I noticed everything's organic.'

'I told you I'd turned my life around. Too healthy?'

'No—no, it sounds great. Go for it. Can I do anything?'

'Yes. Sit down on the sofa there and talk to me while I cook.'

She turned her head and looked at it, squatting there in the 'family room' like a malevolent toad, taunting her with horrible memories.

'Do I have to?'

He looked up and met her eyes, and frowned. 'Hey, what's up?' he asked softly, abandoning the food and cradling her cheek in his hand. It was chilly from the fridge, and it sent a shiver down her spine.

'I don't like that sofa. Not since…'

'Oh, Liv.' Her name was a sigh on his lips, and he drew her gently into his arms and hugged her. 'Come on. We'll sit on it together and chase out the demons.'

And he took her hand and led her over to the sofa and sat her down next to him. 'There. See? It's just a sofa.'

She looked at the coffee table, and he followed her eyes and frowned. 'What's that mark?' he asked, leaning forwards and scratching at a dull, pale patch with his nail.

'You slopped your coffee when you stood up when I told you to go, and I put the paper under it to mop it up, and it stuck.'

He turned his head, his eyes shocked as they met hers.

'It's been there all this time?'

She shrugged. 'It didn't matter. I don't use it.'

He got up, found a sponge in the sink and came back, scrubbing at the stuck bits of paper until they dissolved and slid away. He gave the table one last swipe and straightened up to look at it.

'There, that's better,' he said, and bent and caught her chin in his fingers. 'Much better,' he added softly, and lowered his head the last few inches and kissed her. 'Now stay there, and I'll make you supper and you can talk to me.'

She looked at the mark, now nothing more than a slowly drying damp patch, and realised he was right. It was much better, in every way. Amazing what you could wipe away with a damp sponge…

She settled back into the corner, tucked a cushion behind her head and watched him cook while her lips tingled gently from his kiss.

'Thank you. That was amazing. I loved the cauliflower rice.'

They were back on the sofa, the one where her life had fallen apart last January, and he propped his feet up on the coffee table and rolled his head towards her.

'Don't get too addicted to it. I don't want you getting skinny again. You were way too thin, with all that running.'

'I know.' She looked away for a moment, and he caught her chin and gently turned her face towards him, his eyes searching.

'What?'

She shrugged, forcing herself to hold his steady gaze. 'I've wondered—you know, if that was why I never conceived?'

He dropped his hand and this time it was him who looked away. 'Not necessarily.'

She frowned. There was something he wasn't telling her, and she had a sinking feeling in her gut. 'Nick?'

He swallowed, sucked in a breath and let it go again slowly.

'I had semen analysis,' he said eventually, his voice heavy. 'Three years ago, after the second month you weren't pregnant.'

'And?' she prompted, her heart pounding. If they'd been trying for two years, and all that time he'd known—

'Well, I wasn't exactly firing blanks, but my sperm count was down on the optimum, and the quality wasn't stunning. It wasn't that bad, but it wasn't great, either.'

'So you cleaned up your act,' she said slowly, remembering how he'd suddenly stopped drinking wine and eating rubbish, rejoined the hospital gym, started running—but it hadn't lasted.

'Yes. And you still didn't get pregnant, and it was getting tougher and tougher, so I just let it all slide again. And then just before you found out you weren't pregnant, I had another test.'

Her heart thumped. 'And?'

'It was worse. Not catastrophic, but bad enough that

it could definitely be an issue by then. I'd already decided that if you weren't pregnant I was going to talk to you, tell you the truth, but then when I got the result I was just numb, so I went to the conference, trying to work up the courage to tell you it was probably all my fault, and then Suze asked me what was wrong and I just lost it. And then when you thought I'd slept with her and kicked me out it seemed like the best idea because I thought if you hated me you'd find it easier to move on, but you haven't, and neither have I. But that's really why I didn't tell you the truth about Suze, because I didn't want you taking me back out of pity and going through endless cycles of IVF when you didn't really love me any more anyway.'

She slid her hand into his, threading their fingers together and holding on. 'I never stopped loving you, Nick.'

His fingers tightened. 'It felt like it, when you said you wanted a divorce. It felt as if you hated me, and I could see why, because I hated myself then and I thought if I got out of your life you'd find someone else and have babies the easy way, because IVF's tough, Liv. It can be really tough, I didn't know how tough until I saw others going through it, and you're younger than me, you've got years to find another man who can give you babies—'

'But I don't want another man, Nick, and I don't want anyone else's babies! I want you, and if it was right for us, down the line, I'd want *your* babies, via IVF or whatever other route we had to take so I could give them to you.'

She lifted her other hand and curled it round his jaw, turning his face back to her. 'That's why I never di-

vorced you, because I love you,' she said softly. 'I'll always love you, and I couldn't bring myself to let you go.'

'Oh, Liv...'

He closed the gap between them, his mouth finding hers, sipping, searching, coaxing. She tipped back
her head and his lips trailed down over her jaw, down
her throat, over her collarbone until they met the soft,
clinging fabric of her top.

And then he stopped, motionless for a moment before he lifted his head and dropped the lightest, sweet-
est kiss on her lips and moved away.

'Don't stop.'

'I have to. We can't do this now, Liv. Not yet. Apart
from anything else you're exhausted, you've had a long
day and you need to go to bed.'

'So take me to bed.'

He gave a despairing little laugh and kissed her
again. 'Nice try, but I need to go,' he whispered softly.

'I'll miss you.'

'I'll miss you, too, but it might be good for us. As
they say, abstinence makes the heart grow fonder.'

She felt her mouth twitch into a smile, and she
reached out and cupped his jaw again, her fingers testing the slight roughness of the stubble coming through.
'Promise me something.'

'What?'

'Keep the stubble this time? It makes you look sexy
and a teensy bit badass.'

'What?' he said with a laugh. 'Why would you want
me to look like that?'

'You know what I mean.'

'Yeah. Your bit of rough,' he said self-mockingly,
and she smacked his hand and laughed.

'You are so not my bit of rough. It just makes you look—'

'Badass,' he said on a chuckle. 'Good grief. I don't want to upset my patients.'

'Too late to worry about that. You heard what Judy said about me letting you go. *She* thinks you're hot.'

He frowned and stared down at her. 'Hot? Judy? You're kidding me.'

She rolled her eyes, and he laughed again.

'Seriously?'

'You just have no idea, do you?' she said, shaking her head slowly from side to side. 'Nick, you are *such* a hottie.'

He lifted his hand, fingering his jaw thoughtfully. 'Well, maybe I should get a stubble blade for my razor. You know—just to keep you interested.'

His eyes were sparkling with mischief, and he looked so like his old self that it made her want to cry—or hug him. She did that, as the safest option, and then let him go.

'Go on, go home.'

'I wish,' he said softly, and she felt like crying again.

'I meant back to Sam's. Quick, while I'll still let you.'

He got to his feet and pulled her up, then kissed her again, his mouth lingering on hers for the longest moment before he took a step back out of reach.

'You go on up to bed. I'll put the dishwasher on and clear up before I leave. Shoo.'

She shooed, because she truly was exhausted, but she didn't sleep until she heard the front door close softly, and then the scrunch of tyres as he drove away. By the time the sound of his engine had faded, she was asleep...

* * *

He kept the stubble.

Not because of what she'd said, apparently, but because he had a call from the hospital about Judy Richards, so he'd thrown on his clothes and gone straight there.

By the time Liv went on duty at seven, he'd already been in the hospital for two hours and Judy had had another Doppler ultrasound scan of her placenta because the monitor had shown a slight dip in the baby's heart rate and it hadn't been moving quite as much as usual.

'Is she going to be all right?' she asked him, moving to stand next to him behind the nursing station desk, and he pursed his lips, his eyes still tracking over the scan images on the computer.

'I hope so. Her placenta's certainly not brilliant, but she's going to have another scan in two hours. If there's any change at all, I'm going to deliver it.'

'At thirty-two weeks?'

'Thirty-three today. And every day counts at this stage.'

He turned and gave her a tired smile. 'Talking of which, how are you?'

'Better. I slept like a log.'

'See? I told you you were tired,' he murmured.

'I'm not tired now,' she murmured, 'not looking at that badass stubble,' but he just laughed and stood up.

'No, you're at work,' he pointed out, but he winked at her as he turned away and her heart fluttered. Then he turned back.

'What are you doing this evening?'

'Eating with you?'

He smiled. 'Good. Want to come down to the cabin? I'll pick you and the food up, if you like.'

'Assuming Judy's OK, because I know you and I know she'll come first.'

'Are you jealous of a patient?'

She folded her arms. 'Absolutely.'

He laughed again and walked away, and she stood there staring after him like a moonstruck fool.

'You two seem to be getting on pretty well.'

She jumped and spun round.

'Ben! Do you have to sneak up on me like that? You scared the living daylights out of me!'

He raised his hands in apology. 'Sorry. I didn't mean to startle you, I just wanted your input on a patient,' he said, but his eyes were twinkling and she felt herself colour.

'No, you didn't, you were just fishing for gossip.'

'Not gossip. I'm actually very relieved to see you getting on, on several fronts.'

'Several?'

'Mmm. For a start you're alive, so after worrying us all to death on Friday that's a massive plus. And you're both friends of mine, so it's good to see you to-gether again.'

'We're not "together" together, so don't get over-excited,' she cautioned. 'And anyway, that's only two fronts.'

'Well, he hasn't left yet, so we still have our locum. That's a very fat three.'

She chuckled. 'I can imagine. So, which patient did you want to talk to me about?' she asked, but he frowned thoughtfully.

'Patient? Did I say something about a patient?' he

murmured, and then wandered off, leaving her laughing softly under her breath. *Idiot*...

'Liv, we've got a new mum on the way in in an ambo. Are you involved in a delivery at the moment?'

'No, do you want me to take her?' she asked the duty line manager, and she nodded.

'Please. The baby's OP, and she was in too much pain to get in the car, apparently. It's only precautionary, so it should be pretty straightforward.'

Famous last words.

The back-to-back presentation was always potentially difficult, especially for a first-time mother, and the terrified young woman was in so much pain when she arrived that she refused to move, but without moving she was never going to get her baby out and it was ready to come.

'OK,' Liv said, 'I'll get you some pain relief, and then I'm going to get you up, because you're fully dilated and this baby needs you to push.'

'I can't—'

'Yes, you can, you'll see. I'll be back in a minute.'

She left the mother in the care of another midwife while she went to find Nick. 'Are you busy in the next half hour or so? I might need you.'

'Sounds promising,' he murmured, a lazy, sexy smile playing around his mouth, and she ignored the little shiver of need and rolled her eyes.

'I've got a primipara struggling with an OP labour and she might need a bit of assistance. I'm going to give her some Pethidine and then try and get her up, but I'm not holding out much hope. She's being pretty adamant about not moving.'

'OK. Page me if you need me. I've got a conference call with Ben's brother in an hour to talk about Judy's scans, but if I can help before then, give me a shout. Otherwise it'll be Ben.'

'OK.'

She didn't need him.

Between the painkiller, her partner's physical and emotional support and a bit of cajoling and encouragement from Liv, they got her up onto all fours which expanded her pelvis enough to allow the baby to pass through it, and no sooner was the mother lying down again with the squalling baby in her arms than there was a knock on the door and Nick stuck his head round.

'That answers that question, then,' he said with a crooked little smile. 'Everything OK?'

She smiled back, blinking away the tears that accompanied every delivery these days. 'Perfect, thank you, Mr Jarvis.'

'Good. Come and find me when you're done, please. I might need you.'

She raised an eyebrow, her back to the patient, and he winked and sent her blood pressure rocketing.

The door closed with a soft click, and she blinked again and turned back to the mother with what she hoped was a nice, professional smile firmly pinned on her face.

'You see?' she said. 'I told you you could do it. Well done.'

It was after seven before he finished work and came to pick her up. She didn't mind for herself, because she'd had a nap after she got home, but he'd been at the hospital for fourteen hours and he must be exhausted.

'How's Judy?'

'Fine. OK. Ben's brother Matt was pretty positive about the baby, which was good. It's handy having a prenatal paediatrician on tap like that. What do you fancy for supper?'

'Something quick and easy. You must be really tired.'

He smiled and dropped a kiss on her hair, hugging her gently. 'I am, but I need to wind down. I'm not on call tonight so I shouldn't get called in unless Judy has a crisis, and I'm hoping we've averted that, so I should get eight straight hours in bed.

'Fancy fish and chips?'

'I thought you were on a health kick?'

He laughed. 'It's not a health kick, it's a lifestyle choice, and I can choose to have a treat if I want one. Or if you'd rather, I can knock up a salad. I've got roasted aubergine, braised artichoke hearts, hot-smoked salmon fillets—'

'That sounds gorgeous.'

'Good. Right, let's go because the evening's ebbing away and we're wasting it and we both need an early night.'

He raided the fridge and drove her down to the harbour, pulled up outside the back of Sam and Kate's house and took her into the cabin.

'Oh, it's lovely!' she said, looking round. 'Really nice. And to think I was feeling sorry for you.'

'Oh, don't feel sorry for me, I'm very happy here, it's perfect. Or it is now, now you're here.'

He put the bag down and pulled her into his arms, staring down into her eyes and searching them for answers.

'Can we do this, Liv?' he asked softly. 'Can we make it work? Even if in the end we can never have kids?'

'We can give it our best shot. My mum this morning didn't think she was going to be able to get her baby out without help, but she did it. Maybe that's the clue. Maybe we have to work at it instead of expecting it to look after itself. But you might have to feed me first,' she added with a smile as her stomach rumbled, and he laughed and let her go.

They had coffee after dinner with Sam and Kate, and they could see lights twinkling out on the water, and hear the clatter of the rigging from the boat yard, and she could see why Nick loved it so much.

Then Nick looked at his watch. 'Right, I need to get some sleep because until Judy's delivered I'm just waiting for the call.'

'You need to learn to delegate,' Sam said, which made her laugh.

'He doesn't delegate,' she told Sam. 'He doesn't trust anyone else—a little bit like you, really. I seem to remember you had to check up on me on Saturday morning after the accident.'

'Rumbled,' he said with a grin, and Nick pulled Liv to her feet.

'Come on, I need my bed. Thanks for the coffee, guys.'

'They're such nice people,' Liv said as he started the car. 'Have you told them about us?'

'No. I don't talk about us, you know that.'

'You talked to Suze.'

'Just once, and look where it got me.'

He gave her a fleeting smile, and even the moonlight picked up the sadness in his eyes.

* * *

He pulled up on the drive and cut the engine.

'Oh. Are you coming in?' she asked. 'I thought you were in a hurry to get to bed?'

That made him chuckle. 'Are they mutually exclusive?'

Her jaw dropped a fraction and he stopped teasing her. 'If I kiss you goodnight out here in the car the way I want to kiss you goodnight, Bert and Gwen will probably have a stroke.'

She stifled a laugh and opened her door. 'Well, we can't have that.'

'Absolutely not.'

He followed her into the house, still chuckling, closed the door and leant back on it, pulling her into his arms.

'Oh, that's better.' His mouth found hers, and he felt the smile on it fade as need moved in and swamped them both.

She arched up and kissed him back, tunnelling her fingers through his hair as he plundered her mouth, his hands holding her head steady as he deepened the kiss, his tongue duelling with hers, his hips rocking against her body.

Then he lifted his head and rested his forehead against hers, his breath rasping in and out as if he'd been running.

'I want you,' he whispered roughly, nipping and nibbling over her throat as she arched her head back invitingly.

'So stay,' she murmured, and he wavered for a second then shook his head.

'No, I can't. I have to go. I'm dead beat and I'm on call tomorrow night, so this is my last chance at a good uninterrupted stretch. What time are you on tomorrow?'

'Seven, again.'

'Me, too. I'll pick you up at a quarter to, and we can have breakfast together when I've done my ward round if you're not involved in a delivery by then.'

He kissed her again, just a tender, lingering caress, and then he moved her gently out of his way before he surrendered to temptation. It would be so easy—

'I need to go.'

'I know you do. I love you.'

He groaned. 'Oh, Liv. I love you, too,' he murmured. He kissed her again, then opened the door, got into the car and drove away, wondering what the hell he was doing and why, when he could have been upstairs with her by now, buried in that beautiful, willing body.

He must be mad, but he was also wary and he didn't want to be hasty.

Yes, he loved her, and he needed her, and she clearly felt the same way, but there was so much left unresolved about their infertility, so many things they hadn't tried. They'd hardly got past first base, but their relationship had already crumbled under the strain and he wasn't sure he could face the emotional upheaval of trying to repair their marriage, just to watch it torn down again.

He just had to be sure when they took that next step that they were doing it for all the right reasons, and that meant going back to his own bed.

Alone—but hopefully not for much longer, because the waiting was killing him.

CHAPTER NINE

'YOU'VE GOT STUBBLE RASH.'

His finger traced her top lip, and she had to resist the temptation to draw it into her mouth and suck it. In the hospital café, right in front of everyone, that might not be smart.

'Stop frowning, you'll get wrinkles,' she told him.

'Good. It might stop the patients thinking I'm hot, of all things,' he said, sounding almost disgusted with himself. 'I can't believe I scraped your lip with my stubble.'

She chuckled. 'Well, if you will kiss me like that…'

'Then I'll have to shave. And I fully intend to kiss you like that. Every night. At least.'

She didn't even try to stop the smile. 'Good. How's Judy?'

'Fine. Stable. Her placenta seems to be holding its own and I'm going to get another ultrasound to check if the baby's grown at all. If not, I might have to reconsider leaving her any longer.'

He glanced at his phone. 'Right. I'd better get on.'

'Me, too.' She drained her coffee and walked back towards the maternity unit with him, parting at the lift.

'Lunch?' he asked.

'If I'm free. What are you doing now?'

'I've got my first stint in the fertility clinic.'

She felt her heart hitch in her chest.

'Have fun,' she said lightly, but just the word *fertility* was enough to bring all her fears home to roost. Were they really ready to go back to all that?

'Send me a text when you finish. Failing that, supper?'

'Sounds good. I'll catch you later.'

They fell into a routine from then on.

He picked her up from home if their shifts started at the same time, and if not she walked in, not because she shouldn't drive yet after her concussion, but just because the weather was warmer now and so beautiful and she enjoyed it.

If they could, they shared a break, and if their shifts allowed, they ate together in the evenings, and when they couldn't do either and they weren't working together, he sent her texts. Sometimes cheeky, sometimes funny, sometimes just simply, 'Miss you'.

And bit by bit, over the course of the next week, they started to relax with each other and have fun. And he kissed her. A lot.

And then he rang her at six on Thursday morning, nearly two weeks after her accident, to tell her that Amy Zacharelli was on her way in.

'I'd like you to be her midwife, if that's possible. I think you're on at seven, aren't you?'

'Yes, I am. That's fine, I'll come in now and sort it with my line manager. Don't worry, I'll be there.'

'Good. I'll see you shortly. I'll make sure she's in a side room in the labour ward.'

'OK. Thanks. See you.'

She had the fastest shower on record, grabbed a banana out of the fruit bowl and ate it on her walk in. No time to think about driving, or parking the car, so she walked briskly and arrived just as Leo pulled up at the entrance with Amy.

'Hi, Amy,' she said as Leo opened the door. 'Nick's here, we're all ready for you. Are you OK to walk?'

'I'll be fine, but Leo has to park the car.'

'That's OK, I'll stay with you and check you in. Leo, do you want to park and come back and find us? We'll be on the labour ward on the fourth floor.'

'Sure. Thanks.'

He got back in the car and drove off, and Amy grabbed her hand and held on. 'Oh. Contraction.'

'That's OK. Just relax and breathe through it, there's no hurry. You can lean on me if it helps.'

The next one was three minutes later, just as they arrived on the ward, and the third one came as Leo walked in through the door. She sent Nick a text, and he must have been in his office because there was a tap on the door and he was there just as Amy was undressing, so she slipped out to update him.

'How's it going?'

'Contractions every three minutes, dead on. I haven't had time to examine her yet so I don't know how dilated she is, but so far she's coping well. I don't know what you want to do about pain relief?'

He pulled a face. 'Nothing if she can manage without it, and I'd really rather she didn't have an epidural because she won't have any feedback if her uterus starts to tear along the scar, which she would feel otherwise. Has she asked for pain relief?'

'No, not yet. I just wanted all my ducks in a row.'

'Well, see how it goes. Don't let her struggle.'

'I won't. I'll put her on a monitor in a minute. Do you want to examine her yourself or do you want me to do it?'

'No, you do it, it's your labour. I'm just on standby,' he said. 'I'll come in and say hi, and then leave her with you.'

'Sure? That sounds like delegating,' she teased.

He laughed softly, checked the corridor and dropped a fleeting kiss on her lips. 'Of course I'm sure. I trust you.'

'OK. I'll leave her with you while I get rid of my stuff and tell them I'm here, then I'll be back.'

She was only two minutes, and she found Amy propped up on the bed, with Leo perched on the edge. Nick had put her on the monitor, and the baby's heart rate was nice and steady.

'Good, you're back,' he said, his eyes speaking volumes. 'She could do with a quick check, I think.'

AKA things are moving rapidly. She nodded and snapped on some gloves. 'If you hang on I'll give you a progress report,' she murmured and turned to Amy. 'Right, let's have a look. How are you doing?'

'OK, I think. I wasn't expecting it to hot up so quickly.'

'Everyone's different,' she said comfortingly. 'Still happy to give this a try?'

'Oh, yes. I don't want another C-section, not with two little ones to look after.'

'Well, we'll try and avoid it, but if you start getting any sharp or persistent pains around your scar area that aren't like the contractions, tell us straight away. I'll just examine you and see how far on you are.'

'OK—oh, it's another one.'

'Two minutes,' Nick murmured in her ear, and she nodded as her eyes flicked to the monitor. 'Right, try and relax, let your body do the work. That's it, you're doing really well.'

She watched the baby's heart rate dip a fraction, then recover as the contraction eased. 'OK now?'

Amy nodded and leant against Leo, who was sitting up beside her pillows, his arm around her shoulders.

'Right, Amy, can you just drop your knees out for me and relax as much as you can—that's lovely—wow, you're doing really well. You're nearly there. There's just a tiny anterior lip of your cervix left to pull up and you're ready to go.'

'Really? So fast?'

Liv pressed the call button to summon another midwife. 'Like I said, everyone's different and your baby's obviously in a hurry.'

'I need to push now!' she said, her eyes widening, grabbing Leo's hand.

'Well, that answers that,' she said with a smile. 'Just pant for me, Amy. Don't push until I'm sure that lip's gone.'

'Do you mind if I stay?' Nick asked, and she glanced over her shoulder at him, her smile slipping a fraction. He was such a sucker for a new baby.

'Be my guest,' she said softly. 'There should be two of us and nobody's come yet. Right, let's have a look—OK, it's gone, so on the next contraction I want you to take a deep breath and tuck your chin down and push for me.'

'Can I move? I sort of want to kneel, I think.'

'Sure. Turn round and lean on Leo, or the pillows, whatever's most comfortable.'

'Shall I glove up?' Nick murmured. 'They're pretty busy.'

'If you don't mind.'

His smile was crooked. 'When did I ever mind being present at a delivery?' he asked, and turned away before she could answer.

'Oh, I have to push!'

'OK. Deep breath, chin down, let your breath out as you push into your bottom—that's lovely. Good girl. Well done.'

Two contractions later the baby's head was crowning, and Liv told Amy to pant as she carefully guided the baby's head out and round and checked for the cord.

'Right, little push for me—perfect, well done!'

Amy turned and sat down, and Liv stood back and let Nick lift the baby and pass him to Amy, the tiny slippery body safely cradled in those big, capable hands.

He looked so sure, so natural, so perfect...

He glanced up and met her eyes, and she had to turn away. He wanted this so much for them, needed it so much, and she realised in that moment that she'd go through anything to give him a child.

But what if it never happened for them? What if they went through all the intrusive and gruelling procedures that could be tried and still got nowhere? Would they be able to cope?

She heard the snap as he pulled off his gloves, then felt his arms come round her in a gentle hug.

'Well done, my love,' he murmured, and she knew they had to try, even if they failed, because not to try was to condemn them both to eternal regret.

* * *

Nick stayed just long enough to congratulate them and make sure all was well, then retreated to his office, shut the door and leant back against it with a shaky sigh.

Why did he do this job? He must be a masochist.

And Liv thought working in the fertility clinic was hard for him? He let out a humourless little laugh. Every time he saw a baby born, his heart tore a little more. Delivering babies, handing them to their delighted parents— that was far harder, knowing how out of reach it was to him and Liv.

Sure, it was a wonderful and joyous thing to do, but on a personal level it killed him a little bit more every single time—and watching Liv, he knew she felt it, too.

There was a tap on the door behind him, and he took a deep breath, blinked away the tears he hadn't even known were there and opened the door.

'Hi, Ben. What's up?'

'Nothing, I just saw that Amy Zacharelli's come in. I wondered if you knew.'

'Yes, she's had the baby, I was there,' he said, and turned away, flicking through a file on his desk because he wasn't sure his feelings weren't written all over his face. 'Straightforward easy delivery, mum and baby both doing well. I left them in Liv's hands. She knows where I am.'

'Good. Great.'

There was a pause, and Nick frowned and turned back to look at Ben. 'Was there something else?'

'How are you and Liv?'

He blinked. 'What's that got to do with the price of fish?'

'That's not a straight answer to a straight question.'

He shut the file and forced himself to meet Ben's eyes.

'I didn't think it was a straight question. I would say it was thoroughly loaded and probably none of your business.'

Ben studied him thoughtfully for a moment, then nodded slowly. 'OK, fair enough, but it's kind of relevant. Off the record, Simon's not coming back. Jen's doing OK, but he says it's going to be a long haul and whichever way it goes, they need to be near the family for support, so I'm going to have to advertise the post. I'm going to be blunt, I want you back but only if you and Liv are OK with it. You fit in well, you know your way around, you're a team player, you have additional skills which we need—we don't need to look any further, but I need to know that you're going to stick around if we appoint you. Assuming we do appoint you, which I think is pretty much a given, but we have to abide by the rules and advertise.'

His heart was thumping in his chest, because a part of him wanted this so much it was eating him alive. The other part was still wondering if he and Liv stood a prayer of making it work.

'Of course you have to advertise it. And you don't know what that'll throw up. You might get someone extraordinary apply.'

Ben shrugged. 'We might, although I doubt very much we'd get anyone better than you, but the bottom line is I can't even consider you for the post if you and Liv are going to find you can't hack it, because that's no good for either of you and it's no good for the department. I need to know that you're in it for the long haul.'

He couldn't give Ben an answer. Not yet, not without talking to Liv.

'You said it's off the record.'

'You can talk to Liv. She's the soul of discretion and anyway, her support is key. I realise that.'

He nodded. 'OK. Thanks for the heads up. I'll let you know. When's the closing date?'

Ben laughed. 'Realistically, until we get a suitable candidate, but probably a month at the outside? If you don't apply, we'll have to keep the advert open until we get someone. Talk to Liv, think it over. I don't want to put you under pressure.'

That made him laugh.

'Yeah, right,' he said drily, then shook his head slowly. 'Leave it with me, Ben. I knew it was a possibility, but I hadn't really let myself consider it, so this is a bit of a game-changer.'

'No hurry. This needs to be the right decision.'

He nodded again, but didn't say any more because there wasn't really anything to say. Not until he'd spoken to Liv, and he wouldn't do that until they could talk about this properly, in private.

Leo, Amy and baby Rocco left the hospital at three, just at the end of Liv's shift.

To her surprise Nick came to say goodbye, and Leo put the baby carrier down and hugged them both.

'Thank you so much. I'm so, so grateful. So's Amy.'

'Absolutely,' Amy chipped in. 'I can't believe I didn't need a section, I really didn't think it was going to happen. I'm so glad you let me try, and that you were both there. It made me feel so safe, and that made a massive difference, and so has not having had a section. I couldn't have done it without you, either of you.'

Tears welled in her eyes, and Liv hugged her gently

and told Leo to take her home. 'Go on. Go and show the girls their little brother. I'm sure they'll be thrilled to bits.'

'I'm sure they will,' Leo said, his smile a little crooked. 'I know we are. Look, I don't know if you like eating out, if it's your thing, but if you want to come down for dinner to the restaurant any time, just phone up and we'll find you a table. It would be great to see you again.'

'That's very kind of you, Leo, thank you.'

'It's nothing,' Leo said. 'Remember, any time.'

'That would be lovely,' Liv said, reaching up and kissing Leo on the cheek. 'Thank you. Now take your wife home, please, and spoil her a little. She's done really well today.'

They watched them go, Leo with one arm round Amy and the other carrying their precious cargo, and Liv felt Nick's hand on her shoulder, giving it a quick squeeze.

'You did well today, too,' he murmured. 'Thank you for coming in early.'

'You don't need to thank me, Nick. I did it for Amy. I knew she'd feel better with people she knew around her, especially under the circumstances. That's all the thanks I need.'

'I'm still thanking you. What are you doing later?'

'I don't know. Are you going to tell me?' she asked, looking up and catching a fleeting glimpse of worry in his eyes. 'Nick? What is it?'

His hand dropped from her shoulder and he shook his head. 'Nothing. Nothing to worry about, but there's something we need to discuss and we can't do it here. Yours or mine?'

'Come to the house. I need to put some laundry on

and I could do with washing my hair. I didn't have time this morning. What time do you finish?'

He laughed. 'How long is a piece of string? Hopefully by seven anyway. Judy's OK, so I'm starting to relax on that front, and I haven't got any other mums I need to worry about at the moment—well nothing urgent anyway. I'll give you a call if I get held up but you should probably eat without me to be on the safe side.'

'OK. I'll see you later.'

It was much later.

He rang at six to say that Judy's blood pressure had risen suddenly and the Doppler scan of her placenta showed marked deterioration.

'You weren't worried earlier. Famous last words?' Liv said, knowing what was coming next, and he gave a tight laugh.

'You could say that. Anyway, I'm going to have to deliver the baby and I know I'm not supposed to be here tonight but I promised her I'd look after her and after we've got her this far I'm not going to let her down.'

'Of course you're not, you old softie. Get something to eat before you take her into Theatre, and I'll see you later, maybe.'

'OK, but don't hold your breath. I might have to take a raincheck.'

'OK. That's fine. Just let me know.'

She put the phone down, examined the contents of the fridge and decided to make a Thai chicken curry with cauliflower rice. She knew he liked it, she had all the ingredients and he could reheat it when he got there or she could freeze it.

It didn't take long, and after she'd eaten hers the eve-

ning seemed to stretch out endlessly. There was nothing
she wanted to watch on the TV, she still hadn't washed
her hair, and she really fancied a nice, long, lazy bath.

Probably with a glass of wine, but there wasn't any
in the house, so she made a fruit tea and took it up with
her, ran the bath, added bubbles and found her book before climbing in.

Luxury.

She wallowed until the bubbles had all gone, the
water was tepid and her book was all but finished, then
pulled out the plug, washed her hair in the shower and
dried it.

Did she bother to dress, or should she just put on her
towelling robe and slippers and assume he wasn't coming? Probably a safe assumption. She could lie on the
bed and finish her book while she waited.

By the time she'd turned the last page there was still
no word from him, and it was after ten. She might as
well just go to sleep.

The house was in darkness, apart from a light in the
hall.

Should he go in? He really needed to talk to her, but
she wasn't at work tomorrow so he wouldn't see her
then, and Ben's words were gnawing at him.

And she'd given him keys.

He let himself in, and swore as the alarm started its
entry countdown. He flipped down the cover on the
control panel and punched in his old code on autopilot, but it carried on beeping, the seconds ticking down.
'Dammit, of course, she's changed the code—'

The alarm gave up waiting and wailed into life, and
he frantically keyed in the new number and sighed with

relief as it went quiet. Not before the light went on in Bert and Gwen's house, though. Damn. That was all he needed.

'It's only me,' he called, as their front door opened.

'Is everything all right?'

'Yes, it's fine, Bert. No problem. Sorry to disturb you.'

He shut the door as Liv appeared at the top of the stairs, hastily belting her robe, her hair tousled. 'I'm sorry, I shouldn't have set it but you didn't ring. Was Bert cross?'

'No, worried I think. I expect he thought I'd broken in to give you another black eye.'

She laughed and shook her head. 'No, they know I was knocked down by a car. I told them.'

'Well, thank God for that, I thought he was about to call the police. And I'm sorry I didn't ring you. I thought I'd left it too late, but I just needed to talk to you, and then I saw the hall light on and I thought you might still be awake.'

'Oh, that's my fault as well, I must have forgotten to turn it off.' She ran lightly down the stairs and kissed his cheek. 'Have you eaten? I made a Thai curry for us and there's some left.'

'That sounds amazing. I grabbed a piece of toast from the ward kitchen but that was hours ago.'

'Come and eat, then, and you can tell me all about Judy.'

'She's fine, and the baby's fine,' he said, following her into the kitchen. 'Small, but pretty well. She's in SCBU but she's over thirty-four weeks so it's not too much of a worry. She'll just need a bit of support.'

'Well, that's good. I bet they're really happy.' Liv

took a bowl out of the fridge and put it in the microwave and turned to him with a concerned smile.

'So what was it you wanted to talk to me about?'

He hesitated, then went for it. 'Simon's not coming back,' he said, studying her face for her reaction. 'Ben wants me to apply for the job, but there was a sort of caveat that I'm not going to do another runner.'

'And are you?'

He sighed heavily. 'I don't know, Liv. It all depends on you and the baby thing. If we jump through all the available hoops, have every test, go through every procedure and still fail, will you be to deal with it?' he asked softly.

'Yes—because we love each other, and we'll be all right.'

'Sweetheart, you don't know that. I've seen level-headed, reasonable people take each other apart over this, and it's not because they don't love each other. Look what happened to us before.'

She hitched up onto the stool beside him. 'But we weren't talking. We'd stopped communicating with each other—you didn't even tell me you'd had semen analysis, for goodness sake! We should have shared that right at the beginning, when you had the first test, talked about the result and what it meant.'

'But I didn't *know* what it meant. I didn't know if it was bad enough to make a difference, so I tried to improve it, I changed my lifestyle—'

'And it still didn't work, so instead of talking to me and sharing your fears you shut me out. How much of an improvement was that?'

He stabbed a hand through his hair.

'It wasn't. I know that. But I felt guilty—'

'That's ridiculous, it wasn't your fault—'

'It was my fault, or it could have been. You're right, I should have talked to you about it when I had the first test, never mind the second. But I didn't, because I couldn't, because it was falling apart all around us and we weren't talking about anything by that point.'

'Oh, Nick. Come here...'

Her arms slid round him, and he turned on the stool and took her in his arms, resting his cheek against her hair. It smelt of sunshine and apples and Liv, and he buried his face in it and breathed deeply. He wanted her so much. Needed her so much.

'I just feel—this is a real chance for us, Liv, but I can't muck Ben around, so I have to tell him yes and stick with it or give up on us and get another job somewhere else.'

'You can't do that!' she said, her voice a desperate whisper. 'You can't walk out on us now, Nick. Please? I love you. I need you. And you said you needed me.'

His arms tightened round her. 'I do, more than anything else.'

'So apply for it. From the way Ben's talking, it's yours for the asking, so ask. We know we can work together. If we find we can't live together, then we'll deal with it.'

'You make it sound so easy, but it's not. It's the job I always wanted, the job I'd just secured when we split up. I'm lucky he's even giving me a second chance at it, and I'm so, so tempted, but—he wants me to be able to commit to something I just don't know the answer to and I don't want us to feel trapped. We felt trapped before and it nearly killed us.'

She pushed herself away so she could look up at him, and he met her eyes, open, honest, and so revealing.

'We won't feel trapped,' she promised him. 'Not this time, because this time we'll be going into it with our eyes open. Have you told him about us? About the baby thing?'

'No. That's why I went private for the semen analysis. You know what the grapevine's like.'

'Don't you think you should tell him?'

He swallowed hard. 'They're just about to have their third child. His fourth.'

'So? It's not a competition.'

'It feels like it sometimes—and you know that. It's why you wouldn't come to the conference. Anyway, it's none of his business and it's not relevant to whether or not I can do the job, so he can't legally use it as a reason for not offering it to me.'

He sighed and rammed a hand through his hair.

'The trouble is I just feel I don't have a choice. There aren't any other decent jobs out there and that's taken away any choice over whether or not I apply for this one because I need a job, one way or the other, or I can't pay the mortgage and you'll be homeless. We'll be homeless. I can't do that to you.'

'You can't do this just for money, Nick, and I won't let you! I could pay the mortgage—or rent something, if it came to that. If we want to be together and can accept the fact that we might never have children, and I think we both feel like that, then we should be together, either here or somewhere else. Anywhere, so long as we were happy, but you can't take this job just because you need to earn a living. It has to be because it's what you really, truly want, and only you can decide that.'

He reached out a hand and rested it lightly against her cheek, over the faint yellow stain left by the bruise. He frowned and traced the stain tenderly with his thumb.

'It is what I really, truly want,' he said softly. 'That, and you, as a package. But you first. Always you, front and centre.'

A frown pleated her brow and her eyes were troubled. 'Then what's the problem? Life doesn't come with guarantees, and Ben knows that, but you're talking as if you're expecting it to go wrong between us. It can't work with that attitude. We both have to be behind it one hundred percent, or it won't work. It can't work.'

'I am behind it,' he said. 'I was behind it before, and look what happened.'

Her hand caressed his face, her fingertips gentle against his cheek. 'Yes, look what happened. We didn't talk, we didn't say "I love you", we didn't take care of each other. We just let everything between us grind to a halt because I didn't get pregnant. And we won't do that this time. We *can't* do that this time, because that's not what it's about. It's about the fact that we love each other and want to be together, and we can't let that fail, so why don't we just kick this baby thing into the long grass and concentrate on *us*? Because I miss you, Nick, I miss you *so* much.'

His fingers stroked her cheek tenderly, sliding down to cup her chin as he shifted towards her and touched his mouth to hers in a gentle, lingering kiss.

'I miss you, too,' he murmured gruffly. 'And you're right, we can't let it fail this time. We'll give it everything we've got, no holding back. But on one condition. This baby thing—I don't want to think about it or worry about it until we're feeling confident and settled and we know we're strong enough to face it. I'm almost one hundred percent sure that we'll need help in some form or another, and I don't want to start down that road until we're both sure we're ready. If we ever are.'

She nodded slowly. 'I'll buy that. It's a good idea.'

He kissed her again, the caress tender and sensuous, the passion reined in. But it was there in her, too; he could feel it simmering just below the surface, ready to explode at the slightest provocation, so he drew back.

She curled her fingers over his jaw and let her fingers explore the texture. He could feel his stubble catching on her skin, grazing softly against it, and her pupils darkened.

'You didn't shave today,' she murmured.

He felt her smile against his lips and drew away again. 'No, I didn't have time, and anyway, you said you liked it.'

'I do.' She smiled back and leant in again, kissing him once more, her fingers still curled softly against his jaw. 'Stay with me,' she murmured, and he felt his pulse hammer in his throat. Could she feel it? Probably.

He turned his face into her palm and kissed it, then got to his feet. 'Not tonight. Not when I'm exhausted. I need some sleep, Liv, and so do you. I'll see you tomorrow and we'll talk then.'

'Stay anyway,' she said suddenly. 'You can use the spare room if you don't want to share ours. You've already slept in there, it's not like I've got to find clean sheets for you. I might even bring you early morning tea.'

'No, Liv, I'm going to Sam's. I'll ring you in the morning.'

He cradled her head in his hands and kissed her lightly on the lips, then forced himself to let her go. 'Sleep well. I'm sorry I woke you.'

'You, too. And, Nick? Don't worry. It'll be all right.'

CHAPTER TEN

HE KISSED HER AGAIN, then let himself out, and she listened as he started the car and drove away.

Would they really be all right? She could only hope, because that was all she had left, but at least she *had* hope now. It was more than she'd had for ages, that and determination, and she was going to do everything in her power to make this work.

If he applied for the job and didn't get it for some reason then they'd go elsewhere, because one thing she was sure of, she wasn't losing Nick again, come what may. She'd live in a hut delivering babies in some third-world country so long as she was with him.

She went back into the kitchen to turn off the lights and realised he hadn't had the curry. Poor Nick. He'd be eating toast again, but it was too late now. She threw it out, set the alarm again and went up to bed.

Nick made himself some toast—again—and went to bed alone, racked with frustration and buoyed up by hope.

He'd been so tempted to stay with her, so tempted to scoop her up in his arms and carry her up to bed, but he wanted it to be better than that, better than some random fumble when he was reeling with exhaustion and running on empty.

No. If they were going to make a success of it, they needed a clean slate, and that meant taking it all back to first principles.

A first date to remember...?

He could take her to Zacharelli's. Leo wouldn't have had time to speak to them by tomorrow, but he might get lucky with a cancellation—or, failing that, there'd be somewhere else he could take her to and spoil her.

And then he'd bring her back here.

Sam and Kate were away for the weekend, they'd have the place to themselves—and neither of them was working on Saturday, either, so they could get up when they wanted, or stay in bed all day. No prying neighbours, and even more importantly, no ghosts from their tortured past. No echoes of sadness, no blighted memories, just the two of them alone together with a clean slate.

Less than twenty-four hours and she'd be here with him, in his arms.

The wait was going to kill him.

'Do you have any plans for tonight?'

She cradled the phone in one hand and carried on sorting washing with the other. 'No—I thought you were coming over?'

'I am. I'm taking you out for dinner. We've got a table at seven-thirty. Wear something pretty.'

Her heart jiggled happily in her chest. 'Are you taking me on a date, Mr Jarvis?'

'I am, Mrs Jarvis. I most certainly am.'

'How posh?'

'Oh, nice but not that posh. Smart casual?'

She smiled. Nick did smart casual like no other man she'd ever met. 'Perfect.'

Except it wasn't, of course, because she didn't have anything in her wardrobe that fitted any more that could come under the heading of smart casual. She hadn't had any need for it until now—unless...

She opened her wardrobe and pulled out a subtle blue-grey dress that hadn't seen the light of day for over two years. It had a soft metallic sheen, the fabric almost fluid, and she'd given up wearing it because it hung on her after all the running, but Nick had always loved it because it exactly matched the colour of her eyes.

And, she remembered, he could take it off easily.

A secret little smile on her face, she stripped and pulled it on, and it fitted perfectly again now she was a sensible weight. And she had some ridiculously high heels that were covered in tiny sparkly bits—nothing casual about them, but Nick was a sucker for high heels and she hadn't been able to resist them.

But he'd said they were going for it, holding nothing back, so—underwear? She tugged open the drawer and found nothing that was other than practical and utilitarian. She'd hadn't bought sexy underwear for ages, but she was going to today, and when she'd done that she'd see if she could get a manicure and pedicure. Nick always found painted toenails a turn-on.

Fizzing with excitement, she hung the dress up, pulled on her jeans and a jumper, and went shopping.

She was wearing that dress.

His pulse shot up, and he had to take a deep breath and count to ten. Twenty when he clocked the shoes.

'How do I look?'

'If we didn't have a table booked, I'd slam the front door and carry you upstairs and to hell with everything,' he said tightly, 'but we do, so let's not talk about how you look, eh?'

She smiled the smile he hadn't seen since the day after her accident, and he leant in and kissed her cheek. Her signature perfume wafted over him, and he sucked in his breath and pulled away.

'You look beautiful, Liv. Come on, let's go.'

'Is it far? Only the shoes aren't very practical to walk in.'

He laughed softly and shook his head as he settled her coat on her shoulders. 'No. No, it's not far, but we're taking the car anyway.'

'So where are we going?' she asked as he pulled off the drive and headed towards the sea front.

'On a need to know basis…'

'Nick, tell me!'

'No. It's a surprise.'

'We're not—no, we can't be…'

She trailed to a halt as he pulled up beside the prom, backed into a space and cut the engine.

'Yes, we can. I rang this morning, and Leo has already spoken to his staff.'

'But—it takes months to get a table! It's got two Michelin stars, Nick, for heaven's sake! It'll cost a fortune.'

'I know, and guess what? It's worth every penny just to have you beside me again. This is our first date, Liv. The first mark on our clean slate. Ready to rewrite history?'

The smile lit up her face. 'Absolutely. What a perfectly wonderful idea.'

She reached for the door handle.

'Uh-uh. Wait for me.'

He got out, went round and opened the door, and she stepped out onto the prom and the sea breeze caught her dress and flirted with the hem. She pressed it down with her hand, and for the first time he noticed she was wearing her wedding and engagement rings.

He slid his fingers through hers, lifted her hand and pressed his lips to the rings, then freed his hand and offered her his arm. 'Just so you don't fall over and snap the heel off those shoes before I get to take them off you,' he murmured, and smiled as colour seeped into her cheeks.

'Nick!' she said under her breath, but there was a thread of laughter in her voice and she tucked her hand into his arm, the diamonds sparkling in the evening sun, and he laid his other hand over hers and walked her to the door.

To their astonishment it was opened by Leo, with the baby propped up against his shoulder held securely by his father's hand.

'What are you doing here?' Liv asked, sounding astonished.

'Amy wanted to show him off, so her mother's babysitting the girls for a bit, and we heard you were coming down so it seemed like perfect timing. We've only popped down for a few minutes. Come and join us for a drink, if you're not in a hurry to eat? We've just opened some excellent Prosecco.'

'No, we're not in a hurry but we don't want to intrude—'

'Don't be ridiculous. Come on, Amy wants to see you.'

* * *

Leo handed round the glasses, and they all toasted the baby who seemed perfectly content snuggled down in his father's arms. Leo looked pretty happy, too, and so did Amy, but it wasn't long before the party broke up because little Rocco was beginning to stir and Amy wanted to take him home and feed and change him.

'You know what it's like when they're tiny and your milk's just come in and everything hurts—I just don't want to do that in public yet!' she murmured.

'I can understand that,' Liv said with a smile, and kissed Amy goodbye, trying desperately hard not to be jealous. 'Don't forget, any problems, any questions, either ask your community midwife or give me a ring—I don't mind, any time. Here—my number.' She jotted it on an old envelope in her bag and handed it over. 'Now go and enjoy him.'

'We will. And thanks again.'

'Yes, thank you, both of you,' Leo added. 'I hope you enjoy your meal.'

The maître d' appeared at their sides with a welcoming smile and showed them to their table, and after they were settled Liv looked up and met Nick's eyes.

'I can't believe we're here.'

'No, nor can I. We tried before once—do you remember? It was impossible.'

'I don't remember that. I thought this was our first date?'

His brows tweaked together, followed by a slow, lazy smile as he propped his elbows on the table and leant towards her. 'So it is.' He reached out and took her hand, his thumb stroking softly over the back of it. 'Did I tell you how beautiful you look tonight?'

She felt herself colour. 'You may have done, but I don't mind hearing it again. You don't look so shabby yourself, either, and I see you've shaved.'

'Well, you see, my mother told me that it was bad form for a chap to give a girl a rash on her lip from too much kissing—'

'Did she really?'

His sexy chuckle rippled over her and made her body quiver. 'No, of course not, but we should probably test the theory.'

'Sounds good.'

'I thought it sounded like a thoroughly *bad* idea,' he said softly, and she felt her pulse pick up a notch.

'Excuse me, are you ready to order or would you like a few more minutes?'

'Um—I think that would be a good idea,' Nick said, straightening up, and she had to bite her lip. 'Stop it and read the menu before we get chucked out,' he muttered, trying not to laugh, and she looked down and felt her eyes widen.

'Oh, my life, everything sounds amazing!'

'Doesn't it just? How many courses do you want?'

'Oh, two, max. I can't eat any more than that.'

'Main and dessert? I know you women like a pud.'

'Sounds lovely, and I wouldn't like to appear greedy on our first date,' she said, her lips twitching, but he didn't smile back.

'You can have anything you want tonight,' he said, 'anything at all,' but his eyes said far more than those apparently simple words, and it took her breath away.

'That was the most amazing meal of my life.'

'Mine, too. I can't believe they wouldn't let us pay. Do you fancy a stroll?'

Liv looked down ruefully. 'I do, I'd love to, but they're not really strolling shoes.'

'No, they're not, are they? Maybe on our next date.'

She tilted her head and smiled. 'You want to see more of me?' she asked mischievously, and his mouth twitched.

'Definitely. A lot more.'

'Mmm. I want to see more of you, too.'

The light from the streetlamps caught the beating pulse in the base of his throat, and his voice was low and promising. 'I'm sure that can be arranged. Shall we go?'

She tucked her hand into the crook of his elbow, and he led her to the car, opened the door for her and went round to his side, starting the car in a silence screaming with tension.

Two minutes later they'd pulled up outside the cabin.

'There are no lights on in the house.'

'They're away,' he said, and she thought of the significance of that—the utter solitude, the privacy, no one to see or care what they did so they could be free to be themselves—and a shiver of need ran over her.

The cabin was softly illuminated by a bedside light, drawing her eyes to the bed. The curtains were closed, the bedding crisp and smooth, but not for long. Her pulse picked up and she turned towards him wordlessly.

His hands settled gently on her shoulders and he stared down into her eyes, his own intent and focused solely on her.

'I want you, Liv,' he said, his voice quiet but sure. 'I've never wanted anyone as much as I want you now, but if you're not ready for this, if you don't want it, then tell me.'

She met those serious, steady eyes, his gaze unwavering, and knew she'd never wanted him or needed him more. 'I want it. I want you, Nick. I always have, right from the first moment I saw you, and I don't think I can wait any longer. Make love to me—please?'

His eyes closed briefly, and when he opened them again, passion burned bright in their depths. 'My pleasure,' he said, his voice little more than a breath that whispered over her skin, and taking her hand, he led her over to the bed and slowly, inch by inch, he drew the dress up over her legs, her body, her upstretched arms.

It fell to the floor in a shimmering puddle, and he stood back and looked at her, those hot eyes raking over her body and leaving a trail of invisible fire in their wake.

A fingertip followed, tracing the top edge of her bra, following a strap down from her shoulder, over the swell of her breast, dipping down into the hollow of her cleavage. It swept under the lace, trailing back up, his hand sliding in and following it until her breast was swallowed by his warm, clever hand.

His thumb flicked her nipple oh, so gently, and she gasped. So he did it again. And again, and all the time his eyes were locked with hers.

'Nick,' she breathed, her voice choppy, not knowing what she was asking, but he knew, and he bent his head, his eyes finally releasing hers as his hand pushed the lace out of the way and his mouth found her breast.

His tongue flicked over her nipple, then circled it before drawing it into his mouth, and her hands gripped his shoulders, her breath sobbing now, the ache in her body so intense she could barely stand.

'Nick...'

He lifted his head, tugged back the covers and pushed her gently back until her legs met the bed. She sat down abruptly and he tipped her back, ran his fingertips around the top of her new and barely there lace shorts and peeled them slowly, inch by inch, down her legs.

He reached her feet, eased them over the shoes and then picked up one foot and ran his tongue over the inside of her ankle, up over her calf, behind her knee, then up, along her inner thigh.

She knew what he was going to do, knew just how good he was, how exquisite it would be, and she felt her body liquefy for him.

At the first touch of his tongue she dug her fingers into the bedding, biting her lips to stifle the scream, but she couldn't silence it and she could hear as well as feel his breath as it sawed in and out of his chest.

'Don't hold it in, Liv,' he said, his voice rough with need. 'There's no one to hear you except me, and I want to know exactly what I'm doing to you.'

'Nick, please...'

She felt the tug as he suckled, the flick of his tongue with its unerring accuracy, and she sobbed his name helplessly as her body peaked and everything shattered all around her like shards of light.

Then he was there, holding her in his arms, raining kisses on her face, his chest heaving against her.

'I need you,' he growled softly.

Her hands ran over him, finding silk and cotton

where there should have been skin, and she plucked at his shirt. 'You've got too much on,' she wailed.

'So undress me,' he said, pulling her to her feet, but the buttons were too much for her so he hauled the shirt over his head himself. It landed on the floor near her dress, followed by her bra, their shoes, his trousers and socks and last, his jersey boxers. Her hand closed over his straining erection and a groan shuddered against her hair.

'Liv, no,' he begged, and she moved her hands to his shoulders, stepping back and meeting those fierce, white-hot eyes.

'I need you,' she said, her fingers curling into his shoulders. 'Please, Nick, I need you inside me—'

And at last—at last—he was there, thrusting deeply into her, taking her so close and yet not quite…

'Easy, Liv, easy. I won't last—'

'I don't want you to last. I want you to come with me this time, please, please…'

He drove into her then, every move of his body designed to wind her higher until she felt the starburst start again, spreading out and blinding her to everything but Nick.

He caught her scream in his mouth, his body stiffening as a ragged groan tore through him, and then as the contractions in her body died away he dropped his head against her shoulder, his cheek resting against hers as their breathing slowed and their heart rates came slowly back to normal.

Then he rolled to the side, taking her with him, their bodies still joined, and she opened her eyes and he was just there.

His lashes had clumped together, and she lifted a hand and brushed a tear from his cheek.

'Are you OK?' she asked softly, and he smiled, but it was a pretty sketchy smile and he couldn't stop the tears that leaked from his eyes and dribbled down onto her shoulder.

'I've missed you so, so much,' he said raggedly, and then she lost sight of him because her own tears flooded her vision, but she knew just where he was, and so she kissed him, and held him, and told him over and over that she loved him, until at last he fell asleep in her arms.

He woke in the night and made love to her again, but this time it was slow and lazy and tender, and they didn't wake again until the light filtering through a gap in the curtains cut a bright swathe across their pillows and dragged them out of sleep.

He propped himself up on one elbow and stared down into her eyes.

'Good morning.'

She smiled, a slow, contented smile that lit her eyes from within, and reached up a hand to touch his face. 'I couldn't agree more. It's a very good morning.'

'Mmm. I'm hoping it's going to get even better.' He lowered his head and kissed her gently, then swung his legs over the side of the bed and stood up, stretching hugely.

'Tea?' he asked, and she nodded.

'Lovely. Shall I just lie here while you wait on me?'

'You can. I was going to put the kettle on and then shower.'

'How big's your shower cubicle?' she asked, and he laughed and headed towards the bathroom.

'Not big enough for what you've got in mind.'

'You don't know what I've got in mind.'

'I'm sure I can have a fair stab at it. Just stay there a minute. I won't be long.'

He had the fastest shower on record, shaved—because he intended to kiss her a lot, lot more—then cleaned his teeth and left the bathroom to find her standing by the kettle humming softly to herself.

He walked up behind her, slid his arms around her and cupped her breasts with his hands.

'You're all damp,' she said.

'Because I was in a hurry. The bathroom's all yours. Don't be long.'

Long?

She didn't wash her hair, because she wasn't convinced the cabin had a hair dryer and anyway, she had much, much better things to do with the time, but she showered, borrowed his toothbrush and cleaned her teeth and went back out to find him propped up in the bed with two steaming mugs on the bedside table.

'What kept you?' he asked with a lazy smile, and she crawled across the bed to him and kissed the smile off his face.

'So what now?'

It was much, much later. The tea had grown stone cold, and they'd showered again and put their clothes on, but although she might get away with the dress if they were to go out, the shoes were a bit of a giveaway.

'Well, if we're going to do anything other than lie in bed all day I probably need to go home and get a change of clothes. Shoes anyway.'

'We could go for a walk along the river wall.'

'We could. We used to love doing that.'

'We did. Right, let's go then, and see if you can get inside before Bert clocks you and asks what you were doing last night.'

She laughed at that. It was so unlikely she didn't even waste time worrying about it, but when they got to the house there was an ambulance outside Bert and Gwen's.

'What the hell's going on?' Nick said, and got out of the car. 'Liv, go and change and come back out. I'm going to see if they need help.'

He ran round the end of the hedge and in through their front door, and she let herself in, tugged on yesterday's jeans and jumper with a pair of flat pumps and went straight round to Bert and Gwen's.

She could hear them upstairs, and she ran up, calling Nick's name.

'In the front bedroom,' Nick called, and she went in and found Bert on the floor with a paramedic holding his head steady while Nick massaged his carotid sinus.

'He's in SVT,' he said over his shoulder. 'Can you look after Gwen and follow us to the hospital? I'm going in the ambulance with them but I'm just trying to get this to work first.' She went over to Gwen who was standing to one side, her hands pressed to her mouth, and gave her a hug.

'It's OK, Gwen. He's in good hands.'

'Is he going to die?' she asked, and Liv could feel her trembling violently.

'I don't think so. Let's see if Nick can get this to work.'

'What's wrong with him?'

'His heart's started beating very fast. What Nick's

doing is stimulating the nerve beside his carotid artery, which sometimes gets the rhythm back to normal. It's not hurting him, and it often works.'

Just then Bert groaned, and Nick stopped and laid his fingers over the artery and nodded.

'That's got it. Hi, Bert, it's Nick,' he said calmly, taking the old man's hand. 'How are you feeling?'

'Tired. Chest feels really tight. Need my spray.'

'He's got angina,' Gwen said, and she handed a GTN spray to Nick and then started to cry. 'I thought he was dead,' she whispered brokenly, turning her face into Liv's shoulder for a moment until she'd recovered her composure.

Liv found a box of tissues on the bedside table and handed one to her. 'Here. Mop yourself up and give him a hug,' she said softly. 'He's looking a better colour now. I expect they'll take him to hospital soon and sort him out.'

Gwen crumpled the tissue into a ball and crouched awkwardly down beside her husband, clutching his hand as Nick got to his feet and came over to Liv.

'Well done, you,' she said with a smile, and he pulled a face.

'Thanks. I thought it was worth a shot.'

'Definitely. Hadn't they tried?'

He shook his head. 'They'd only just got here. Once I said I was a doctor they just stood back and let me get on with it.'

'I'm so glad we came back.'

'Me, too. Are you all right to drive?'

'Yes, I'm fine. My head's perfectly all right now, I just haven't bothered. I'll shut up the house with Gwen and follow you there.'

* * *

By the time they left the hospital it was almost one.

'Lunch?' Nick suggested, and she nodded.

'How about the pub on the river? We could go for a walk along the river wall afterwards.'

'Good idea. I'm starving.'

They went back to the house to swap cars and for her to change her pumps for trainers, and they ate lunch outside on the terrace overlooking the river, basking in the glorious spring sunshine and watching the boats swing lazily on their moorings.

'I could watch the river for ever.'

'Me, too. Shall we stroll?'

'Mmm. It might work off some of those gorgeous chips.'

'Don't work too many off. I rather like your new curves. It's like having the old you back again.'

'Well, ditto. You'd let yourself get flabby.'

'Flabby?' he said, sounding disgusted, and she laughed.

'Well, not flabby, that's going a bit far, but certainly not as toned and luscious as you are now.'

'Hmm. I like luscious better than flabby.'

'Me, too. I might have to check out your lusciousness again later.'

'Only if I can check out your curves.'

She gave him a cheeky grin. 'Be my guest. But maybe not here or now.'

CHAPTER ELEVEN

'SO WHERE ARE we spending the night?' he asked later when they were back at the house. 'Here, after we eat, or in the cabin?'

'I rather like the cabin,' she said, but then she frowned as they heard a car drive up, pause for a moment and then drive away after the door slammed, and she went to the window and saw Gwen letting herself in next door.

'Gwen's back. Should we offer her supper?'

Nick gave a wry smile. 'That would be nice—and if she's back, we really ought to be here. I don't like the thought of her on her own.'

Liv tipped her head on one side and stared at him. 'They drive you mad!'

He laughed ruefully and pulled her into his arms. 'I know, but they're harmless and he looked such a poor old boy, I just—they've been married for ever, Liv. What must it feel like to know you're getting near the end and one or other of you is going to go first? They'd be lost without each other.'

'I was lost without you,' she said, tipping her head back and meeting his eyes. 'So lost.'

'Me, too, but I'm back now, Liv, and I'm staying.'

'Good. And I know it won't necessarily be easy, but we can make this work, Nick.'

'Yeah. You're right. And if it gets tough, we'll just have to bite the bullet.'

'Wasn't that what people in the trenches used to do before their legs were amputated without anaesthetic?'

He laughed and drew her into his arms. 'I'm hoping it won't go that badly wrong,' he said, and then his mouth found hers and feathered a gentle kiss on her lips.

She looked up at him. 'So are you going to apply for the job?'

'Yes. Definitely. And I'll move back in here.'

'Sure?'

He kissed her again. 'Yes, I'm sure.'

'Even with Bert and Gwen watching our every move?'

'Even so.'

She felt the smile bloom in her heart and spread to her face. 'Good. Let's go and talk to Gwen and find out how he is.'

He moved back in the following day, while she was at work on a late shift, and when she got home that evening the light was on in his study.

It hadn't been on to welcome her home for so long, and her heart was filled with the sort of deep happiness and contentment that she'd only ever felt in their first years together.

There was only one thing missing, and she was used to that by now and it didn't dent her happiness.

He must have heard her car because he opened the front door, shut it behind her and pulled her into his arms.

'Welcome home, Mrs Jarvis,' he murmured, and it had never sounded so good.

He'd been working on his CV, he told her, and the next day he applied for the job, went through the formal interview process a fortnight later and found her in the ward office afterwards.

He pushed the door shut and let out a long, slow breath.

'God, that was tough. Ben really grilled me.'

'That was mean.'

'No, it was fair. They had a couple of very good candidates and the hospital seems to be able to attract them. This department's got a great reputation. I just hope I've done enough.'

She got up from the desk and hugged him. 'Of course you have. And if not, we'll go elsewhere. I don't care where I am so long as I'm with you.'

'What about our friends?'

She shrugged. 'We can make new friends. There's only one friend I'm really bothered about and that's you. Come on, let's go and get lunch, I'm starving. I've been waiting for you because we've got a lull, which means all hell's going to break loose later, so let's make the most of it.'

'There's a second interview round,' he told her the next day as he checked his phone over breakfast.

'Really?' Liv felt her stomach tighten, and she pushed away her cereal. 'Did you know that was on the cards?'

He shrugged and put his phone away. 'It was always a possibility. Oh, Liv, I hate this uncertainty.'

'It's only a job. There'll be others—and anyway, I'm

still sure you'll get it,' she lied, her stomach in knots. 'I need to go, I'm due at work in a minute.'

'You haven't finished your breakfast.'

'No, I know. I'm not hungry yet, it's too early.' And she was way too stressed to worry about food. 'I'll see you later.'

The second interview was in three days, he told her later, and by the time it arrived they were both living on their nerves. The only thing that made it all go away was the time they spent together at night, when the lights were off and everything was quiet and she was in his arms.

Sometimes they talked, sometimes they made love, sometimes they just held each other, and in those times everything that was wrong seemed to right itself.

He got through the second interview, but that night he told her it was worse than the first and he was beginning to doubt Ben's friendship.

'Of course he's still a friend. He just has to be your boss, too—he's the clinical lead and he's way too ethical to do anything other than give everyone the same treatment. You can be sure he was every bit as mean to them.'

'He wasn't mean, he just asked some really tricky questions—what would you do in this or that circumstance, that kind of thing. Really tricky cases where there's no definitive answer, and your brain just goes to mush.'

'I'm sure yours didn't,' she told him comfortingly, but the tension was getting to her and she wasn't sure she could stand the wait much longer. 'When will they let you know?'

'Ben said a couple of days, perhaps? I got the feeling the board were divided.'

She was off the next day, and because Nick was at work and she had to do something to keep herself sane, she went into her little study upstairs—the nursery that had never been needed—and settled herself down at the desk to read up on hypnosis as a form of pain relief in labour, but she couldn't concentrate.

Stress? Or an after-effect of her concussion? She didn't know, but it wasn't working, so she went downstairs, put the kettle on and reached for the instant coffee, then pulled a face.

She just didn't fancy coffee. Or tea, come to that. Or food. No, that wasn't true. There were some things she couldn't get enough of, like chocolate. And pasta. She could eat mountains of pasta and pesto. Maybe she was just hungry.

Or maybe she just needed to know what on earth was happening in their lives, and where their future lay?

She went for a walk, popped into the little local supermarket for some more bread and pasta and heading for the till she felt the blood drain from her head, and reached out and grabbed a nearby shelf. She'd walked down the aisle with personal products—feminine hygiene, condoms, pregnancy tests...

Pregnancy tests?

They were right there, in front of her. She'd bought countless numbers of them in that dreadful time, but she'd always done the test before her period was due, and if she'd only waited she would have had her answer for nothing.

But she'd lost track, between Nick coming back and

her accident and the job thing. She'd had one period, but that had been weeks ago.

More than four?

Her fingers shaking, she reached for a packet, put it in her basket next to the bread and pasta and went to the till.

'Liv?'

She must be out, he thought, and ran upstairs to change—and stopped dead.

Lying on the bed was the open packet of a pregnancy test.

His mouth dried and he felt sick. God, no. Not back to this again.

He changed into jeans and a thin T-shirt and sat down on the edge of the bed, staring at the open packet as if it was a bomb.

Why? They'd agreed on the rules—no trying, no thinking about it, no worrying, just accept that it wasn't going to happen for them without help and not until they were ready, but—no. She couldn't do that, and suddenly he wondered if she really loved him, really wanted him, or if it had just been a way of getting him back so she could use him as a stud, a sperm donor.

Jeez. He pressed his hand to his mouth, holding in the hurt, the rage, the overwhelming disappointment. The betrayal. And then he heard her call him.

He didn't want to answer. He'd promised they'd talk, promised they wouldn't let this destroy them again. Kick it into the long grass, she'd said, but there it was again, just when he'd burned his boats and taken the job, and he didn't know what to say to her because he didn't know if it was all a lie.

His heart in his mouth, he stood up and walked out of the bedroom.

'Where are you?' he asked, and followed the sound of her voice to the little room they'd never quite dared to call the nursery.

She was sitting at her desk, the test wand in her hand, and as he went in she turned her head and looked up at him and her face was streaked with tears.

'Why now?' he asked quietly. 'Just when everything was looking promising—why now, Liv? I thought we weren't going to do this?' he said, trying to keep a lid on his hurt, his anger. 'Dammit, you promised me we wouldn't do this!'

Her face froze, and she dropped the wand and stared at him. 'Nick—'

'No. I can't cope with it any more. I told you that, I warned you—'

He turned on his heel and walked out, and he was halfway down the stairs when something hit him on the head.

'What's *wrong* with you?' she sobbed. 'You can't cope with it when I'm not pregnant, and now, for God's sake, you can't cope with it when I *am*! What kind of a person *are* you?'

He slowed to a halt and turned and looked up at her. His heart was climbing out of his chest, his mouth was dry, and...

'I don't understand,' he said numbly. 'You can't be. I warned you my semen analysis was rubbish, we knew this wasn't going to happen—'

'No—no, Nick, you're wrong,' she said, shaking her head. 'Look at it! Look at the wand!'

He glanced down and saw it lying on the hall floor.

His hand trembling, he bent and picked it up, and read the word in the little window.

Pregnant

He stared at it blindly, until the word blurred in front of his eyes. 'I don't understand.'

She came slowly down the stairs and sat just above him on the second step. 'I'm pregnant—we're having a baby, Nick. We're having a baby—'

Her voice cracked, and he looked up from the wand and met her eyes. 'How?'

She laughed then, the sound music to his ears. 'If you don't know that by now, Nick, you're *really* in the wrong job.'

He sat down next to her, his heart still pounding, and put his arm round her. 'But—why now and not then?'

She shrugged.

'Think about it. I was too thin, your diet was appalling, you were possibly drinking too much, having tons of coffee, not exercising, I was running every chance I had, we only made love when the techie runes told us to—and now we're healthy, we're relaxed, and we're making love every chance we have. It's not rocket science.'

She was pregnant. He felt the smile first, and then his eyes prickled and her face blurred, so he shut them and pulled her into his arms and held her, pressing his cheek against her hair.

'I thought you'd lied to me. I thought you didn't love me, you just wanted me back so you could keep on trying. I never dreamt…' He broke off to kiss her, then cupped her face in his hands and stared down into her eyes. 'I love you,' he said raggedly. 'I love you so, so much, and I can't believe it's finally happened for us.'

Her hand came up and stroked his cheek, wiping away the tears. 'Nor can I. Now if we could only hear about the job—'

'I have.'

Her mouth opened and she looked up at him, her eyes hopeful and fearful at the same time. 'And?'

'I got it. I got the job,' he told her, and she put her hand over her mouth and let out a sobbing laugh.

'Really? You got it? We can stay here in Yoxburgh, in this house, near all our friends, take our baby to the park…?'

'Yes. We can stay here. We sort of have to. I promised Ben we would.'

'Oh, Nick, that's amazing!' She flung her arms around him and hugged him so hard his ribs crunched.

'Ouch.' He laughed, and eased her away. 'I'm glad you're pleased. We can celebrate that later. Right now I'm busy dealing with the fact that we're going to have a baby.'

Her eyes were soft, almost luminous, and her smile lit him up from the inside out.

'I know. I might have to share your study.'

'You might—if you have time for that when you're a mum. I still can't quite believe it's real.'

'I can't believe you've got the job, either. It's like we've reset the clock on our lives and gone back to where it all went wrong and put it right, and this is our reward.'

'Oh, Liv.' He hugged her again, then scrubbed his hands over his face and sniffed hard. 'I'm a mess.'

'You're a lovely mess. I was a very unlovely mess

earlier, because I'd managed to convince myself that
you hadn't got the job, and there we were pregnant and
with nowhere to go and no visible means of support. It
wasn't a good moment.'

'I'll bet. Poor you. How are you feeling now?'

'All right. I'm fine so long as I eat chocolate in in-
dustrial quantities,' she said, and he laughed again and
hugged her.

'I'll add it to my regular internet shop,' he said drily,
and then got to his feet and pulled her up. 'Come on,
let's go and tell Bert and Gwen. Their grandchildren
live hundreds of miles away, and I reckon they'll love
having a baby next door.'

'Can you bear it?'

'What, them? They're fine, Liv.'

'Bert thinks you saved his life.'

'Well, he might be right. We'll let him think it. If
he feels he came that close, he might let me take over
the hedge cutting.'

She started to laugh, and once she'd started she
couldn't stop, so he turned her into his arms and they
leant on each other and laughed until their sides ached.

'Better now?' he asked eventually, and she nodded.

'Never better than this. The job, the baby, you back
in my life for keeps—what more could a woman want?'

'Diamonds?'

'No. Cold, hard—and they don't hug you. I wouldn't
swap your hugs for anything. Come on.'

She took his hand and stood up, only instead of heading out of the door towards Bert and Gwen, she turned
towards the stairs.

'Where are we going?' he asked, and she just smiled.

'Up here. We've got a nursery to plan…'

EPILOGUE

NICK CLOSED THE door behind the midwife and went back into the family room, where Liv was curled up on the sofa in her towelling robe with the baby asleep in her arms.

'Cup of tea?' he asked, but she shook her head.

'I'm going to drown if I drink any more tea. Come and sit here and admire your daughter.'

She shifted her feet out of the way, then plonked them back on his lap as he sat down.

'Happy?' she asked him, and he gave a tired laugh.

'Yes, my darling, I'm very happy. A teeny bit stressed, but I might have known you'd want to be different.'

'I didn't plan a home birth. She was just in a hurry.'

'And I was in a clinic. I only got here by the skin of my teeth. I'm an obstetrician, for goodness sake, and I didn't even realise you were going into labour.'

'I'm a midwife. It's all I deal with, and I didn't recognise the signs. We're both rubbish.'

'No, we're not. We're amazing. Look at her. How could two rubbish people create anything as amazing as that?'

'Want a cuddle?'

He reached over and took the baby from her, staring

down into her dainty, screwed up little face with its tiny button nose and rosebud lips. 'She's so perfect—such a miracle.' He looked up and met Liv's eyes and tried to smile, but it was too hard so he gave up.

'Have I told you lately how much I love you?'

'Only a million or so times.' She sat up with a little wince and put her arms around him and kissed him. 'But don't stop. I'll never get tired of hearing it.'

'I love you,' he said softly, and then propped his feet up on the coffee table, right over the tiny mark that he'd wiped clean, and rested his head back against the sofa and smiled at her.

Life had never felt so good...

* * * * *

If you enjoyed this story, check out
these other great reads
from Caroline Anderson

THEIR MEANT-TO-BE BABY
BEST FRIEND TO WIFE AND MOTHER?
RISK OF A LIFETIME
SNOWED IN WITH THE BILLIONAIRE

All available now!

ONE NIGHT THAT CHANGED HER LIFE

BY
EMILY FORBES

Published in Great Britain 2017
By Mills & Boon, an imprint of HarperCollins*Publishers*
1 London Bridge Street, London, SE1 9GF

© 2017 Emily Forbes

ISBN: 978-0-263-92665-1

Printed and bound in Spain
by CPI, Barcelona

Dear Reader,

A feisty midwife and a gorgeous obstetrician with come-to-bed eyes… What could go wrong?

Plenty, it would seem. Starting with Huntington's Disease.

HD is a genetically inherited disease that fortunately is fairly rare but, while advances *were* made in the late stages of last century, for which there is still no cure. It presents a lot of challenges and poses a lot of questions for which there is really no right or wrong answer. So, while the subject matter might not be the most light-hearted, it certainly made for an interesting storyline. I hope you can empathise with Brighde and stick with her as she searches for her happily-ever-after.

I'd love to hear from you if you've enjoyed this story or any of my others. You can visit my website, emily-forbesauthor.com, or drop me a line at emilyforbes@internode.on.net

Emily

For Felicity.

Thank you for your love and support.
It means so much to me that you read
and enjoy my stories! This one is for you. xx

Wishing you a very Happy Birthday!

With all my love,
your goddaughter,
Emily

Books by Emily Forbes

Mills & Boon Medical Romance

The Christmas Swap

Waking Up to Dr Gorgeous

The Hollywood Hills Clinic

Falling for the Single Dad

Tempted & Tamed

A Doctor by Day...
Tamed by the Renegade
A Mother to Make a Family

His Little Christmas Miracle
A Love Against All Odds

Visit the Author Profile page
at millsandboon.co.uk for more titles.

CHAPTER ONE

BRIGHDE HID BEHIND a conference banner as she stabbed her finger at the screen of her phone. Her hand was shaking as she tried to end the call and it took her two attempts to press the right spot. She took a deep breath, fighting to remember her yoga breathing as she fought back the tears that threatened to spill from her eyes.

She was happy for Nick, really she was, but her brother's phone call had confirmed her worst fears.

Good news for him could only mean bad news for her.

She struggled with the clasp of her bag, eventually managing to open it, and shoved her phone inside before snapping the clasp shut. She needed a drink. A strong one.

There were plenty of free drinks on offer in the hotel ballroom where one of the major pharmaceutical drug companies was hosting the end of conference party but Brighde didn't feel like going back into the crowd. She needed space almost as much as she needed a drink.

The ballroom was on the hotel's mezzanine floor but on the floor below she knew there was a bar adjoining the lobby. She looked at the staircase; the expanse of carpet between her and the stairs looked immense and she wasn't sure if she'd make it. Her knees wobbled as she took the first step and she focused on putting one foot in front of the other until she could reach for the banister. She clutched it tightly, steadying herself for the descent. The simple task of negotiating a staircase suddenly seemed to require enormous effort. Was that a sign? She knew difficulty with motor skills was often one of the first obvious symptoms of the disease, impaired voluntary movements like gait and balance were hard to ignore, but surely that would be too much of a coincidence.

Get a hold of yourself, Brighde, she admonished herself. *You're only twenty-eight—you're not about to fall apart yet.*

She hoped she was right but it was hard to discount the feeling of mounting panic. Her chest was tight and she was finding it hard to breathe. She was surprised by her reaction to Nick's phone call. She'd always suspected that she would be dealt the bad hand and she hadn't expected to be so shocked.

This was what she'd always dreaded. It wasn't exactly a surprise but, at the end of the day, it obviously didn't matter how prepared she thought she was; the truth of it was no one wanted to know they were going to an early grave.

Somehow she managed to get down the stairs and into the bar on her wobbly legs without taking a tumble. She perched on a stool and ordered a vodka Martini. She had no idea if she liked Martinis—she drank vodka—but she felt she needed something more potent. Something that would numb the pain and a Martini sounded like it might do the trick. She didn't want to ask the bartender for suggestions; she just wanted to anaesthetise herself.

She plucked the olive from the toothpick as she drained her glass.

Martinis weren't too bad, she decided as she ordered another.

'Brighde! What are you doing down here?'

Brighde turned at the sound of her name and found Sarah, her best friend, colleague and roommate all rolled into one, making a beeline for her across the room.

'Just collecting my thoughts.'

'Looks like you're collecting more than thoughts,' Sarah said as the bartender put a fresh cocktail on the bar.

Sarah was watching her closely as she pulled out another bar stool and sat down.

'Who was on the phone?' she asked. She'd been standing next to Brighde when she'd taken the call.

'Nick.'

'Is everything okay?'

'He got his test results back.'

'At nine o'clock at night?'

Brighde shook her head. 'No. But it took him a while to figure out how to tell me.'

'Was it bad news?'

'Not for him.' Sarah and Brighde had been friends for ten years since meeting at university, where they'd both studied nursing. Brighde had no secrets from Sarah. 'He had ten repeats.'

'He tested negative?'

Brighde nodded.

'That's great news.'

'Yes. It is,' she said, fighting to speak past the lump in her throat. She still felt like crying, even though nothing she'd heard in the phone call should make any difference. Nothing had really changed. She had her reasons for not getting tested and those reasons hadn't altered. She could go on just as before. Nick's results didn't affect her future plans but she knew they solidified her fears. His results didn't confirm her suspicions but they definitely strengthened them.

'You don't seem happy,' Sarah said.

'We each had a fifty-fifty chance of inheriting a faulty gene. There's only two of us,' Brighde explained. 'What do *you* think the chances are of both of us dodging a bullet?'

'You know the answer to that. It's still fifty-fifty. Just because Nick is clear doesn't mean you won't be. The chance of you inheriting the gene or not hasn't changed. Nick's results have no bearing on you.'

Brighde knew Sarah's facts were correct. The reality was her chances of inheriting the mutated gene hadn't changed but she still felt the odds were not in her favour. She'd always felt that. Which was why she never intended to get tested. Who wanted to know that they were going to die young? Who wanted that fear confirmed?

Not her.

'I know you're right. In theory. But I've always felt that I was going to draw the short straw and knowing Nick is okay just reinforces all those feelings. Huntington's Disease is dominantly inherited and I can't believe we'd both dodge the bullet. I don't think we could both be that lucky.'

'And I don't think there's anything you can do about it tonight,' Sarah said as she shook her head at the bartender, who was clearing Brighde's glass and asking if she wanted another. 'Come and dance, have some fun. The band's playing some good music—dancing will take your mind off it.'

Brighde let Sarah convince her to vacate the bar in favour of the dance floor. She didn't really feel like dancing but she felt less like going back to the hotel room and staring at the walls. She was feeling miserable enough already.

Xavier nursed his beer as he watched the dance floor. It was taking him a little while to get back into beer drinking. He hadn't realised he'd acquired such a taste for whisky in his years of living in Scotland, but when in Rome… Or Edinburgh.

What he was getting accustomed to far more quickly was the plethora of attractive young women at the conference. The band had been playing for some time and the dance floor was full. His eyes were drawn to a petite blonde in a sapphire dress. He'd been watching her for a while now; she'd been late onto the dance floor but even among the crowd she'd stood out. He'd tried to look elsewhere but his gaze continued to return to her. He believed you could tell exactly what a woman was like in bed by the way she moved on the dance floor. The blonde had rhythm and energy. Her dress shimmered under the lights and her hair shone, contrasting brightly against all the black outfits in the room. She was striking to look at. She wasn't smiling, she looked focused, but she danced as if she enjoyed it and he'd put money on her enjoying sex too. She looked fit and flexible and carefree, all admirable traits in his opinion, and he was hooked.

He waited until she left the dance floor. He wasn't

going anywhere until he'd spoken to her. He could dance, but he wasn't about to dance in front of hundreds of his fellow medicos. He'd rather dance *à deux* and so he waited.

The band were playing a love song that was impossible to dance to without a partner. She needed pop music. Something she could lose herself in. She gestured to Sarah—she was going to grab a drink—and made her way to the bar at the side of the ballroom.

She had intended to get a water—dancing had taken her mind off the earlier phone call—but once she stopped dancing and reached the bar all her doubts returned. She'd have a water later. She needed another drink to numb the pain.

'Can I buy you a drink?'

Brighde's skin tingled as she felt, rather than saw, someone behind her. His voice was deep and quiet and although she couldn't see him she knew he was addressing her. She closed her eyes, imagining a face to go with the voice, before she turned around, hoping she wasn't going to be disappointed.

She wasn't.

She turned to find the most gorgeous man she'd seen in a long time at her side. How had she not noticed him in the room? Okay, there were hundreds of people at the conference but seriously, he was magnificent. She must have been more distracted than she'd realised.

He watched her as he waited for her answer. His dark eyes studied her, captivating her with his gaze.

'The drinks are free, you know,' she replied.

'In that case, I'll get you two.' He grinned at her,

lightening the seriousness of his dark stare, and Brighde lost the last remnants of her composure.

He looked like European royalty. No, he wasn't clean-cut enough for royalty. His dark hair was slightly too long, exploding around his oval face into soft curls that just begged her to reach out and touch them. His jaw was covered in designer stubble, his eyes were dark and his forehead was strong. He was dark and swarthy and sexy as hell. Confidence oozed from him. He was impeccably dressed—his dark navy suit hung from his shoulders and fitted his frame, the pants were slim, encasing powerful thighs. He looked like a European polo player. Something out of a Jilly Cooper novel. He looked rich and successful, although of course she had no idea if that was the case, and he wanted to buy her a drink. If there was a downside to his offer she couldn't think of one.

'What are you having?' he asked. He didn't wait for her to accept his offer. He just assumed she wouldn't refuse. Was that confidence or was it simply an assumption based on the fact it was an open bar? She didn't know but she also didn't care. She wasn't going anywhere. Not now.

She shouldn't mix her drinks but the bar wasn't offering Martinis and she knew she needed more than water if she was going to be brave enough to keep up her side of the conversation with this gorgeous man. 'I'll have a white wine,' she said as she perched on a bar stool. She didn't need to sit down but she needed to take a step back. He was standing close to her; that wasn't a problem but she wanted to get a good second look at him and she needed a bit of distance to do that.

He ordered and handed her a glass. His fingers

brushed hers and a spark arced between them, setting her already nervous heart racing. It had been several months since she'd shared a drink with a man but she knew it wasn't the length of time making her react this way.

Was the touch accidental? she wondered as he tapped his beer glass against her wine and made a toast. 'To new experiences.'

He held her gaze a fraction longer than was polite and her stomach flipped and she knew his touch had been deliberate. Her body was responding to him in a way it never had before. She'd never felt such immediate attraction or, if she was honest, such blatant lust before. He made her think of naked bodies and tangled sheets and raw, amazing sex and she knew exactly how this night would end. 'Indeed,' she replied as a sense of delicious anticipation flooded through her. She smiled and added, 'I'm Brighde.'

'Xavier.'

She didn't need to know any more than that.

'Have you enjoyed the conference?' he asked her.

So he was part of the conference and hadn't just snuck in for the free drinks.

'It's been really good,' she said as she put her glass on the bar and crossed her legs, pleased that she'd had a little bit of free time to lie by the hotel pool and work on her tan. 'But I could do with a few days off to recover before I go back to work. I'm heading home tomorrow, back to work on Monday.'

'That's a pity. I'll be here for a few more days.'

'Work or pleasure?' she asked.

'Purely pleasure.' He kept his dark eyes fixed on her as he reached past her shoulder, picking up a napkin from the bar. His arm brushed against her skin and she could feel his words on her cheek, soft little puffs of air. She knew he didn't need the napkin, she knew it had just been an excuse to lean in but she wasn't complaining. She could feel the electricity surging between them. They could power the room with the heat that was being generated between them. She wasn't aware of the music, the dancing, of anything that was going on around them. She was lost in the sensation he was evoking in her. She could feel his charisma wrapping itself around her as his pheromones enveloped her. Her nipples hardened and she squirmed in her seat. She pressed her thighs together as heat pooled low in her belly.

'I've been working in Scotland,' he told her, 'but the conference seemed like a good way to keep the taxman happy and visit my family.'

'Family?'

'My parents live here.'

'You're travelling alone? No partner? No wife?' She played with the ends of her hair, feigning casualness. She had to know the answer. She had rules and standards. She knew she would have sex with this gorgeous stranger—having sex would be a far healthier, and much more entertaining, distraction than drowning her worries with alcohol—but first she needed to establish some ground rules. She didn't want to make any mistakes.

'No wife. No girlfriend. No significant other.'

Now it was her turn to smile. 'Good to know.' She kept her gaze fixed on him now, wanting him to know where she stood. What she wanted. She didn't need to know anything else about him. She knew she wouldn't see him again. He was only visiting; she was leaving tomorrow. She hadn't had sex for ages and a one-night stand with this gorgeous man was a good option all round. No commitment, just a bit of fun and a good way to keep her mind busy. She didn't want time to think about her brother's phone call. She wanted something to take her mind off her situation. This was perfect.

She wanted Xavier.

And she wanted him to know that.

But Xavier was looking to his right.

Sarah had joined them.

Brighde watched her friend looking from her to Xavier and she knew she was taking in the distance, or lack of, between them. She watched as Sarah, quite blatantly, checked him out.

'I'm off,' Sarah said when she'd finished her inspection. 'Are you coming?'

Brighde thought about it for a second—okay, to be honest, a millisecond—she didn't need any longer than that when Xavier was looking at her with his come-to-bed eyes. 'No, I think I'm going to stay here for a bit.'

She knew Sarah's question had been rhetorical. She knew her plans for the rest of the evening were written all over her face but she didn't care. She wasn't even looking at Sarah as she answered; she couldn't make herself tear her eyes away from Xavier. He oozed sex appeal and she knew it was only a matter of time before she would be in his bed. She could feel it. She knew he wanted it too. She could feel the desire coming off him in waves and he was just what she needed. Taking a gorgeous man to bed ticked all the right boxes and it was a habit she had no intention of breaking. Okay, so she didn't do it all that often—she could barely remember the last time she'd even had sex—but a one-night stand was the perfect way to scratch an itch.

She needed sex but she didn't need a relationship. One night was enough. There was no need to go into details, no need to reveal anything personal about herself. She didn't consider sex to be personal—sex with a stranger couldn't hurt her, not as much as revealing her fears. She could happily share her body but not her mind. Her body was going to let her down one day; she owed it nothing.

Sarah nodded and smiled. She lent forwards and kissed Brighde's cheek. 'Have fun,' she whispered into Brighde's ear.

Brighde watched her go and when she turned back to Xavier she found he'd moved closer to her. His thigh pressed against her knee. She shifted forward on the bar stool, sliding her knee against the inside of his thigh. Their intentions were perfectly clear.

She looked up at him to find his dark eyes watching her. Her reaction was immediate and primal and she could feel her nipples jutting against the cool silk of her dress. She saw his gaze drop lower, saw him take in the peak of her nipples against the fabric of her dress. When he looked back at her his gaze was so intense and full of heat she thought she might melt into a pool of desire at his feet.

'Can I offer you a nightcap upstairs?' he asked as he lifted her glass from her hand. He reached across her to put her half-finished drink on the bar and the back of his hand brushed across her chest, grazing her nipple. Brighde felt as if she might climax on the spot.

She swallowed and nodded as she licked her lips. Despite everything she'd had to drink her throat was suddenly dry and she was having difficulty breathing, let alone speaking. She was experienced in the art of seduction but not in relationships. She didn't communicate with words. She sought the comfort of sex when she needed it, emotionally or physically. Tonight she needed it to distract herself. It had worked in the past and, looking at Xavier, she was sure it would work again today.

He took her hand and helped her off the stool. Once again her legs had turned to jelly but she barely noticed this time. She was too aware of the tingling in her belly and the intense weight of expectation and excitement in her groin.

Xavier held the door for her as she stepped into the lift. The lift had four other occupants and Brighde stood slightly apart from Xavier. She needed to keep some distance, otherwise she was in danger of throwing herself at him in front of a crowd. He pushed the button for the sixteenth floor while she leant against the wall of the lift; she needed something solid to keep her upright. She wanted to lean against Xavier but didn't dare while they had company. She didn't trust herself to maintain a sense of decency.

'What floor would you like?' one of the other passengers asked her.

'Sixteen,' she replied as she tried to avoid eye contact with Xavier, the gorgeous stranger.

Over the heads and shoulders of the other people sharing their lift she was totally aware of him. The man exuded sex appeal. Tall, dark, handsome and well-built. His dark hair was thick and just long enough to show the wave through it. There was no grey in his hair but a hint of it lightened the tidy stubble that darkened his jaw. He was well-groomed but definitely all man and he was watching her with his dark chocolate eyes as she studied him. His eyes were slightly hooded; he reminded her of a predatory bird. She felt like a sparrow in the piercing gaze of a falcon and she knew she was firmly in his sights.

The lift stopped several times but it wasn't until the fourteenth floor, when the doors closed, that it was finally just the two of them who remained.

She continued to study him. His hands were large, as were his feet. Even his slightly hooked nose was on the generous side. Brighde was twenty-eight years old and she was a midwife, she knew anatomy, and even though it was purported to be an old wives' tale she knew you could judge the size of a man's appendage by the size of his hands, feet and nose. She swallowed. She wouldn't have to wait long to test her theory.

His eyes hadn't strayed from hers and she knew he was visualising what was under her dress, just as she was imagining what she might find under his clothes. The idea gave her a rush of lust and she stepped a little closer as the lift doors eased shut.

He smelt fantastic. She was tempted to press the emergency stop button but she didn't want to be surprised by a maintenance team coming to rescue them. She could wait two more floors. Maybe.

She was aware of her breathing now. Heavy and laboured.

He reached out one hand and put it on her waist and she could feel the heat of his fingers through the thin silk fabric of her dress. He pulled her closer until she was pressed against him. She could feel his desire now, a thick, hard bulge pressing into her. She tipped her head back and looked up at him as the lift stopped and the doors slid open.

CHAPTER TWO

SHE LEANT AGAINST HIM, not trusting her legs to support her, as he led her to his room. He swiped the electronic key card over the door and held it open for her.

The room was a carbon copy of hers, with the exception of the bed. She was sharing with Sarah so their room had twin beds. Xavier had a room to himself, and a king-size bed that she intended to put to good use dominated the space.

She stepped inside and somehow managed to wait until he stepped in behind her and closed the door. She turned around and his mouth was instantly on hers. His hands at her back.

She wasn't interested in talking. She didn't want to know anything about him. She didn't *need* to know anything about him. His voice was deep and velvety smooth and it did funny things to her insides but she didn't need to hear it.

She parted her lips and his tongue delved deeper, exploring her, tasting her.

She pulled his shirt free from his trousers and undid the buttons, running her hands over his chest. The muscles were firm and warm under her fingers and dark hair covered his skin.

She could feel wetness pooling between her thighs. She pressed against him, wanting to feel the thickness of his erection, knowing she wouldn't be disappointed.

She closed her eyes and the room started to spin. Just a little, just enough for her to recognise she'd had more to drink than she'd realised. Drunk and emotional. That wasn't a good combination. But she wasn't so drunk that she didn't know exactly where she was and what she was doing, she thought as she felt his hand slide up under her dress. She opened her eyes as his hand cupped her buttock. He lifted her off her feet and continued to deepen the kiss as she wrapped her legs around his waist.

He carried her to the bed. She knelt on the edge as he opened the bedside drawer and retrieved a little foil packet. He put it on the bedside table, watching her as he let it go. His intentions were clear and Brighde knew he was asking for her acquiescence. In reply she reached up and slid his jacket and shirt from his shoulders, letting them drop to the floor. She wasn't changing her mind now.

He kicked off his shoes as she fumbled with the buckle of his belt. Finally, the belt came loose and she undid his trousers, letting him step out of them.

She swallowed as she looked at him standing before her. He pushed his boxer shorts off his hips and his erection sprang free.

He was even more impressive than she'd imagined. Thick and proud. He was glorious.

He reached for her again and she lifted her arms above her head as he whipped her dress from her body. She wasn't wearing a bra; she was as naked as he was save for her knickers and heels.

She stood up, brushing her breasts across his chest, and watched in fascination as his chocolate-brown eyes darkened further.

She spun him around, pushing him lightly backwards, making him sit on the edge of the bed. She needed to control this.

She stepped out of her underwear and put her legs either side of his, straddling his thighs.

She pushed him gently again, forcing him to lie back, as she climbed onto the bed and sat across him.

She plucked the foil packet from the bedside table and tore it open, sheathing him and protecting herself.

She was in a hurry now. Foreplay had been dealt with at the bar and in the lift. Silent communication and agreement had got them this far and she was ready and eager for the satisfaction she anticipated.

She put one hand on each side of his head and lifted her hips as he guided himself inside her, filling her. She closed her eyes as she concentrated on the sensations swamping her. The thickness of his shaft, the slight stretch of the muscles in her inner thighs as she spread her legs wider to take him deeper inside her.

She leant forwards as she raised and lowered her hips, sliding up and down his length. She opened her eyes and watched as his lips parted, listened to his sigh of pleasure. His hooded eyes were darker now, even more intense. She felt his hands on her skin and then his breath as he lifted his head and took one breast into his mouth.

Brighde moaned as waves of pleasure consumed her and her body came to life.

His hands were on her bottom and she could feel each individual finger against her skin. He wasn't controlling the pace though; his hands were just following her movements, following her rhythm and pace. She was setting the tone. She was in control.

She sat up and felt her nipple peak as the cool air replaced his warm mouth. She wanted to watch him as they made love. She wanted a chance to commit it all to memory.

She reached behind her back and down between his thighs. Her fingers searching. She cupped his balls in her hand; they were hard and tight and cool in her grasp. She rolled them in her hand before circling his shaft with her fingers, following its movement to feel it disappear inside her. Deep inside her.

Her knees were shaking but the muscles in her buttocks and between her thighs were tight. She was panting quickly now, her breath coming in short, shallow gasps almost as if she were forgetting to breathe. She didn't have enough muscle control spare to focus on breathing.

She couldn't wait much longer. She could feel the waves of an orgasm threatening to break over her.

His hands had moved to her hips now, keeping her in place. Not that she had any plans to go anywhere. Maybe he was just holding her up.

She could barely keep her eyes open. Every cell in her body was focused on pleasure and there was nothing left for the basics. Nothing left to spare on breathing or thinking.

Brighde let herself go, giving in to the burst of light that wanted to explode in her.

'Now,' she begged and she felt him shudder and heard herself cry out as they climaxed together.

She collapsed, exhausted, spent and fulfilled onto his chest.

He wrapped his arms around her and she felt him kiss the top of her head. She closed her eyes and breathed deeply, inhaling his scent. She'd had a few one-night stands—she considered them her only practical option as she wasn't willing to risk having a real relationship—but she couldn't say she'd ever found them terribly satisfying and she definitely couldn't ever remember one as immensely gratifying as tonight.

She wouldn't mind repeating it, but that wasn't in her rule book.

One night only. With single men. And only with men she knew she wouldn't bump into at work or in the supermarket.

But Xavier was on holiday from Scotland. Maybe she could stretch it to twice. But she was leaving tomorrow. Going back to Melbourne and back to work. She only had one night so she'd have to take her second chance tonight and surely twice in one night didn't count.

She lay with her head on his chest and her fingers splayed across his stomach and listened to the rhythm of his heartbeat under her ear. She closed her eyes and let the silence drift over her.

She woke an hour later. The hotel room curtains were open and the city lights lit up the room. Xavier's arm was draped over her shoulder and she slid out from under it, careful not to disturb him. She needed to go.

She ducked, naked, into the bathroom but when she returned to collect her clothes he was awake. He was lying on his back watching her. The covers were off and he made no attempt to hide the fact that he was ready and willing to make love again.

Brighde forgot all about getting dressed as she let him pull her back into bed.

But this time she took care not to fall asleep afterwards. She waited until he drifted off before she dressed and snuck out in the early hours of the morning.

There was no exchange of phone numbers or even last names. She didn't know anything about him and that was the way she wanted it. She would never see him again. She felt a tiny twinge of disappointment but even though he was magnificent she wasn't about to break her own rule.

She didn't do weekends. She didn't do relationships. One night was enough.

There was no danger of falling in love in only one night.

Brighde changed into scrubs ready for another night shift. Her fifth straight. She was exhausted; the maternity wing had been really busy. That wasn't unusual; Parkville Private Hospital had the largest private maternity service in Melbourne and they were always busy, but the past few shifts had been ridiculous. The nurses were blaming the full moon; there was no scientific evidence to back up their suspicions but years of experience had taught them that a full moon seemed to trigger labour, not only in the women who had reached full term but also for those who were overdue as well as for plenty who were a week or two away from their due dates. The department was bursting at the seams and Brighde was looking forward to a few days off at the end of this shift. Only eight hours to go.

She tied the laces on her sneakers and headed for handover, hoping that tonight would be quiet.

'Brighde, you can take over from Jacqui. She's got delivery room three.' The charge nurse distributed the patients among the new staff.

'I've got Kirsty Jones,' Jacqui told her.

Brighde remembered Kirsty from prenatal appointments. 'First baby, husband is Matt, right?' she clarified.

Jacqui nodded. 'She's been in labour for about twelve hours and in active phase for a few hours now. Seven centimetres dilated, contractions four minutes apart. She probably hasn't got long to go. Do you want me to stay until she delivers?'

It was common for the midwives to extend their shifts if they thought their patients were close to delivering. It made for good continuity of care and the mums appreciated having one midwife throughout. But it wasn't always possible. Lots of babies took far longer than one shift to make their appearance.

'Is there much else happening at the moment?' Brighde asked, meaning, *Are we likely to be run off our feet?*

'No.'

'Go home, then,' she told Jacqui. 'I know Kirsty. I've got this.'

'Thanks. I've called her doctor. He's on his way. Dr Davey is on holidays and Dr O'Donnell, the new OB/GYN is covering for him.' Jacqui was already untying her ponytail, getting ready to leave, as she gave Brighde the final information.

'OK, all good.'

'Kirsty, how are you?' Brighde stepped into delivery room three and greeted Kirsty and her husband. Kirsty

looked tired and Matt didn't look as if he was faring
much better. 'We've had a shift change, it's my turn
now but you won't have any more changes after this. I
promise I'll be here when your baby is born.'

'You'd better be,' Kirsty panted. 'Your shifts are
eight hours, right? If this baby isn't out by then, I'm
leaving.'

Brighde smiled.

'What?' Kirsty asked.

'We hear that a lot at this stage, when you've had
enough, that's when we know you're getting close.'

Kirsty grimaced as she was gripped by another contraction.

'How are you doing, Matt?' Brighde asked as she
waited for Kirsty's contraction to ease. This stage was
hard on the partners; she knew he'd be feeling useless.

'I'm okay but isn't there anything to do to speed this
up?' he asked.

'Sorry, not at this point. She's very close. We've just
got to let things take their course. Natural is best.'

Jacqui had attached a monitor to Kirsty's abdomen to
record the contractions and Brighde checked the read-
out. The contractions were now two minutes apart, last-
ing for around sixty seconds and getting stronger.

'I'm just going to take a look to see how your labour is progressing,' Brighde said as she pulled a pair
of gloves on.

'Eight centimetres. You're getting there,' she said.
'You're in the transition phase now. It won't be much
longer.'

'We haven't even seen the doctor,' Matt said.

'He's on his way. There's nothing for him to do yet.
Trust me, you don't want the doctor in early. If things
are going well you don't need him until the end.'

Kirsty's labour seemed to be progressing as expected and Brighde thought they wouldn't really need the doctor at all but she also knew that at Parkville Private the patients paid for, and expected to see, the doctor.

Kirsty cried out as another contraction took over. She was getting restless. 'God, it hurts.'

'If you think you can manage to get onto all fours that might ease the pressure on your back,' Brighde told her. 'Matt, you could run a flannel under hot water and give Kirsty's back a rub.' That would hopefully distract Kirsty, ease her discomfort and give Matt something useful to do. 'You'll meet your baby soon.'

Matt had followed her suggestion and returned from the en suite bathroom with a warm flannel. Brighde let him look after Kirsty while she checked the equipment, making sure she had everything she needed for the delivery at arm's reach. As she worked she listened to Matt as he tried to reassure Kirsty. She could hear the love and affection in his voice, along with concern, and it made her wish that she had someone to share her life with. Someone who would love and support her. But she knew that would be asking a lot. She'd vowed long ago that she wouldn't put someone through what she'd been through. She'd made a pact with herself that she would stay single. She wanted to be loved but she wouldn't risk it.

Thinking about being in love led her to thinking about her brother. After all the pledges they'd made, the promise not to get tested, Nick had fallen in love with Imogen and everything had changed. The pact she and Nick had made years before, agreeing not to have genetic testing, had ended when Nick had fallen in love. He wanted to start a family and he needed answers. Brighde couldn't blame him for that. But now she knew her decision to stay single and free was justified. She had watched her mother's life disintegrate and she'd vowed not to put herself or loved ones in that same position. Which meant not allowing herself to fall in love. That was the only way to avoid the heartache. To avoid the risk. She had to stick to her plan. As much as she'd like to share her life with someone, she couldn't commit to anything more than one night.

The last night she'd spent with someone had been with Xavier. She wondered how he was. Whether he was back in Scotland. Whether he ever thought about her. She couldn't deny she'd been thinking about him. A lot. In the maternity suites she'd found herself comparing all the partners to Xavier. Wondering what he would be like in the same situation. Would he be the bossy, know-it-all expectant father who'd read all the books? Or would he be the kind, gentle, supportive partner who was only concerned about his wife. Not that it mattered. Her silent imaginings were a waste of time. Xavier was gone.

She had to stick to her plan and even if she wanted to change her mind Xavier wasn't around. That boat had sailed. That was why she'd let her hormones carry her away that night. Because she'd known she'd never see him again. But she hadn't been able to get him out of her head, despite the fact that the night she'd spent with him was now almost eight weeks ago. She really needed to get him out of her system.

She'd expected the sex to be good—the sparks she'd felt between them had been too huge to ignore—but she hadn't expected it to be the best sex of her life. But that didn't mean she couldn't have better. Xavier might have become her new benchmark but that didn't mean someone else out there couldn't match up or even improve on him.

Maybe that was the answer. Maybe she just needed to have sex with someone else. She needed to erase the memory of him. Something about Xavier had got under her skin but she couldn't afford to get fixated on someone she'd never see again. That had been the whole point. Anonymous sex was the only way to go. She didn't get involved. She didn't do relationships and she really didn't have time to spend thinking about him. She needed to get this baby delivered, and however many others decided to be born tonight, and then she'd go home, get a good eight hours sleep and tomorrow she'd start to wipe all traces of Xavier from her mind. She'd go back to the old, independent Brighde. She didn't need a man; she was fine.

She didn't *want* a man she told herself as she prepared to check Kirsty's progress again.

She was now nine centimetres dilated and Brighde could see the baby's head. She wondered how far away the doctor was. If he wasn't already here he was likely to miss the delivery altogether.

'Almost there, Kirsty. You're doing really well. Not long now.' She stood and pulled off her gloves. 'I'll fetch the doctor.'

Brighde stepped out of the delivery room and was surprised to find Sarah just outside the door. She was working a late shift too but she was working in the nursery. Maybe she was collecting a baby. But she grabbed Brighde's arm.

'Good, I'm glad I found you.'

'What's the matter?'

'There's something I need to tell you,' her friend said as she dragged her towards the nurses' station.

'What is it?' Brighde had no idea what could be so urgent. 'I'm in the middle of a delivery.'

'I know,' Sarah said, 'but this is important. Dr O'Donnell—the doctor covering for Dr Davey—you're looking for him, aren't you?'

Brighde nodded.

'That's him.' Sarah tilted her head to her left a few times in quick succession, nodding towards the nurses' station.

Brighde frowned. 'Who is?'

'Dr O'Donnell. It's him. From the conference.'

Brighde saw the back of a head. Her eyes took in the thick, dark, slightly curly hair. The tall, broad, masculine shoulders. Her stomach flipped as recognition slapped her. He wasn't someone she knew from staff but he wasn't a complete stranger either.

He turned, maybe a sixth sense alerting him to the fact he was being scrutinised, and their eyes locked.

Brighde took a deep breath and held it. The man she'd shared the best sex of her life with was standing six feet away.

CHAPTER THREE

'OH, MY GOD.'

He wasn't supposed to be here.

Brighde turned to Sarah, dragging her eyes away from Xavier's perfect face. Her heart was racing. 'What the hell is *he* doing here?'

Sarah shrugged. 'He's the new OB/GYN.'

'Seriously?'

'Yep.'

She swore under her breath.

Be cool, Brighde, she told herself. *No one needs to know anything.*

But she had to fight the urge to turn on her heel and run out of the door.

She looked back at him. He didn't look nearly as surprised as she felt. Maybe he was just better at hiding his feelings. He nodded in her direction, a half-nod, and smiled and Brighde's heart did a little flip. How the hell was she supposed to handle this? She was always so careful to ensure that she didn't mix her private and professional lives, yet here was the man who had quite literally swept her off her feet, had seen every naked inch of her and given her the time of her life, standing in front of her expecting to work together. She'd never, ever been in this situation before.

Her flight and fight responses were having their own private battle inside her. She was very tempted to go with flight but she knew that wasn't going to give her the answers she wanted or make the problem go away. If he was, as Sarah had said, the new OB/GYN, she had to assume he was here to stay.

Maybe she could just ignore him, she thought as she half turned away, giving herself a moment to try to get her reactions under control. But she knew that was impossible. He was the doctor she was looking for. He was the one she needed to deliver Kirsty's baby. They'd be working together, which meant she wasn't going to be able to ignore him.

And now he was beside her. She knew he was. She could feel him. Ignoring him was definitely not going to be an option. Thankfully, Sarah still stood to her left, giving her moral support. She needed it.

Sarah had heard Brighde's recount of the night spent in Xavier's bed many times over the past eight weeks but Brighde had never expected the two of them to meet. She felt her cheeks redden as she thought about the intimate details she'd shared with her best friend.

'Hello, Brighde. I didn't expect to see you here.'

His deep voice washed over her and she fought the impulse to close her eyes and give in. His tone was seductive. She knew he probably didn't mean it to be but that was the effect it had on her. She glanced at Sarah, wondering if Xavier affected her the same way, but she seemed completely relaxed whereas Brighde felt as if someone had tied her up in knots while she wasn't paying attention.

Was he pleased or disappointed to see her?

She shouldn't care.

But she did.

And she couldn't ignore him. Not while he stood beside her. She turned towards him, lifted her head and willed herself to keep it together as she looked into the depths of his dark eyes.

And there it was. The same seductive come-to-bed expression that had drawn her to him the first time. Different circumstances, same reaction. She was in trouble.

Her eyes drifted lower, away from his carnal gaze, as she fought temptation. She couldn't afford to go to pieces here. She had a job to do.

He was wearing scrubs. Shapeless blue hospital scrubs that did nothing to disguise the width of his shoulders, the length of his legs and the flatness of his stomach. She could still remember how every ridge and groove of his abdominals felt under her hand. She closed her eyes briefly and when she opened them she was looking at his hand. He had his fingers wrapped around a coffee mug. She could remember when those fingers had been cupped around the cheek of her arse.

Her breath caught in her throat.

She couldn't breathe. She needed to breathe.

She looked at Sarah in desperation.

Sarah stuck out her hand. 'Hi, I'm Sarah, one of the midwives. I don't think we were ever properly introduced.'

'Nice to see you again,' Xavier replied as he took her hand.

He was all charm. He even remembered Sarah.

'Brighde is looking after your patient,' Sarah said,

obviously figuring she'd given Brighde enough time to gather her wits. 'She'll take you to the delivery room.'

'Lead the way.' He was looking at her again. She was caught, spellbound, by his gaze. *Come on, get yourself together.*

Sarah gave her a gentle push, making Brighde's feet move. She doubted she would have been able to put one foot in front of the other otherwise.

Okay. Focus, Brighde. Just do your job and worry about Dr O'Donnell and his bedroom eyes later. That's the way. Think of him as Dr O'Donnell and not Xavier. Separate him into two parts, professional and private, and just remember to keep them separate. Pretend you've never met him. He's nothing to you. And, whatever you do, don't start a personal conversation.

But she was aware of his body heat as they walked side by side down the corridor. His scent. She even imagined she could hear him breathing. And she had the feeling once again that her cells were straining towards him. She concentrated hard to make sure she kept walking in a straight line. She could feel herself veering towards him. She needed to stay on track.

She breathed deeply as she put her hand on the door to the delivery room.

Focus, Brighde.

'Our mum-to-be is Kirsty, twenty-nine years old and forty-one weeks' gestation with her first baby, so a little overdue. No complications with the pregnancy. She's been in labour for about twelve hours but just reached nine centimetres. Kirsty is tired but the baby is fine, although it's quite large. Around four kilograms. Her husband is Matt.'

Xavier pushed open the door and strode into the

room, full of confidence. No one would ever imagine he was new to the hospital. He looked as if he'd been here for ever. He looked completely comfortable. *She* was the one who was unsettled.

Xavier introduced himself to Kirsty and Matt while he washed his hands. He pulled on a pair of gloves while Brighde fastened a gown over his scrubs and resisted the temptation to run her hands down his back. She stepped away as soon as she was done; the further away she could stay the better.

'Let's see what's going on, shall we?' Xavier said as he crossed to the bed.

Kirsty was still kneeling on the bed with Matt supporting her as she rocked. Brighde expected Xavier to reposition Kirsty. She expected him to ask her to lie down, as that would make it easier for him to see what was going on, but she was pleasantly surprised when he pushed a small wheeled stool over to the bed with his foot and sat behind Kirsty.

'Good news,' he said as he finished his examination. 'You're fully dilated and I can see the baby's head. Everything's good. Are you comfortable in that position?' He was calm, relaxed, friendly, engaging. He was perfect.

'No,' Kirsty half laughed as another contraction gripped her.

'Sorry, bad choice of words,' Xavier admitted. 'What I meant was, would you like to stay in this position or did you want to try something else? From my experience this is often the most comfortable position to give birth but it's up to you.'

'I don't think I can move,' Kirsty said.

'All right, stay just like you are. Are you okay, Matt?'

Matt would need to support Kirsty in that position. Kirsty was leaning on his shoulders and he had his arms wrapped around her waist. It was an awkward position for both Matt and Xavier but Xavier didn't seem fazed by it. Brighde didn't know many obstetricians who would happily make their own job more uncomfortable. Most still went for the standard, 'lie on your back, bend your knees and push'.

Brighde had to force herself to focus on the task at hand. She couldn't afford to be distracted by Xavier although it was hard when all she could see was the width of his shoulders, the dark curls on the back of his head and his long fingers as they rested on the bed. His voice alone was enough to distract her without the additional fact that he was sitting mere inches from her. Her fingers itched to reach out and slide through his hair. She stepped away to check that she had a warm blanket ready for the baby. Knowing she did but needing an activity to keep her hands busy.

But she kept one eye on him.

'Your baby is doing fine,' he said as he checked the foetal heart rate monitor before checking Kirsty again. 'When you feel the next contraction I want you to push. It's time to meet your baby.'

Brighde took up her place at Xavier's side, ready for the delivery.

'Okay, here we go. Push!' Xavier instructed. 'Stop now, breathe. Okay, nearly there, you're doing great, Kirsty. All right, you can push again.'

He delivered the baby's head before letting Kirsty rest again. The baby's shoulders would be next and Xavier had to reach and contort himself for this part due to the position he'd left Kirsty in. 'Okay, one last push. You're almost there.'

The baby slid out into Xavier's waiting hands. 'Congratulations. A healthy boy.'

Kirsty collapsed back onto her haunches and Brighde helped her to lie down. Xavier handed the baby to his mum, laying him on her chest.

The next few minutes were busy but Brighde knew Kirsty and Matt would barely notice as Xavier gave the required injections and Brighde did the Apgar scores. They worked smoothly together and as Xavier got ready to deliver the placenta Brighde took the baby to be weighed, measured and attach the identification bands.

She loved this part of her job. She took any chance she could to hold and cuddle the babies, getting her fix, as she didn't plan to have children of her own.

'He's absolutely perfect,' Brighde said as she handed him back to Kirsty. 'I'll give you some time together,' she said once the new parents looked settled, 'and I'll be back in a little while to help you shower.'

She would attend to the rest of Kirsty's care later. For now, they just needed some time alone to get acquainted with their new arrival.

Xavier followed her out of the room, untying his apron as he walked. They threw their dirty aprons and gloves into the rubbish and stood, side by side, at the sinks to wash their hands.

Brighde's skin tingled with his proximity. She still couldn't quite believe he was here. One part of her wanted to tear off his scrubs, another wanted to scream at him and a third part of her wanted to burst into tears. She had no idea why she felt like crying. She'd been highly emotional lately but she'd been blaming the fact that her brother had found love along with her own inability to stop thinking about Xavier and now he was here, standing beside her, smiling at her, and she had no idea what she was supposed to do.

He wasn't supposed to be here and he *definitely* shouldn't be smiling at her, turning her insides to mush and her legs to jelly.

His pull on her was magnetic. It felt as if all her cells were straining towards him, giving the impression that, if it were possible, they'd leap out of her body and into his. It felt as if he could absorb her, as if she could disappear into him and all that would be left of her would be her empty skin pooled on the floor at his feet. All traces of her gone.

She'd never felt anything like this before.

All her one-night stands had been just that. One night. She'd never seen any of them again and she'd never had to think about how she would feel if she found herself in this exact situation. She certainly hadn't expected to feel such a strong attraction and her reaction frustrated her.

'What the hell are you doing here?' Her voice was quiet but her tone was anything but friendly. She was irritated with herself and annoyed with him. She didn't want to cause a scene but she had to have some answers, otherwise she knew she would go crazy. 'Why aren't you back in Scotland?'

'Because I live here now.'

What? She *never* would have slept with him if she'd known he was going to turn up on her doorstep.

'You live here?'

'Yes.'

'What about Scotland?'

'I said I'd been working in Scotland; I didn't actually say I was going back.'

Her brow creased and he knew she was trying to recall the scant conversation they'd had. They hadn't spent much time talking. She probably knew as little about him as he did about her. Although he could recall every curve of her body, the softness of her skin and the touch of her hand, he didn't know much beyond that. He hadn't needed to at the time. He hadn't even known she was a midwife. He'd assumed she worked in the health profession because she was at the conference but he hadn't given any thought to what she did for a living. He hadn't been interested in that.

But now he praised his good fortune in accepting this job at Parkville Private. Working with Brighde could turn out to be a pleasant surprise, although her tone suggested she wasn't quite as excited about the idea as he was.

'But you're not supposed to be *here*!' she said, confirming his suspicions that she wasn't especially pleased to see him. '*Why* are you here?'

'Have dinner with me and I'll tell you.'

'No, thank you.'

'No?' He wasn't sure that he'd heard right. She was turning down his invitation. 'Really?' He couldn't remember the last time he was knocked back.

'Haven't you ever had anyone say no to you before?' she asked, but she was still frowning as if this was all very serious rather than the pleasant coincidence he saw it to be.

'Not often,' he admitted. And never straight after

he'd spent the night with someone. 'So, what's your objection to dinner?'

'I didn't expect to see you again.'

'Nor I you, but that's no reason not to share a meal.'

'And I never would have slept with you if I'd known we'd be working together.'

'It's just dinner, Brighde. You can show me around Melbourne.'

'I don't think so.'

'Why not? Are you seeing someone?' That was a possibility he hadn't thought of until now but it was quite likely. The conference and the one night they'd shared was now months ago. Maybe she wasn't single any more. That wouldn't surprise him but it would definitely be a shame.

'No.' She shook her head and the golden curls that had come loose from her ponytail bobbed around her shoulders.

'Well, in that case, how can I convince you to change your mind?' He wasn't one to give up easily. And, besides, sex with Brighde had been incredible and he was more than willing to get to know her better and see if she could be persuaded to give it another go.

'You can't.'

'There's nothing I can do?'

She shook her head again. 'It's not you. It's me.'

Xavier almost laughed until he realised she wasn't kidding. 'Seriously? That old chestnut.' What could he have done to offend her so terribly that she wouldn't share a meal with him?

'I mean it. I don't date and I don't do dinner.'

'Ever?'

'Never.'

He'd never heard anything so ridiculous. Who didn't date? Even his disastrous last relationship hadn't put him off the idea of dating. If you didn't date you were destined to spend your life alone and who wanted to do that? Not him. 'Why is that?'

'I'm happy on my own.'

'That's a very male attitude. Don't all women want a partner?'

'You don't know much about women, do you?' she countered.

'I actually thought I knew women pretty well. I have four sisters and I work as an OB/GYN. I work with women every day.' Hormonal ones too, but he thought better of mentioning that.

'Maybe so but there are always exceptions. You can't put us all in the one basket.'

So it would seem.

'I don't need a man to complete me,' she continued. 'I might need him for sex but there is more than one way to skin a cat.'

'You're very direct.' Her directness was appealing. Another tick in the box. After playing guessing games with his ex, Brighde's honesty was refreshing. But it wasn't getting him what he wanted.

'I don't see the point in playing games. Life is short; I intend to live my life by my rules. So, why didn't you go back to Scotland?'

She looked as if she'd have him on a plane right then and there if it was up to her.

'I'm Melbourne born and bred. I've come home.'

'So you don't need me to show you around Melbourne, then.'

'No.' He laughed, trying to ease the tension he could feel emanating from her. She was wound up tight. 'Guilty as charged. But I warn you, I will try again. I'd like to have dinner with you. Just dinner; we won't call it a date. No expectations, no strings.' He wasn't looking for a serious relationship but Brighde wasn't even looking at him any more.

'I need to get back to Kirsty,' she said as she dried her hands. And then she was gone. Leaving him alone and completely confused. And naturally intrigued. She'd thrown him a challenge by knocking him back and he wasn't about to retreat.

Anyone listening to her would think she was mad. *He* probably thought she was mad. But she'd prefer to risk being considered crazy than to risk falling in love. That was not on her agenda. She needed to get away. Far away. From his easy charm and his come-to-bed eyes and his to-die-for body before she made any more mistakes. She could totally understand why he wasn't often rejected. He was completely gorgeous and the sex had been fantastic but he wasn't for her. She couldn't afford to relax her rules. She didn't do second dates or dinner or whatever he wanted to call it. She couldn't accept his invitation, no matter how much she was tempted.

So she walked away, even though it was hard to do, and returned to Kirsty and her baby. She had a new mum to care for. A job to do. There was no time to think about what-ifs and to wish things were different.

She helped Kirsty to breastfeed her baby, then shower and dress. She settled her into her room and left Kirsty and Matt alone with their baby. She was due for a tea break but she didn't want to risk having it in the staff kitchen and bumping into Xavier so she escaped to the nursery, looking for Sarah. She needed to debrief.

Brighde offered to take over from the other nurse on duty so she could take a tea break which allowed her to talk to Sarah without interruption. The nursery was quiet. It was three o'clock in the morning and most of the babies were with their mothers. Sarah was feeding a premmie baby and there was another who needed changing. Brighde picked her up, changing her nappy before holding her for a while. She loved the weight of a newborn baby in her arms. Loved the new baby smell. She would love one of her own if things were different.

'Are you going to tell me how it went?' Sarah asked as she settled her charge.

'Fine,' Brighde replied. 'Good, even.' Xavier was a good doctor but Brighde hadn't been able to think straight. She needed a plan. A way of knowing she was going to be able to hold herself together and do her job. She couldn't afford to be distracted.

'And?' Sarah queried. 'You obviously have something on your mind. Spit it out.'

'He asked me out.'

'And you said yes?'

'I don't do second dates. You know that.'

'Technically, it's not a second date. You never really had a first one and a good bonking is not the same thing as a candlelit dinner. And I've never seen you so obsessed.'

'I'm not obsessed,' Brighde objected.

'Fascinated then.'

'Well, there's a lot to be fascinated about,' she admitted.

'There's no harm in going on a date with him. Especially as you can call this a first date.'

'I don't need anyone else in my life. I have you and Nick and now Imogen.'

'Would it be so terrible to have one more?'

'You know I can't afford to let other people close.'

Brighde would love to fall in love but that was a risk she couldn't afford to take. She was worried she wouldn't be able to resist Xavier. She was worried that he'd only have to look at her with those eyes and she'd melt into a pool of desire and do whatever he asked of her. She got all hot and bothered just *thinking* about him.

'Well, say no then. It's as simple as that. You have two choices. Yes or no.'

'It's hard to say no to the best sex of my life.'

'In that case—' Sarah sighed '—maybe you should have another go. Perhaps you're putting him on a pedestal. Perhaps it will be easier to let go if you find out he wasn't so fantastic after all.'

Brighde didn't think that would be the conclusion she'd come to. She couldn't possibly sleep with him again. That would be risking too much. The way her body reacted to him, she knew the fire would burn just as brightly the next time. The heat would be just as intense and she couldn't afford to let her guard down. Something about Xavier made her feel that it would be all too easy to lose control. There was something insanely attractive about him. She *had* to resist. It would be too dangerous not to.

'I can't,' she said. Not sure who she was trying to convince.

She had thought that perhaps more sex was the way to put him out of her mind but she didn't think that more sex with Xavier was the answer.

But it was an answer.

CHAPTER FOUR

BRIGHDE HAD MANAGED to avoid Xavier for the best part of a week but her luck ran out on Wednesday night, when she last expected to see him. She knew he had Wednesday afternoons off—she'd checked—so she was surprised to quite literally bump into him in the hospital corridor.

Just the sight of him set her heart racing. Her palms were sweaty and her throat dry throat as she struggled to form a coherent sentence. 'I thought it was your afternoon off.'

'There was a baby with other ideas,' he told her. 'But I'm finished now. Safely delivered. Are you on your way home too?' he asked and she saw him glance at her bag that was slung over her shoulder.

Brighde nodded.

'Can I walk you to your car?'

'I'm catching a bus.'

'At this time of night?'

'I do it all the time. I only have to get to North Carlton.'

'Let me give you a lift,' he offered as they headed out of the hospital. 'My car is in the doctors' car park.'

That was closer than the bus. Brighde didn't think

it would count if she let him drop her home. She didn't have to ask him in. And she would be home much faster. She could think of a dozen good reasons to accept his offer. So she did. 'Thanks, that would be great.'

She sank gratefully into the leather seat. The car smelt new but in the close confines she could also smell Xavier. She remembered his scent. Part shampoo with traces of pear and honey and part man.

Her stomach growled as he turned the car into Lygon Street. 'Do you want to grab something to eat? Not dinner,' he clarified with a quick glance at her, 'just a snack.' She could see him smiling. In profile the corner of his delicious mouth turned up; he obviously thought he was going to win this round.

But she *was* starving. Surely there was no harm in grabbing a quick bite to eat in a public place? No risk.

'Okay.'

'Really?'

She nodded, pleased that she had surprised him. 'I'm starving,' she admitted, just in case he thought it was his company she couldn't resist.

'Italian?' he asked as he pulled to the kerb.

It was close to midnight and there weren't a lot of restaurants still open but Italian sounded good. They ordered bowls of pasta accompanied by a glass of wine. The pasta smelt fantastic but the wine left a metallic taste in Brighde's mouth. She pushed it to one side and concentrated on her pasta.

They chatted about work and which football teams they supported. Nice, neutral, typically Melbourne conversation and Brighde wondered if this was how normal people felt. Was this what it felt like when you actually wanted to get to know someone? Was this what a proper date felt like? Was this how people behaved when they hoped it might lead to something more? She'd never been out with anyone she'd slept with before. Things always ended after that. She'd never let herself have a second date.

She waited until Xavier was halfway through his dish before asking, 'So is now the time you tell me why you came back to Australia?'

'Was that part of the deal?'

Brighde nodded. 'I think it was.'

'There were lots of reasons. I'd been away for four years and my parents aren't getting any younger. I wanted to spend some time with them.'

'Are you close to your family?'

'I am but it's kind of hard not to be. I'm the middle of five siblings, two older sisters, two younger sisters. It's impossible not to get caught up in all the craziness.'

'Wow! Five!'

'And eight nieces and nephews.'

Hearing that made Brighde wistful. Her family had been torn apart, and then depleted, due to disease. Her father had left when she was only nine. Unable to cope with her mother's illness, he had abandoned his family and Brighde had never come to terms with that. How could someone walk out on the people that supposedly meant the world to them? People they loved? She would never put her faith in love. Happily ever after endings were for other people. Other families.

Her mum had succumbed to the disease and for the past five years it had just been Brighde and her brother. That was all that remained of the Campbells now and she wouldn't be adding to the family tree, although she was looking forward to Nick and Imogen having a family. It was nice to think their family would still grow even if it wasn't going to be her doing.

'Do you want kids?' she asked.

'Definitely.'

He sounded so certain and Brighde knew then that she had to cross him off her list. Her silly fantasies about what might be had to stop. She should get up and walk out right now. There was absolutely no point in getting to know him—their paths were headed in completely different directions—but she couldn't make herself leave. Not yet. She could share a meal with him tonight and tomorrow she'd start again.

'What about you?' Now it was Xavier's turn to ask the questions.

'I'm in no hurry,' she said, using her usual excuse. 'I get my fill at work.' She couldn't answer honestly. She couldn't bring herself to tell him 'no'. She knew that would just open her up to a whole lot of questions that she didn't want to answer.

The waitress cleared their plates and Xavier ordered dessert. One serve of tiramisu with two spoons. Brighde didn't think she could fit another thing in but when it arrived it looked so good she couldn't resist. She wondered what was happening to her willpower. She'd have to watch herself around Xavier.

'So, how come you haven't found the mother of your children yet?' She steered the conversation back to him. 'You didn't fall in love in Scotland?'

A dark expression flashed across his face. It could have been sorrow or pain but it was gone so quickly she wondered if she'd imagined it and she certainly didn't have time to interpret it. Maybe he was just tired or didn't like being questioned. Maybe he really wasn't the talkative type. They certainly hadn't talked much on first meeting.

'No. Scottish girls are not my type.'

'So you've come home to settle down?'

'No. It was always my plan to come back at some stage. Now seemed like a good time but my focus at the moment is work. I'm in no hurry to start a family. I'm going to focus on my work. Build up my practice, get established back here. I don't have time for other distractions.'

Brighde relaxed. It didn't sound as if he was looking for anything more than she could offer at the moment. Maybe they could share one more night without any expectations.

'None?' she teased.

'Well, maybe a couple of distractions would be okay.' The corners of his mouth lifted into a smile. His gorgeous lips were closed; it was only a half-smile but she knew exactly what he was thinking. She could see it in his eyes. They were dark and languid. Just begging her to take him to bed.

Was she prepared to break her own rule? Just this once?

She knew it would be dangerous but she was sorely tempted.

He stood and pulled some cash from his wallet and tucked it under his wineglass before holding her chair for her. He held out his hand to help her up and kept hold of her hand as they left the restaurant. It felt nice, almost as if they were on a real date.

Her house was only a couple of blocks away. They didn't talk as he drove her home. Brighde couldn't think of anything sensible to say. All she could think of was what she should do when they got home. She knew if she invited him in he would accept. It was a big risk but one worth taking. She wanted one more chance. She wanted one more opportunity to commit everything about him to memory.

'It's that house there,' she told him as they drove past a single level terrace house. 'You can drop me out the front if you like,' she offered. Maybe that was one way to resist temptation. The only way.

But Xavier was going to be a complete gentleman. 'No, it's late and it's dark. I'll just find a gap and walk you to your door.'

Sarah was working a night shift and the house was in darkness but Brighde knew the porch light would come on as soon as she opened the front gate.

Xavier parked the car several houses away—parking spaces were hard to find—and followed her through the gate and up the front path. The outside light clicked on and Brighde slid her key into the front door and turned to thank him for the lift.

He was standing centimetres from her. His eyes were dark and serious and she knew exactly what he was thinking.

'Don't look at me like that,' she said.

'Like what?' He grinned and his eyes lightened. 'Like I want to peel off all your clothes and make love to you again?'

Brighde nodded. She was lost for words. That was exactly the look in his come-to-bed eyes.

She couldn't think when he was looking at her like that.

'But that's exactly what I want to do,' he said. 'Are you going to invite me in?'

Brighde's eyes were fastened on his mouth, reading his words as they fell from his lips.

She started to speak, intending to be strong, intending to tell him 'no', but Xavier bent his head and claimed her lips with his, silencing her words and dissolving all her objections.

She lifted her hands, intending to put them on his chest, intending to push him away, but instead she found her arms winding around his neck, holding him closer.

She thought about telling him to stop but as his tongue parted her lips her final resistance crumbled.

She wanted this. She wanted one more night.

Was that really so bad?

His hands were under her buttocks and he scooped her up. She wrapped her legs around his hips as he pushed the unlocked door open with his foot and carried her inside.

'First door on the left,' she managed to tell him.

He didn't let her go until they were in her room. He lowered her to the bed but by now her fingers were tearing at the buttons on his shirt. She pulled his shirt from his trousers before unbuckling his belt and unzipping him. Now that she'd made her decision she wasn't about to change her mind.

Xavier pushed his trousers from his hips, exploding from the confines of his clothing, as he stepped out of his shoes.

The only light in the room came through the curtains from the porch but that was enough to illuminate him in all his glory.

He bent over and slid his hands under her skirt. His fingers were warm and firm as he slipped them beneath the elastic of her underwear and pulled them off.

Next his fingers slid the zips down on her boots and he removed them and tossed them to one side as she reached for him.

Her fingers wrapped around his erection. His shaft was thick and hard and he moaned and moved closer.

Brighde was on the edge of her bed, still almost fully clothed but she didn't care. There was no time to get undressed; she was in too much of a hurry.

Xavier knelt on the floor and parted her legs. His fingers slid inside her. She was warm and wet and ready.

She inhaled and let her knees fall further apart. Then his fingers were gone and she was about to beg him not to stop when she saw he was reaching for his trousers. He pulled his wallet out, searching for protection. He rolled the sheath on and she lifted her hips and wrapped her legs behind him as he thrust into her, filling her.

His arms were under her shoulders, controlling her movements, holding them together. Brighde threw her head back but fought to keep her eyes open as waves of pleasure rolled through her. She wanted to watch him. His eyes were fixed on her, taking it all in as he took her.

They were keeping time to the same orchestra, their bodies perfectly in tune. Xavier rolled his thumb over her swollen sweet spot and Brighde thought she was going to burst into a thousand tiny pieces.

'Oh, God, Xavier.'

She heard him hold his breath, felt him start to come and she cried out as he knelt between her thighs and brought them both to a climax.

Xavier collapsed on the bed beside her and wrapped her in his arms.

'Can you stay?' she asked, hating the fact that she

was asking but she really didn't want him to leave. She wanted him to stay the night. She wanted to get completely naked and make love again, one final time. She wasn't ready for it to end just yet.

He nodded and kissed her.

She sat up and unzipped her skirt, sliding it from her body. She lifted her arms and Xavier pulled her shirt over her head. He undid her bra with one flick of his fingers and bent his head to her breast. Brighde lay back as Xavier's tongue circled her nipple. Their initial frenzied desire had been sated; she knew that she would have a chance to take it slow this time, to savour every second and commit it all to memory.

She'd broken all her rules for him in just one night. She never spent a second night with a man. She never invited them to her house and she definitely had never slept with someone she worked with. But she was finding him difficult to resist. She'd have to come up with a new plan but that could wait until tomorrow. For tonight she was staying right where she was. She fell asleep in his arms, her head on his chest, lulled to sleep by the rise and fall of his chest and the sound of his breaths.

'Good morning.'

Brighde woke to the sound of his voice. He brushed a strand of hair from her cheek as he leant down to kiss her. He was already out of bed and dressed. 'I need to get home and shower for work,' he said. 'What are your plans for the day?'

Brighde took a moment to remember what day it was. 'I'm having brunch with my brother and his fiancée and then I'm on another afternoon shift.'

'Shall I come and pick you up after work? I could give you a lift home again.'

It was clear he wanted to continue on from last night. Brighde liked the sound of that. She was flattered but she knew she shouldn't accept. She couldn't start something with Xavier. They shouldn't have even had last night.

'I'd like that,' she said, meaning to add *'but I can't'* but the words never made it out.

Xavier grinned and kissed her again. 'I'll see you later then,' he said.

She rolled over in bed and watched him leave. She wondered what it would be like to be like normal people and make real plans for the day or the week or next weekend. She knew she needed to be careful; Xavier was testing the limits of her willpower. She knew she would never make plans for the rest of her life but waking up with someone and knowing she would see him again felt nice.

Was this how it had started for Nick and Imogen? Had Nick's plans crumbled in the face of his feelings for Immy? She'd love to ask him but she didn't want that to lead to questions about what was going on in her life.

Nick and Imogen were waiting for her at the café.

'Are you feeling okay?' Imogen asked her as she gave her a hug.

Brighde knew she looked pale and washed out. Hardly the glow of someone who'd spent a passionate night in bed with the sexiest man alive. She had dark circles under her eyes and really needed to spend more than two minutes on her make-up but she'd run out of time and hadn't wanted to keep Nick and Immy waiting.

'I didn't get a lot of sleep last night.' She knew they'd assume it was because of work and she was happy to let them think that. She wasn't prepared to talk about Xavier. Talking about a man would be completely out of character for her and would only invite questions she wasn't prepared to even think about, let alone answer.

'We've got some good news,' Nick told her as the waitress took their order. This was a regular meeting spot for them and Brighde always ordered the same breakfast. Eggs Benedict with Hollandaise sauce.

'You've picked a date for the wedding?' Brighde guessed.

'No, that's next on our to-do list.' Nick held Imogen's hand. A gesture that looked so tender and sweet that Brighde felt a pang of longing. 'We're having a baby.'

'It's a bit sooner than we planned but we're really excited,' Imogen said.

'A baby! Wow.' Brighde sat back in her seat as she digested the news. 'I'm going to be an auntie.'

She smiled. It was good news. Happy news. Nick's negative test results meant that he and Imogen could start a family without any concerns about passing on the mutated gene. Brighde would love to have a family of her own and while she knew that was a possibility with the assistance of genetic testing she wasn't going to risk putting her own children through what she and Nick had gone through with their mother. Watching their mother deteriorate and eventually die at a young age had been horrific and it was something Brighde had no intention of repeating. But Nick and Imogen didn't need to worry about that. That worry was Brighde's alone now.

Brighde didn't want to think about how alike she and her mother were. Nick and Brighde had the same colouring—they were both blonde and with the same blue-grey eyes—but Nick was tall and lean and his face was longer than hers, not as square, although he still had a very defined jawline. They were similar enough that people recognised them as siblings but Brighde was the spitting image of her mother while Nick had more of their father in him. Because of the similarities in appearance between her and her mother she had always assumed they'd be alike in other ways too. Right down to the faulty DNA.

But Brighde didn't want to think about her mother today. It always made her sad and today she wanted to be happy for Nick. 'Congratulations. I'm really happy for you.' She stood up to hug them both again, determined not to let her dark thoughts ruin their excitement.

'We thought it might take longer to happen, so as soon as we got my test results we started trying.'

'How many weeks are you?' she asked Imogen.

'Only eight, but we couldn't wait to tell someone. We knew you'd understand.'

She did understand the excitement and she was happy for them but it didn't stop her from wishing things were different for her. She'd have to be content with being an auntie—that was almost as good as having a family of her own.

'We'll have to move the wedding forward now,' Nick was saying. 'I'd like to be married before the baby comes. Make an honest woman of you.'

He was looking at his fiancée with such adoration that it made Brighde's heart ache.

'That shouldn't be hard,' Imogen replied. 'There's only a few people we really want to be there with us. You,' she said, looking at Brighde, 'my parents and my sister.'

'What about Dad?' Brighde asked. She knew that Nick had some contact with their father. She had severed all ties with him when he'd walked out on them and their mother but, as an adult, Nick had reconnected with him and they caught up occasionally.

'That's up to you,' he said. 'If having him there would make you uncomfortable then we won't invite him. It's more important to me—to us—' he smiled and picked up Imogen's hand '—that you'll be there. We'd like you to be our witness.'

Brighde smiled. 'I'd be honoured.'

'Thank you,' Imogen said as she stood up. 'I'll be back in a minute.'

'I really am happy for you, Nick. The two of you are going to have a beautiful life.'

'You might be able to have the same. Have you thought any more about getting tested?'

Brighde shook her head. 'Nothing has changed for me. I didn't want to get tested before and I definitely don't want to get tested now. I don't want to know and part of me feels even more certain that it would only be bad news. I'm okay as I am.' She was more convinced than ever that she had inherited her mother's DNA and she really didn't want to know that she'd be going to an early grave. It was far better just to avoid going down the path of marriage and babies.

Imogen returned to the table carrying two glasses of champagne. 'I can't have any but I thought we could toast the baby,' she said as she handed Nick and Brighde each a glass.

'To your family,' Brighde said as she raised her glass. She put it to her lips to take a sip but the yeasty smell turned her stomach. She forced down a sip so she didn't appear rude and then put her glass on the table.

'I might just wait until I've had something to eat,' she said. Drinking on an empty stomach and on top of a limited amount of sleep seemed like a recipe for disaster.

'You sound like how I feel in the morning,' Imogen said. 'I'll be pleased when my morning sickness stops.'

'Well, I don't envy you that.'

Brighde didn't finish her champagne and even her breakfast sat heavily in her stomach as she walked home. She was feeling a little queasy. Perhaps she was coming down with a cold. She'd felt a bit flat for the past few mornings, she realised, but once she'd got to work and was busy she'd been okay.

Her symptoms were mimicking Imogen's morning sickness but Brighde knew she was only thinking that way because of all the baby talk at brunch.

She couldn't be pregnant.

But her last period had been exceptionally light.

Surely that didn't mean anything?

The idea of it made her feel queasy and her legs were shaky. She stopped walking and rested her hand on a street bench as she waited for the queasiness to pass.

She looked up and saw she was outside a pharmacy.

There was only one way to make sure.
She went inside and bought a pregnancy test kit.
She took it home and went straight to the bathroom.

CHAPTER FIVE

'WHAT ARE YOU doing in here?'

The bathroom door opened and Sarah stepped in. Her hair was dishevelled and Brighde realised she'd just woken up after working a night shift.

Brighde hadn't realised how long she'd been sitting in the bathroom. She hadn't been able to make herself move after taking the test. Waves of nausea had swamped her and she'd vomited a couple of times. But she refused to think the vomiting was symptomatic; she was sure it was stress-related.

'Are you sick?' Sarah asked.

'Not exactly,' Brighde said as she pointed to the stick sitting on the side of the bath.

'Oh, my God.' Sarah was looking at her in shock. 'You're *pregnant*?'

Brighde nodded.

'How the hell did that happen?'

'I don't know.' She was on the Pill and she took it religiously and also practised safe sex. She'd always been afraid that one mistake would mean something like this might happen.

'Didn't you use a condom?'

'I think so.' She honestly couldn't remember. It was

weeks ago. It would have been very unlike her to be so careless but she really couldn't recall. How could she not remember? How could she be so reckless? But what did it matter now? The *how* was irrelevant. She was pregnant and what mattered now was doing something about it and there was only one option in her mind.

'Are you going to tell Xavier?'

She shook her head. 'No. He doesn't need to know. I'm not going to keep it,' she said before bursting into tears. Termination had always been her fallback position and she knew that was her only option, but she wished just for a moment that things could be different.

Sarah hugged her. 'My God, you're freezing.'

Brighde had been sitting in the bathroom for so long the cold had seeped into her bones. She was shaking now with shock and cold.

'You need to go to bed,' Sarah told her. 'There's nothing we can do about this right now. I'll bring you a cup of tea and then I'll call the hospital and cancel your shift.'

'Xavier!' Surprise was written all over Sarah's face when she opened the front door, answering his knock. 'What are you doing here?'

'I heard Brighde was sick,' he said. 'I brought her some of my mum's chicken soup.' He held up the container as evidence of his good intentions.

'That's really sweet but I don't think that's going to help.'

'What's wrong with her?' he asked. She'd been fine that morning so when he'd heard that she'd called in sick he'd figured it couldn't be much more than a gastro bug or something similar.

'She's in bed—do you want to see her?' Sarah asked as she took the soup and stepped back, letting him into the hall.

He followed Sarah to the back of the house, walking past Brighde's room. 'I'll just wash my hands,' he said. He didn't want to expose Brighde to any more germs but as he washed his hands he realised Sarah hadn't answered his question. He dried his hands and returned the towel to the hook that hung over the rubbish bin. A box for a pregnancy test kit poked up out of the bin and caught his eye. He reached for the bin and then hesitated. Was this any of his business?

He dropped his hand to his side, resisting the urge to pick up the kit.

But his heart was beating furiously in his chest and his mouth had gone dry. He needed to see the kit. He needed to see the result.

His hand shook as he picked up the empty box and exposed the little stick that lay in the bin underneath.

He could see two pink lines in the window.

Someone in this house was pregnant.

He lifted the stick from the bin and carried it out of the bathroom.

Sarah was in the kitchen, boiling the kettle. She turned when she heard him enter. 'Would you like…?' The question died on her lips when she saw what he was holding.

'Is this yours?' he asked.

Her eyes were wide with fright but she shook her head and he had his answer.

His heart was hammering in his chest. He could feel the blood pumping in his neck, flooding his carotid artery. Sarah was biting her lip. Was she wondering what he was going to do next?

He felt dazed, sucker-punched, but he knew he had to talk to Brighde. He had to find out what was going on.

He left the kitchen, still holding the test stick, and knocked on Brighde's door. He didn't wait for permission to enter. He was going in, no matter what she said. They had things to discuss.

'Brighde?' he said as he pushed the door open. Her bedside lamp was on, bathing the room in a soft yellow light. Her blonde hair was tousled and thick. Her face pale and tearstained.

He sat on the edge of her bed and put the stick on her bedside table. He saw her eyes dart to the stick, widen and then look back at him.

'Where did you—?'

'I found it in the bathroom,' he said, cutting her off. 'You're pregnant?'

Her eyes were enormous, grey and frightened, as she nodded.

'Is it mine?'

Brighde wanted to be offended that he'd asked her that but she knew it was a legitimate question.

'Yes. There hasn't been anyone since you and I...' She drifted off, letting him fill in the blanks. Despite the impression he might have of her, she didn't jump in and out of men's beds on a regular basis. Once or twice a year for one night didn't make her promiscuous. Not in her opinion anyway, but she wasn't about to share the finer details of her love life with him.

She sat up in bed. This wasn't the place she'd envisaged having this conversation. If she was going to be brutally honest, she hadn't planned on having this conversation at all. She had thought the best thing to do was not to say anything to him and just deal with it as she thought best. She knew he would want to keep the baby and that was not her plan. The less said the better, in her opinion. But it looked as if that option had been taken away from her.

'Wow.'

He said nothing more for a moment. He just sat and stared into the distance.

Brighde waited. She had no idea what to say so thought it best to stay silent.

'This is huge,' he said eventually. 'We have to work out what we're going to do.'

'There's nothing to work out,' she told him. 'I know what I'm going to do and don't worry, I won't put any pressure on you. I don't intend to keep it.'

'*What?*'

Xavier sat back, reacting as if she'd slapped him, his gorgeous face showing his complete shock. But he shouldn't be so surprised. She'd told him she wasn't ready to have children of her own. Ironic that she'd only mentioned it last night.

'I know you said that you get your fill of babies at work,' he said, clearly remembering the conversation, 'but surely this has changed things?'

She shook her head. 'No, it hasn't.'

'I understand this is unexpected, a shock even, and it may be sooner than you would have planned but you're *pregnant*. That *must* change things?'

'No.'

'Surely you haven't come to that decision so quickly? Surely you'll consider your options?'

'To be honest, I didn't decide overnight not to go

ahead with the pregnancy. I decided that a long time ago. I never intended to have children.'

'Never? You must have planned to have children of your own at some point.'

'No.'

'We're not even going to discuss this?'

'There's nothing to discuss. I'm not keeping it.' Brighde took a deep breath. 'I know you want kids but I didn't think you wanted them right now. You told me you wanted to concentrate on your work. I imagine your plan of fatherhood is vastly different to this situation too. I can't imagine you thought you'd have a baby with someone you barely know. You didn't sign up for this and I definitely didn't.'

She was counting on the fact that he wasn't any more prepared to become a parent than she was.

'I realise it's not ideal,' he said, 'and maybe I'm not the man you had in mind to be the father of your children, but can't we discuss this?'

'This isn't about you and what sort of parent you'd be. I've never even *thought* about the type of man I'd look for as a father to my kids. It was a moot point, considering I decided a long time ago that I wasn't ever having children.'

'But that's crazy! That must have been a hypothetical discussion you had with yourself? Surely this situation changes things?'

Brighde shook her head. 'No, it doesn't.'

'How can you say that? I think you should take some time, we both should, and let this sink in.'

'I'm not going to change my mind.'

'How do you know?'

'It's complicated,' she said. Although that was a lie. It wasn't complicated, in her opinion.

'I think you owe me an explanation.'

Brighde sighed. 'I know I do.' It was only fair. To him. Not to her. None of this was fair to her. She'd always tried to ensure she would *never* find herself in this position. Nothing about this was fair. And there was no easy way to start this conversation. She took a deep breath. 'Have you ever had a patient who suffers from Huntington's Disease?'

'Huntington's Chorea?'

She nodded.

'Not that I can recall.'

'Do you remember anything about the disease from your training?'

He frowned. 'A little. It's an inherited condition, right? That causes degeneration in the brain and affects movement. Which is where the term "chorea" comes from.'

'It's a genetic mutation that ultimately kills the nerve cells in the brain. It affects mood, memory and movement and results in premature death. There is no cure.' She hesitated very briefly, dreading the idea that she had to have this conversation but knowing she couldn't avoid it. 'As you said, it's an inherited condition. It runs in families and my mother had it.'

'Had?'

Brighde nodded. 'She died five years ago. She was forty-nine. The mutation is a dominant one. There's a one in two chance of children inheriting the fault and therefore developing the disease. I have one brother; he doesn't have the mutation.'

His face went pale under the dark stubble that lined his jaw. 'Are you telling me you do?'

'There's a strong possibility.'

'Don't you know? You said there's no cure but surely there's a test for it?'

'There is but I've never been tested.'

'So there's a good chance you don't have it?' Xavier's shoulders relaxed as he let out a breath she hadn't noticed him holding.

'I wouldn't say a good chance. My brother tested negative. If there's a fifty-fifty chance of inheriting the gene and he didn't get it, I reckon the odds are not in my favour.'

'But why haven't you been tested to make sure?'

'I don't want to know.'

'How does that work?' He was frowning now. 'How can you not want to know?'

Brighde, like many other people whose lives had been affected by Huntington's, had her reasons and, to her, they sounded logical, sensible and reasonable. But she had to try to explain it in a way that would make Xavier understand. She knew that was vitally important.

'Imagine if you were told today that you were going to be hit by a bus and killed in five years' time. Would you want to know? Would it change the way you live your life?'

'I think it probably would.'

'What if you were told you were going to be hit by a bus at the age of forty and that you'd survive but you wouldn't be able to walk or talk any more? That, more than likely, you'd lose your memories and you wouldn't be able to communicate. Would you want to know that your future looked like that?'

'That doesn't sound appealing.'

'Trust me, it's not. Nick and I watched our mother suffer that exact fate and it's horrible. Knowing your life is heading in that direction might make you determined to pack as much into the days you have left, but what about when your fortieth birthday gets closer? What about when it's a month, a week, a day away—how do you think you'll feel then, knowing what is about to happen? How would your family cope with that scenario? I don't want to know if my life is going to end prematurely. I watched my mother die and I don't want to know if that is my future too. I'm happier not knowing. That's why I haven't been tested.'

'I think I understand but I don't see how this means you want to terminate a pregnancy. You don't know if you have the faulty gene and you don't know if our child does either. We're talking in hypotheticals.'

'There's every chance I have the mutation. Nick and I nursed our mother until we couldn't manage. We had to put her into care and then we watched her deteriorate a little more every day until she died. I'm not going to put anyone I love through that and especially not my own child.'

'But don't you see, you don't know for certain what you're faced with?'

'But what if *I've* passed on the gene? How do you think you would feel watching your child die before you? I can only think of one thing worse than watching my mother die and that is watching my own child suffer and die. I can't do it.'

'But you might not have to. You could get tested and then make a decision.'

Xavier picked up her hand and held it. It was a surprisingly comforting gesture but it didn't change anything.

'You're not listening to me,' she said as she pulled her hand from his grasp. She couldn't think when he was touching her. 'I really don't want to know what my future holds. I don't think Nick and I could both be that lucky and I don't want to live with the knowledge of a premature death and what that looks like. I don't want to pass on this gene. I don't want to be pregnant.'

She was scared. She was terrified. She couldn't do this.

'I think we're probably both in a bit of shock. There's a lot to think about but we don't need to make decisions tonight. We have time. It's what…ten weeks since the conference?'

'Nine and a half.' Which made her eleven and a half weeks pregnant.

'Please. Don't make any hasty decisions. Can we both take some time to think about what this means and talk about it some more?'

He could talk about it all he liked but she wasn't going to change her mind. But she nodded anyway. It was easier to give in for now. It didn't mean she had to change her mind and she was going to go crazy if she had to talk about it any more tonight.

'Do you want company?' he asked.

'No.' She shook her head. 'I want to be alone.' Seeing Xavier would just remind her of the situation she was in. If he wasn't there she could pretend it was all a nightmare.

Xavier's head was spinning when he left Brighde.

She was pregnant!

He was going to be a father.

He wanted kids, had always wanted them, and he made no secret of the fact to those nearest to him. He'd grown up in a close family, doted on by his sisters and, in turn, he doted on his nieces and nephews but he wanted children of his own. He'd actually thought he'd be a father already—he'd certainly thought he was on the way with his ex until she had ripped his dreams from him. But that hadn't deterred him. To acquaintances he said he was concentrating on his career but that was what people expected a man to say. He'd always intended to have children, a family of his own, and he knew he could do both. Granted, this current situation wasn't exactly what he had in mind but that didn't mean he was prepared to give up his dream. Not again.

He wanted to be a father. He was *going* to be a father, only that wasn't Brighde's plan.

He could understand her anxiety but to him things were black and white. He dealt in facts and figures, not in suppositions. He knew emotions could influence decisions—he saw that every day in his job—but he didn't believe that emotion should be the deciding factor, not without the facts. Brighde was making decisions based on assumptions. He wasn't discounting her experiences but she wasn't being reasonable. In his experience, you gathered the facts and then you dealt with them. You didn't worry about things that hadn't happened yet.

He could acknowledge her fear but he wasn't going to give in to it. She *had* to get tested. He couldn't let her make such a monumental decision without gathering all the facts. Ultimately, he might not stand in her way but that was a discussion for another day. A day when they had some facts to deal with.

He started his car and pulled into the traffic.

He didn't want to go. He didn't want to leave her alone. She'd said she needed space and he would respect that, but it was hard to leave.

He wanted to comfort her but he realised he probably also needed some time to clear his head. They obviously had differing opinions on this situation and if he was going to convince her to see his point of view he needed time to work out a strategy. There was a lot of information to take in, a lot to think about.

She was scared; he got that. He wanted to erase her fears but he needed information.

She was talking about terminating the pregnancy. He wanted her to keep the baby and he needed to work out how he was going to achieve that.

He needed a plan.

Brighde had three days off work and she managed to avoid any further discussion. She ignored Xavier's phone calls and only replied to his text messages very briefly, telling him she wasn't ready to talk yet. But after three days she was going stir crazy in the house, alone with her thoughts.

She pounced on Sarah when she walked through the door after her shift. 'How was work?' she asked, desperate for news of the outside world. Of Xavier. Not that she would admit it.

'Quiet. No dramatics today.'

'Who were you working with?'

'Paul Davey,' Sarah replied. She paused slightly before she added, 'You could always call him, you know.'

'Who? Paul? What for?'

'You know I don't mean Paul. Xavier.'

'Have you seen him?'

'Yes.'

'Did he ask about me?'

'No.' Sarah shook her head. 'I'm sorry.'

Was it a good thing or a bad thing that Xavier wasn't asking about her? Brighde didn't know. Part of her wanted him to worry about her. She wanted him to tell her everything would be all right, even though she knew that was unlikely. If he was worried about anything it would be about the baby and what her plans were.

'I think you should call him,' Sarah said. 'You need to talk about this. You can't keep avoiding the topic. It's not going to go away on its own.'

Brighde knew that. She knew she would have to make a move. She couldn't delay the inevitable. She had to make plans but she didn't have to discuss them with Xavier, yet she knew that was the decent thing to do. She was going to have to continue to work with him. She couldn't pretend this hadn't happened and she couldn't terminate the pregnancy without another conversation with him. He was no longer an anonymous one-night stand. He was her colleague and she knew more about him than she wanted to. He seemed like a good person; he deserved some consideration. This wasn't all his fault; she had to take some of the blame, and therefore some of the responsibility. She knew she needed to speak to him but it was a daunting task.

She still intended to terminate the pregnancy. She didn't need Xavier's permission but part of her wanted it. In her mind, when she'd thought about what she'd do if she was ever faced with this decision, there was never a father of the baby that needed her consideration. She'd never envisaged this scenario.

But now there was very much a father in the picture. She couldn't deny that but she still wasn't ready to see him. She didn't want to give him an opportunity to try to talk her out of her decision.

But she knew she couldn't avoid him for ever. She was due back at work tomorrow.

She had half hoped he wouldn't be on the ward today but she'd barely finished handover when he found her.

'Hi, how are you?' His voice wrapped around her like a comforting hug and made her want to step into his arms. She could use a hug.

'Good,' she lied, as she fought back tears. She was an emotional wreck and she knew she looked like she'd been through the wringer. She was pale, tired and unhappy. Xavier, by comparison, looked gorgeous. His eyes were bright, his hair was shiny, thick and healthy, his skin lightly tanned.

'Brighde, I have four sisters and I work with women all day. I can tell when a woman is lying.'

'Okay. Since you asked, I've been throwing up constantly—' morning sickness had arrived with a vengeance '—I'm exhausted, physically, emotionally and mentally. I've barely slept. The whole thing is a nightmare. Is there anything else you want to know?' She had a slight sense that she was being cruel but she couldn't help it. This situation was partly his fault. Why should he get off scot-free? If he pulled her up for being harsh she could always blame a lack of sleep and an excess of hormones.

'I need to ask you something.' He put his hand on her elbow and steered her towards a quiet spot in the corridor.

'Oh, God, Xavier, not now.' He couldn't possibly want to have the conversation she'd been trying to avoid, here at work? She felt her eyes widen with panic and her heart was racing. Was she going to throw up again? Early shifts were perhaps not the best for her in her state and if he was going to put her under the pump she didn't think she would cope with that *and* morning sickness.

'What do you take me for?' he said and she could hear the offence in his voice. 'It's a work question.'

'Oh. Sorry.' Perhaps she wasn't giving him enough credit. He hadn't really done anything wrong.

Except get her pregnant.

'You're taking over Amelia's patient in labour, correct?'

'Yes.'

'I'm the obstetrician. There's a slight problem and I told Amelia I would discuss it with you.'

'With labour?' Brighde frowned. It was unusual for the doctors to seek out the midwives in order to discuss their patients. Usually any issues were raised during handover.

'Not exactly.'

'Don't you want to work with me?' Maybe that was what this was about. Nothing to do with the patient and everything to do with trust?

'No, it's nothing like that. I have no issue working with you.'

Did he have other issues with her? She supposed it was highly likely but she was happy to avoid that topic as he continued. 'Labour is going well but this delivery isn't totally straightforward and I wanted to talk to you about it in private.' He paused and took a deep breath, giving Brighde the impression that he was steeling himself for something. 'The baby has Down Syndrome.'

'Do the parents know?' Brighde asked before she held her breath, waiting for his answer. She hated those deliveries where the parents were expecting a normal, straightforward delivery of a healthy baby and things didn't quite go to plan.

'They do.'

Brighde breathed out. That was good. No surprises was a good thing.

'And they are looking forward to a normal delivery and to welcoming this child into their family. They want the experience to be joyful and they have specifically requested that the staff are aware of their wishes and that the staff will respect the fact that this baby is loved and wanted. I need to know how you feel about that. Whether you can give them what they want or if you want to swap patients with one of the other midwives?'

'You think I can't do my job?'

'I don't know.' He was watching her carefully. Perhaps he was worried she was going to lose the plot completely. 'Given our last conversation, I wasn't sure how you would cope with this. I need to know that you can give the parents the support and attention they want and need and deserve.'

'Of course,' she replied. The parents had made their decision and she would respect that. Just because she would choose differently didn't mean she would treat them differently or without respect. 'I am not going to judge people for their decisions, just like I hope I'm not judged for mine.'

Let him think about that!

Brighde managed to hold herself together through the delivery and while she settled the new parents and their baby. The baby was beautiful, ten fingers and ten toes and big blue eyes, and Brighde felt the usual pang of longing. But it wasn't enough to convince her to change her mind about her own pregnancy. If anything, despite what she'd told Xavier, she was more adamant now than ever about termination. This family had chosen to welcome their child into the world but there was a difference. This child had Down Syndrome and would lead a normal life within those parameters. In all likelihood, he would lead a long life and wouldn't experience any dramatic changes in quality of life once into adulthood. In Brighde's opinion, one couldn't compare Down Syndrome to Huntington's Disease but when it came down to it the real issue was with her. Bottom line, she didn't think she was strong enough to go through the trauma of suffering from Huntington's herself or watching her child suffer.

But what if she didn't have the mutation? She knew that was a possibility.

Could she be that lucky?

Was she strong enough to risk finding out?

She let the tears that she'd been holding back flow as she washed her hands in the sluice room, hoping for some privacy. She was super emotional at the moment and every emotion—happiness, sadness, fear—all seemed to be magnified. Especially fear.

'Are you okay?'

His voice made her jump. Was he going to follow her around, constantly checking on her?

'I don't know. I don't even know why I'm crying.' She rinsed her face as she tried to work out how she was feeling. *What* she was feeling. Confused. Guilty. Sad. In equal parts.

'Why don't you come for a walk with me? Get some fresh air and clear your head. You're on your lunch break now, aren't you?'

Xavier needed to talk to her. He'd done some research and he wanted—needed—to talk about their options. He had some suggestions to make and a walk in the garden next to the hospital might be the perfect place to have a neutral discussion. If they walked and talked Brighde wouldn't need to maintain eye contact and then she might feel less like he was pressuring or interrogating her.

'Yes, but surely you don't have time?' she replied.

'I do,' he said. 'Unless another expectant mum goes into labour, I'm good. I want you to know that I'm here to support you and that starts now.'

He waited until they were out in the autumn sunshine before he began. 'I've been doing some research. I was surprised I'd never come across Huntington's Disease, except in theory, but when I found out there are only sixteen hundred Huntington's sufferers in Australia it made more sense.'

'Only sixteen hundred that we know of,' Brighde said.

'But, with the genetic testing that's available now, in a few more generations there could be none. The disease could be eradicated.' He thought this was incredible.

'If people choose to get tested.'

'That's my point. Why wouldn't you get tested if you've got the option?'

'Would *you* want to know that you're going to die a premature death?' she asked again.

Xavier had thought about this since she'd first posed the question days ago. 'I think I would. I'd like time to prepare.'

'You can't prepare for something like Huntington's Disease. It's not like getting killed in a plane crash,' she said. 'It's not sudden. It's a horrible, debilitating disease. It takes your life slowly over several years. There's no cure. I don't want to know if that's what my future holds.'

'So instead you want to terminate what could potentially be a perfectly healthy pregnancy?' Xavier knew he needed to stay calm and in control but he was really struggling to follow Brighde's logic.

'I know you want children, Xavier. I know that's in your plans for the future but I'm not the one to give them to you. I'm pregnant but it wasn't planned and I don't have to stay pregnant. It's my prerogative.'

'We can do this together.'

'There is no *together*. There is no *we*. We don't have a relationship. And even if we did, this disease destroys lives. My own father walked out when I was nine. He promised to love my mother through sickness and in health and that didn't last. It wasn't enough to make him stick around when the going got tough. How could I expect you to stay and support me if we start out with nothing substantial between us in the first place? I've made my decision. I'm not having this baby. I've made an appointment to see Julie Stewart to discuss a termination.'

Xavier felt as if she'd punched him. His stomach lurched and he had a pain in his chest. If he didn't know better he'd think he was having a cardiac episode but he knew the pain was caused by Brighde's words. He couldn't comprehend that she could so blithely announce that she was going to deprive him of his child. He'd lost a child once before and he couldn't bear to think of it happening again and he would do anything to ensure it didn't. He needed to have some control this time. He knew that would be difficult but he refused to back down quietly. This was his child and he would do everything in his power to make sure he would meet this one.

'Brighde, please. I'm begging you. Can't we discuss this some more?'

She shook her head. 'You're an obstetrician. Surely you've had patients who have had terminations arranged by you? There must be some instances where you agree that it's the right thing to do?'

'Yes,' he admitted. On a couple of occasions where it had been best for the baby or for the mother's health, physically or emotionally, he'd been involved but that was different.

'So what's the difference now?'

'Now it's *my* child we're talking about.' It couldn't be *more* different, in his opinion. But he knew Brighde could do as she pleased. 'But I guess it doesn't matter what I think or what I want. You hold all the cards.'

A termination wasn't necessarily what Brighde wanted either. She would love to be a mother but this was what was best. She didn't need, or even want, Xavier's permission but she did want him to understand her decision. And, hopefully, support it. She didn't want him to think she was being selfish or unemotional. She wanted him to like her. She thought he was fabulous and she wanted him to think the same of her. But she knew that was unlikely, especially given these circumstances, and she wasn't willing to trade her decision for his approval.

Xavier stopped walking and turned to her as he said, 'I know I don't legally have any say in this decision, I understand that, but there's something I'd like to tell you.'

'What is it?' she asked, even as she wondered if she should warn him that there was nothing he could say or do that would convince her to change her mind. She should warn him he was wasting his breath but he looked so desperate to be heard that she couldn't refuse to listen.

He sat on a park bench and Brighde sat with him.

'I wasn't totally upfront with you,' he told her. 'Remember you asked me if I'd fallen in love in Scotland?'

Brighde nodded. 'You said Scottish girls weren't your type.'

'I did. Which wasn't quite true. Three months before I came back home I broke up with my girlfriend.'

'Oh.' Brighde thought about that for a moment, wondering what that had to do with their situation.

'We'd been together for two and a half years.'

Again, Brighde wondered what relevance that had. Then she remembered the expression on his face when she'd asked about his girlfriends. That look she hadn't been able to decipher. Sorrow or pain. Maybe it had been both. 'Were you in love with her?'

'At the time I thought so. And I thought she loved me.'

'You couldn't work things out?'

'No. Things got complicated.'

'What happened?' Surely things couldn't have been more complicated than the circumstances he found himself in now?

'She was pregnant.'

He'd been in this situation before? And last time he'd been in a relationship and things still hadn't worked out, yet he seemed to think they would be able to muddle their way through this. As if things weren't difficult enough.

Was. He'd said was. Something must have happened. Something must have gone wrong because she knew Xavier didn't have children. 'Did she lose the baby?' she asked. That might explain Xavier's expression, might explain the pain and sorrow she'd seen in his eyes, but it didn't necessarily explain the break-up.

'No. We hadn't planned it, hadn't even talked about it really, but I was over the moon. Until she told me that she'd been having an affair. She told me it had started because I spent too much time working. I was doing my speciality training so I figured that it went without saying that I would be doing ridiculous hours, but she figured that seeing I was studying OB/GYN my hours were always going to be ridiculous and she felt she was never going to be my first priority. And then she told me there was a chance the baby wasn't mine.'

No wonder he'd asked if Brighde's baby was his when he'd discovered the positive pregnancy test.

'Anyway, it turned out she was right: the baby wasn't mine.'

'She's had it?'

He nodded.

'And you're sure it's not yours? You're not going back to Scotland to check? To have tests?'

'No. We did the tests while she was pregnant. We did a prenatal paternity test at fourteen weeks. You know the one, a blood sample from her and mouth swabs from the possible fathers. I was excluded as a potential father based on the DNA testing. The baby wasn't mine. And that's when I decided to come home. I needed to come home. I needed a break, to take some time out. Once I got here I realised how much I'd missed Australia and I decided to stay.'

'Are you asking me to have the same test? Is that why you're telling me this?' Was that why he'd told her this story?

'No. You've told me the baby is mine and I believe you. You didn't have to tell me that. You're probably regretting the fact that you did, given what your plans are, but it seems to me that you're making some big decisions, huge decisions, without all the facts. And these decisions affect me too. And our baby. Won't you at least get the baby tested? Then we'll know what we're dealing with.'

'But that's just it,' she replied. 'I don't *want* to know what we're dealing with. I made the decision long ago *not* to get tested and if I test the baby and the result comes back positive then I will know my fate too. I'm not ready for this.'

Xavier was nodding but he wasn't finished. 'Can I ask you one favour then?'

'What is it?'

'Before you make any further plans would you please have an ultrasound? I'd like a chance to at least see my baby.'

CHAPTER SIX

BRIGHDE LAY ON the exam table and pulled the shirt of her scrubs up and eased the waistband of her pants down, exposing her midriff.

She was a lot quieter than he was used to. She wasn't even giving him any grief and she definitely wasn't making eye contact. He expected she'd agreed to the ultrasound out of a sense of obligation but he didn't care. He was desperate for a glimpse of his baby. He was amazed at how important this was to him. He'd made no secret of the fact that he wanted to be a father, that it was in his plans for the future, but he'd anticipated that, like a lot of other fathers he'd spoken to, the sense of responsibility and love for his offspring wouldn't eventuate until he held his child in his arms. But he already felt an overwhelming sense of responsibility and an urge to protect his unborn child. And that was his second reason for asking Brighde to let him do an ultrasound. He hoped that once she saw the image of her baby—*their* baby—on the screen, she might be more willing to discuss alternatives.

This baby was a gift he hadn't expected and one he would do everything in his power to keep. Despite what had transpired with his ex, or maybe because of it, his dreams of fatherhood were strong. He would have to wait and see how he and Brighde would get through this together but he was determined that they would. Their relationship might not be a traditional one but he wasn't going to let go of his dream. He wasn't going to give up his child without a fight and he was pinning all his hopes and dreams on this scan.

But the procedure wasn't going quite as he'd anticipated. Brighde had given him clear instructions as to how this was going to work. She had agreed to an ultrasound but only an abdominal one. She'd said no to a pelvic one, claiming that seemed far too personal, which was ridiculous considering they'd had sex, but she'd been adamant—he could do the ultrasound abdominally or not at all. But that was okay and it was definitely better than nothing. She was twelve weeks pregnant; an abdominal ultrasound should give him a clear picture.

Her face was stony, expressionless, set, as if she was deliberately blocking all thoughts on what was about to happen. She'd told him she didn't want to look at the monitor. She didn't want to see the baby.

He knew she'd prefer not to be pregnant and he assumed that she didn't want to see the image because that would make it real. He wished she would change her mind but he wasn't about to argue with her now. He was grateful that she'd agreed to the ultrasound at all and he wasn't going to jeopardise this opportunity. She might not want to see their baby but he sure as hell did.

Had she suspected that his motivations for the ultrasound were not completely altruistic? He should have thought about the chance that she would refuse to look at the images. She was a midwife; she'd seen plenty of scans before. She would know what to expect and she would know what to expect and she would prepare for it. This was obviously her way of preparing—by denying it all. It seemed to be her way of coping.

But this pregnancy was really happening and he just wanted time to convince her not to end it prematurely. He was counting on this ultrasound, but she was playing tough.

Her head was turned away from the monitor. It looked as if she was going to stick to her decision. While he was all for a woman knowing her own mind, Brighde's stubbornness was infuriating. He knew he was only irritated because she was refusing to agree with him or listen to his point of view and he had enough grace to admit that that was part of the problem, but he was also terrified that he would either run out of time to convince her that he was right or that she was going to go ahead and make a decision without him. He knew she was perfectly entitled to do that but he'd be damned if he was going to make it easy for her.

He looked at her exposed stomach. Her skin was pale and soft. Her stomach flat. She was only twelve weeks along but it was incredible to think that his baby was in there.

His hand shook as he picked up the ultrasound head. He was unbelievably nervous. He'd done hundreds of ultrasounds for all sorts of reasons but he'd never done one where he'd be looking at an image of his own child. It was an incredible moment.

He squeezed the gel onto the machine, flicked the switch and pressed the transducer into Brighde's abdomen. The picture came onto the screen—white stripy muscle fibres, a black womb.

Brighde's head remained turned away from him although he'd angled the screen so she couldn't have seen even if she wanted to. He moved the ultrasound around as he searched for the baby.

There! He felt a goofy smile spread across his face. That was his child. His trained eye took in the details. At twelve weeks the shape of a little person was easily identifiable. The foetus was about two inches long and he could see the head and body as well as four limbs. It looked perfect.

He moved the head of the ultrasound lower, trying to see if he could change the angle and see the baby in profile. He lost the picture and had to search again. The baby had changed position. Flipping itself around to face the opposite direction. Or had it?

He frowned and moved the transducer head higher again. It took him a moment to figure out what he was seeing.

Brighde could feel Xavier moving the ultrasound over her belly. He was stopping and starting as if he was having trouble getting a clear view. Or looking for something. She started to worry. She'd seen hundreds of ultrasounds. She knew the routine and he seemed to be having trouble making sense of things. Was he having trouble getting a good view? Was something the matter? She was getting nervous.

She turned her head to look at him. 'What is it? What's wrong?'

'Nothing.'

She still couldn't see the screen but she could see Xavier's face. He was smiling. He didn't look worried.

'What is it?' she asked. 'What are you looking at?'

He was looking at her now and she could see tears in his eyes.

Brighde's heart was in her throat. Why was he crying? What was wrong with her baby? 'Tell me,' she insisted. 'What's the matter?'

Xavier shook his head but the wide grin remained. 'It's twins,' he said.

'*Twins?* Are you sure?'

'Absolutely. I can see two sacs and two heartbeats.'

'I want to see,' Brighde said. She couldn't resist looking now. She'd been hoping that the ultrasound would show nothing, that it would tell her the pregnancy test had been a false positive. She'd known that was a long shot—she'd done three pregnancy tests now and all three had returned a positive result—but she had still held on to that hope. But now that the ultrasound had confirmed the pregnancy she had to see for herself.

'You do?'

She nodded and Xavier turned the screen to face her. The screen was black. He moved the transducer head around, pressing on her stomach.

'There. Twin A.'

Brighde caught her breath. She was tiny and perfect.

Xavier pressed a couple of buttons and Brighde could hear the printer spitting out a picture. She wanted to ask him for one for her as well but she couldn't bring herself to ask the question. If she wasn't going to keep the baby did she really want a reminder of her decision?

Xavier was moving the transducer head again and the image disappeared briefly before another one took its place.

'There's Twin B.'

A carbon copy of the first appeared on the screen.

She could hear Xavier clicking buttons again as the printer whirred in the background but she couldn't take her eyes from the screen. She could see the little flicker of a tiny heart beating.

'Can I hear the heartbeats?' she asked.

Xavier turned on the speakers and the thump-thump of two little hearts echoed in the room. It was the most beautiful sound she'd ever heard.

She blinked back tears.

She was pregnant with twins.

'They look perfect,' Xavier said.

She nodded. They did. But she knew looks could be deceiving. The babies might look perfect on the out-side but that was no guarantee. There were no physical signs of Huntington's Disease until much later in life. Who knew what terrible gift she might have passed on to her babies? How was she going to fix this? Now that she'd seen her babies—both of them—the decision to terminate was going to be almost impossible but she was still afraid.

She was afraid to ask the questions. Did she have the gene? Did her babies?

She was scared of the answers and of what the an-swers might mean.

Being in a state of denial was preferable but was it too late for that now? This was *exactly* why she didn't want to know her status. She didn't want to deal with her own mortality or make tough decisions. It was bet-ter not to know. Ignorance was bliss.

She couldn't stay in that state any longer. She knew that.

But what were the chances that she would have es-caped inheriting the mutated gene? Surely either she or

Nick must have it. They couldn't both be lucky enough to escape.

It was better when they'd both been oblivious. If she hadn't escaped she didn't want to be talked out of the termination. But she knew she had until twenty-four weeks. She had some time. Maybe she could hold on a little longer. Pretend everything was normal, live in denial and enjoy being pregnant.

But she worried that the longer she took the harder the decision would become.

Brighde hesitated at the door to the hospital nursery. She needed to collect a baby to take to her mother but through the glass she could see Xavier. He was standing by a crib, holding a newborn, and Brighde was certain it was the one she was coming for.

She'd avoided him for twenty-four hours. Since the ultrasound. They hadn't discussed it. She needed time to work out what she was going to do and she suspected that Xavier hoped the ultrasound would make her change her mind. She hadn't changed it yet but she was wavering. And she couldn't handle any increased pressure, however subtle, from him. She was barely holding things together without throwing additional emotion into the mix.

She took a minute to watch him holding the baby. He hadn't seen her; he was too caught up in the moment. The baby was clutching his finger and looking up at him, no doubt transfixed by his mesmerising eyes. Seemed like he had the same effect on females of all ages. His lips were moving as he held a one-sided conversation with the baby. He cradled the baby like an expert and she could just imagine him with his own child. He looked utterly gorgeous.

God, she wished things were different.

She shook her head as she punched in the access code and pushed open the door. There wasn't really any room in her head for what-ifs.

'What are you doing in here?' she asked him. There was normally no reason for him to be in the nursery and she hadn't seen him there before.

'Just a quick visit to see how my deliveries are faring. I know they're not my responsibility any more but I like to know how they're going and Shadow here was a bit grizzly so I thought I'd see if I could quieten her down.'

'I've come to take her to her mum,' Brighde said.

'Can you ask her what they were thinking, naming her Shadow?' he asked. 'I can't say I've heard that one before.' He smiled and her heart pounded in her chest, beating frantically like it always seemed to whenever he was near.

'It's not the worst name we've heard,' she replied. She'd seen or heard of many more ridiculous names than Shadow. 'And at least people will be able to spell it,' she added. She'd always hated the fact that no one could spell her name.

Xavier bent over and put his lips to her ear. Brighde's skin tingled as he started to whisper. 'I think we should stick to something simple for our children, like Mary and James.'

Brighde hadn't changed her mind about the fate of her pregnancy but she liked the way 'our children' sounded on Xavier's lips, though she wasn't about to admit that to him.

She knew he wanted kids. Could she really deprive him?

As long as the risks were still there, she knew she could and would. She would much rather deprive him than have him suffer the agony of watching his child die before him.

She locked her gaze onto his. 'Xavier, nothing has changed. Not the risk and not my mind. I can't give you what you want.'

She could work with him professionally—at the moment she didn't have a choice—but there could never be anything personal between them. He wanted things she couldn't give him. It would never work.

She reached out and took the baby from his arms, using Shadow as a shield to separate them in distance while she willed herself to stay strong and reasonable. 'I'm sorry, Xavier, but this would never work.'

She needed to leave now. She needed to get away from the pain she could see in his eyes. She hated knowing that she was hurting him. That she was potentially taking away something he cherished, but the pain now would be nothing compared to the pain later if his children had inherited the mutated gene.

She turned around, leaving him standing there empty-handed. She felt as if she was taking his dream away as she left the nursery but she had no other option. He didn't realise how easily his dream could become a nightmare. She was doing this to protect him. To protect them both.

Her way was still the best way.

The only way.

* * *

'Brighde Campbell?'

Brighde glanced at Sarah as the receptionist called her name. Xavier had offered to accompany her to her obstetrics appointment but Brighde didn't want him there. She deliberately hadn't told him when it was. She didn't need someone with a different opinion or agenda to her clouding the issue. She was confused enough already. It was important to her to retain control of the situation but she'd needed some moral support and, besides her brother, Sarah understood what she was going through better than anyone.

She had made an appointment with Julie Stewart. She'd worked with Julie many times and liked her skills and manner. She needed someone calm and unflappable who she hoped would listen to her concerns and help her through this difficult and confusing time.

'Do you want me to come in with you?' Sarah asked.

Brighde shook her head. 'No, I'll be okay. It was the waiting part I was worried about.' Brighde hadn't trusted herself to go through with the appointment, but having Sarah to keep her company had stopped her from fretting or fleeing. The rest she needed to do on her own. The rest was up to her, completely her decision, and she needed to be strong and independent and take responsibility for her decision.

'Brighde, congratulations. Fourteen weeks, I see, from Xavier's referral,' Julie said as she welcomed her into her office. 'You don't want to see him for your antenatal care?'

Brighde shook her head. Xavier had written the referral for her but that was the last thing she was going to ask of him. 'No,' she replied. 'He's done enough already. He's the father.'

'I see. He didn't want to come to the appointment today?'

'I didn't ask him to. He knows about the pregnancy,' Brighde added quickly when she saw Julie's expression. She knew that was the next question. 'I just didn't want him here today.'

'I don't need to ask if you've had the pregnancy confirmed.'

'Xavier did an ultrasound. It's twins. Two placentas so we're not sure if they're identical or not.'

'Twins is exciting but, as you know, that can be a little more complicated. However, the first appointment is routine either way.'

'It's not quite as routine as you might hope. There's some family history I need to talk to you about. A genetic abnormality.'

'What are we talking about here? Cystic fibrosis? Down Syndrome?'

'No.' Brighde shook her head. 'My mum had Huntington's Disease.'

'Your mum?'

Brighde nodded.

'But not you?'

'I don't know,' she admitted. 'I haven't been tested.'

'Do you want to get tested? I would need to refer you to a genetic counsellor.'

'I want to discuss a termination.' Brighde tried to stay strong. And focused. But she could hear the slight waver in her voice as she tried not to think of the two tiny life-forms growing inside her. She hoped Julie didn't pick up on it. Her hand itched to rest on her belly.

A protective gesture and one she resisted. Her body was at war with her mind but she needed to stay resolute.

'Have you discussed this with Xavier?'

'I have. He knows about the Huntington's and he knows my thoughts but, as I understand it, I don't need his permission.'

'That is correct.'

'I don't want to take a chance that either my children or I could develop Huntington's. I've seen what it does. I've lived through it with my mum and I know I couldn't go through it again. I don't plan on letting it take my life if the worst comes to the worst and I don't want to put my family through that, nor do I want to see my family suffer the same fate.'

'Well, the simple answer is yes, I can arrange a termination. We'll need to do an ultrasound scan so I can confirm your dates but we have until twenty-four weeks' gestation. It's better to do these things as early as possible. After that you would need to get a second specialist to support my recommendation. It's a big decision and I want to know that you've considered all options. I'd like you to have an appointment with a psychologist prior to scheduling a termination, if that is what you decide on. I insist on that for all my patients. You have some time so I'd like you to think about it and call me after you've seen the psychologist to schedule a time, if that's still what you want to do. But if you change your mind and want me to organise a referral to the genetic counsellor that's fine too. The other alternative is testing the foetuses. I can do an amniocentesis if you choose.'

'No. I don't want that. If one of the babies tests positive then I'll know my prognosis too.'

'Fair enough,' Julie replied as she handed her a card with the psychologist's details on it. 'Call me or schedule another appointment once you've seen the psychologist, okay?'

Brighde took the card as she agreed with Julie's conditions. She needed to get out of there. She needed to think.

'How did it go?' Sarah asked when Brighde reappeared.

'I'm not sure.'

She waited until they had left the rooms. This was not a conversation she wanted to have within earshot of any other mothers or pregnant women.

'Julie will perform the termination if I want her to but she insists on an appointment with a psychologist first.'

'That makes sense.'

'Am I doing the right thing? What if the babies are perfectly fine?'

'Only you can make that decision, Brighde.'

'I spoke to Nick and Imogen about testing the other day.'

'Are you thinking about it too?'

'I still don't know but the fact that I even want to talk about it worries me. I'm second-guessing myself now. I was always so sure, so convinced that I would never have children and everything has changed overnight. Nick and I spent so many years being adamant that we wouldn't get tested. I understand why Nick changed his mind but I wanted to know what they would have done if he'd tested positive. I wanted to know if Nick would still marry Imogen, knowing what we went through with Mum. Whether he would have been prepared to put Immy through that.'

'And what did he say?'

'He said no. Which was what we always thought, and that's effectively where I stand too, but Imogen said yes. She said they would still get married but they would have done pre-implantation genetic testing done on any embryos to make sure they didn't inherit the mutation. I can see her point of view but I don't have that option. I'm already pregnant.'

'But you could test the babies. An amnio would tell you what you need to know, right?'

'Yes. But it might also tell me my fate, one way or the other, and I'm not sure if I'm ready to know that.'

'Brighde, if I'm honest, this is about more than just you now. I understood your reasons for not getting tested but this isn't just about you any more. I know you're battling with this decision and you need to ask yourself why. I know you're scared but I also know you want these babies. You have to find out what you're dealing with. You need some answers so you can make decisions with a clear conscience. I know it's hard but we will support you, Nick, Imogen and me.'

She noticed that Sarah hadn't mentioned Xavier. Did she presume he wouldn't support her decision?

But Sarah was right. She couldn't in good conscience go through with a termination without all the facts. She put the psychologist's business card in her pocket. She would save that number for later. She had another decision to make first. Who should she test? Herself or her babies?

Brighde switched her phone on as handover finished and her shift officially ended and saw two missed calls from the same number. The number wasn't programmed into her phone but she recognised it instantly. It was the genetic counsellor's number.

It had been three weeks since she'd called her obstetrician and asked for a referral to the genetic counsellor and two weeks since she'd had blood taken for the test. The counsellor had promised to get the results rushed through. The results must be in. This was it.

She saw Xavier walking along the corridor and felt the blood rush from her head. She wasn't ready for this.

She was vaguely aware of darkness swirling at the edges of her vision and she could feel the floor rising up to meet her as the room started to spin. She reached for the desk, trying to steady the room, to steady herself, but her hand found only thin air.

'Brighde!' She heard Xavier's voice. He sounded miles away.

'Brighde?'

She opened her eyes to find herself in Xavier's arms, pressed against his chest, as he carried her along the corridor.

How did she get there? 'What happened? What are you doing?'

'You fainted.'

'Fainted?' She wasn't a fainter. 'Where are we going?' she asked as he pushed open a door to an examination room.

'To check you out,' he said as he laid her on the bed and reached for the blood pressure cuff. He wrapped it around her arm and she watched his long fingers fix it in place.

She wanted to sit up. She felt perfectly fine but something must have happened. Something must have triggered the fainting spell. She lay still and tried to re-member what had happened. The counsellor!

The blood pressure machine beeped and the moni-tor showed one-ten over seventy. 'That's a little low.'

'It's normal for me,' she told him.

'Is fainting normal too?'

'No.'

'Then we should find out what caused it.'

'I know what caused it,' she said as she patted her pocket. 'Where's my phone?'

'Here.' He pulled it from the pocket of his trousers and handed it to her. 'What's so important?'

Brighde's hand shook as she took her phone from him. 'I saw a genetic counsellor a couple of weeks ago. I had blood tests done.' She swiped the screen as she spoke; she couldn't bring herself to look at him.

'Why didn't you tell me?' She could hear the hurt and confusion in his voice. The one thing he'd been asking her to do and she'd done it behind his back.

'I didn't tell anyone,' she explained. 'I thought it would make the wait worse if other people were also expecting news.' And she didn't think she was strong enough to handle the weight of expectation. If no one else knew, she could pretend for a little longer. And she didn't want to answer questions until she had the results. 'I didn't want to make any promises I couldn't keep. I just got a message on my phone. The test re-sults must be back.'

'What did the message say?'

'I don't know. I haven't listened to it yet. That's what I was doing when I fainted.' She hit voicemail and held the phone to her ear.

'Do you want me to wait outside?'

She shook her head. She thought she might chicken out if left on her own. Xavier's presence was the catalyst she needed to listen to the message. His calm demeanour and physical size gave her a sense of strength she didn't have if left to her own devices.

'He wants me to go in to his office,' she said as she ended the call. 'He's there until six o'clock today.'

'Is that all he said?'

She nodded, knowing what Xavier was asking. 'He won't open the results until I'm there.'

'Where is his office?'

'South Melbourne.'

'I suppose you want to catch the tram,' Xavier said but his tone was teasing and there was warmth in his dark brown eyes. 'Would you like me to drive you?'

'I don't know if I'm going to go yet. I'm not sure I'm ready to hear what he has to say.'

'Brighde, I know this must be daunting for you. Just making the decision to get tested must have been difficult and I understand if you need more time but you don't have to go alone. I imagine the suggestion was made to bring someone with you?' He waited while she nodded. 'I can do that for you. No pressure. Just a friendly face. Someone to hold your hand.'

She didn't want to go on her own. She knew she wouldn't cope. She could ask Sarah to go with her but she wanted Xavier. She felt safe with him. She wanted to be back in his arms. She wished she could stay there for ever and she wished she could make everything else go away. She wished she could be normal. They might not have a future together but she needed him with her just for now.

And besides, if Xavier heard the results it might be

easier to persuade him that she was right. She felt bad that she couldn't give him what he wanted but maybe letting him accompany her would make up for that somehow.

Xavier noted that Brighde introduced him to the counsellor only as a friend, not as the father of her twins. It seemed she was determined to keep him at arm's length. He supposed he should be thankful that she'd allowed him to accompany her for this meeting even if he obviously still wasn't going to be asked for his opinion. He wondered what it would take to get her to let him into her life properly. He was determined to be a part of it; she had got him thinking about the future, imagining a life with his children and with her. Very definitely with her. She was stubborn but fragile, independent but wounded and he wanted to take care of her. He wanted to give her peace and security, even though he knew that might be out of his control. She brought out all his protective instincts and he wanted her to feel protected and cherished. But he knew he had some work to do if he was going to convince her that he should be part of her life. She was so set on shutting him out.

'How much has Brighde explained to you about testing?' Tuan asked after the introductions had been made.

'Not a lot,' Xavier replied. Although the honest answer would have been 'nothing'. If he'd known Brighde was being tested he would have done his research. He hated being unprepared. He'd done a bit of background reading on the disease early on, trying to get inside Brighde's head, trying to understand her thought processes, but he hadn't spent a lot of time on the science of the testing procedure. 'I am an obstetrician so I'll understand the facts, but Huntington's Disease is not something I've had first-hand experience with.'

'All right then. I'll just explain what we are looking for in the testing process. Huntington's Disease is caused by a mutation in the HTT gene which is instrumental in making the Huntingtin protein. The faulty gene produces an oversized version of the protein which builds up in the brain and attacks the neurons, causing the symptoms we see in Huntington's Disease. We still don't know why the faulty gene only attacks the nerves in the brain but that's what happens. In order to determine whether an individual is likely to develop Huntington's Disease we need to count the number of CAG trinucleotide repeats. Normally a CAG segment is repeated between ten and thirty-five times within the Huntingtin gene. In people who are going to develop Huntington's Disease the number of repeats will be anything in the range of forty to more than one hundred and twenty. Thirty-six to thirty-nine repeats is considered the grey area where individuals *may* develop the disease.'

Tuan's desk was clear except for a single white envelope. He reached for the envelope and picked it up, looking at Brighde. 'These are your test results. Do you have any questions before we open it?'

'We're hoping for a number less than thirty-six?' she checked. She knew that her brother's tests had shown ten repeats and that had been good news but she had never bothered to investigate further than that. She was still of the opinion that ignorance was bliss.

'For you to test negative, that's right. Have you thought about what you will do if the test is positive?'

Brighde nodded. 'If I have Huntington's Disease I will terminate the pregnancy.'

'You understand that even if you test positive the babies could still be fine? They may both have inherited the healthy gene.'

Brighde understood exactly what Tuan was telling her. Which was that if she tested positive but didn't test the babies she wouldn't know their fate for certain; therefore, she could be terminating perfectly healthy foetuses. She got that, but this wasn't something she was prepared to negotiate. Huntington's was a genetically dominant disease. If Brighde tested positive the chances of both babies escaping the mutation was not impossible but it was improbable. 'Yes. But I watched my mother die and it was the worst thing imaginable. If I have the disease I don't want to put my own children through that. And I won't.'

'All right,' Tuan continued. 'It's not my job to tell you what to do; it's my job to give you the facts. Are you ready?'

Brighde looked at Xavier. She was terrified but it was time to find out.

He squeezed her hand and she looked back at Tuan and nodded. He slit open the envelope and pulled out a single piece of paper.

The piece of paper that would determine her future and possibly that of her unborn children too. It didn't look important enough to Brighde.

She held her breath.

'You have twenty-nine repeats.'

Brighde breathed a sigh of relief. Tears came to her eyes. She couldn't believe it. 'I'm going to be okay?' She and Nick had *both* had a win in the genetic lottery? She was safe. She'd dodged a bullet. It was hard to comprehend; she'd been so certain her test would be positive. She hadn't dared let herself believe her result could be anything else. How could they both be so lucky?

Her hands and her knees were shaking. Adrenalin coursed through her. Fear was replaced with relief, leaving her light-headed. She took a deep breath. 'So I won't develop HD?'

'That's right.' Brighde felt like bursting into tears of relief. '*You* won't develop HD…'

She could hear a *but* in Tuan's voice. Why was there a *but*? She'd tested negative. She was going to be okay. She frowned. 'Is there more?' she questioned him. 'What aren't you telling me?'

'Fewer than thirty-six repeats means that you won't develop the disease but there's a range termed the unstable range.'

'Which is what?' Her voice shook. Fear was back.

'Between twenty-seven and thirty-five repeats.'

'And I'm in there? The unstable range?'

Tuan nodded.

'And what does that mean?' Xavier asked.

'It means things can be a little ambiguous.'

Brighde didn't like the sound of that at all. What did Tuan know that she didn't? She could feel herself starting to panic. Xavier was still holding her hand and she was squeezing his fingers so hard she feared she would cut off his circulation but he wasn't flinching.

'It means you won't develop HD,' Tuan continued. Brighde watched his lips carefully. He sounded as though he was speaking underwater; she knew it was because her brain was fuzzy, and she had to concentrate hard to make sense of what he was telling her. 'But there's a possibility that the CAG gene could expand when passed from a parent to a child.'

Her fainting spell had passed but she now thought she might vomit as Tuan's explanation sunk in. 'Are you telling me I won't develop HD but my children might?'

CHAPTER SEVEN

BRIGHDE STARED AT TUAN. 'So, I'm safe but the babies might not be? I might still have passed on a faulty gene?'

'It's more likely that the gene could continue to expand when the gene is passed through the father's side. We're not certain about the mother.'

'But you don't know for sure?'

Brighde fought back tears. The test results hadn't helped at all. They had made things worse, not better, and given her more questions than answers.

Tuan was shaking his head. 'No. I'm sorry.'

Xavier started to speak but Brighde held up her hand. 'Stop.' She couldn't look at him. She was seconds away from bursting into tears, from losing her composure completely and she knew that if she looked at Xavier and saw compassion or concern in his eyes she wouldn't be able to maintain her composure. She needed to think. She couldn't afford to go to pieces. 'I need a moment.'

She wasn't coping. Not at all. This was even worse than she'd imagined. She'd been prepared to hear that she had the mutation but to learn that she would be okay but she might have condemned her unborn babies was devastating. She'd chosen not to test the babies since it might have given her an insight into her own future anyway. If one of the babies had tested positive it would have confirmed that she carried the gene. But to find out she might have passed on the gene *without* testing positive herself—that she hadn't expected and she wasn't sure how to deal with it.

She took a deep breath and kept her eyes fixed on Tuan. 'What do I do now?' In her mind, it was still a question of her options. The decisions were still all hers. This was her family's legacy; Xavier was just a bystander.

'That's up to you,' Tuan replied. 'You can test the foetuses or terminate the pregnancy. The only way to know for sure is to have an amniocentesis but the choice is yours. You've got time. You have got until twenty-four weeks before a termination gets complicated but you need to make sure you're okay with whatever decision you make.' Tuan stood up from behind his desk. 'You'll need some time to process this. You're welcome to stay in here for as long as you need and if you want any more information or would like to discuss anything further, today or in the future, I'm available. I really am sorry.'

He left them alone. Brighde knew she was in shock. Xavier was silent too; she supposed the shock was just as great for him. Worse, maybe. She'd always expected that she would have the repeat so she should have anticipated bad news. But to hear what she thought was good news and then to have it tainted by premonitions of disaster was almost more than she could bear.

'Are you okay?' he asked.

'No. I'm definitely not okay.'

'You didn't know the significance in the different numbers of repeats?'

'No. I knew nothing about unstable ranges or grey areas.' She'd never researched testing as she'd never intended to get tested. She'd preferred to live in a state of denial.

What had she done to her babies?

Her hand was resting on her stomach. An unconscious, protective gesture she'd found herself making more and more often.

She dropped her head, imagining for a moment that she'd be able to see her babies. What would she tell them?

I'm so sorry. I never meant to hurt you.

I never meant to have you.

But now that she was pregnant she knew she couldn't terminate the pregnancy without knowing what hand she'd dealt them.

Everything had changed yet again. If the twins had escaped the mutation then everything was good. She would be around to see her children grow up. But if they hadn't she would have to go ahead with a termination. She couldn't stand the thought of passing on the faulty gene. She couldn't do that to her own children.

She felt Xavier's fingers under her chin. He lifted her head and she could see the worry in his dark eyes. Was it her worry reflecting back at her or was he just as concerned?

His thumb brushed across her cheek and she could feel dampness on her skin. She hadn't been aware that she was crying but now she could feel the tears gathering on her bottom lashes and spilling over onto her cheeks.

'I'll take you home,' Xavier said.

She nodded mutely. She just wanted to curl up in a

ball in her bed in the darkness and wait for this all to go away. She hadn't prepared herself for this news at all and it was overwhelming. She didn't know if she was strong enough to cope with the decisions that she still faced.

Xavier's phone rang just as he pulled up in front of her house. He'd been silent on the drive home and Brighde was grateful. She didn't feel like talking. She didn't think she was capable of holding a conversation. Her brain wasn't holding any thoughts at all. It kept jumping from one thought to another. She was completely unsettled.

She climbed out of the car and walked up the path. Xavier followed her up the path, talking on his phone.

'Is Sarah home?' he asked as she unlocked the front door.

'No. She's working a late. Why?'

'That was the hospital. One of my patients is in labour. I should go but if you like I can call someone to cover me so I can stay with you.'

'No. I'm fine,' she lied. She wasn't fine but she didn't know if she wanted company. She just wanted to be left alone with the consequences of her actions and her grief.

She wanted everything to go back to normal.

'Is there someone else who can come and stay with you? I don't think you should be alone. What about your brother?'

Brighde shook her head. 'No. I'm okay.' She still hadn't told Nick she was pregnant and she wasn't about to tell him today. Definitely not today. 'It's all right. Go.'

Brighde had a restless night's sleep. She dreamt in vivid Technicolor. Disturbing dreams. She finally fell asleep again as Saturday dawned, only to be woken later by a knock on the front door. She waited to see if Sarah would answer before remembering that she'd been doing a late/early and would already be back at work.

She stumbled out of bed and pulled her curtains back at the corner, craning her head to see who was disturbing her.

Xavier.

'What are you doing here?' she asked as she opened the door. Was he checking on her or the babies? Worried about her or only about them?

'I came to see how you are. Whether there's anything you need.'

She shook her head as she stepped aside to let him in. She couldn't stand in the doorway dressed in nothing but an old T-shirt. 'I'm fine.'

The expression on Xavier's face told her he didn't believe her but he didn't argue.

'In that case I have a suggestion.'

'What is it?'

'How would you like to get away for the weekend?'

'Why?'

'Why not? I know Sarah is working this weekend. Which means you'll be home alone. I don't want you staring at the walls and worrying.'

'Maybe I want to be alone,' she grumbled.

'If you won't listen to me, would you listen to my sister? I've learnt that in order to live a stress-free life it's wise to listen to her. She suggested that a change of scenery might be good therapy. Please, won't you give it a shot? Twenty-four hours, that's all I'm asking for.'

What else had she planned for the next twenty-four

hours? Nothing at all. He was right. She would just sit and fret. She sighed. 'What do I need?'

Xavier grinned and her spirits lifted instantly. She could think of worse ways to spend the next day than in his company. 'Walking shoes, a warm coat. Something a little smart for dinner and a smile.'

'Where are we going?'

'That's a surprise.'

'Brighde? We're here.'

Xavier's voice roused her from sleep. She hadn't been able to keep her eyes open once they'd hit the highway out of Melbourne; the steady thrum of the car engine had lulled her to sleep and she still had no idea where Xavier had taken her.

'Welcome to Daylesford.'

'Spa country?'

Daylesford was famous for its mineral springs, spa retreats, restaurants and natural beauty and it was putting on a magnificent display today, Brighde thought as Xavier drove through the picturesque country town. She'd heard about the area but never visited. It looked spectacular. The myriad trees showed off their autumn colours. Gold, fiery red, burnt orange, a touch of green against a crisp, clean blue sky. It was one of those beautiful Victorian days when the weather was being kind and anything seemed possible.

Xavier turned off the road into their accommodation that sat on the edge of the lake. Brighde had heard about this five-star restaurant and hotel. 'Are we staying here?'

'As long as you've got no objections,' Xavier said

as he switched off the engine. He smiled at her and Brighde's stomach flipped.

He jumped out of the car while Brighde sat for a moment to gather her thoughts. This wasn't a romantic couple's weekend away; this was Xavier's version of R&R. He'd promised to give her time and space to rest and recover but she couldn't afford to let her guard down. She needed to keep her wits about her and remember what was at stake. She still had some decisions to make. Big decisions. And she couldn't get too comfortable with Xavier as it was more than likely that her decisions would destroy any chance they might have had at any sort of relationship.

'Are you hungry?' Xavier opened Brighde's door and reached for her hand. She took his hand without thinking; it was warm and large and reassuring and his touch sent her stomach tumbling again.

She wasn't hungry or tired. She was restless. She had to move. Had to get busy. Had to get her mind off Xavier and his smile, his come-to-bed eyes and his warm hands and how he made her feel. Maybe it was the pregnancy hormones but she was feeling very much like ripping his clothes off.

'Not really.' She was dying to see their room—she wondered if he'd booked one or two—but she could see the lake from the car park and it looked so peaceful and serene and it called to her. 'After we check in I might go for a walk.'

Xavier checked them in—just the one room, she noted—and they followed the porter.

The door swung open to reveal a light-filled space with views of the lake through expansive windows set either side of a pair of French windows. The king-size bed had a plush bedhead upholstered in a black and white fabric, the bathroom was as big as her kitchen with a bath the size of her dining table and a couch was positioned in front of the window to catch the view but also angled towards a gas fire. The black and white theme continued in the soft furnishings of the room and into the bathroom with hints of gold. Brighde had never seen anything as luxurious as this suite.

She spun around slowly, taking it all in. 'Wow! This is gorgeous.'

'You like it?' Xavier asked as he tipped the porter.

'It's amazing.'

'I didn't intend to book just one room—it was all they had left at short notice but I thought you could have the bed and I'll take the couch.'

Brighde looked at the couch. It looked comfortable but not nearly long enough to accommodate Xavier's six-feet, two-inch frame. She would offer him the bed but she'd leave that discussion for later; she knew he wouldn't accept now. 'Are you sure?'

'Positive. This weekend is all about giving you a chance to recharge. I want you to have a good night's sleep.'

Sleep was the last thing on Brighde's mind. The first thing wasn't wise though so she went for option two.

'I think I'll go for a walk around the lake while the weather holds,' she said. The Victorian weather was notoriously fickle and locals learnt to take advantage of clear skies whenever possible. The weather could change in an instant. 'Would you like to come?'

They were able to step out through the French windows onto a small deck from where stairs led down onto the lakeside path. The gardens were planted with Australian natives and Brighde could hear frogs croaking in the reeds and a kookaburra laughing in the distance. She wasn't watching where she was walking, mesmerised by her surroundings, and she missed the bottom step, stumbling slightly. Xavier grabbed her hand, preventing her from falling, and he didn't let go even as she recovered her feet. Brighde wondered if she should pull her hand away but it felt so good she decided not to make a fuss. Her body was flooded with pregnancy hormones, which made it difficult to think straight. Her brain felt like complete mush at times while at other times she was so sexually charged she couldn't think about anything else. But it was strange how those times only occurred whenever Xavier was near.

They walked in silence and Brighde savoured the peace and the sensation of having her hand in Xavier's. Her situation could be so perfect if it wasn't built on mistakes and haunted by her fears.

'Was this really your sister's idea?'

She was curious to know what Xavier had told her family about her. She liked the idea that they knew about her. It meant she existed in his life.

Did she want that?

She did but she doubted she'd get what she wanted. That would be too much to ask for and she'd learned not to ask for, or expect, too much.

For the moment, it was enough to know that she was free of the possibility of inheriting HD. That was good news and she needed to remember to cherish that outcome. Could she dare to hope that both her babies had also been spared? If they hadn't then she and Xavier didn't stand a chance.

'She suggested the change of scenery. I chose the location.'

'You've done well,' Brighde said as she watched a pair of black swans glide serenely past them on the lake. 'Which sister was it?'

'Mary. She's the eldest and the bossiest. It's good to let her get her way occasionally and I think she got it right today.'

'What about the others?' Brighde was enjoying the chance to talk about someone else's family for a change. Hearing about his life meant she didn't have to think about hers.

'Eve is number two. She's not quite as serious as Mary. A bit more of a free spirit. She's pregnant with her third child; Mary has four. Then, Angie and Gabby, the twins, are younger than me.'

'You have twin sisters?' Brighde was surprised that he hadn't mentioned that before.

He nodded.

'Why haven't you told me about them?'

'Would it make any difference?'

'I guess not.' It was irrelevant to her situation, she supposed, but it felt like another connection to his family and she liked that idea. 'But what was it like having twins in the family?'

'Awful,' he said but he was grinning. He really was irresistible when he smiled. 'I was four when they were born and they made my life hell.'

'Did they really?'

'Of course. But I adore them. Now. But I imagine they were hard work to begin with. I'm sure my mum would happily pass on any words of advice about raising twins if you're interested.'

Brighde wasn't sure she was ready to go there. Either to meet his mum or to talk about raising twins. That would be admitting that she was going ahead with the pregnancy.

When she didn't reply he continued. 'I just remember a lot of bottles and nappies and crying. I can't say I'm an expert on raising kids but I'm getting plenty of practice with my sisters' tribes.'

'You've got eight nieces and nephews, you said?'

'Yep, plus one on the way and a couple of godchildren as well.'

'That sounds busy,' she said as she wrapped her scarf around her neck a little more tightly. They had reached the far side of the lake and the wind was blowing more steadily on this side and there was a bit of a chill in the autumn air.

'It is,' he said as they approached a picturesque red-roofed weatherboard kiosk. 'Shall I get us both something hot to drink?' he asked, leading her onto the deck of the kiosk that extended out over the lake. 'Would you like to sit inside or out?'

A row of brightly coloured paddleboats was tied to the bank and several had been rented and were drifting on the water. Despite the wind, the views were pretty. 'Outside, I think.'

Xavier found a table and chairs on the deck that was partly sheltered from the elements. Brighde sat and thought about his large family as she waited for him to return with their drinks. His family sounded close and she tried to imagine her babies with a heap of cousins. She and Nick only had each other. Their parents had both been only children but her babies would have cousins on both sides *and* of similar age. She wondered what her family would think about this whole situation. What would her mum have thought of Xavier? What she would have said if she'd known Nick and Brighde were both going to give her grandchildren.

Xavier put Brighde's hot chocolate on the table but she didn't acknowledge his return. She was gazing across the lake, lost in her thoughts. But she didn't look relaxed. She looked like she had the weight of the world on her shoulders. He'd brought her here hoping to give her a chance to relax, rest and replenish her reserves. He knew she wouldn't be able to make sensible decisions if she was exhausted and emotional. He knew she hadn't been sleeping well. Sarah had mentioned it but he could see it in her face. She'd lost weight and had dark circles under her eyes. Her energy seemed to have been extinguished and she'd lost some of her spark. Seeing her like this made him feel terrible. He'd done this to her. He'd put her in this position.

But there was some good news in all of this. She had tested negative. She was going to be okay.

That should be one less concern for her but he knew she was still stressed about what she might have inflicted on their children. He'd hoped that bringing her to Daylesford would help to get her mind off that. It had to be better than leaving her home alone, with only her thoughts for company. He didn't want to put any pressure on her but he'd hoped a change of environment might allow her to forget her worries and fears. Even a temporary reprieve had to be a good thing, but it didn't look as though his plan was working.

'Is everything okay?'

She jumped in her chair. 'Sorry, what did you say?'

'I asked if you were okay.'

'Yes, I'm fine.'

'If you want to talk I'm a good listener. My sisters have taught me that as well. Whether by accident or design, I'm not sure, but they talked so much it was always hard to get a word in so I learnt to listen.'

He was rewarded with a smile. Her smile was fantastic. Wide and sincere. Although this one didn't quite reach her eyes. What was on her mind?

'I was just thinking about my mum. Wondering what she would think of my situation. And what she would do.'

'What do you think she would do?'

'I don't know. I guess her situation was completely different to mine. Things have changed so much since I was born. Not in terms of any treatment for HD but in terms of the genetic testing. Almost all the worthwhile discoveries about the disease and all the useful advances that have been made have happened since I was born, but none of it is going to help me.'

He begged to differ. The tests that were available today gave them a lot more information than ever before. Information that could be used to make informed decisions. And he was all for that. He still couldn't understand how testing could be a bad idea. Or an idea that wasn't on the table for consideration. But he'd promised that he wouldn't pressure her. This weekend was all about peace.

'The Huntingtin gene wasn't identified until 1983 and genetic testing wasn't an option until 1994, five years after I was born, so by the time Mum could have learned that she was going to develop HD Nick and I were already born. And pre-implantation testing has only been possible since 2003 so Mum didn't have any of the options that are available today, but I still wonder what she would have done if she'd had access to testing. Would she have taken a chance and had a family?'

'You never asked her?'

Brighde shook her head. 'No. We never really spoke about the future. We were too busy trying to survive in the present. I wish I had though—not that it would have changed anything, really. Her only option would have been not to have kids. But it's too late to know now and it's a regret I'll have to live with. I guess I just wonder what advice she'd have had for me.'

'Have you spoken to your brother?'

'No,' she said as she picked up her hot chocolate.

'Why not?' He was curious to know why she hadn't said anything to her family.

'We've had enough bad news in our life. He's happy now. He's getting married and they're expecting their first child. I don't want to take the gloss off their news with my troubles.'

Xavier finished his drink and checked his watch. 'I made a massage appointment for you,' he said. 'I wasn't sure if you'd like it but there weren't many spots available so I took the liberty. If you'd like it we'd better head back.'

'That sounds fabulous—thank you.' She drained her hot chocolate, leaving a dusting of chocolate powder on her top lip.

He reached across the table and wiped the chocolate from her lip with his thumb. Brighde's blue-grey eyes widened and her pupils dilated and he fought the urge to lean across the table and kiss her soundly.

He wished things were different. Less complicated. He was still prepared to try to work things out but so many of the decisions were Brighde's alone to make. He really didn't have much influence over how things were going to turn out. There was nothing much he could do except to try to show her that he was there to support her and hope for the best. He knew there were no guarantees in life but he didn't doubt that, if Brighde was willing to give him a go, they could have a future together. But it was all up to her.

He stood and held her chair for her and kept her company as they walked back around the lake.

Brighde stretched out on the couch in front of the fire. Housekeeping had been to their room while they were at dinner and had turned down the bed and turned on the fire. The room was lit by lamps and by firelight, casting a warm glow.

Xavier picked up a chocolate that had been left on the pillow by Housekeeping.

'After-dinner chocolate?' he offered.

Brighde groaned. 'I couldn't eat another thing.' Dinner had been divine. Poached pheasant with autumn vegetables, followed by a pear and rhubarb tart. She couldn't remember when she'd had a nicer meal. 'I should go to bed but I don't think I can move.'

'That's my bed, don't forget; you'll have to move at some stage.'

'Come and sit with me.'

Xavier sat on the floor at her feet, leaning his back against the couch. That wasn't what she'd intended.

'That doesn't look very comfortable,' she said as she sat up and shuffled to one side to make some room. 'You can sit up here.'

He sat in the corner of the couch, his long legs stretched out in front of him towards the fire, and pulled Brighde down again so she could lie with her head in his lap. She closed her eyes and breathed out slowly as he stroked her hair.

'Have you had a good day?'

Brighde sighed. 'I've had a great day. Thank you.'

'How are you feeling? Apart from full?'

She felt safe but she wasn't about to share that with him. She wasn't used to revealing her innermost thoughts. 'I'm feeling relieved.'

'About testing negative?'

She rolled onto her back, opened her eyes and looked up at him as she nodded.

'I kind of ignored that yesterday. I was so worried about what still might be that I sort of forgot that Tuan told me I'd be okay. I'd always been so certain that I would test positive so it didn't sink in that the tests were negative. But it's a double-edged sword. On one hand I'm relieved, but if I wasn't pregnant I'd be absolutely ecstatic, not just relieved. But knowing that I still might have inadvertently affected my babies is hard to come to terms with. In a way I think it would have been easier to deal with if I *had* tested positive. But it's ironic, isn't it? If I wasn't pregnant I never would have got tested and I wouldn't have this sense of relief. I've got one answer from the test results but more questions.'

'About the babies?'

'Yes.'

'I know I said I would just listen,' he told her. 'That

all decisions were yours, but from a purely medical point of view the sooner you make decisions the better. Particularly regarding a termination.'

'You do agree that a termination is okay in certain cases?' she asked. 'I've been thinking about the ramifications a lot, particularly since delivering the baby with Down Syndrome. There's a difference between that and HD. That child will grow up with the syndrome; they won't know any different, their life will be constant. A child who has the mutated HTT gene will lead a completely normal life for thirty or forty years and that means that when the symptoms start it will be a massive blow. They will lose all normality. That's what worries me. That seems cruel. It *is* cruel. I lived through it with my mother and I can't do it again. I need to know how you feel about that.'

She'd been avoiding asking him direct questions. She'd been making assumptions about what he would say but maybe he had changed his mind. She hadn't asked. But now she was struggling with the decision-making. She didn't want him to feel excluded but she also didn't want to make all the decisions. He'd shown her his support and she felt she needed to show him some consideration.

'I need to know for certain one way or another before I would be happy with a termination,' he replied. 'The babies might be fine and then we're worrying for no good reason. Will you have an amnio to find out?'

She'd been thinking about this. A lot. Her babies might be fine and part of her would love her own happily ever after—a husband, children, a family of her own—but she was still scared. When Xavier was around it was easy to forget all the bad things that could happen and she found herself thinking ahead to the future, daydreaming about falling in love and living a long and happy life. But if she was ever going to get a chance at that she needed to make some decisions and she knew she didn't really have a choice. It wasn't the testing she had to consider now—she knew that was inevitable—it was what would happen next. Whether Xavier would agree with her decisions once they got the results or whether he'd still want her to continue with the pregnancy.

'Would you agree to a termination if the tests came back positive?' she asked. She had to know. She couldn't go ahead with the tests if he would give her grief over her decisions if the tests *were* positive. Legally she didn't need his consent but she wanted his support. They might not agree on everything but he was entitled to his opinion, although, in this case, she was going to do what she believed was best.

'Can I have some time to think about my answer? It's a big decision and I'm just not sure how I feel about the termination when, regardless of the genetic make-up, our babies will be perfectly healthy well into adulthood.'

'Have you ever seen, with your own eyes, someone with late stage Huntington's? Not read about it or watched videos but actually seen for yourself what it does?' she asked.

He shook his head. 'No, I haven't.'

'Then you have no idea what this disease does to someone. Not just the person who has the disease but the entire family. It destroyed ours.' She sat up on the couch and turned to face him, sitting cross-legged on the cushions. She didn't know how to make him understand the horror of this disease. 'You can spend thirty or forty years of your life being perfectly fine and then, one day, your world starts to crumble. Just little things at first, a slight change in your personality or moods, some forgetfulness—things that you probably won't even notice but your family will. And then depression might be the next thing or your motor functions will deteriorate. You'll start to stumble or have trouble holding your knife and fork. Over the next fifteen or twenty years your body and your brain decay and there's nothing you can do.

'Nick and I watched our mother suffer through this. Our father left us to do that alone. I was nine years old when her symptoms started. We did what we could until we couldn't cope any more. When I was twenty we had to put her into full-time care. She was forty-nine when she died. That is too young. Way too young. And the only reason she lived that long was because of us. I think she would have given up long before if it wasn't for us.

'That is why I didn't want to know if I carried the gene. I've seen what it does and it scares me. It terrifies me. But now I know. And that should be good news but now I'm frightened of what it means for my children. You need to understand what this could mean. I know how much you want children and, believe me, this isn't an easy decision. I would love children too but not if I have passed on a faulty gene.' She shook her head. 'Not Huntington's. It's too awful and I could never forgive myself. You need to understand what it is like.'

'What are you saying?'

'I want you to go and see someone who is suffering with late stage HD and then tell me if you could imagine seeing your own children suffer the same fate.

Once you've done that I will agree to an amnio but *only* if you agree, in writing, that the pregnancy should be terminated if the tests are positive. If we don't get them tested while they are in utero then we have no control over anything and I can't have these babies without knowing their fate. And I can't have these babies if the test is positive either. If we don't get the tests done now then once the children are born they would have to wait until they turn eighteen before they could request testing and then, at this stage, if the test is positive there is *still* nothing that can be done. I want you to see what this disease looks like and I need you to remember that, right now, there is no cure. There is no way to stop the suffering.'

CHAPTER EIGHT

XAVIER STOOD IN the car park. He wasn't sure about this. He had agreed to Brighde's request as he couldn't imagine her terminating the pregnancy without doing an amniocentesis. And if he had to visit the care facility in order to meet her terms then he would.

She hadn't offered to accompany him and he hadn't asked her to. He knew she would refuse. She wouldn't want to see the patients here—he'd learnt that denial was her preferred way of coping—but she had given him the address. He wondered if this was where her mum had spent her last days or months or years. He didn't know. There was so much he didn't know. She didn't volunteer a lot and he was reluctant to ask her. He had no idea where he stood within the framework of her life. Did she trust him? Would she want to confide in him? How did she view him? Did she see him as the enemy? Someone who had gotten her into this position in the first place? Someone who wanted a different outcome from her? Was there a chance she could see him as someone permanent in her life or was she eager to cut him out of her life as quickly as possible? Would seeing him always remind her of this situation she was in? This awkward, unwanted situation? How did she feel about him? How did he feel about her?

There were far too many questions to tackle at the moment. He'd take one step at a time and the first step, before it was too late, was to try to convince Brighde to find out exactly what they were dealing with. To find out exactly what situation they were in. He didn't want to play guessing games and if he needed answers he needed to go inside the building. From the outside it looked harmless enough, ordinary even—a two-storey brick building, surrounded by gum trees. He could hear birds chattering and water flowing.

He was nervous but he couldn't stand outside all day. He headed for the front entrance. A fountain bubbled in front of the building. From the outside everything seemed calm and peaceful. In complete contrast to how he was feeling.

An elderly woman staffed the reception desk. Xavier hadn't really thought of how he was going to explain his visit here but he'd been hoping for a younger staff member. In his experience they were less likely to question his motives once they knew he was a doctor and, if he was honest, a young female employee wouldn't hesitate to let him have his way when it came to work.

'Good morning.' He flashed his best smile, deciding against the full charm offensive. He needed to present himself as a professional. That was the angle he was going to use. He pulled his identification from his wallet, his driver's licence and business card, and slid them onto the desk. 'My name is Dr O'Donnell; I was wondering if there was someone I could speak to regarding Huntington's Disease.'

The woman, who according to her badge was named

Joyce, studied his ID before returning it to him. She looked up. 'What is it you want to know?'

'I'm an obstetrician and I have a patient who is pregnant and the baby has tested positive for Huntington's Disease.' He'd stretched the truth marginally but refused to feel guilty about a slight exaggeration of the facts. They were mostly accurate. 'She is considering a termination and I really don't have much idea about the disease and what she's dealing with. I'd like to get a better understanding of the condition.'

'You need to see Dr Baird,' came the reply, 'but she's not here at the moment. We don't have doctors on site. Would you like me to take your details and pass them on to her?'

Did he? He really wanted to see some of the patients. That was the task Brighde had set him. 'Is there someone else I could talk to while I'm here, one of the nursing staff maybe?'

Joyce frowned. 'I'm not sure,' she said. 'I'd have to check with the manager.'

'If you could, I'd really appreciate it.'

Joyce made a call. 'If you go up to the first floor, to the east wing, Steve, one of our RNs, will meet you there. But you'll need to sign the visitors' book first,' she told him as she handed him a visitor badge.

Xavier did as he was instructed; he signed in and then made his way to the east wing, where Steve was waiting for him.

He was a big burly man in his early thirties. His hair had a buzz cut and he was heavily tattooed but his uniform was neatly ironed, his shoes were polished and his nails clean. He looked like ex-defence force and Xavier wondered what made him work here. His look was unexpected but he must have chosen to work here and if he was here because he wanted to be, not just for the pay cheque, then Xavier had learned from experience that would make him an excellent nurse. It was a vocation, not just a job.

'Dr O'Donnell?'

'Xavier, please.'

'You want some information on HD?'

Xavier nodded and repeated his reason for the visit.

'We are one of the only care facilities in Australia to have a specialised HD unit. We can accommodate twenty sufferers at a time,' Steve told him as they walked along a corridor. 'Most people are cared for at home initially, until it gets too much for the families, either physically or emotionally. The majority of our HD patients need twenty-four-hour care, which becomes virtually impossible in a home environment.' Steve punched a code into an electronic keypad at the end of the corridor and pushed open the door. 'This is our day room.'

Steve stopped just inside the room and his voice was low and quiet as he explained the situation further to Xavier. 'The majority of our patients are late stage and many have lost the power of speech so you won't be able to talk to them. Many sufferers choose not to get to this stage; some choose to find another way out. Huntington's is hard on the sufferer and on the families. There's no cure. No hope. It's a waiting game; the end is just a matter of time.' Steve paused as Xavier looked around the room.

He saw several wheelchair-bound residents. Some were being fed but many had naso-gastric tubes, obviously no longer able to swallow. The room was large and light with pretty views out to the gardens and the gum trees but Xavier knew these patients would never walk out there and might not even remember what it was like to be mobile.

'You're wanting to know more about the impact on a family rather than the symptoms and progress of the disease, correct?' Steve asked. When Xavier nodded Steve added, 'Give me a minute, would you?'

He left Xavier and went to speak to an elderly woman who was spoon-feeding a younger woman. Xavier watched the interaction.

'Merilyn is happy to talk to you,' Steve said when he returned. 'She can give you her perspective if you like. Why don't you grab a coffee and take her outside?' he suggested. 'She could do with a change of scenery. She spends a lot of time with her daughter.'

Xavier bought sandwiches and coffee from the café on the ground floor and followed Merilyn to a wooden bench.

'You want to know what it's like living with Huntington's?' Merilyn asked as she sat down.

Xavier nodded. 'My partner—' he really had no idea how to describe Brighde and he suspected she'd have a fit if she could hear him but she wasn't there; this was all up to him and he was determined to find out everything he needed today; he didn't plan on coming back '—is pregnant. HD runs in her family and she is understandably concerned about the risk. She nursed her mother through the disease but I have no experience with it whatsoever and I'm trying to get an idea of what she went through. Of what we might be facing in the future.'

'You didn't use pre-implantation testing? That's been an option for years now.'

'We didn't plan the pregnancy,' Xavier admitted.

He could see the look of surprise on Merilyn's face but it was only there briefly before her expression went blank. She obviously had an opinion about their recklessness that she had decided to keep to herself.

'Are you going to test now? Before the baby is born?' she asked.

Xavier was appreciative of the fact that Merilyn had agreed to talk to him and he wanted to be honest even though he had no idea how she might interpret his candidness. 'I want to do the test but my partner wants to terminate. I'm not sure that I agree with her and that's why I'm here—to try to see things from her point of view.'

'Well, I can't speak for her but I can speak on behalf of the families of sufferers. I love my daughter and I would never wish that she hadn't been born but I *do* wish that she hadn't been born with HD. I wish that every day. It is a horrible disease.'

'But you chose to have a family.'

'The disease runs in my husband's family. Elise is forty-nine now and things were different fifty years ago. The disease was never talked about, never discussed, in his family and it was like that in many families who suffered the same fate. Because of the shortened life expectancy of sufferers, most die somewhere between their forties to sixties; many of us had already had children before we learned that there was a family history. It was brushed under the carpet and not spoken of, certainly never by its correct name, and a lot of sufferers were diagnosed with other afflictions—dementia, alcoholism and the like. Not a lot was known about HD when Norm and I got married—the gene was only identified in 1986—and even less could be done. Testing wasn't available when I had my children and pre-implantation testing wasn't available until Elise was nearly thirty-four. By then my husband had died from the disease. Elise and her sister had watched their father succumb to the disease.' She paused before asking, 'Are you sure you want to hear all this?'

Xavier nodded. 'As long as you don't mind talking about it.'

'My husband became aggressive and mean,' Merilyn continued. 'We had to keep reminding ourselves that this was a result of the disease, that he couldn't control it, but every day was a struggle to keep our family to-gether. Elise was profoundly affected by the changes in her father and she decided early on that she wouldn't have children. She became a kindergarten teacher and those kids became her surrogate children.'

Brighde's choice of career sprang to Xavier's mind. She'd told him she'd never planned to have children, that she got her fill of babies at work. Had she chosen her career because of her family history?

Was he being unfair? Was he putting undue pressure on her? He hoped that if the babies were okay that she would be happy. But maybe she still wouldn't be. How did she really feel? She had told him she would love children of her own providing she hadn't passed on the gene but he had no idea if that was true. Maybe she re-ally didn't want children, no matter what, and was using HD as an excuse. He really wasn't sure of the answers.

'I have two daughters and they both chose to get

tested as soon as that was an option. Sometimes I wish they hadn't.'

'Why is that?'

'Carmel tested negative, Elise obviously didn't and that put a terrible strain on their relationship. They'd always been close until then. After the diagnosis, Elise got depression—it's a very common outcome—and that changed her long before her symptoms became apparent. Sometimes I think the diagnosis was the beginning of the end. She had no symptoms yet but everything changed from that day.'

Again, Xavier was able to see the similarities between Merilyn's family and Brighde's. Brighde and her brother had made a pact not to get tested for HD but what effect had Nick's change of mind had on Brighde? Would she be even more worried now, not only about her test results, but how that might affect her relationship with her brother? There were so many things to consider. So much more than just the physical aspects of the disease. He was beginning to understand just how complicated this all was and the stress that Brighde would be under.

'Elise's physical symptoms started about nine years ago but, by then, we had battled with her depression for six years already. Her balance was one of the first things affected. She had been a competitive swimmer but gymnastics might have been a better option to counteract the decline in her balance. At this stage the disease has affected her ability to walk, talk and think. Next to go will be her ability to swallow and she will end up being tube fed. I am seventy-four years old. It's taken forty years of my life and people would say I'm the lucky one, that I don't have the disease. But I've lived it twice over.'

Merilyn had nursed her husband and now her daughter. Xavier knew she'd been beaten down by the disease; he could hear it in her voice and see it in her face. Listening to Merilyn, he could hear how difficult her life had been. Not only had her husband and daughter been afflicted but even Merilyn's memories of them were being replaced by more recent, devastating memories. Her story was heartbreaking and he suspected it was very similar to Brighde's story.

He was so relieved that he hadn't asked Brighde to accompany him today—he hadn't really had any idea how emotional this would be—but, talking to Merilyn, he felt like he could be talking to a future Brighde. Her mother had died at forty-nine, the same age as Merilyn's daughter was now. That surely would have brought Brighde's memories to the fore and he was glad he hadn't subjected her to that.

He knew Brighde had watched her mother suffer, had nursed her through the early stages of the disease and was now facing the possibility of doing it all over again with her own child. *Their* child. And, potentially, both babies could be affected. Xavier knew he couldn't put her through that. It wasn't only the person with the faulty gene who suffered; it was the entire family.

'Do you have any words of advice for me?' he asked.

Merilyn shook her head. 'I'm not going to tell you what is right or wrong. I'm not going to give you any advice except to say that everyone has their choice to make and don't judge someone for what they choose to do or not to do. Not before you've walked a mile in their shoes.'

Xavier nodded and stood up. 'Thank you for talking to me; I really appreciate it.' And now he needed to talk to Brighde.

Sarah answered his knock on the door.

'Hi. Is Brighde home?'

'She's just gone down to the shops. Are you okay? You don't look well.'

He felt awful. Merilyn's insight had been an eye-opener for him. He'd done his research and thought he had been prepared for the visual side but he hadn't been prepared for the emotional side. Listening to Merilyn had been confronting. An awakening. An emotional punch in the face—there had been so many parallels between Brighde's life and Merilyn's. He wasn't surprised to hear he looked terrible. It had been a lot to absorb. 'I've just been to see some HD patients.'

'Oh.' Sarah stepped aside, holding the door open. 'I think you'd better come in. Brighde won't be long. Can I get you something to drink? You look like you could use a whisky.'

He would love a drink to take the edge off the pain he was feeling but he knew that was nothing compared to what Brighde had been through. 'No. Thank you, but I need to keep a clear head.'

'So, how did it go?' Sarah asked as he followed her inside. 'It's pretty confronting, isn't it?'

Xavier nodded. 'It was one of the worst things I've ever experienced and, considering I've been a doctor for ten years, that's quite a statement.'

'So you see why Brighde feels the way she does?'

'Yes, I can.'

'What are you going to do?'

'I'm going to speak to her again about having an amnio.'

If he wanted her to have the test he knew he had to agree with her conditions. If he didn't she could terminate the pregnancy without his consent *and* without getting tested. The amniocentesis was the only chance he had of convincing her to have the babies; therefore he had no choice but to agree to her decision regarding the pregnancy if the babies had a positive score on their CAG repeats. He knew that was the only way.

'If she agrees to the amnio you can't ask her to go through with the pregnancy if the test comes back positive. It would destroy her,' Sarah said. 'No matter what happens, she's already a victim of the disease. She lost her mother and lost contact with her father because of it. She's scared. You need to understand and respect that.'

Brighde held all the cards. He knew that. She'd lost both her parents because of the disease and he couldn't ask her to go through it again with her own child. She might not have the symptoms but if she had passed on the mutated gene she wouldn't escape the suffering or the guilt and he couldn't ask her to spend half a lifetime with her child only to then watch that life disappear in a terrible fashion. But he also couldn't agree to take a life now without knowing the future. If Brighde would agree to an amniocentesis, he would agree with her subsequent decision.

'I do. I get it. She's agreed to having an amnio on certain conditions. Having seen what I did today, I'm prepared to agree to her terms,' he said as they heard the sound of Brighde's key unlocking the front door.

Brighde was surprised to see Xavier sitting in her kitchen. She didn't think they'd made plans but she couldn't be one hundred per cent sure. She'd been extremely forgetful of late. She didn't think it was pregnancy brain, more likely a symptom of everything that was on her mind. There was no room for the little day-to-day things when her head was so full of big decisions that needed to be made.

'Hi. Sorry, have I forgotten something?'

'No,' he said as he stood up.

He looked uncomfortable. Uncertain. It was the first time she could remember seeing him ill at ease.

'Is something wrong?' she asked. He didn't look his usual robust self. He was still gorgeous—she doubted he could look anything else—but he looked exhausted, drained.

'You were right,' was all he said.

'About what?'

'Huntington's Disease and what it does.'

'You went to the care facility?'

He nodded.

'Are you okay?'

'Not really,' he admitted as they sat at the kitchen table. 'But this isn't about me. I spoke to a woman there. A mother. She was visiting her daughter. She'd nursed her husband and then her daughter. She was strong but you could tell it has destroyed her. You were right; I didn't understand what it was like. I'm not sure I really do, even now, but it's a lot clearer. The pain, the helplessness. I'm sorry I've made this difficult for you.' He picked up her hand. 'If you will have the amnio I will be guided by you when we get the results. It's all up to you.'

'Are you saying that if the result is positive you won't fight a termination?'

Xavier nodded. 'That's what I'm saying. But I need to ask: if the tests are negative what are your plans then? Would a negative test result change your mind about having a family of your own? Would you have the babies?'

'Of course.'

'You're happy about the pregnancy?'

'Not completely,' she admitted. 'Not yet. I never thought I would have children—you know I never planned to—but *if* the test is negative, if everything is okay, then yes, I will be happy. But I can't allow myself to think like that yet. I'm scared I might still be disappointed, that it will all come crashing down and that would be devastating.'

'There's something else,' he said. Brighde expected him to look pleased that she would be prepared to give him the children he was so desperate for but there was still a crease of concern running between his brows. 'Have you thought about what would happen if only one twin tested negative? What would you do then?'

Brighde frowned. It was a possibility, given that they suspected the babies were non-identical, but, once again, it was another thing she hadn't thought through. 'I'm not sure. Would selective reduction be an option, do you think?' She knew it was possible to abort one twin but she didn't know the details.

'Yes. But the further along the pregnancy is, the more difficult that becomes. And there's also the risk of losing both. The longer you wait, the harder it is.'

'Even if Julie can do the amnio this week it will take a couple of weeks to get the results back. I'll be twenty weeks by then.' Her voice was laced with worry; she could hear it.

'That's okay, but it's something you need to think about over the next fortnight. I know you'd rather not have to deal with it but, if it comes to that, time will be of the essence. It's better to think about that scenario now so you're prepared.'

Brighde could see Xavier's point. She had to get all her facts straight. She needed to get her ducks in a row and then she'd be able to make informed decisions. That *had* to be better than making decisions based on guesswork.

She would make an appointment with Julie for an amniocentesis.

'Are you okay?' he asked as she sat on the edge of the examination bed. She'd asked him to accompany her this time. He was calm, unflappable and knew what to expect. She wouldn't have to explain anything to him or worry about him coping with the procedure. Sarah would have accompanied her but having Xavier there was the right thing to do. And she wanted him there.

She had never gotten over her father leaving her and Nick to cope with their mother's disease on their own and she was terrified of having to face more tragedy without support. 'I'm scared.'

It felt as if she was permanently afraid of late. This pregnancy was very real to her now. Her body was changing: her boobs were bigger, her stomach a little rounder. Her morning sickness had almost resolved and this morning she'd felt flutterings in her stomach that she knew was the babies moving. She would have loved to share that information with Xavier but she still didn't want to invest too much emotion into this pregnancy. It would destroy her if she got too attached, only to find out she had to terminate.

Her whole attitude had changed and now she was praying that her babies would be okay. She couldn't imagine the alternative. Not any more.

Xavier held her hand. 'I'm right here. You don't have to do this alone,' he said as Julie came into the room.

'Good morning. How are you feeling, Brighde?'

'I'm really nervous,' she admitted. 'And apprehensive.'

'About the test itself or the result?'

'Both.'

'The amnio may be a little uncomfortable—'

Brighde shook her head and interrupted. 'It's not the discomfort that's bothering me. It's the risk.'

'There's a small risk of miscarriage associated with amniocentesis,' Julie told her, 'The risk decreases after fifteen weeks' gestation so that's good news for you at eighteen weeks. There's no clear reason as to the cause of miscarriage; it may be due to infection or trauma to the amniotic sac. Here in Victoria it's about one in two hundred into the second trimester and my statistics are a bit better than that. In theory, about one in twenty women miscarry before twelve weeks but you do already have an increased risk because of a twin pregnancy. But, with regard to the amnio, because your twins are fraternal I need to take two separate samples. So the risk is the same but the likelihood of a miscarriage is slightly higher because you are having two needle aspirations. That's the facts. I'm not sure if that will help to put your mind at ease but you do need to know the risks before we go ahead. Do you still want to do this?'

Brighde knew she didn't really have a choice. As frightened as she was of having the procedure, she was more afraid of passing on the gene. This was the only way to know for sure. She nodded and squeezed Xavier's hand a little more tightly.

'I'll do the amnio under ultrasound guidance,' Julie said as she switched on the machine, 'so let's have a look at your babies.'

Brighde lifted her shirt and turned her eyes to the screen as Julie moved the transducer head over her abdomen.

'There's Twin A,' Julie said as the image of one tiny baby came onto the screen.

'He's a little footballer. Look at him kicking,' Xavier said. If Brighde hadn't been so nervous she would have smiled at the note of pride in his voice.

'Girls can play football too,' she said. With the way the baby was positioned she couldn't see anything to suggest the sex and she knew Xavier was just using a figure of speech but she was convinced both babies were girls.

Julie paused the image and clicked buttons, measuring the foetus. 'Fourteen centimetres. Just what we hope for at this stage.' She printed a picture and then moved the machine onto Twin B.

'She's sucking her thumb!' Brighde exclaimed.

'Do you want me to take the measurements for foetal anomalies?' Julie asked as she measured Twin B's length.

'Can you do the amnio first?' Brighde asked. 'I want

to get that over and done with.' She really was nervous about the test and wanted it out of the way as soon as possible.

'Of course,' Julie replied. 'Now, the results are about ninety-nine per cent accurate. Do either of you have any questions before I begin?'

Xavier and Brighde both shook their heads.

'I'll just put a bit of local anaesthetic on your tummy, Brighde, and call the technician to monitor the ultra-sound.'

Julie gave the anaesthetic time to work but when she pulled out the long, thin biopsy needle Brighde turned her head. She didn't want to watch the procedure. She held on tight to Xavier's hand and kept her eyes focused on his gorgeous face. He smiled at her and kissed her. The kiss was unexpected and Brighde's heartbeat picked up its pace. If his intention was to distract her it was working.

Xavier had been so gentle and considerate recently. He was thoughtful and gorgeous and just what she'd imagined she'd look for in a boyfriend if she'd ever let herself have one. But even though they were spending time together she hadn't slept with him again. She was trying hard to keep some distance between them. She didn't want things to become messy or awkward so, no matter how much she longed to share physical intimacy, she knew she couldn't risk it. Her heart was conflicted enough with the idea of a pregnancy; she couldn't afford to throw an intimate relationship with Xavier into the mix. She would love to be able to say he was her partner or boyfriend but that would be taking things further than she could handle at the moment.

'Do you want to know the sex of the babies?' Julie asked. 'The test will be definitive on that too.'

'I'm not sure,' Brighde replied. Even though she felt they were girls she hadn't actually thought about finding out. She hadn't dared to think too far ahead.

'Do you want to know what I think?' Xavier said.

'What?'

'I think we're having a pigeon pair. A boy and a girl.'

He sounded so certain that Brighde wondered if he'd glimpsed something on the ultrasound that she'd missed. 'Did you see something?'

'No—' he grinned and Brighde's heart did a little flip in her chest '—did you?'

She shook her head.

'What do you think they are?'

'Two girls.'

'Why?'

'I have no idea.'

'Shall we have a bet on it?'

'I am *not* betting on the sex of our children.'

'Why not?'

'I don't trust you. I think you saw something.'

'Cross my heart. Shall we find out officially?'

'No.' She didn't want to know for sure until they had the results and she'd made a decision about what would happen next. She felt knowing the babies' sex might strengthen the attachment she was beginning to feel and that would only make things more difficult if the results came back positive. She couldn't afford to get too attached. Just in case.

'Okay, I'm all done,' Julie said.

'Thank you,' Brighde said to Xavier.

'What for?'

'For distracting me.'

'Did it work?'

'Yep.'

'All right, next question,' Julie said. 'The anomaly scan?'

'I'm not sure,' Brighde said as she looked at Xavier. This test would check for other more common anomalies like Down Syndrome. Brighde didn't think she would terminate a pregnancy in that case but, like many other things, she and Xavier hadn't actually discussed this.

'It's not just for Down syndrome,' Julie said when Brighde posed the question. 'There are a whole host of things we look for. You know that. I will check the heart, kidneys, spine, palate and stomach plus take some further measurements of the head, abdomen and thigh and also check your placenta.'

Xavier was nodding. Of course he'd want the tests done. He liked to be prepared.

'Okay,' Brighde agreed.

It took another hour to scan both babies, by which time Brighde thought her bladder would burst, but Julie hadn't finished with her yet.

'Miscarriage will usually occur in the first seventy-two hours after testing so I recommend that you take it easy for the next few days,' she said as she helped Brighde to sit up. 'You don't need bed rest but you have got time off work, right?'

Brighde nodded. 'Three days.'

'Good. Tell me if I'm singing to the choir, won't you, but I know from when I was pregnant myself that being on the other side of the fence is a very different experience. So much of your medical knowledge seems to disappear into the ether when it's your own children. So, don't forget about what can be perfectly normal happenings after an amnio. Things like mild, period-like cramping abdominal pains with some light spotting. You can take paracetamol to help ease the pain. The results will take a couple of weeks. I'll call you to schedule an appointment when the results are back.'

'You know,' Xavier said once Julie had left the room, 'during the amnio you said "our children". That's the first time you've said that.'

Brighde frowned. 'No, it isn't.'

'Yes, it is. You've said "my children" and "your children" but never "our children". Does that mean you've been thinking that we might be able to make a go of this? That maybe we could have a future. Not just co-parenting but the two of us, together.'

'What do you mean? Together?'

'I think we should get married.'

'What? Why on earth would you want to get married?'

'It's not about getting married. It's about showing you my commitment. To you and the babies. Showing you that, whatever happens, you can rely on me. That I'll be there to support you.'

'Marriage is no guarantee of that. Trust me, I know. And I'm still no closer to knowing what I'm going to do yet, Xavier. I'm not making any more decisions until we get the results of the amnio back. I'm not doing anything until I know my children's future.'

'Our children.'

'Our children.' She did like the sound of that phrase and she couldn't disagree—he'd been very considerate and supportive of her so far—but marriage was no guarantee of commitment. She'd seen evidence of that first-hand with her own parents.

'Would you think about it at least?' he asked. 'If not from your point of view, how about from the babies'? Surely having parents who are married gives them that stability and surely that is best for them?'

She couldn't help but wonder if his suggestion was only tied in to his desire to be a father. Was it his way of making sure she couldn't leave him out?

'Don't be ridiculous. The babies won't know and won't care if we're married. Having two parents who love each other is best for children. Having parents who are going to live a long, healthy, happy life is best for the children. As a matter of fact, having a parent who would not choose an early death sentence for a child is best for the child. Marriage isn't the answer.'

'But it's my promise. My way of showing you that I will be there for you and our children,' he argued.

'You can't promise that. And I've told you, I'm not going to inflict this disease on my children—that's why we're doing these tests—and if they have escaped the mutation there is still no reason to get married. Any promises you made would only be false ones if there's no relationship between us to begin with.' Xavier wasn't in love with her. How could she trust him to stick around and support her if they started out with nothing substantial between them in the first place? 'I don't *want* to get married.'

'Why not?'

'Because relationships don't last. Marriages don't last. Not even love is enough to get people through the tough times and there is no way I can trust a marriage that is based on a misguided sense of duty to survive.'

'It's more than duty,' he said. 'We have plenty of chemistry. That's something. I know marriages that have started with less.'

'Chemistry isn't enough to get us past our first wedding anniversary, let alone all the obstacles we could be facing. Neither of us should expect everlasting married happiness, given what we've seen. Your girlfriend cheated on you and my father walked out on us.'

'We are not those people. What they did doesn't define us.'

But Brighde had spent too many years avoiding relationships to change her mind that easily now. There was a reason she didn't date. She didn't want to fall in love. To fall in love was to risk everything.

And while knowing she wasn't going to develop HD had unlocked an alternative door to her future, she still couldn't afford to think about marriage yet—no matter how much she wanted to. She had to wait for the results of the amniocentesis now before she could think ahead and, regardless of those results, she couldn't have it all. Xavier wasn't offering his love and she refused to be married to someone out of an obligation.

She shook her head. 'I can't marry you.'

'I don't know what to do.'

Xavier sat at his sister's kitchen table, nursing a whisky. Mary's husband was putting the kids to bed and Xavier was picking Mary's brains. Her suggestion to get Brighde out of Melbourne and into a fresh environment had prompted their trip to Daylesford and he hoped she'd have more good advice this time. 'I know Brighde's stressed about the amnio results but she's barely speaking to me.'

'You can't blame her for being stressed. From what you've told me, it's a terrible disease and she must be worried sick that one or both of the twins might have it. She must be terrified and I can't imagine that she's got the energy to worry about you too. I know what it's like. Sometimes there's a limit to what you can focus on. Give her time.'

'But we need to think about the future.'

'That's a bit difficult at the moment. The future might change in the blink of an eye, depending on the amnio results. If you want my advice, I'm telling you to just be patient. I know it's not always your forte. I know you don't like to wait, but there's nothing you can do about the test results and I don't think you can expect Brighde to move forwards until she has those.'

'I promised her that if the test results came back positive I wouldn't oppose a termination, but I don't think I can give the babies up.' Xavier could see Brighde's point of view about a termination but he still couldn't imagine ending the life of a child—his child. But he was fast running out of ideas of ways to get around her concerns.

'So what are your options?'

'I don't really have any. It's all up to Brighde.'

'As long as she knows you're there for her. That's what she needs at the moment.'

'I'm not sure that she wants that either. I asked her to marry me. She said no.'

'Why?'

'Why what? Why did I ask her to marry me or why did she say no?'

'Both, I guess.'

'I wanted her to know she has my support and I

thought getting married would show her I meant to stick around. I thought she'd appreciate it after her father walked out on them when she was very young. That's really messed her up and I thought I was doing the right thing.'

'Her parents were married, weren't they?'

'Yes.'

'And her father still left. In Brighde's mind, marriage probably isn't the promise you think it is.'

'But marriage makes sense.'

'Getting married only makes sense if you love each other. Do you love her?'

Did he?

'She's going to be the mother of my children,' he replied, not sure he was ready to give an answer. He thought he'd been in love with his ex-girlfriend but that was nothing compared to the way he felt about Brighde. Brighde was different—she lit up his life and he couldn't picture his future without her in it. He thought he could be falling in love with her but she kept pushing him away.

'That's not necessarily love. Would you marry her if she wasn't pregnant? I know you love the idea of settling down, getting married, having a family of your own, but there are lots of ways to do that. Marriage may not be your only future. Brighde can still be in your future without marriage. There's nothing wrong with choosing to co-parent. Plenty of people opt for that and do it successfully. Marriage isn't for everyone.'

'But it is for me.'

'I know that but maybe it's not for Brighde. Give her some space. Don't crowd her but don't desert her either.'

'How do I do both?'

'You're a smart man. You'll figure it out. She *will* need you. She might not need a husband but she will need your support, no matter what happens. And if everything goes well she will need a father for her children—your children. Don't muck this up. Give her what she needs.'

She needed him.

No, she didn't.

But she did need someone to love her. And that someone was him.

He would tell her how he felt. He would give this one last shot. All or nothing, he decided. Go hard or go home.

Brighde opened her eyes and checked her alarm. Something had woken her but it was still half an hour before she needed to get up. She had taken three days off after the amniocentesis but she was due back at work today.

As she lay in bed she felt a fluttering in her belly. Maybe the babies had woken her. She smiled and put her hand on her stomach. She was scared to admit it but she had bonded with her babies and with every breath she took she hoped that they would be all right. That maybe they would all get through this. But she knew she wouldn't relax until the test results came back. There was still too much at stake.

She rolled onto her side. She would stay in bed for a little longer; there was no hurry to get up. She would lie still and see if she could feel any more tiny movements. She liked to think of the twins communicating with each other as they wriggled and kicked.

She waited until her alarm rang before getting out of bed but she had only taken four steps into the hallway when she felt a sharp pain in her side. That wasn't a fluttering; it was a strong cramp. She clutched her side and put her other hand on the wall to steady herself as she took a deep breath and waited for the cramp to pass. It subsided but, before she could move, she felt something warm running down the inside of her thigh. She put her hand between her legs. It came out red.

CHAPTER NINE

'SARAH!'

Brighde's voice echoed in the hallway, bouncing off the floorboards and the walls, and Sarah burst out of her room, spurred on by Brighde's cries. She took one look at Brighde, who was leaning against the hallway wall, her hand and legs smeared with blood.

Sarah's eyes were wide. 'We need to get you to the hospital.'

Brighde nodded mutely. Her heart was racing and her knees shook. She didn't want to lose her babies.

Sarah grabbed a cardigan and wrapped it around Brighde's shoulders. She yanked a towel from the linen cupboard, picked up her keys and both of their phones from the hall table and bundled Brighde into her car. 'Is Xavier's number in your phone?' she asked as she put her seat belt on.

Brighde nodded again and Sarah called the number. She heard her leave a message.

'Xavier, Brighde is bleeding. I'm taking her to Parkville.'

Sarah ended the call and pulled the car into the traffic as Brighde sobbed quietly in her seat. She had her hands resting on her stomach, willing these babies to stay put. These babies she'd never dreamed she would have were now the most important things in her life. She couldn't bear to lose them.

Sarah drove her car into the turning circle at the front entrance to the hospital and Xavier was the first thing Brighde noticed. He was pacing up and down the driveway, an empty wheelchair abandoned to one side. The moment he saw Sarah's car he was by the door, opening it almost before Sarah had stopped completely. He scooped Brighde into his arms and carried her to the wheelchair.

'I'll take her upstairs,' he said over his shoulder to Sarah.

He pushed Brighde into the foyer; avoiding the emergency department, he wheeled her to the lifts. 'I've called Julie. She'll meet us in Maternity,' he told Brighde as they waited. He didn't tell her everything would be okay. She knew he couldn't but she longed to hear those words anyway.

He wheeled her into an exam room and lifted her onto the bed.

She curled herself into a ball and faced the wall. She couldn't bear to look at him.

She wondered if it was something she'd done. Maybe she'd strained something? But she couldn't imagine how; she'd barely done anything for the past three days but that didn't stop her from worrying. From feeling guilty. She'd never forgive herself if she had caused this and she couldn't bear to look at Xavier. She couldn't bear to see any recrimination in his dark eyes.

She didn't need anyone else questioning her actions or wondering what had gone wrong. Because in her heart she knew that something was wrong. Something was *very* wrong.

There was way too much blood.

She heard the door open, heard Xavier greeting Julie.

She turned her head as she listened to Xavier telling Julie the little he knew.

Someone had to help her. Someone had to do something.

'I think I might be losing the babies,' she said as she burst into another flood of tears.

Xavier was by her side. He pulled a chair closer to the bed as he grabbed some tissues from the dispenser on the wall and pressed them into her hand. He sat beside her and stroked the hair back from her face.

'When did the bleeding start?' Julie asked as she snapped on a pair of surgical gloves.

'Maybe an hour ago,' Brighde told her. She wasn't really sure what the time was. Everything was a blur since she'd started to bleed.

'Are you in pain?' Julie asked as she attached monitors to Brighde to record her blood pressure, heart rate and oxygen saturation.

She was scared and anxious and felt as though her heart was breaking but she knew that wasn't what Julie was asking. 'No.' She'd only had the one cramp and, while it had been painful, it didn't come close to the pain in her heart.

Maybe it was nothing. Maybe it was just a bit of spotting. But in her heart she knew that wasn't the case.

Something had gone wrong. She could feel it.

'Any temperature?'

'I don't think so,' Brighde replied as Julie picked up the thermometer and popped it into her ear.

'That's normal,' she said as the thermometer beeped. 'Let's have a look, shall we?'

Brighde had come to hospital in the old T-shirt she'd worn to bed. She had Sarah's cardigan wrapped around her and a towel between her thighs. Her underwear was soaked in blood. Julie lifted Brighde's shirt and removed the towel. Brighde saw the look that Julie and Xavier exchanged as they examined the towel.

It was stained with dark red blood.

'I'll need to do a scan,' Julie said. 'That will show us what's going on.'

Brighde waited in silence while Julie got the machine ready and ran it over her abdomen. She couldn't speak. She couldn't think straight. All she wanted was to hear that her babies were fine.

Julie kept the screen turned away from Brighde and she didn't think she could bear the suspense. 'What can you see?'

'Twin B is fine. I can see a heartbeat and the rate is perfectly normal,' Julie said, keeping her eyes on the monitor.

'And Twin A? What about Twin A?' Brighde could hear a trace of hysteria creeping into her voice as Xavier picked up her hand and held it. Tight.

Julie was shaking her head. 'I'm sorry, Brighde; there's only one heartbeat.'

'No!'

'Let me see.'

'Brighde—'

She heard the note of warning in Xavier's voice but she knew she wouldn't believe it until she'd seen it with her own eyes.

She turned to face him. His eyes were brimming with unshed tears. Shiny and bright.

'I need to see.'

He nodded slowly as Julie turned the screen to face her and moved the ultrasound head around, capturing the picture.

Two sacs, two tiny babies, but only one heartbeat.

Tears streamed down Brighde's cheeks. The front of her T-shirt was soaking wet. 'No! Why? What happened?'

'Often we don't know why these things happen,' Julie said as she lifted the transducer head from Brighde's stomach and the image disappeared.

Brighde lifted one hand, reaching for the screen, trying to bring her babies back. 'But they were both fine three days ago.'

'You had a viable pregnancy three days ago, but that's all we know.'

'Was it the amnio?'

'It could have been but I think it's more likely to be unrelated. The amniotic sacs are both intact and you don't have a temperature so I don't think there's an infection but I'll take a blood sample and we'll check that. As you know, there is a much higher rate of miscarriage with twin pregnancies. I'm sorry.'

'What happens now?' Brighde felt like she should know but her brain seemed to have completely shut down. Nothing made sense.

'I'm going to admit you. I want you to have bed rest for a few days.'

'I have to stay here?'

'I think it's the best place for you. We can keep an

eye on you here. We need to make sure the bleeding stops and I need to monitor the other twin.'

'You think I might lose the other baby?'

'I couldn't say for certain. The twins were dizygotic and dichorionic—two sacs and two placentas—and being non-identical reduces the risk of both miscarrying. Plus your general health is good. These things are all in your favour, which lessens the likelihood of a second miscarriage, but I can't make any promises. So, for now we wait. There's nothing you can do. I'll take some blood and you rest and I'll see if I can get the amnio results through a little faster.'

'Once the bleeding has stopped, what then?' Brighde asked as Julie took a blood sample. 'What happens to the babies?'

'If you don't have any cramping and the blood tests are normal, so no sign of infection, then once the bleeding stops I will discharge you. We shouldn't need to do anything more except closely monitor Twin B.'

'And the other baby? What happens to the other baby?'

'The sac is intact. Both babies can stay in there for as long as possible. Given the chorionicity, your gestational age and your health, letting your pregnancy continue is low-risk. I don't want to do any unnecessary procedures.'

'Can you tell me if Twin A was a boy or a girl? I'd like to know.' She didn't ask Xavier. She had to know now.

'A boy.'

Brighde closed her eyes. She'd lost their son.

She opened her eyes. 'And the other one?'

'A girl.'

Xavier had been right. She turned to look at him. He had tears in his eyes but he hadn't said a word.

Did he blame her? Did he think this was her fault? She knew how much he wanted these babies; he'd made that perfectly clear on many occasions. Would he think this was her fault?

She didn't dare ask what he was thinking; she was too scared of the answer.

'We'll get you cleaned up and admitted,' Julie said, interrupting her thoughts. 'I'll be back to see you later.'

Brighde was in a private room, attached to a drip and various other electrodes, lying in bed while Xavier hovered. There was nothing for him to do; there was nothing he *could* do and his presence was irritating her. She still didn't want to look at him, still couldn't bear it. She didn't want to see her loss and despair reflected back at her from the depths of his eyes. She was feeling terrible enough already.

'Don't you have patients to see?' she asked.

'I've rescheduled or postponed them,' he replied. 'I can stay as long as you need me.'

'I don't need you. I think you should go.'

'What? Why?' She could see the confusion in his eyes. But that was better than accusations.

'Don't you see? I shouldn't even *be* pregnant. I've just lost one baby and I might lose the other one too. I shouldn't *be* in this position and I wouldn't be if it wasn't for you. Every time I look at you I'm reminded of what I've lost or might still lose. I don't want to see you. I just want to be alone.'

'Brighde, you don't have to be alone. I'm here for you.' He'd stopped pacing and was standing by her bed, a worried expression on his gorgeous face. He reached out one hand towards her but when she folded her arms across her chest, blocking him out, his hand dropped to his side. 'I'm hurting too, Brighde.'

'It's not the same. You've never lost anyone.'

'This baby was ours. Yours and mine. I've lost just as much as you have. Don't shut me out. I want this baby more than anything.'

Was that part of the problem? She knew it was. Xavier wanted the baby but he wasn't talking about wanting her any more. Had his suggestion of marriage been his way of making sure he was in his children's lives? Making sure she couldn't cut him out? She had never intended to do that but, right now, she just didn't want to see him. She needed some space. 'I don't want you here,' she said bluntly and she could see she'd hurt him but she was hurting more.

He stood, watching her silently, for what seemed like hours before, eventually, he nodded. 'I will go now but I'm not walking out of your life. You can keep sending me away but I'll keep coming back. I can be just as stubborn as you.'

Brighde closed her eyes and turned her head away, waiting until she heard him leave, until she heard the door close.

She was better off alone.

That was what she'd always thought but meeting Xavier had made her believe, just for a short while, that maybe she could have a happily ever after. But it seemed she'd been wrong.

This was all his fault. If she'd never met him she wouldn't be pregnant. If she'd never met him she wouldn't be grieving for a child she'd never expected to have.

How could it hurt so much?

She just wanted to be loved. For her life to have a happy ending. But that was a foolish dream. Everything was unravelling. Everything was out of her control. She never should have let her guard down.

She'd always believed nothing good would ever come of letting someone into her life, into her heart. Well, now she had the proof.

If she'd had any tears left to cry she knew they would be falling. She didn't think her heart could take any more.

CHAPTER TEN

XAVIER LEFT THE room but he wasn't about to leave the hospital. He had nowhere else to go. He'd cancelled his lists so unless someone went into labour he had nowhere to go *and* nothing to do. He didn't think he could face delivering someone else's baby today. His heart was bruised, aching.

He'd lost his child. His son.

Brighde had said he'd never lost anyone before but that wasn't true. He'd lost once before. He remembered when he'd found out that his ex was expecting another man's child, that she wasn't pregnant with his baby. He remembered the day she'd taken that dream from him. He'd thought he could never feel worse than he had that day but to physically lose his own child, his own flesh and blood, was devastating. Heartbreaking.

These babies were real to him and he couldn't bear to think about potentially losing them both or not being allowed to have anything to do with the surviving twin. His daughter. If she made it.

He had to convince Brighde to let him back into her life. He wasn't prepared to lose another child or his chance of fatherhood.

He needed a plan. Another one. And this time it would have to be the perfect plan. Flawless. Because he was in love with a woman who couldn't bear to look at him.

He hadn't had a chance to tell her that he loved her. Or maybe he just hadn't taken the chance. He'd been caught up with other priorities. Had his ex been right? Had he, once again, put too many other things before the important people in his life? Had he not given Brighde the priority she deserved?

He'd have to make things right. He had to let her know how he felt.

He gave her as much time as he could. He tried catching up on paperwork but found he couldn't concentrate. He tried catching up on journal articles—that was even worse—so eventually he gave up and returned to Brighde's room. She'd have to see him. There were some things that couldn't wait.

He was several rooms away from hers when he saw a couple knock on her door and enter. He couldn't see their faces but the woman was petite and dark and the man was tall and slim with hair the colour of Brighde's with the same thick wave. Was that her brother and sister-in-law? He hesitated. There were some things that couldn't wait but there were also some things that could only be said in private and this was certainly not a discussion he wanted to share with Brighde's brother on their first meeting.

He pulled a chair along the corridor and positioned it outside her room. He'd wait.

He sank into the chair. The adrenalin that had been pumping through him at the thought of declaring his feelings continued to surge through his body but, with no release, the energy it had created left him feeling exhausted. He stretched his legs out and leant back against the wall.

He could hear voices, snippets of conversation, coming from Brighde's room. He didn't mean to eavesdrop but he didn't have the energy to stand and walk away.

He was done walking away.

'You're pregnant?'

A female voice. The sister-in-law?

'Why didn't you tell us?'

Brighde's brother.

Xavier strained to hear her reply. He was interested—very interested—in the answer. He hadn't realised she'd kept her pregnancy a secret. Had she kept *him* a secret?

'Lots of reasons. But mostly because I didn't know what I was going to do about the pregnancy. I didn't know if I would go through with it. I didn't know if I *could.* I was worried about telling you—especially when Immy is pregnant too. I was worried about HD and how you would react if I chose *not* to be pregnant. This wasn't planned. Not at all.'

'What are you going to do?'

'I still don't know. I'm waiting on test results.'

'And the father? Who is he?'

'No one important.'

Pain pierced Xavier's chest. A pain so sharp it made him catch his breath. Was that really how she felt about him? He was imagining a life with her and yet she could dismiss him so easily? Her words cut him to the core. Surely she didn't mean them?

'Does he know about the baby?'

'He knows.'

'And what does he think?'

'That doesn't matter. This was all a mistake. A big mistake.'

Xavier had heard enough. He summoned his energy and stood and walked away. He would retreat but he would return.

His problems were multiplying. He was in love with a woman who wanted nothing to do with him. That presented a challenge but he wasn't defeated. Not yet.

It had been forty-eight hours since their loss and Brighde was still refusing to see him. Sarah had given him some brief reports but nothing she said eased his concerns. Brighde was barely talking to Sarah either and Sarah suspected she wasn't eating properly. Xavier was concerned she was in real danger of sinking into a depressed state of mind.

He had snuck in late at night to watch her sleeping. She'd been curled into a tight little ball, elbows flexed, hands tucked under her chin. A defensive position. She hadn't looked relaxed even though she was asleep and his heart ached and his arms longed to hold her.

He had finished his morning visits and was hovering near Brighde's room, hoping to catch Julie as she finished her rounds. He saw her walking towards him, a frown between her eyebrows.

'What's going on?' she asked him as she approached.

'What do you mean?'

'I've just seen Brighde to give her the results of her second blood test.'

'Her *second* test?' His heart hammered in his chest. What was wrong now?

'Yes. I asked if she wanted to wait for you. She implied you weren't here.'

'I'm here. I've barely left the hospital for the past few days. What did the blood work show?'

'You know I can't give you Brighde's results,' Julie said as she shook her head. 'You'll have to ask her.'

He hated the rules. The fact that Brighde was the only one with a say. That the father had no rights. 'She's not talking to me,' he admitted. 'She doesn't want me anywhere near her and, from what I hear, she's not doing too well. I'm worried about her but she's not telling me anything.'

Julie considered him carefully before she spoke and he could almost see the wheels turning in her mind. 'Can I ask your professional opinion about one of my patients?'

'Sure.'

'She's a first-time mum who has just lost a baby, a twin. All her blood work has come back clear, no sign of infection, and she's generally healthy.'

'No infection, you said?'

'That's right. I think the miscarriage was probably related to the twin pregnancy. Maybe there was something wrong with the baby but everything seems okay now and she's recovering well, physically, from the loss and I could discharge her but I'm worried about her mental health. We are still waiting on some other test results so I'm considering keeping her here for a couple more days until those results come back. It's not really necessary but I'd feel better if I could keep a close eye on her. What would you do if she was your patient?'

'I'd definitely keep her in.'

'I thought so. Right. Thanks.'

Imogen had been in several times over the past four days, bringing with her pictures of wedding dresses, wedding cakes and bouquets. Brighde knew she was trying to distract her but she wasn't able to get enthused about anything at the moment. Her concentration was shot and she just wasn't interested in what was going on in other people's lives. It was very unlike her but she couldn't shake herself out of the despondency that had settled over her. She wasn't sleeping or eating properly either, which she knew was only making things worse, but her appetite had deserted her along with her sense of humour.

Now it seemed it was Sarah's turn to try to jolly her out of her slump. Although she'd chosen a strange topic to try to cheer Brighde up.

'So, have you seen Xavier?' Sarah asked as she rearranged a bunch of flowers on the bedside table, pulling out a few sad, droopy stems in an effort to revitalise the display.

Brighde wished she could do the same to her. Pull out the sad pieces of her heart and plump it up with some fresh water. She wished it was that easy to bring her back to life.

'No.' She still wasn't ready to see him. To see the sadness in his eyes. She didn't have the energy to deal with his grief as well as her own.

'You can't put it off for ever. He is still going to be the father of your child.'

'I know.' But there was still a possibility that she could lose this baby too and then there would be no need to see Xavier. There would be no need to have anything to do with him. She was convinced he was only interested in their child and where did that leave her? 'But I could lose this one too. There's no point in speaking to him until I know for certain what's going on. I haven't even got the amnio results back yet.' The lack of information was hanging over her head like a big black cloud.

'You are nineteen weeks pregnant. This baby looks perfectly happy; there's no reason to think anything untoward will happen. If everything comes back clear, which I'm sure it will, then I think you two need to have a serious conversation.'

'About what?'

'Life, the universe and everything in between. You are going to have to find a way to work things out. You'll be tied together for ever through this baby. If you wanted to you might even get to live happily ever after.'

'I don't think so,' Brighde said with a shake of her head. 'He doesn't love me.'

'Has he told you that?'

'He hasn't told me he does. Everything he's done has been about the baby,' she replied just as her OB/GYN entered the room.

'Good morning, Brighde,' Julie said as she breezed in. Everyone's spirits seemed high today, Brighde thought. Everyone, that was, except for her.

'Please, can I wait just a bit for another ultrasound?' Brighde asked, assuming that Julie was planning another scan. She'd been checking the baby regularly and Brighde knew her little girl was developing well. Julie would show her the images on the screen but Brighde always had to battle to avoid thinking about the baby Julie *wasn't* showing her. Her little boy. Where there had been two babies to keep an eye on, now there was only one. Where there had been two heartbeats there was now only one and Brighde wasn't feeling up to coping with that today. Not straight after her conversation with Sarah, which had filled her head with thoughts of Xavier.

'I'm not here to do an ultrasound,' Julie replied, pulling a letter from the pocket of her white hospital coat. 'I have the results of your amniocentesis.'

'Oh.' Brighde could feel sweat gathering on her upper lip.

This was it. She would no longer be able to put things off. No longer be able to hide behind the excuse that she didn't have all the facts. She was about to find out, once and for all, just exactly what she was dealing with.

'Do you want me to look at the results first or would you like to do it?' Julie asked.

Brighde shook her head. 'You do it,' she replied. She knew she wouldn't be able to even open the envelope. Her hands were shaking and she was terrified of what she might find. No, it was much better to be told the results. She couldn't bear to have to read it for herself.

'Do you want to wait for Xavier?' Julie asked.

Did she? She wasn't sure.

No. It was better to get this over and done with quickly, like pulling off a sticking plaster. She didn't want to delay the inevitable and this way there would be time then for her to digest the information before she would have to share it with anyone else.

She shook her head. 'No. I'll tell him later.' Once she'd had time to compose herself, if necessary.

She reached for Sarah's hand and held it tight as she closed her eyes. 'Okay.'

She could hear the rustle of paper as Julie opened the envelope and pulled out the contents. Brighde held her breath and kept her eyes closed.

'Two tests,' she heard Julie say. 'Both negative.'

She hadn't passed on the defective gene. She felt the tears well up as reality took hold. Both her babies would have been fine. If they'd both survived. But she'd already lost one.

Sarah was by her side before the sadness could overcome her. She wrapped her arms around Brighde, providing comfort. 'It's okay. You'll have a healthy child who will have every chance of living a long life,' she said, understanding what was going through Brighde's mind while reminding her of what was important.

Everything she'd been worried about hadn't come to pass. She had much to be grateful for. She would have a healthy baby. She needed to be strong and focused now. She could still mourn her loss but her daughter deserved all her attention now.

It was hard to believe. She was going to be a mother and Xavier would get the child he wanted. Their daughter.

Xavier.

'Shall I get him?' Sarah asked.

'Get who?'

'Xavier,' came Sarah's reply and Brighde realised that she'd spoken his name out loud.

She nodded. He deserved to know the outcome.

She had no reason to delay. They would have to work out their arrangements. They needed to have a discussion about what would happen next.

Brighde caught her breath when Xavier walked into the room. She hadn't seen him for four days but it felt like weeks and she'd almost forgotten how gorgeous he was. His familiar scent of honey and pear followed him in, wrapping around her. God, she'd missed him.

He looked divine but he also looked miserable.

She'd done that to him and she felt terrible. This separation had all been her fault. She knew she had been unfair. She couldn't put all the blame on him but it had been easier to shut him out than to see him. Seeing him just reminded her of what she'd lost.

But she hadn't lost everything—she was going to have a healthy baby—but her behaviour meant that she had lost more than she needed to. She'd lost one baby and pushed Xavier away. Xavier who, just possibly, might have been the love of her life.

But she was too proud to admit that.

'Sarah said you wanted to see me?' He looked utterly dejected. She wanted to put a smile back on his face and she hoped her news would do that. She hoped she hadn't made such a mess of things that she couldn't fix it. She hoped she hadn't left it too late.

She nodded. All the anger she'd felt had dissipated and now she was just sad that that things hadn't worked out. Tears welled in her eyes but she fought them back. This wasn't a time for tears. Crying would be self-indulgent. She owed Xavier an explanation. She owed him the truth. There would be time for tears later.

He took a step closer. 'What's happened?' he asked. Had he seen the tears in her eyes?

'Nothing,' she replied as the tears spilled from her lashes; triggered by the concern in his voice, she couldn't hold them back.

'Shh.' He was by the bed now. He sat down and took her in his arms. She closed her eyes and leant against him as he stroked her hair. 'It's okay. I'm here.'

He kissed her forehead and waited for her to calm

down. Waited for her tears to subside. She sniffed as she got her emotions under control.

'Are you sure everything's okay?' he asked as he passed her a tissue.

She nodded again and took the tissue from him, aware that she was still clutching the piece of paper that Julie had left with her.

'I'm glad you asked for me,' he said as she blew her nose. 'There are some things I need to tell you.'

Brighde steeled herself for bad news. She couldn't believe that today could only bring good news. That wasn't how her life worked. Good news was always followed by bad.

'I need to talk to you,' he continued. 'I've had some time to think since you banished me.' He put a finger on her lips as she opened her mouth to protest. 'It's okay, I probably deserved it. I realise that I might have made too much of an issue about your pregnancy and the babies and not enough about you. This isn't just about the baby. I want the whole deal. The baby and you.'

'Xavier, we've discussed this. You don't have to make promises just to ensure you see your daughter. I'm not going to cut you out of her life.'

'That's not what I'm doing. I know I didn't give your feelings, your needs priority. I didn't give *you* priority. I was doing exactly what my ex-girlfriend accused me of, putting everything else ahead of a relationship. My work, the decisions about our children, and forgetting about you and what you need. I made a mistake. One I'd like to rectify if you'll give me a chance. I don't want to lose you. You're too important to me. I want you in my life, not because you are the mother of my child but because I love you.'

'You love me?'

'I love you and I want to share my life with you. Not co-parenting. I want it all. I want us to have a future together, a family together.

'You know, you were right, this wasn't how I would have planned to have a family, but I'm glad it's you. You captivated me from the moment I first saw you and when I learned you were pregnant I could imagine us as a family, but now, even more than that, I can imagine us as a couple. You are strong, brave, honest and beautiful and I don't want to think of my life without you in it. Things happen for a reason and I think we were supposed to meet.

'You challenge me, you can be stubborn and opinionated but, according to my sisters, I need that, and according to me I need you. And I'd like you to give me a chance. To see if there's any way you could love me too. We've got four months to ourselves. To spend some time together. You might even decide you like dating me. And then we can work out what is best for us as well as for the baby. I promise not to mention marriage again, not until you're ready, but I want us to do this together. What do you think?'

'I like the sound of that.' Brighde smiled, almost afraid to believe this was really happening. 'I'm sorry I shut you out.'

'It's okay. I know you were scared. There were so many things we couldn't control but I meant it when I told you I had no intention of going anywhere. I know you felt alone and I was trying to make sure you knew I would be there for you, but I should have told you sooner how I felt. I'm not about to walk away from the best thing that's ever happened to me. And, just to be clear, I'm talking about you. Our baby is the icing on the cake. I know you are reluctant to make any commitments until you have the test results back but I wanted you to know how I feel *before* then. I can be patient, despite what my sisters might tell you. I can give you the time and space you need, but it was important to me to tell you how I feel. I love you and I want to be a part of your life. Regardless of what happens with this pregnancy.'

'We need to talk about that. That's why I needed to see you. I need to speak to you about the baby.' She held up the piece of paper. 'I got the amnio results back just now.'

'Oh.' That worried look was back in his eyes but this time Brighde knew she could erase it. He loved her and she had a chance of getting everything she wanted. They both did. 'And?' he asked.

Brighde grinned. 'She's fine. She tested negative.'

'Everything is okay?'

She nodded.

'Really? You're certain?'

She handed him the results and waited while he scanned the page.

His answering smile was enough for her. More than enough. But he followed it with a kiss. A lingering kiss on her lips that brought her back to life. He loved her. His kiss was the water for her damaged heart and it swelled with love for him as his kiss nourished her.

'So, what do you think?'

'Do you really love me?'

'I do.'

She didn't think she would ever get tired of hearing that. 'I find it hard to believe I can get good news and to have two lots in one day, it's almost too much.'

'Every day can be a good day if we are together.'

'I can't believe I almost blew my one chance at my own happily ever after.'

'You didn't blow it. I'm right here and here I intend to stay, if you'll have me. Do you think there's room for me in your life?'

'Yes,' she said as her smile threatened to split her face in two. 'Definitely.'

'What do you think of this one?' Xavier asked as he pushed a pram back and forth on the shop floor. 'We can add a toddler seat to it later.'

Brighde didn't mind which pram they got; she just wished he'd hurry up and choose one. Her back was aching and she wanted to get home and put her feet up. She knew they had to choose a pram, and a bassinette of some description, as they were running out of time to get organised. She was booked in for a Caesarean section next week, but she was having trouble concentrating. She rubbed her stomach as a ripple of pain ran across her abdomen.

'Are you okay?'

'I think I need to sit down,' she replied as a second spasm gripped her, hard and fast and low in her belly. She gasped as the pain made her catch her breath. That was way too close to the first one.

'Was that a contraction?' She could hear the concern in Xavier's voice. She didn't want him to worry. She needed him to keep her calm.

'I'm not sure,' she said, but what she really meant was, *It's too soon. I'm not ready to have a baby.*

And then Xavier was beside her. Right where she needed him to be. He took charge, took control, took care of her and she felt her panic ease. As long as he was beside her she would be okay.

'Congratulations. She is perfect,' Julie said as she handed Brighde her daughter.

She was early and tiny but she was perfect. Ten fingers, ten toes and downy blonde hair. She grasped Brighde's finger and looked up at her with blue-grey eyes.

'Hello, Bessie.' She and Xavier had agreed to name her after Brighde's mum. It was the perfect name; she was a miniature version of her grandmother.

'You did it.' Xavier leant over and kissed her fore-head.

Brighde lifted her face, meeting his lips with hers. 'We did it.' She smiled. 'Together.'

'Xavier?' Julie interrupted. Xavier straightened up and Brighde held her breath as Julie passed her husband a second blanket-wrapped baby. Their son.

'Can I hold him?' she asked.

The midwife took Bess. 'I'll clean her and do her name tags,' she said as Xavier laid their baby boy on Brighde's chest.

'Hello, my darling.' He was exceptionally small, still the size he had been at eighteen weeks, but he was rec-ognisable as a tiny person. Brighde's eyes filled with tears but she refused to be sad. Not today.

She held him for a long time but her arms longed to hold Bess too.

'There's a cuddle cot in here,' Xavier told her. 'Would you like to use that and then you can say goodbye when you are ready?' Had he seen the longing in her eyes? The dilemma she was facing? She wasn't ready to say goodbye but she needed to cuddle Bess. Her arms needed to hold her daughter.

She nodded. The refrigerated bassinette was the perfect solution. She could keep her son with her until they were ready to let go.

Xavier lifted him from her arms and the midwife returned Bess to her.

'Are you okay?' he asked.

'Yes.' She had Xavier beside her and their daughter. She had more than she'd ever thought possible. 'I am.' She smiled at the father of her children. 'I have everything I need.'

'There's one more thing I need,' Xavier told her as he put their son into the chilled bassinette and wheeled it closer to Brighde. 'I need us to be a proper family. I love you and I want to be your husband. I want to give you commitment and security and love. I want the world to know we are a family. Will you marry me?'

EPILOGUE

BRIGHDE STOOD AT the end of the aisle and took a minute or two to savour the moment. She'd never dared to dream that she would have this day—a wedding of her own—and she wanted to be able to remember every second. She only intended to do this once.

'Are you ready?'

She turned to her brother. He stood beside her, strong and steady, waiting patiently to walk her down the aisle. For so long it had been just the two of them but now Nick had a wife and baby of his own and today it was her turn to extend the family just a little more.

She nodded and tucked her arm through Nick's as the organist started to play. She was vaguely aware of the guests swivelling in their seats as they turned to watch her make her entrance but she only had eyes for Xavier.

He was waiting for her at the altar. Her stomach did a little flip as he met her gaze with his come-to-bed eyes. She hoped she never got used to the effect he had on her whenever she saw him.

She kept her eyes on him as she walked down the aisle. He was wearing the dark navy suit he'd worn on the night they'd met. His hair was a little shorter but still had the wildness in the curl and his thighs were just as lean and powerful under the fabric, his shoulders just as broad. The suit wasn't necessarily traditional wedding attire but Brighde suspected she'd fallen in love with Xavier on that very first night and she wanted a little reminder of that evening. Although, she conceded, the suit was probably unnecessary as Xavier held another, far more precious reminder in his arms. Their four-month-old daughter, Bess.

Nick put Brighde's hand into Xavier's and took his niece, leaving Brighde and Xavier alone at the front of the church.

Xavier squeezed her hand and smiled. 'You look beautiful.'

Brighde got lost in his eyes and, despite her plan of memorising every minute, she scarcely heard a word the priest said. All she could focus on was Xavier, the love of her life, and the fact that they were about to officially become a family.

'I now pronounce you husband and wife.'

Brighde tuned back in as the priest said the words she'd been waiting to hear.

'You may kiss the bride.'

Xavier turned to her. He was grinning from ear to ear as he cupped her face in one hand and tilted her head towards him before bending to kiss her.

She closed her eyes as his lips found hers. She reached for him, her fingers curling around the back of his neck, holding him to her, never wanting to let him go as they sealed their commitment to each other.

'And now, if the godparents could bring Bess up to join us,' the priest invited as Xavier and Brighde finally broke their kiss.

Today was going to be a double celebration. While family and friends were already gathered, Brighde felt it was the perfect time to christen Bess as well. Sarah carried Bess to the baptismal font, her maid of honour duties temporarily suspended as she, along with Xavier's sister Mary and her husband, took on their responsibilities as godparents.

'Brighde and Xavier, what name have you given your child?'

'Elizabeth Marie O'Donnell.'

Bess had been named after both her grandmothers, although she remained the spitting image of Brighde's mum. Brighde thought about the son they'd lost. He was a constant presence in her subconscious and she knew she'd never forget him. Each milestone Bess marked would be another reminder but the pain and sorrow Brighde felt was lessening with time. She had a lot to be thankful for and plenty to look forward to.

Mary held Bess above the font as the priest continued the proceedings. 'Elizabeth Marie, I baptise you in the name of the Father,' he said as he poured warm water over her blonde curls, 'and of the Son—' Brighde waited for the tears to start but Bess was quiet until the second wetting '—and of the Holy Spirit.'

She started crying in earnest now, reaching her chubby little hands out to her father as Mary lifted her from the font. She settled the moment she was in Xavier's arms. She was such a daddy's girl but Brighde could understand why. She loved him just as fiercely and felt just as safe and secure when she was in his arms.

She smiled as she looked at her family. It was a perfect day, surrounded by everyone she loved, and she couldn't ask for anything more.

* * * * *

*If you enjoyed this story, check out these
other great reads from Emily Forbes*

*A MOTHER TO MAKE A FAMILY
WAKING UP TO DR GORGEOUS
FALLING FOR THE SINGLE DAD
A LOVE AGAINST ALL ODDS*

All available now!

MILLS & BOON®

MEDICAL ROMANCE™

THE ULTIMATE IN ROMANTIC MEDICAL DRAMA

---

sneak peek at next month's titles...

In stores from 5th October 2017:

Sleigh Ride with the Single Dad – Alison Roberts
and **A Firefighter in Her Stocking** – Janice Lynn

A Christmas Miracle – Amy Andrews *and*
Reunited with Her Surgeon Prince – Marion Lennox

Falling for Her Fake Fiancé – Sue MacKay *and*
The Family She's Longed For – Lucy Clark

Just can't wait?
Buy our books online before they hit the shops!
www.millsandboon.co.uk

Also available as eBooks.

MILLS & BOON®

EXCLUSIVE EXTRACT

Dr Grace Forbes is reunited with old flame ER Chief
Charles Davenport – can the single dad and his adorable
twins make her Christmas wish come true?

Read on for a sneak preview of
SLEIGH RIDE WITH THE SINGLE DAD
the first book in the magical CHRISTMAS IN
MANHATTAN miniseries

But there was something else there as well.

A… twinkle…

Of amusement, laced with something else.

Appreciation maybe.

No… it was deeper than that. Something she couldn't
identify.

'What?' she heard herself whisper. 'What are you thinking?
That you'll never leave me in charge of your kids again?'

One corner of his mouth lifted into a smile that could only
be described as poignant.

'I'm thinking,' he said quietly. 'That I've spent the last three
years trying to be both a father and a mother to my kids and
keep their lives as predictable and safe as I can and then someone
comes in and, in the space of a few hours, wrecks my house
and shows me exactly what I didn't realise was missing.'

Grace's brain had caught on the comment about wrecking
his house.

'I'm sorry,' she murmured.

Charles was smiling back at her and that twinkle in his
eyes had changed into something else.

Something that was giving her a very distinctive shaft of
sensation deep in her belly.

Attraction, that's what it was.

A very physical and very definite attraction.

Maybe Charles was feeling it too. Maybe that was why he
lifted his hand to touch her hair.

'Chocolate,' he told her.

'I know…' Grace made a face. 'You might find you need to wash the boys' hair in the morning, as well.'

'It's not a problem.' Charles was touching her cheek now, his finger feather-light. 'You've got some here, too.'

Grace couldn't say anything. She was shocked by the touch and the electricity of the current it was producing that flashed through her body like a lightning bolt to join the pool of sensation lower down.

The smile on Charles's face was fading fast. For another one of those endless moments, they stared at each other again.

Fragments of unformed thoughts bombarded Grace. Memories of another time when they'd looked at each other just like this.

Join Britain's BIGGEST Romance Book Club

- **EXCLUSIVE** offers every month

- **FREE** delivery direct to your door

- **NEVER MISS** a title

- **EARN** Bonus Book points

Call Customer Services

0844 844 1358*

or visit

llsandboon.co.uk/subscriptions